Big business and equally big politics provide the themes for this skillfully tailored novel of Montana today—its timbered valleys, its executive suites, its capitol . . .

Englishman Jack Random's entrance into the small lumber town of Tozabe, Montana, where he was to begin work as general manager of the Anglo-American concern, Kennaway-Jardine Paper and Pulp, Inc., was little short of spectacular; for he brought in his car with him the body of a man found shot to death on the road, and that man turned out to be his boss, Harry Jardine. Not only had Harry been a big wheel in business in the state, but he'd also been a politician—he had planned shortly to announce his candidacy for the U.S. Senate.

Harry's widow, Grace, is a woman of uncommon beauty, and Jack Random immediately falls in love with her, and she with him. With equal zest, she plunges into supervision of her husband's complicated business and political interests. Of particular stress on the business side of things is the fact that rich mineral deposits have been found in timbered Limbo Valley, and whether the company will destroy its natural beauty for the sake of the mineral wealth is a question that threatens to disrupt the community.

PHOTO CREDIT

Jon Cleary has had a long and prolific career as a writer—to date he is the author of nearly thirty novels. With his wife, Joy, Mr. Cleary has lived in many parts of the world and presently resides in Sydney.

A Sound of Lightning

Jon Cleary

A Sound of Lightning

William Morrow and Company, Inc.
New York   1976

Printed in the United States of America.

1 2 3 4 5   80 79 78 77 76

Library of Congress Cataloging in Publication Data

Cleary, Jon (date)
  A sound of lightning.

    I. Title.
PZ3.C58So3   [PR6053.L4]   823   76-1859
ISBN 0-688-03030-0

To JOY

We loved in silence
But for the drum of blood
Our hearts were deaf
And never heard
The scream, a sound of lightning,
That sparked the storm
And brought murder
To the quiet day.

Chapter One

I

They called it the Big Sky country, though Random had seen bigger skies: any man who had stood in the Empty Quarter of Arabia or on the Nullarbor Plain of Australia had some appreciation of the immensity of the heavens. But so far he had not seen the Great Plains of Montana and perhaps out there the sky really was as big as they claimed; Americans seemed to make a fetish of size, as if that way lay fulfilment. King-size beds, giant hamburgers: if they liked to think their skies were bigger than anyone else's, it did no harm. At least it didn't bring on indigestion or make them buy sex books to find out how to fill the space in their vast bedroom playgrounds.

'Beautiful!' He had a habit of talking aloud to himself, although he didn't always listen; it had been a mannerism that had irritated his ex-wife, especially when the time had come when he had ceased to listen to her, too. 'Absolutely beautiful!'

Binoculars pressed to his eyes, he swung his head slowly, taking in the landscape below him. He lowered the binoculars, feeling his vision cramped rather than enlarged by them. The valley stretched away below him, the Limbo River glittering like swiftly moving shards of glass as it carved its way through the trees and meadows. Ridges rose and fell, giving light and shade to the forest that covered both sides of the steep valley. He recognized the different types of trees, though there were many that he had never seen before growing in their natural state. He could see the tall ponderosa pines and higher up the lodge-poles; on the next ridge to that on which he stood a stand of Englemann spruce ran down to the river. Along the river itself cottonwoods and quaking aspen clustered like expectant fisher-men, the aspens' rippling heads a green twin of the glittering silver stream.

'My domain,' he said and smiled to himself at the conceit. He had listened to himself that time and he wondered if the ghosts back home in England had heard him. There had been a time when the family had used the word *domain* without conceit or amusement, but that was a part of history that had faded almost to the point of invisibility.

He caught a glimpse of movement on the ridge to his left and he put the binoculars to his eyes again. A narrow gravel road ran up through the trees and a black bear was crossing it, shuffling along unhurriedly with all the assurance of an animal that knew that, today at any rate, it was safe from guns and other inter-ference. It's his domain, too, Random thought, and made an acknowledging bow to the oblivious bear. Then, binoculars still to his eyes, he saw the other movement down on the road that ran along the floor of the valley.

Two cars were drawn up on the side of the road beneath a thin overhang of trees, a large car and a small sports car. A man and a woman were standing beside the sports car, the woman's blonde hair bright as a golden helmet in the rays of sunlight that came through the overhang, the man's face hidden by a wide-brimmed hat. Random kept the glasses on them for a moment; he was about to look away when he saw the man slap the woman's face. She fell back against the car, an arm going up in front of her face as if she expected to be hit again. But the man had turned and walked swiftly across to the big car; Random, with an eye for colour, saw that the man's blue shirt appeared to match exactly the colour of the car. The man got in, slamming the door, and a moment later the car, engine roaring so loudly that Random, a quarter of a mile away, could hear it, spun out on to the tarred surface of the two-lane road and sped down the valley. It went round a bend with a scream of tyres, disappearing from Random's sight, and then suddenly the sound of it was also gone. Silence, but for the soft whisper of a breeze in the trees, settled on the valley again.

Random put the binoculars back in their case, embarrassed at what he had seen and angry at the man's behaviour. He and Jennifer had fought a lot, but he had never hit her. If one had to strike a woman to score a point he would rather lose the argument. As he had invariably done with Jennifer . . . He wondered if Women's Lib welcomed fisticuffs as another measure of equality.

As he turned back towards his own car he saw another movement on the next ridge: a car was coming slowly down the gravel road. But he only glanced at it, then got into the rented Gremlin. He had been wary of the size of American cars and had settled for the bug-like Gremlin; every mile on the way down from Seattle had made him happier with his choice. The back of it was stowed with the four suitcases he had brought with him on the Polar flight from London; ever since his divorce eight years ago what passed for home had been contained in those four scuffed and dented bags. He had learned that he did not need possessions to identify him, at least not to himself. But he was honest enough to admit that perhaps he was more fortunate than most: the Random identity, faded though it might be now like a long-neglected banner, was still recognized in East Anglia. Five hundred years of a name provokes its own constantly recurring echoes, faint though they may be.

The car was stifling hot and he regretted that he had not thought to ask for one with air-conditioning. It had been cool and wet when he had left Seattle, but as soon as he had crossed into Idaho the rain had ceased and the temperature had climbed. Now that he was in the thin high air of the Montana Rockies the July sun was mocking him for his oversight. He started the car, leaning his face out against the breeze as he took the Gremlin down the winding road to the floor of the valley.

Leaning out of the driver's side he almost passed the girl before he saw her. He had put her and the man who had slapped her out of his thoughts; he had developed the knack of closing doors in his mind against involvement with strangers. It gave him a coolness of attitude that some people took for a cold heart; only he knew that the doors of the mind were a defence against a heart that could be too warm for its own good. Still, he now pulled the Gremlin into the side of the road, got out and walked back.

'Having trouble? Perhaps I can help. I know a little about engines.'

'Maybe you can at that.' She had a pleasant voice, though it sounded a trifle strained; her cheeks were smudged, as if she had been weeping. 'You might know something about an MG. You're British, aren't you?'

'Yes.' English, his father would have said; but that would be too much to explain to a foreigner. 'I had one like this once. This very model.'

It was an MG about ten years old, painted what used to be known as British racing green. He and Jennifer had driven down to Spain in one like it on a second honeymoon that they had hoped would save their marriage; that car and the marriage had both finished up on the scrap heap. The girl stood back as he peered at the engine, soon found the trouble and fixed it.

'One of the distributor leads was loose. Try it now.'

The girl, one hand on her cheek as if not sure that the slap mark had faded, had been looking at him with cautious interest, curious about him but still too upset to want to be distracted by any conversation. She saw a man of just above medium height, possibly in his mid-thirties, slim and straight-backed; he was dark-haired, good-looking in a more refined way than the men she was accustomed to, and had an amused tolerance to his gaze that suggested he could be arrogant in certain circumstances. For his part, with the eye of the quick, trained observer, he had seen a girl with bright, straight blonde hair, a handsome rather than beautiful face that was softened just now by hurt eyes, and a full-bosomed figure with a carriage as erect as his own. But, though he didn't know it, he read her less well than she had read him. There was no way of knowing whether she was amused by, tolerant of or arrogant towards the world.

'Try it now,' he repeated.

She frowned a little, as if she didn't understand him; then abruptly she nodded and slid into the driver's seat of the MG. The engine started at once and he stepped back, nodding appreciatively.

'Thank you.' She stared at him; then, without smiling, said, 'Are you a male chauvinist?'

He was not one to show surprise at surprising questions. 'About things mechanical, yes. But if it upsets you, I'll pull the lead off the distributor again, get into my car and drive on. I don't think I'd want to go to war over my male superiority as a mechanic.'

'I wasn't thinking about things mechanical.' She had turned her head away, was looking straight down the road to the bend where the man in the big car had disappeared.

'I don't slap women's faces.' Her head swung back, the hurt in her eyes suddenly intense. Instantly regretting what he had said, he apologized. 'I saw it all by accident. I didn't mean to be a Peeping Tom — '

He had to step back hurriedly as she slammed in the gears and took the car away in a burst of gravel-hurling wheel-spin. The MG lurched out on to the macadam and in a few moments had disappeared round the bend where the big car had gone five minutes earlier. Random dusted himself down, stood watching the empty bend in the road. Puzzled, annoyed, he tried closing another door in his mind; but he had the feeling the device might not work this time. He would know tonight, in the darkness before sleep, when doors started *opening* in the mind, blown in by winds of imagination and memory.

He went along to the Gremlin, was sliding gingerly on to the hot vinyl of the seat when the shot rang out.

He looked up and about him, startled by the unexpected loudness of the shot on the thin clear air; an echo came back at once, almost as sharp-edged as the original sound. Then he heard the crashing in the undergrowth on the steep slope that rose up on the opposite side of the road. The stand of trees on the slope was sparse, thinned out perhaps by the steepness; but the undergrowth was thick and a long section of it was quivering from the passage of whatever had plunged down through it. Then the bushes were still and the echo of the shot died away. The valley was still again but for the thin singing of the river as it ran over shallows somewhere beyond the trees to the right. Random got out of the car and scanned the slope opposite. He wondered if someone in the car he had seen earlier up on the gravel road had decided to shoot the black bear out of season.

Then he heard the sound of the car's engine somewhere up behind the trees. He looked for the car but couldn't see it because of the angle of the slope. It went up the ridge, still hidden, then the hum of its engine died away and once more the valley was silent but for its natural sounds.

Random hesitated, then reached for his binoculars. It took him only a moment to focus on the dark heap sprawled among the bushes half-way up the slope; but it was not the black bear. It was a man in a blue shirt; hanging on a bush further up the slope was a wide-brimmed hat. Random put the binoculars back in the car, crossed the road at a run and clambered up the slope, pushing his way through the bushes, grabbing at them to haul himself up. Then he was crouched beside the man, not needing to check that he was dead. The bullet that had gone in through the throat and come out below the ear had done its job.

He was a big, good-looking man; if anyone dead is good-looking, Random thought. His wide-staring eyes were pale blue, paler perhaps in death than they had been in life; the mouth was open as if for a last angry shout that it had never managed. Despite the bruises and scratches that reduced its dignity, it was still an aggressive-looking face, that of a man used to having his own way; but he had had his own way for the last time, knew now, if there was any knowing, that all authority was only temporary. Random closed the eyes, began to go through the man's pockets. He did it without any feeling of intrusion; he had searched dead men's pockets before. As a Coldstream Guards officer in the 1960s he had never fought in any large war, but small wars left men just as dead and demanding attention. He wondered what small war this stranger had been engaged in.

He paused, looked up and about him; but he knew the killer was now probably miles away. He went back to the dead man's pockets; it was hard to believe any man would carry so little on him. A packet of cigarettes, a book of matches, a handkerchief; no wallet, no loose change, no concertina of credit cards. Random sat back on his haunches, then stood up and climbed further up the slope to the gravel road. The big car, a blue Cadillac, was parked there in the middle of the road; Random wondered why the dead man should have set up such an obvious road-block. Then he saw the tyre tracks in the gravel, just in front of the Cadillac. It looked as if the other car, the murderer's, had been the road-block.

Random shook his head, trying to close another mental door

against playing detective. He searched the Cadillac; the glove-box, pockets and the trunk were full of odds and ends. But nothing that told him the man's name. He got out of the car, stood for a moment wondering what to do. He heard a car or a light truck pass along the tarred road below him, but its sound was soon gone. Then he heard the snapping of a twig, looked up and saw the black bear further up the ridge. That decided him.

He noted the registration number of the car, went down the slope, took the dead man under the shoulders and, awkwardly and none too gently, slid the body down to the tarred road. He paused when he reached the flat, listening for an approaching car; but all he could hear was the singing river and, like a counter-note, the cry of a bird somewhere in the trees. He was beginning to appreciate what he had read about Montana, that it was a state almost empty of people.

He propped the dead man up in the passenger's seat of the Gremlin, got in and tried to start the engine. But all he got was the still unfamiliar, still annoying buzz: the seat-belt of even a dead man had to be fastened before the engine could be started. America, Random thought, had as usual gone too far. He clipped the belt across the body, re-fastened his own belt, started up the car and headed it down the road. The dead man fell sideways with the movement of the car, his head lolling against the open window like that of a man made sleepy by the heat.

Random drove at a sedate pace, as if the Gremlin had now become a hearse. He crossed the river by way of a narrow bridge, looked back and saw the valley from another angle. Tomorrow he would be responsible for all this through which he drove, the forests and lands of Kenneway-Jardine Paper and Pulp, over a hundred square miles of the finest lumber country on the east slope of the Rocky Mountains.

'It will be the biggest job you've had so far,' his father had told him, stating the obvious with his usual precision. Nigel Random treated both his sons as if not quite certain that either of them had inherited his intelligence; the fact that both of them were more intelligent than he, and had been since puberty, seemed to have escaped him. His wife might have set him right, but, having bequeathed *her* intelligence to her two sons, she had departed for the grave and the intellectually stimulating life she believed lay beyond it.

'Just don't let the family down,' Nigel Random had said. 'Hate to think someone might mention nepotism.'

'Dad, you're only one of eight directors on the British – sorry, English board of Kenneway-Jardine. With the way the Establishment has interlocking directorships in this country, half the public school old boys would have to emigrate or go on the dole to avoid any hint of nepotism.'

'No need to sound like a Communist,' said Nigel Random.

Random had let that pass: his father thought Karl Marx was still roaming around loose in Highgate Cemetery. 'I got this job on my merits – or anyway I like to think so. If I prove no good, from what I've heard Harry Jardine will soon tell me I'm not wanted.'

'Good luck, then. Just don't let the Americans push you around. Understand they're very good at that, especially that fellow Kissinger.'

'I don't believe he works for Kenneway-Jardine. But we English were rather good at pushing people around, too. You should have heard the Australians while I was out there.'

'We did it with more finesse,' said Nigel Random, as if that forgave everything.

That had been a week ago, in the old house in Suffolk musty with ghosts and his father's illusions. A long way and a long time from here, at this intersection where the signpost said *Tozabe 8 miles*. Random turned left, heading south, now on a main highway. There was more traffic here, but still sparse; a few cars with out-of-state plates, summer tourists, a few local cars and pick-ups, several trucks laden with logs. After four or five miles he went by two or three houses, each of them set well back from the road in land cleared among the trees; then he saw the first of the roadside signs telling him what he would find in Tozabe. The best beds, the best food, the best sport: Paradise lay only two miles down the road. Random looked at the dead man, wondering if he had been one of Tozabe's 4978 Happy Citizens, the boast of the last sign he had passed.

The town came on him suddenly: he rounded a bend in the road and at once he seemed in the middle of it. He slowed the Gremlin, all at once feeling conspicuous, as if the dead man was strung across the front of the car like those trophies he had seen in pictures of hunters returning to town. Though the town was tightly clustered together, hemmed in by the forest on all sides, there was no jam of traffic or people in the streets. Tozabe, though the county seat, was evidently not a busy town, at least not at mid-morning on a hot July Thursday.

Random saw three men standing on a corner outside a drug store and he slid the car in beside them. He had to lean across the dead man to speak to them.

'Can you tell me where the police station is?'

The three men, all of them middle-aged or close to it, lean and weathered as fence-posts, looked at him and his passenger with astonishment.

'Jesus Christ!'

Random, still leaning across the corpse, the seat-belt gripping him like an arresting officer's arm, felt the ridiculousness of his situation. 'I found this man out along the road – '

'Christ Almighty,' said one of the men and looked at his companions. 'It just ain't possible!'

'Anything's possible, I guess.' One of the men had a wall-eye: it seemed to stare at the dead man as he bent down and, face close to that of the corpse, looked in at Random. 'You better take him down to the sheriff, mister. Follow me.'

All three men jumped into the cabin of the yellow pick-up parked at the curb. As it pulled out in front of him Random saw the sign on its door: *Kenneway-Jardine Paper and Pulp Inc.* Within the next hour, he guessed, everyone at Kenneway-Jardine would know how the new general manager had come into town. He looked at the corpse and cursed it. It was as if he knew that the dead man, like some warlock, was about to blight his stay in Tozabe County.

He had to hurry to keep pace with the pick-up; it raced down the main street as if heralding a birth instead of a death. It skidded to a stop in front of a large two-storied building set in what looked like a school yard. The three men got out of the pick-up and came back as Random got out of the Gremlin.

'Hec and Gus will look after him while I take you in to the sheriff,' said the wall-eyed man. 'My name's Peeples, Chris Peeples.'

'Random. John Random.'

An eyebrow went up and the wall-eye seemed to grow larger. 'That so? Well, we better get Bill Gauge. This used to be the junior high school, but they just built a new 'un out the edge of town. They're building a new jail, too – that's why the sheriff is here, waiting to move into his new quarters.' He paused at the top of the steps, shook his head. 'It just don't seem possible. But I guess everything's possible, right?'

'I suppose so,' said Random, and then added a little impatiently, 'Now do you mind if I meet the sheriff? I want to be relieved of that dead man as soon as possible.'

'You ain't going to be relieved of him too easy,' said Chris Peeples, good eye as suddenly blank as his wall-eye. 'That's our boss out there, yours and mine. Harry Jardine.'

2

Bill Gauge had been sheriff of Tozabe County for twelve years, but this election year he had begun to feel uneasy. It no longer seemed enough to run just on your record, though he knew his record was a good one; the crime rate in the county was the lowest in the state and you couldn't ask much more than that of a law officer. Also he hadn't, as far as he knew, trodden on the toes of any of those whose crimes, if they'd committed any, he hadn't unearthed; he had learned long ago that any officer running for election had to pay as much attention to the law-abiding as to the law-breakers. One of those he had paid a lot of attention to had been Harry Jardine.

He followed Random and Chris Peeples from his office out to the crowd gathered round the Gremlin. He was a big man with a wide, open face on which frowning lines were scratched like graffiti, a protruding belly, a behind that was heading the opposite way like a counterweight, and a deep loud voice that, somehow, curiously lacked authority. He told the crowd to go about its business, but no one took any notice of him other than to make way for him to look in at the dead man.

'It's him, all right.' He sounded as if he hadn't quite believed what Random and Peeples had told him in his office. 'You say you found him up the Juniper Creek road?' He looked at Random and then said in a voice made ever louder by the shock he was feeling. 'Mister, I'm talking to you, you hear me?'

Random had been staring across the top of the car at the green MG parked down the street and the golden-haired girl walking hurriedly towards it. He hadn't seen her in the crowd when he had first come out of the sheriff's office, but he was certain she knew who lay in the front seat of the Gremlin. Then he became aware that people in the crowd were looking at him and he turned back to the sheriff.

'Sorry, sheriff. You were saying?'

'You found him up on Juniper Creek, the road up there?'

'If that's the road that comes in over Lodgepole Pass, then yes. I'm a stranger here, sheriff.'

'You certainly are, mister. Bringing in Harry Jardine like that and not knowing who he was.'

'I tried to identify him, but he had nothing on him to tell me who he was. I'd have recognized the name if he'd had a card or something.'

'He didn't need no card. Darn near everybody in the whole state knew Harry Jardine.' There was a loud murmur of assent from the crowd; they sounded to Random like a Greek chorus. The king was dead . . . 'Ain't going to see the likes of him again.'

'No, sir,' said the crowd.

'Well, we better get him outa your car and take him inside. Peter Rasmussen will want to look at him. That's the county coroner,' Gauge explained to Random. 'You better come back into my office with me while I get a few more particulars. Chris, you and the boys bring the deceased inside, willya? Better put him in that old locker room. Treat him careful.'

'He ain't going to worry if we don't,' said Peeples.

'I wouldn't let his missus hear you say that.'

'Didn't mean any disrespect.' Peeples sounded suddenly apologetic and looked directly at Random.

It took Random a moment or two to realize that he was the one who was being appealed to. He hadn't yet signed in, but already Peeples had recognized him as the new general manager, the man with the ear of the boss's widow. He nodded reassuringly to Peeples, pushed through the crowd and followed the sheriff up the steps and into the school building. He glanced quickly down the street, but the green MG was nowhere in sight.

'Harry Jardine owned this town, just about. He was against the new buildings they're putting up, but the Governor over-ruled him.'

'Was Mr Jardine in politics?'

'You might say he was.' Gauge looked sideways at Random. 'Politics out here would be a bit different than where you come from, I guess?'

'Possibly,' said Random, refusing to be drawn. He could feel a cobweb of involvement being spun around him: Chris Peeples, the sheriff, the unknown girl, all of them were laying strands on him, without malice, perhaps even without design. But he knew that the less he said, at least until he was more at home in this scene, the better his future position would be. He wondered if the sheriff would know who the golden-haired girl was; but he wasn't going to ask. Not yet, anyway. Not till he met her again, if he could, and asked her why she had walked away from the murdered body of a man who was obviously more to her than just a passing acquaintance. 'I suppose I'm going to find a lot of things are different here.'

'You come direct from England?'

'If you mean right now, yes. I was in Australia, Tasmania, up till a month ago. Kenneway, the English side, have paper and pulp interests out there, too.'

'Yeah, well – ' The sheriff was not interested in what went on outside his county. He sat down heavily in a chair that looked as if it had been waging a losing battle with his weight over a number of years; it creaked and tilted back to a dangerous angle. 'Well, we better get all the facts down.'

The interview took much longer than Random had expected. Bill Gauge made work and worry for himself. He seemed incapable of taking yes for an answer; such easy acquiescence only seemed to make him suspicious. He split every fact into a number of small facts; at the end Random wondered if the sheriff would ever be able to sort them out into a coherent report. But that was none of his business, he told himself, and tried to shut another door in his mind.

At last he stood up. 'I'm afraid that's all I can tell you, sheriff.' Though he had told him nothing of the golden-haired girl; that might have meant his being here all day. 'Has anyone told the widow yet what happened?'

'The widow? Oh, you mean Grace Jardine? No, not yet. I had to get all the facts down first.' As if the widow at once was going to ask for all the facts. He looked at the facts scrawled in a large hand all over several pages of a yellow legal pad; then he squinted up at Random, his face suddenly old and worried behind its veil of lines. 'Don't suppose you would want to tell her? No, I guess not,' he said as he saw the look on Random's face. 'Man gets some shitty things in this job.'

'If she lives in town, someone may already have told her.'

'Live in town?' The sheriff laughed harshly. 'Money don't live in a place like this. Not Jardine sort of money. No, she'd be down at their ranch or maybe down at their place in Helena. Well, I better go looking for her.' He stood up, the leather cushion of the chair letting out what sounded like a sigh of relief. 'Where you going to be staying, Mr Random?'

'I'm not sure. I understand there is a general manager's residence here in town – it comes with the job.'

'Oh, sure. Yeah, it's on the edge of town.' The sheriff seemed to be having trouble fitting Random into the local picture; but then the whole local picture had been fractured by what had arrived on his doorstep less than half an hour ago. In twelve years as sheriff he had had to deal with four murders, but none of them had had the impact that this one would have. Jesus Christ, and in an election year, too! 'You just go straight down Main and you'll see it the other side of the church. Red-brick place, it's got a big Doug fir in front of it.'

Random went out to his car. Most of the crowd had gone, but some people were still congregated in a loose, gossiping group on the sidewalk. They stopped talking as soon as Random appeared and he felt the atmosphere – curiosity, suspicion, antagonism? – as he walked down the steps and across to the Gremlin. He got in, switched on the ignition and the irritating buzz chided him again. Almost angrily he buckled his seat-belt.

Then Chris Peeples was standing by the car. 'I called Wally Fletcher, told him the news. He's expecting you down to his house. Sorry – ' he grinned, the first relaxed expression Random had seen on a face since he had arrived in town. 'Your house I guess it is now.'

Random nodded, returning the smile. 'What's your job with the company?'

'Sawmill foreman. A helluva way to meet, ain't it? Well, Wally's expecting you, like I said.' He slapped the top of the car. 'Good luck.'

Why should I need luck? But Random didn't query him. He put the car in gear and drove down Main Street, glancing in his mirror at the bank of faces, bright in the sun above their dark clothes, turning to stare after him.

'You could have chosen a better day to arrive,' he said aloud and, for once listening to himself, nodded emphatically.

Tozabe would have won no prizes as a pretty town. The stores that lined Main Street looked like red-brick packing cases; a traveller would have had to be dying of thirst and starving to have pulled up at any of the two or three bars and the two diners. Even the houses, most of them built of timber, looked as if they had been bought wholesale and dumped on the vacant lots. Random passed a gas station and it looked the smartest set-up on the street; next to it was a motel and it, too, looked smart. It was called the Fort Tozabe Inn and the cut-out wooden figure of a fur trader stood at the entrance, the look on his face suggesting that he was a dissatisfied guest rather than a welcoming stand-in for the owner. But the town, Random noticed, was clean, the grass in front of the houses was cut short and some of them had gardens. If the town looked drab, then it was the fault of Kenneway-Jardine: after all, it was virtually a company town.

He found the general manager's house without trouble. A man sat on a garden bench beneath the giant Douglas fir, a plaster-clad leg stuck out in front of him like a white, rotting log. 'You could've picked a better day to arrive.'

'Yes. Someone just told me that. How's the leg?'

'I feel like taking it down to the mill, getting 'em to saw it off. Goddam fool thing to do at my age, trying to cross the river jumping from rock to rock.'

Fletcher was a thin, balding man whose age would have been hard to guess from the time he had reached his thirties. He had a weathered face in which every muscle showed when he smiled; and he looked the sort of general manager who had spent as little time as possible behind his desk. 'You ever been a general manager before?'

Random shook his head. 'I've been a forester and a plant superintendent. I've never had a job as big as this.'

'If you know how things work – '

'I do.'

Fletcher nodded. 'Then you're not going to have any trouble with the guys working for you.'

'But?'

Fletcher smiled. 'You got a sensitive ear or I'm getting careless.' He squinted up at the mountains, then looked back at Random. 'You're going to be working for bosses who know what they want but aren't going to tell you.'

'You don't know me,' Random said carefully. 'Are you going to tell me more or do you think you've told me too much?'

Fletcher studied him for a moment, then he said, 'What do you think of this valley of ours?'

'I like it. It's beautiful.'

'You'll like it even more when you come to know it. Because the whole valley is privately owned, it's never been spoiled by tourists. I was down in Yellowstone, the national park, couple of summers ago. Place was chock-a-block with goddam campers, tents side by side like goddam tenements. Up here we let in hunters and fishermen, but we limit them. And the company has done its timber cutting intelligently – you must've seen that when you were driving down. No ecologist could come in here and complain about what we've done.'

'But?'

Fletcher laughed more than smiled this time; he seemed utterly relaxed with Random. '*But* again. Yeah. Well, there's something going on and I don't know what it is – though I got my suspicions. We had some hunters in here last fall and then some guys came fishing in the spring. Nothing in that, except we found out they had some mining survey equipment with them. They got outa here before we could nab 'em – though I don't know what we could've charged 'em with, except maybe trespassing. I told head office down in Helena, but I heard nothing more. But while I've been in hospital with this leg, orders started coming in telling me to sign up sub-contractors for cutting. What the hell for? Unless they're planning to cut down every goddam tree we own.'

'Whom did the orders come from? Harry Jardine?'

'Harry never signed an order in his life. He might come up here and bawl you out, tell you to do something verbally, but he never put his name on anything but the annual general report. Harry had delusions of grandeur – when he was drunk he used to call himself the King of Montana. I think he thought he was the natural successor to Daly, Clark and Heinze. You ever hear about them?'

'I read about them.' Random had read all he could about Montana and its history when he had learned of his posting; that was the old army training, know the enemy terrain. Though he had not really expected to be coming to enemy terrain. 'They were the copper kings. But Jardine wasn't in copper, was he? I thought the Anaconda Company had all that tied up in this state.'

'Harry Jardine would be in anything that made him money. And so would the guys who helped him run his empire.'

'Who are they?'

'Speak of the devil!' Fletcher tried to sit up straighter, but was hampered by his leg. He stared at the silver-blue Mercedes that had drawn up out on the road behind Random's car; then he looked directly at Random. 'I'm trusting you to keep your mouth shut. I want my retirement to be peaceable.'

'I shouldn't think of disturbing it,' said Random and stood up as the two men got out of the Mercedes and came across the lawn towards them.

'You heard the news yet?' said Fletcher bluntly.

'What news?' The bigger of the two men was smiling affably, his hand held out to Random. 'You must be John Random. Part of our reason for coming up here today was to meet you. I'm Jim Coulson. Karl Shooberg.'

The other man seemed to stand in the shadow of Coulson, but Random had the feeling it was from choice rather than because he had been put in his place. He seemed built entirely of bone with a cover of skin stretched over him; it was difficult to imagine there were any soft areas of flesh on him. He took the black holder with its cheroot out of his slit of a mouth, put out a hand of bones and said in a soft rasping voice, 'Glad you made it okay, Mr Random.'

'He didn't,' said Fletcher, still blunt. 'That's the news. Harry Jardine is dead – murdered. Random here brought the body in.'

Coulson reared back as if he had been hit in his big, beefily handsome face. Shooberg put the holder back in his mouth and said round it, his voice still soft but a little more rasping, 'You're a joker, Wally, but not a sick one.'

'I'm not joking, Karl. Harry's dead. Ask Mr Random.'

Random, keeping his own voice level and unemotional, keeping the facts down to the necessary minimum, told the two new-comers what had happened. But he still left out any mention of the girl. 'If I hadn't stopped to look at the scenery, I suppose his body would still be out there.'

'Where's the – the body now?' asked Coulson.

'Up the street in the sheriff's office. They were waiting on the coroner to look at it.'

'Anyone told the newspapers down in Helena yet?' said Shooberg.

'I wouldn't know. All I know is that the sheriff was going to tell Mrs Jardine.'

'We better get up there, Jim.' Shooberg took the cheroot butt out of the holder, dropped it in the grass and ground his heel on it. He seemed to step out of Coulson's shadow, literally and figuratively. 'It'll be an hour before the reporters can get up here from Helena. We'll try and get the body back to the ranch before then. If they want any statements, we'll make them from Helena.'

Coulson nodded, still dazed. Random looked at him, then at Shooberg, recognizing him as the boss for the moment. 'Do you want me to come with you?'

Shooberg put the holder away in the pocket of his shirt. He looked cool, undisturbed, completely in control of himself and the situation. Utterly in contrast to Coulson, who looked like a man who had escaped only by inches from being felled by a falling tree. He was sweating and he had taken off his wide-brimmed hat and was running his hand through his thick grey hair.

'Not right now,' said Shooberg. 'But you better come back to the ranch with us – we don't want the reporters worrying you just yet. Can you be ready in twenty minutes?'

He and Coulson went back to the Mercedes and Random looked at Fletcher. 'Which of those is the senior man?'

'Neither, as far as I know. We used to call 'em the palace guard – I guess they still are, only there's no king any more. Jim Coulson usually did all the talking, but he's had the wind knocked out of him today.'

'Would the wind ever be knocked out of Shooberg?'

'Don't reckon so. He had a son, his only kid, he got killed

in Vietnam. He didn't even take the day off when they gave him the telegram from Washington. Just worked right through and then went home and told his wife. Coldest bastard I've ever known.'

'I'm beginning to think you chose a good time to retire.'

'I didn't choose it. But you're right – it's a good time. You want to take a shower before they come back for you? You look a bit sweaty.'

'I don't quite understand why they want me to go down to the ranch with them.'

'Maybe they want to make sure you don't say too much to the press. That's one of the few things Harry Jardine was never able to buy in this state, the newspapers.' Fletcher stood up with difficulty, leaned on his stick. 'Down at the ranch you may also get to meet the boss's wife. Grace Jardine. She's quite a gal. Though I think she may miss Harry less than the rest of us.'

3

'That son-of-a-bitch Wryman,' said Coulson. 'Who the hell does he think he is?'

'He's the County Attorney,' said Shooberg, 'and he's on our ticket. So we're stuck with him.'

Random sat in the back of the Mercedes and did his best not to be too interested in the conversation up front. Wryman, the County Attorney, had refused to release Jardine's body until it was claimed by a next of kin. There had evidently been a great deal of argument up at the sheriff's office because it had been almost an hour before Coulson and Shooberg had called back for Random. By then the newsmen had arrived from Helena, two reporters, two photographers, a television crew and a radio man; they were now in two cars and a truck tailing the Mercedes back to the Jardine ranch. The tiny convoy had climbed out of the Limbo Valley over a road that skirted a narrow gap in the mountains, had come down into a much bigger valley, wide and shallow enough almost to be called a plain, and were now approaching the Lazy J. On the half-hour trip Random had offered no comment and made only the necessary answer when either of the two men up front had spoken to him.

The convoy passed through wide white gates and went up a

long avenue of cottonwoods to a large low house built of stone and timber. Random caught a glimpse of sun-baked lawns, a swimming pool and, down at the bottom of the low hill on which the house stood, a large complex of red-painted sheds and white-railed yards. It looked as if the Lazy J, the dead king's palace, had been meant as a show place.

As the Mercedes pulled up Random said, 'Am I expected to repeat all the details again to Mrs Jardine?'

'Don't worry about Grace, if you have to tell her,' said Coulson. 'She's got more guts than any ten men in Montana.'

The sheriff's car was in the driveway, a deputy standing beside it. On a nod from Shooberg, he stepped forward and held up a hand as the newsmen scrambled out of their cars and tried to follow Shooberg, Coulson and Random into the house.

'Far enough, fellers.'

Random heard the loud protests behind him as he went through the wide front double doors; he had read about the freedom of the American press but he hadn't expected it to be so clamorous. Grief, according to American newsmen, was evidently not a private right.

Or perhaps the reporters knew Grace Jardine too well. She stood, small, composed and beautiful, before a huge stone fireplace in the big living room. It was her beauty that first struck Random: it was startling, almost too perfect. Thick dark hair, bone structure that had the clean line of classical sculpture, a generous mouth and eyes that seemed to change colour from dark blue to violet as they turned in the light coming through the window-wall at the far end of the room. Quite a gal, just as Wally Fletcher had described her.

She greeted Coulson and Shooberg, then came towards Random with her hand outstretched. He took it, feeling its firm warm grip, and only then did he notice her composure. Any grief she was feeling was not for public display. He had the impression that if she allowed the newsmen in here she would handle them with the authority of a national editor-in-chief. She would provide her own copy and they could take it or leave it.

Later he would be surprised at his quick appraisal of her: he had never been an expert on women, though, unlike so many Englishmen, he was always at ease in their company. But he had never been so attracted to a woman; she looked straight into his face and he wondered if she read what he was thinking. But his own composure must have equalled hers. He raised her hand to his lips, an un-English thing to do, one of his few idiosyncrasies, and said, 'I wish we were meeting under happier circumstances, Mrs Jardine.'

One of her thick dark eyebrows had gone up at his gesture, but she didn't turn and invite Coulson, Shooberg and the sheriff to share her reaction. She withdrew her hand gracefully, as if she were accustomed every day to having her hand kissed by gentlemen callers, and waved him to a chair, moving across to sit on another chair close to him.

'Sheriff Gauge has told me all the details, so I'll spare you having to repeat them.' She had a low, controlled voice, perhaps a trifle too controlled.

Random looked up at Shooberg, but the latter was ushering the sheriff towards the front door. Coulson, recovered now, nodded at Random and ventured a weak smile. 'We told you you wouldn't have to worry about Grace.'

'Were you worried about me, Mr Random?'

'Perhaps I was more worried for myself. I'm not a good bearer of bad news.'

'Neither was my husband. He used to lose his temper when – ' She stopped and he waited for her to break down; but she looked across at Coulson and smiled sadly. 'It's hard to realize we won't hear Harry any more.'

Coulson nodded. 'Right.'

But he didn't appear relaxed and Random had the feeling that he was not welcome with the big man, that Coulson wished Shooberg had not invited him to the ranch. Then Shooberg came back, walking with the quiet tread of a man who wanted to be noticed as little as possible. Yet Random was sure that the bony, bald-headed man was neither shy nor modest.

'If we want Harry's body released, Grace, you'll have to come up to Tozabe with us.'

Grace Jardine stood up. 'We'll bring him back here, have the mortician come out and prepare him. Prepare him – ' She shook her head, a wry amused look in her dark eyes. 'Harry was always prepared for everything. But not this.'

'We'll have the funeral as soon as possible,' said Shooberg. 'But we'll have to give people time to come in here for it.'

'Jesus Christ!' Coulson suddenly exploded, jumped out of his chair and stamped about the room. 'He's not even cold yet and you're talking as if you're organizing some goddam political meeting. He's not running for the Senate any more. He's dead, Karl, cold fucking dead!'

'Watch your language, Jim,' said Grace Jardine quietly. 'We know he's dead – you don't have to tell *me* that.'

'Sorry, Grace.' Coulson simmered down, waved a frustrated hand. 'But you know how I felt about Harry – he was more than just the boss. When some murdering son-of-a-bitch shoots him – '

Grace moved to him, put a hand on his arm. 'I know and I understand. That he was murdered is something all of us are going to take a long time to get over. But he's dead and he's got to be buried. And funerals, whether you or I like it or not, are a business.' She turned to Shooberg. 'Karl, I'll leave it all to you. He'll be buried from here. I'll choose somewhere on the ranch for the grave.'

Shooberg, who Random suspected would look on the whole of life from birth to burial as a business, nodded. 'I'll get back to Helena now, send out the notices right away. You going to talk to the newspaper guys?'

'It has to be done,' Grace said, and looked at Random. 'Excuse me, Mr Random.'

She went out with Shooberg, and Random was left alone with Coulson in the big room. Coulson got up, walked to the window-wall and stared out. Random watched him, aware of the tension in the big man's heavy frame; Coulson, he thought, would be the sort who would fight his way physically out of any situation that was too much for him. *I'm not going to have an easy time with the palace guard.*

Coulson turned round, walked across to the large bar in one corner. 'I could do with a drink. What's yours?'

'I only drink beer during the day.'

'Your choice.' He opened a refrigerator hidden beneath the bar. 'There's American, Dutch, German, Scandinavian, English. Harry catered for everybody.'

'I'll have Carlsberg, if it's there.'

While Coulson poured the drinks, Random looked around him. Usually he took little notice of his surroundings when he was indoors; the furnishings that occupied so many people so much meant nothing to him. The old house outside Long Melford in Suffolk had been furnished long before he was born; he couldn't remember one item in it that had been bought by his parents. He supposed there was a refrigerator and a modern stove in the kitchen, but he had never bothered to look. He had never learned to judge anyone by their possessions.

But now he could not place Grace Jardine in this room. She seemed to him as feminine as any women he had ever met, without resorting to the giggling of certain of his cousins or the attacks of the vapours of one of his more elderly aunts; she was feminine without being soft or helpless. But there was little, if any, of her personality in this big male room. The dead owner stared out at the room from a large, silver-framed photograph: Harry Jardine, ruggedly handsome, smiling broadly, standing proudly beside a muscular stallion that, Random was to learn later, was one of the quarter-horses he bred: this was his room and no doubt about it. The walls, timber or stone, were hung with hunting equipment and trophies. *Machismo* is the message, Random thought, this is the room of a man who swung his balls like cymbals. Elk, deer, a black bear, a big-horned sheep: it was like being in a dead zoo. Random, eye inexperienced in such detail, looked for the touch of a woman and saw none.

Coulson brought the drinks, sat down, ran a hand through his grey curly hair. 'Cheers, or whatever you English say. A helluva day to arrive.'

'I keep hearing that. Perhaps I should have come yesterday. At least I'd have met Harry Jardine. I mean while he was still alive. Did he have many enemies?'

'That's a helluva question.' But Coulson looked at his drink, then at last said, 'He had a few. You didn't see the car that drove away, the killer's?'

'No, I told the sheriff that. There *was* a car up on that road earlier, but I only caught a glimpse of it.'

'Yeah. Jesus – !' He shook his head, took a long swallow of his bourbon. Then he said abruptly, 'Why did London send *you*?'

Random noted the underlining of *you*. 'I suppose they thought I was the best man for the job. And my youth – ' He smiled, but there was no reaction from Coulson. 'That may have helped. Our top man in British Columbia, the only one with any real experience of North American forests, is like Fletcher, just about to retire. I was told to expect to be here indefinitely. Unless, of course, I rubbed some of the local people up the wrong way. Jardine, for instance.'

'Well, you don't have to worry about Harry.'

'No.' Random sipped his beer, looking straight at one of the two men he might have to worry about.

If Coulson caught the point of the direct gaze, he ignored it. 'Your father is on the London board, right?'

'Yes. But there was no question of nepotism. My father was at pains that you should understand that.'

'Nepotism?' As if he were puzzled by the word; then he nodded. 'Oh, sure. Right. No nepotism. Your father, he thinking of coming out here? Or any of the other London directors?'

'I don't think so. Not unless someone comes for the funeral.'

'We better tell 'em not to bother. It's a helluva way to come just to pay your respects – ' He looked out through the window-wall. 'I wonder where she'll put the grave?'

'I gather some people like to be buried on a hill. As if there's some sort of view from a high grave.'

'Harry never looked at a view in his life. Not unless it had a dame smack in the middle of it.' He looked back at Random, seemed to think he had said too much. 'Well, that was Harry.'

He sat back in the deep leather chair, lapsed into silence. Random sipped his beer, content to let the other man run the conversation. He was full of mixed reactions to all that had happened today, but he had not been made uncomfortable by them. He had the self-confidence that generations of Randoms had had bred into them, that certainty of themselves that was both the protection and the weakness of the English upper classes.

At last Grace and Shooberg came back into the house. 'They've gone,' said Shooberg. 'The sheriff with them.'

'What did you say to them?' Coulson asked.

'The usual,' said Grace. 'Widows aren't expected to make memorable speeches. Not recent widows.'

'Did they ask any awkward questions? Goddam newsmen, they're always the same. Think they own the rights to your privacy.'

Well, there's one American who thinks like I do, thought

Random. But was already wondering how many other things he and Coulson would agree upon.

'They asked her if she had any idea who might've shot Harry,' said Shooberg.

'Sons-of-bitches! Asking a question like that – ' Coulson went across and put his empty glass down on the bar with a thump.

Random had risen and moved back against a wall, trying to stay beyond the tight circle of the others' preoccupation. But he was watching Grace, aware now of the strain in the beautiful face. He was not surprised that she showed no signs of having broken down on the news of her husband's death; grief, he knew, could be banal and therefore covered up. Even death could be banal; but not murder. And whether Grace Jardine grieved or not at her husband's death, she was shocked at the way in which he had died. Random was certain of that.

'We're never going to find out with that guy Gauge in charge of the investigating,' said Shooberg.

'Don't interfere, Karl,' said Grace quietly. 'Let them do it their way.'

'Whatever you say.' Shooberg was smoking a cheroot again, the holder moving up and down in his mouth as he spoke. Random wondered if his voice had developed its rasping note because it had always had to force its way out past the holder. 'I'll go back to Helena now, Grace. I'll call the Governor, tell him you won't be at his reception tonight.'

'I'll be there.' Grace looked calmly at both Shooberg and Coulson as they stared at her. 'I don't think Harry would mind.'

The two men exchanged glances; then Coulson shrugged. 'You know what you want to do, Grace.'

Grace nodded, but didn't answer him. Instead she turned to Random, who, still not wanting to intrude, had now moved across to the window-wall. 'Mr Random, unless you are too bushed, would you like to come to the Governor's reception tonight? You may not get another chance to meet the people who run this state, not all in one bunch.'

Random was about to decline, when he saw the two men behind Grace exchange glances again. They don't want me there, he thought; and said, 'I think it would be a good idea, Mrs Jardine. Especially if I'm going to have to stay in Tozabe most of the time.'

'Oh, we'll see you don't have to do that.'

She let her gaze remain on him just a moment or two longer than was necessary; she was not being coquettish with him, he guessed she was too intelligent for that, but he had the feeling he had already been sized up and passed as acceptable. His reaction to a woman's acceptance or rejection of him in the past had been casual; there had been no real pain when Jennifer had finally told him she wanted a divorce. But now he felt an unaccustomed pleasure that Grace Jardine had not dismissed him as just another man.

'You go back to Helena with Karl,' she told Coulson. 'I'll drive Mr Random back to Tozabe and bring him into town with me this evening.'

'Do you think that's wise?' Random saw Grace's face stiffen; and so did Coulson. The big man added hastily, 'I mean, maybe you'll need me up at Tozabe to handle that County Attorney.'

'I can handle him,' Grace said and there was a cold edge to her voice that both Coulson and Random caught. She could handle any man, Random thought; and looked at her this time with caution. 'Don't fuss over me, Jim. You know me better than that.'

'Right!' Coulson seemed to change his attitude; he became crisply co-operative. 'You sure never were one for being fussed over. Okay, Grace, we'll see you at the Governor's place tonight. You too, Random.'

'If you bump into any newsmen,' Shooberg said to Random, 'refer 'em to us. I guess all you'll want to do is get on with your job.'

Grace took Shooberg and Coulson to the front door, then came back into the living room. She paused in front of Random and looked him up and down. She was short, no more than five three, he guessed, but she held herself straight and she looked taller than she was. She had a full-bosomed figure and, a feature he always appreciated in women, good sleek legs. He became aware that he was studying her as much as she was him, and he smiled.

'What are you smiling at?'

'I'm sorry. I shouldn't be smiling at a time like this.'

She frowned and for the first time he saw something like pain in the beautiful eyes. She sighed, turned away from him. 'You have a lot to learn, Mr Random. Are you ready?'

33

'To learn?'

It was her turn to smile. 'No, to go back to Tozabe.'

She drove a Lincoln Continental and she drove it well, though he thought she looked ridiculously small in the huge car. 'It eats up the gas,' she said. 'Maybe with the energy situation the way it is, I ought to drive something smaller. Do you believe in setting an example, Mr Random?'

'I can't say I've ever bothered. I leave that to my father and my elder brother. My brother is an MP. A Member of Parliament,' he explained as he saw her look at him.

'My husband was planning to be a US Senator, but I don't think it occurred to him to set an example.' He had been noticing her voice; she had obviously worked on it. There was a veneer of education to it, but only a veneer; a stranger to American regional accents, it was difficult for him to put a finger on what distinguished her voice. It was more in her *arrangement* of words, an occasional stiffness, than in any accent. She did not speak *naicely*: those women in England he recognized before they had uttered half a dozen vowels. There were supposed to be no classes in America, but he guessed that Grace Jardine, beginning God knew when, had been gradually moving up the line from station to station. 'What's the matter? Have I said something wrong?'

He hedged, recovering. 'Probably not. It just seemed strange to hear you say your husband *planned* to be a Senator.'

'My husband was like that. It would have been the first time in his life he had ever run for office and he wouldn't have run if he hadn't been guaranteed election. Oh, he planned to be a Senator, all right.'

Random had turned to look out at the wide shallow valley through which they were driving. The fields stretched away on either side, sun-bleached and dry, sharp as glaring brass against the eye. Angus cattle stood in pools of shadow as black as themselves. On the slope of a hill grey Charolais cattle, less substantial than their shadows, moved like a mirage through the brilliant, eye-paining light. Along the tops of the hills pines, like a black-green wall of quartz, divided the yellow-brown glare of the land from the bright blue glare of the sky. Random could see no sign of any men working in the whole wide landscape.

'Is this all your land?'

'The whole valley. And the Limbo Valley too. That is, until we

34

went into partnership with Kenneway, I mean with the Limbo. My husband was the biggest landowner in the state.'

They began to climb through the mountains, speeding up the road that skirted the narrow gap that was the entrance to Limbo Valley. 'That's called Massacre Gap. It happened back in 1870. An army cavalry troop came through here looking for Indian horse thieves. There were some Blackfeet camped down by the river there. The cavalry didn't ask any questions, just went in. They killed over a hundred of the Indians, men, women and children.'

Random looked down into the gap, at the silver river, the narrow green meadows on either side, the trees like dark mourners ranked below the cliffs: the scene could not have been more peaceful. Blood was a stain that soon faded, especially on exposed ground: he had seen that when in the army. He wondered how many memories or consciences had been stained by the Indian blood. It was hard to tell about Grace Jardine. She had mentioned the massacre matter-of-factly, as she might have pointed out any other, less gruesome landmark.

'Is there any sort of memorial down there?'

'No. The Indians wanted to put up one several years ago. They had no money, so they came to my husband. But he was never a sentimentalist, he didn't believe in memorials.'

'Will you put up one?'

'Who to? Him or the Indians?'

'Both.'

She looked at him out of the corners of her eyes: they seemed even another colour now, almost black. 'You're an interesting man, Mr Random. I just wonder how long you're going to last up here.'

'That's a question I ask myself everywhere I go.'

'Do you look for trouble?'

'No, not really.'

'It wouldn't be wise to try. This state has a history of trouble-makers. None of them ever got to be a winner.'

4

The Governor's mansion in Helena was not what Random had expected. Passing the grand copper-domed State Capitol, he had assumed that the Chief Executive's house would be in the same rather ornate style. Instead it turned out to be a large red-brick house that looked like nothing more than the home of a successful businessman, one without too much imagination. At one end there was an angled walled balcony that might have been meant to suggest the prow of a ship of state; but to Random it suggested no more than a brick barge that had been left high and dry by a receding tide of public opinion.

The mansion stood on the slope of a hill and from the main reception room one looked down across the city towards a flat valley and a distant range of mountains. The city itself, from what Random had seen of it as Grace Jardine had driven him through it, had also been something of a disappointment. As the state capital he had somehow expected it to be a bigger, bustling city; instead it looked no more than a somnolent country town. But he said nothing, worked his face into an expression of interest at everything they passed. He was not going to be a trouble-maker, not even by the sin of omitting to show pleasure when it was expected.

As they drew up in front of the mansion Grace had put on a pair of tinted glasses. 'Maybe I should've brought some really dark ones. There will be some old biddies in there who'll be standing on top of me to see if I've been weeping. Are widows expected to weep in England, new ones?'

'I don't know. I'm afraid I never really concerned myself with what one was expected to do. Not in that sense.'

'You're right.' She took the glasses off and put them in the glove-box of the car. 'I've never worried about convention before. Why start now?'

He got out of the car, flinching as the early evening heat hit him after the Lincoln's air-conditioned interior. He had driven down from Tozabe to the ranch in the Gremlin, waited while Grace showered and changed, then come on with her, glad now that he had accepted her invitation to do so. He was dressed in his best, his *only* suit; he wore a cream silk shirt he had bought in Hong Kong on his way back to London from Australia; and he had put on one of his two ties, the Guards one. He felt like a new boy on his first day at school, about to be presented to the head-master; he remembered his father taking him to Eton, the boring admonitions to stand up straight and look intelligent. Half-

36

smiling, he straightened his already straight back and tried to look intelligent.

'You always seem to be enjoying some private joke,' said Grace. 'Do we really amuse you so much?'

'Actually, I was smiling at something my father used to say to me. It had nothing to do with you or Montana, Mrs Jardine. I'm here to please, not to be amused.'

She looked at him sceptically. 'I doubt it. Are you going to kiss the ladies' hands tonight?'

He smiled at her this time. 'Their husbands may not be amused.'

'No one will be amused tonight, Mr Random. We don't lose a king every day, not in Montana.'

As soon as he stepped into the entrance hall behind Grace, Random felt the eyes settling on him like a small plague. He heard Grace accept the condolences of the trim, grey-haired man in front of her, then she was saying, 'Governor Mackintosh, this is John Random, our new general manager up in Limbo Valley.'

Random felt the firm grip of the hand, remarked the brisk nod of the crew-cut grey head. He had read about Hugh Mackintosh, the career army general, the Vietnam war hero who had been spoken of briefly as a Presidential possibility, who had entered politics as his state's governor and, nationally, hadn't been heard of since. 'Welcome, Mr Random. It's a pleasure to have you with us, even on such a sad day for your corporation. And for our state, too, I must add.'

He *sounds* like a politician, Random thought. He murmured a reply, got another crisp nod from the Governor, wondered if he should have saluted, and moved on.

Grace was already besieged by a platoon of women throwing sympathy like shrapnel. Other women (like Indian scouts, he wondered) watched him suspiciously as he drifted towards the far end of the room where the view was of the outskirts of the city and the flat valley. The valley now was crumpled with shadows in the slanting evening light. Four helicopters, like overweight ducks, took off from the city airport and lumbered away in ragged formation towards the south. A few lights began to glitter, like cheap gems, and a fire truck spun the red ruby of its light down the string of the state highway. The view was hardly one that he could go on admiring all night.

'Do you drink beer this time of day, too?' Coulson appeared beside him with a drink waiter in tow.

'Scotch, just with ice.' The waiter handed him the drink and he raised the glass to Coulson.

'Cheers,' said Coulson, sounding as if he didn't say it too often.

'Yes.' He doubted if Coulson was a man to whom you explained that Guards officers did not say cheers; he would not be interested in or understand the little snobberies and affectations of foreigners. 'Has the funeral been arranged?'

'Day after tomorrow. That won't give your London fellers time to get out here. Guess it can't be helped. The dead don't wait, isn't that what they say?'

'Who, the dead?'

But Coulson had turned away to catch the arm of a tall, pretty woman and turn her round to face Random. 'Honey, I want you to meet John Random. I was telling you about him. My wife, Pet. Petula.'

'Mr Random, it must have been just terrible for you – I mean, what a welcome for you.' Pet Coulson was not as pretty as Random had first thought, though she may once have been. But there was a dullness to her grey eyes, a pale opaqueness that drained her face of vitality; Random was reminded, looking at her dull fair hair and long oval face, of women he had seen in Renaissance paintings, flattened and dimmed by coatings of varnish. He guessed that Mrs Coulson's varnish might be liquor, because she said to her husband, without looking at him, 'My glass is empty, honey.'

For a moment it looked as if Coulson was going to refuse to take the held-out glass. Then he shrugged, took it and went away after a drink waiter. Pet Coulson didn't look after him, but kept looking at Random, as if afraid that she might lose her focus on him.

'What do you think of our state, Mr Random? It's called the Treasure State, that's its nickname, you know? Though God help us, and He doesn't very often, there isn't much treasure left. Though some people have some.' She looked around the room, blinking her eyes, trying to focus on the fortunate ones. But she gave up, looked instead at her husband as he came back with what seemed to Random a very weak drink. 'Ah, here's *my* treasure. Right, honey?'

'Right.'

'But you water the drinks, honey. That would have been an indictable offence in the old days.' She looked at her glass, then at Random. 'Don't tread on any toes, Mr Random.'

She suddenly slipped into the crowd, as if washed away unresistingly by it. Coulson shook his head. 'My wife has a little problem. She worries too much.'

'Who doesn't?' said Random, not wanting to be involved in any domestic confessions.

'Right.'

Then Grace, apparently unscathed from the barrage of sympathy, came up to them, her hand resting lightly on the arm of Governor Mackintosh. The latter held himself straighter than any man Random had ever seen, as if he had an iron pipe for a spine; the arm under Grace's hand looked like a clothed angle-iron. Only his face was not under firm control; he looked awkward, even embarrassed, yet boyishly pleased. He looks as if he could be in love with her, Random thought.

'I was telling the Governor that you had been an army career officer.' Random raised a querying eyebrow and Grace smiled. 'I looked up the dossier on you.'

Random wondered what else the dossier on him had told her. He looked at the Governor as the latter said, 'Were you in the army long, Mr Random?'

'Eight years. I went to Sandhurst, then into the Coldstream Guards. But I never saw any real fighting, not a war anyway. Just a few shots fired in anger in various places.'

'I was in Korea,' said Coulson, aggressively defensive, as if the two ex-professionals were trying to shove him into a rear-echelon area. 'The Governor was CO of our outfit, right, Hugh?'

Mackintosh nodded, but ignored Coulson to continue his conversation with Random. 'You must come and visit with us, Mr Random. More privately, when there's less of a crowd. I'm a great admirer of the British Army, unlike some of my professional colleagues.'

'But no army talk tonight,' said Grace, and the Governor smiled at her: like an obedient lover, Random thought. 'Here comes Bonnie.'

The look on Mackintosh's face didn't change: it was still full of love, but of a different nature. 'Mr Random, I'd like you to meet my daughter.'

The golden-haired girl put out her hand, her face bland and empty of recognition. 'Mr Random. And what brings you to Helena?'

Chapter Two

'Well, what did you think?' Grace said.

'I liked the Governor.'

'Hugh? Yes, he's a nice man. I don't like the word *nice*, but it fits him. He's just not really happy in politics, that's all.'

'What about his daughter? She didn't look happy, either.'

'Bonnie? My, you're observant – you couldn't have been with her more than a minute. Do you usually size women up that quickly?' He gave her his half-smile, and after a moment she went on, 'You're right, she is unhappy, I think. She's a reformed hippy. Most reformed people are never entirely happy, are they? What did you think of the rest of the crowd?'

'They are friendly. Unless their friendliness is hypocritical.'

'No, it's genuine. Something of the hospitality of the Old West still lingers on here. We live a lot in the past, you know.'

We do indeed, she thought, none more than yours truly. But it had not always been so; only in the past twelve months when she had realized that she and Harry no longer had a future together. *Oh God!* she felt the beginning of tears, a sudden filling-up of emotion. She couldn't tell whether it was grief or self-pity; and hated herself if it was the latter.

'Careful!' the man beside her said.

She straightened the speeding car, concentrated again on her driving, became aware again that the man beside her was not Harry. Harry, a nervous passenger, had always been telling her to drive carefully. But in stronger language than this Englishman had used.

'You're starting to feel it, aren't you?' said Random solicitously. 'The day, I mean. Everything that's happened. Do you want me to drive?'

She pulled the car into the side of the road, allowed him to take the wheel. She sat beside him in the big moving room, the light sliding by outside like the blurred negative of a dead world. It was still early, only nine o'clock, and they were less than thirty miles from the city; but it could have been the middle of the night and they could have been in the middle of a remote wilderness. A wilderness that I now own, she thought.

It had not been easy for her to go into Helena to the Governor's reception; and now, thinking back, she was not quite sure why she had. Defiance, she guessed: that had been the trumpet call of her life. Never of triumph or plain joy: always just defiance. But there had been no call for it tonight and she knew she had made another mistake. A mere dead man's widow might make an appearance out of a sense of duty; but a murdered man's widow was expected to show shock, anger, anything more than just grief. Jesus God, she prayed, why don't You occasionally hold me back?

But nobody had been able to hold her back, neither God nor herself. And least of all her parents, Clyde and Rose Hagen, the honyockers.

'What is your family like?'

Random took his eyes off the road for a moment. 'Wasn't that all in the dossier on me?'

She noticed the soft sarcastic edge to his tone. 'Only that your father is a baron or something – '

'Baronet.'

'What's the difference?'

'A baron is a peer, a lord. My father is a knight, but the title is hereditary – my brother will inherit it. There's an old definition – a baronet is one who has ceased to be a gentleman but not become a nobleman. It's a distinction that probably doesn't mean much to an American.'

'Does it mean much to the English?'

'Not to my father. The Randoms have been baronets since 1620. My father considers any barons created since Queen Victoria's time are just upstarts.'

'Do you?'

'I never think about titles.'

'Are you still a gentleman then?'

She saw his smile in the glow from the dashboard lights. 'I try to be. A gentleman would never keep a dossier on someone else.'

'You resent that?'

He retreated a little and she wondered if it was because he didn't want to offend her personally. 'I'd like to see the dossier first. If it's about my work, okay. If it's personal – ?'

'I'm afraid it is.'

And abruptly she shared his resentment. What if someone kept a dossier on her? Would Harry have done such a thing to her? But then she knew he wouldn't have. Harry, for all his faults, had never been a spy. The dossiers in the Kenneway-Jardine files would have been compiled on the orders of Karl Shooberg. She would talk to Karl tomorrow, order all the personal notes in the files to be destroyed.

Random took the car in through the main gates of the Lazy J and up the long avenue of cottonwoods to the front of the house. A car stood in the driveway and Grace frowned, not recognizing it. She didn't want to face strangers, not tonight.

'Will you come in for some supper? You haven't eaten.' She was not really concerned that he might be hungry. She turned to him as the only immediately available defence, someone to act as a buffer between her and whoever was in the house.

'You have a visitor.'

'That's why I want you to come in with me.' She had always been too frank as a young girl; later she had tried to practise subtlety but there were still times when her honesty got the better of her.

He seemed to consider her for a moment, as if afraid of committing himself. She felt a momentary anger, at herself for her candour, at him for his independence. Then he said gently, 'If I can be of any help, I'd like to. It's not going to be easy for you, these next few days.'

Of its own accord her hand reached out and touched his: she had once been full of such generous gestures. 'I'll see that the dossier on you is destroyed.'

'Can you do that?'

'Why not? I'm the boss now.'

She said it lightly, but her own remark echoed in her ears as she led the way into the house; and she would hear it again later. Lee, the Chinese houseboy, opened the door as she reached it. He had worked for Harry for twenty years, a self-contained Oriental in the world of a man who had thought of anybody but a white Montanan as a foreigner. She wondered how Harry's death would have affected the quiet Chinese, but she could not ask him.

'A visitor, missus. A Mr Pendrick.'

'My first husband,' she told Random and failed to keep the note of surprise out of her voice.

'You won't need me, then.' He turned to go.

'I asked you in for supper. Is something prepared, Lee?'

'In the dining room, missus. I set only one place.'

'Make it two.' She read the question behind the inscrutable face. 'Mr Pendrick won't be staying, just Mr Random.'

She went on into the living room, preparing to face Cliff for the first time in twelve years. He lived in Miles City in the eastern part of the state and, as far as she knew, rarely came west to Helena. He had been a railroad engineer while they were married but he had left that job years ago and now had the biggest farm equipment dealership in Miles City. The last time she had seen him was when he had come to offer his condolences the day after Oscar had been killed. It was almost as if he were here now to remind her that he was a survivor, one she hadn't been able to destroy.

He was standing looking out at the dark landscape through the window-wall, a glass of beer in his hand. He had always been a beer-drinker, she remembered; it was beginning to show in the heaviness round his middle. He turned as she and Random came into the room, a man she now wondered she could ever have loved.

But she went forward, put out her hand. 'It was kind of you to come, Cliff. It's been a long time.'

'Too long, Grace. We only seem to see each other on occasions like this.' So he remembered; but then he had always had a good memory. 'I was over this way, seeing some people in Helena, when I heard the news. I'm sorry, Grace.'

She thanked him, then introduced Random. 'It was Mr Random who found Harry.'

Pendrick had a wide, open face made more open by his blunt features and his receding blond hair. He had a deep voice with a perpetual chuckle in it, the wrong sort for an occasion such as now. He compensated by lowering his voice even further, so that it sounded like a deep grumble. The men in my life, Grace thought. Cliff, who now looks just middle-aged and fat and dull; Oscar, the lucky one, who died while I was still in love with him; and Harry. She closed her eyes for a moment, knowing Harry would keep her awake tonight.

'Pity you didn't get to talk to him first. You interested in ecology, Mr Random?'

It was a surprising question and Random looked at Grace. She too, was surprised by it. 'Cliff, Mr Random is here to work for the company. I don't think he wants to answer questions like that, not right at this moment. Is that what *you* are interested in now?'

'Among other things. But like you say, now isn't the time to talk about them. Well, I better be getting along. I'm planning to be home in Miles City before daylight.'

'It's a long way, Cliff.' But she didn't offer to let him stay the night. Hospitality had its bounds of decency: you didn't offer a bed in your house to your first husband on the night your third husband had been murdered. *Murdered* . . . the word was wounding in itself.

'Got a big day ahead of me tomorrow. Like to get some sleep before I start it. Goodnight, Grace. I'm sorry about what happened to Harry. I never met him, you know that? I was looking forward to it.'

'How's that?'

'That was what I came over to Helena for. I've put my name down for the Republican candidate for Senator. Nobody wanted to run, you probably heard. Figured it would be a waste of time and money running against Harry. Don't reckon I gave myself much chance, but I thought *someone* should run. Maybe I do have a chance now.' He put out his hand to Random. 'Nice meeting you, Mr Random. I guess you'll get to understand our politics if you stick around here long enough.'

Random murmured something, but Grace didn't hear it. She led Pendrick to the front door, looking at him with revived interest. In the hallway she said, 'It would have been interesting, Cliff – two of my husbands running against each other.'

'Yeah, I thought of that.' His big face closed up for a moment with sincere concern. 'But that wasn't why I was doing it, Grace. Believe me.'

'I do, Cliff.' She leaned forward and kissed his cheek. Once she had kissed him passionately; but that had been another woman, a girl with a different name. 'I always believed you. You were always an honest man.'

'That's all you seemed to think I had to offer you,' he said and went quickly out the door, leaving her with pain that she had never thought him capable of inflicting.

She went back into the living room and Random said, 'I'll go now. You don't need me.'

'You're welcome to stay. You still haven't eaten.'

He shook his head. 'I'm bushed, as you say. There's tomorrow – I have to start work.'

'Of course. You've been kind. Thank you.' She held out her hand, expecting him to shake it, but he raised it to his lips. 'Do you always do that?'

He smiled. 'It started out as a joke, when I was in the army. The colonel's wife was heard to say that Englishmen, especially army officers, thought all gallantry began and ended on the battlefield. She thought we'd prefer to get a medal rather than a woman. From then on every time I met her I kissed her hand.'

'What happened?'

'She thought I should be promoted. The colonel thought I should be shot.'

'I agree with the colonel's wife. Keep it up. Unless you're afraid the people around here might think it's – queer?'

'I don't really care what people think.'

'Somehow I didn't think you would.'

She closed the front door on him, heard him drive away. She stood in the hallway, then became aware of the silence of the big house, the beginning sound of loneliness.

Harry Jardine was buried two days later, at the height of summer in what was to have been the high year of his life. People, not all of them mourners, came from all over the state for the funeral; the avenue of cottonwoods, half a mile from the front gates to the house, was lined both sides with cars. Passers-by on the main highway, if they had been out-of-staters, foreigners or out-landers as Harry would have called them, might have been forgiven if they had thought there was a party or a wedding taking place. The grave was hidden from the road, on a small rise behind the rise on which the house stood. If anyone remarked that the grave faced east, the direction from which Grace, and not Harry, had come, no mention was made of it. None of them knew that it was the only revenge Grace had allowed herself on her late husband. He had always maintained that nothing and nobody good had ever come out of the East; in his drunken, more savage moments he had included her in his abuse. He could lie there now for eternity facing the direction where he had always reckoned Hell began.

The minister, long face set in planes of professional mourning, eulogized Harry, a man he hardly knew and who hadn't been in a church since his wedding day. People stood with their heads bent, not listening, their eyes, moving back and forth under their lowered brows like mice, scanning those who stood around them. Grace did the same, only her head was not lowered, her gaze was frank. *Who among you murdered Harry?*

She had thought about it over the past forty-eight hours. Harry had had enough enemies, God and the world knew. Friends by the score, hangers-on who dropped his name as if they were friends, women who loved him or anyway loved his attention to them: he had been far from *un*popular. But lurking somewhere among the court (she still thought of him as king. It was a silly title, given him by a newspaper editor in sarcasm, but it had stuck) had been someone who hated him enough to have done this . . .

'Sent him to his grave before his time,' intoned the minister.

Black clouds were coming in from the west, over the mountains. There had been little rain in the past two months and this might prove no more than a quickly passing storm. Thunder rolled along the horizon and a baleful grin of lightning split the bruised-looking sky. The minister looked up as if he had heard a private word from God, began to gallop through the final prayers. Harry Jardine went down into the earth with unseemly haste, the rain began to spatter and the crowd was already turning away before the grave-diggers began to throw the first sods on the coffin.

Everyone raced for their cars, uncertain whether Grace wanted them in the house and not wanting to risk being rebuffed by her. In any event today was a working day; it was only a holiday for the dead and the close mourners. Thunder crashed about the ranch, lightning flared, rain drove like silver lances into the dry brown earth. A traffic jam built up between the cottonwoods, horns blared, drivers wound down their windows and shouted at each other, tyres spun in the developing mud. Three cars ran into each other, a fourth ran into one of the cottonwoods . . .

'Trust Harry,' said Grace. 'He couldn't leave on a quiet note. That thunder sounds a bit like his laugh, especially when he was drunk.'

'I didn't know you were poetic,' said Pet Coulson, nodding at her husband to get her a drink. The living room was almost full: these were the real friends. Or those who had stayed behind to get the early news of who had succeeded the king. 'But I wouldn't blame Harry if he was laughing. You'd rather he was like that, wouldn't you, instead of lying out there in the rain, mournful as hell?'

'Pet — ' The two women were side by side, separated for the moment from the rest of the crowd. 'I think you and I may be the only sincere ones here.'

'*In vino veritas*, honey. That's all I got out of three years of college — some Latin phrases. Oh, and Jim. My nearly-All-American end. He *is* the end sometimes, too. Thank you, honey.' Coulson came back with her drink. 'I was telling Grace what the University of Montana gave me. You never did go to college, did you, Grace?'

'I went a couple of times with Harry,' said Grace sweetly. 'To give them a cheque.'

Coulson broke up into laughter, coughing into his drink. His wife just nodded approvingly at Grace: she is long past being offended, the latter thought. 'Keep your sense of humour, Grace.

And don't forget – I'm on your side. Us sincere ones have got to stick together.'

'Right,' said Grace, and moved on, glad of the company in the big house but wishing she could have been more selective of those who had stayed.

'Are you going to stay on out here?' Karl Shooberg, cheroot and holder in his mouth, spoke to her from a corner. Karl, she thought, was always in a corner somewhere, but she never had the feeling he was hiding. Harry, never a man for corners himself, had once explained to her that you could see just as much of a room from a corner as from anywhere else, but the bonus was that the angle of the walls enabled you to hear more. She wondered how much of what was being said in the room was being stored away in Karl's computer brain.

'No, I'll go back to town. I always thought of this place as Harry's.' She looked around the big room, suddenly hated it. 'It's not where I want to be just now.'

'It could be lonely out here for you.' Annabelle Shooberg had been a Basque girl from Idaho and Grace had never understood why she had married Karl. She was a plump, lazily sensual woman, dark-haired and still pretty, and Grace knew that many men, including Harry, had tried to get into bed with her and been quietly told where to get off. Grace, glancing at Shooberg and mentally shaking her head in wonder, could only imagine that Karl was a marvel in bed. On the surface it seemed that he offered nothing else to Annabelle.

'It may be lonely in town, too.'

Annabelle looked sideways at her husband, then back at Grace. 'Men don't understand a woman's loneliness, do they?'

Shooberg said, as if he hadn't heard his wife, 'You ought to take a trip, Grace. That would be best.'

'Are you trying to get rid of me, Karl?'

Shooberg wasn't flustered by the question. 'Why would I want to do that? You know Jim and I have only got your interests at heart.'

'Have you seen Harry's will?' She knew she sounded as if she was needling him, but she couldn't stop herself.

'Not yet.'

'That's strange. You and Jim are the witnesses to it, so Harry told me.'

'I meant I hadn't seen it officially.' It was the first time she had seen him flustered; even then, if she hadn't been watching him so closely, she would have missed the sign. The cheroot and holder rose just a trifle in his mouth, as if his teeth had tightened their grip. 'He didn't add any last-minute codicil, did he?'

'Why would he have done that? I don't think he was expecting to die, do you?'

He looked squarely at her; a flicker of lightning, coming through the window-wall, lit up one side of his bony face. She was reminded of the stone heads of helmeted knights she had seen in French cathedrals on the only trip she had ever made to Europe: the stone eyes had had the same cold challenging look. She stared squarely back at him, aware of Annabelle standing in the corner beside them, seemingly unaligned.

'Do you have something on your mind, Grace?'

'Only Harry's murder.'

Annabelle uttered a soft gasp, but Shooberg's voice didn't alter. 'You don't think I killed him, do you?'

'No, Karl,' she said truthfully, 'I don't. But things are going to be different from now on. I just wanted you to know that.'

He stared at her a moment longer; then he abruptly nodded and walked away. 'Good for you, Grace,' said Annabelle surprisingly, and followed her husband with her slow lazy walk that had always made Harry want to pat her ass. I wonder if he ever did? Grace thought.

Grace was about to move on, to circulate, as Harry had often advised her to do, when she stopped herself. She was not playing hostess to this crowd; she was the widow to whom they had come to pay their respects. She stood and, as if on cue, they began to come forward. She listened to a mixture of sincerity and regret, echoes of another occasion when she had been a widow. But Oscar had been only a shadow of Harry, a smaller version cut from poorer cloth: when he had gone he had left no void other than that in her own life. And that had soon been filled by Harry.

Governor Mackintosh took her arm and led her aside. 'I'm rescuing you, you know that. I can see the boredom on your face.'

'No, you can't, Hugh. I'm a better actress than that. But I wish they would all go home.'

'I can arrange it. I can leave and announce in a loud voice that I think we should all be going.'

'You're a sweet man, Hugh. But this isn't the army, this crowd doesn't take orders or even hints.' She pressed his arm, frowned when she saw the fleeting look on his face. She was experienced enough in men to recognize the look and she felt disappointed in him. *He thinks I'll soon be available.* And realized she had never really looked closely at him before, had always been put off by his military bearing, his crisp no-nonsense attitude. She took her hand away, looked around. 'Is Bonnie with you? Though there's no reason why she should be. At her age she should be avoiding funerals.'

'Oh, she's here.'

She mistook the note in his voice and looked back at him. 'You didn't *order* her to come, did you?'

He didn't smile often and when he did it looked like an effort. 'I've run an army better than I was able to run her. Bonnie doesn't respond to orders. No, she came of her own accord. She's over there, with that Englishman.'

Grace saw Bonnie Mackintosh and John Random standing together out in the hallway, just beyond the arch that led into the living room. There seemed a tension between them and she wondered if Random, the Englishman, the outlander, had said something that Bonnie resented. But she didn't believe Random could be so undiplomatic.

'Let's go and talk to them.'

Bonnie Mackintosh, head bowed over her drink, looked up startled as Grace spoke to her. 'Has Mr Random been treading on your toes? You look as if you don't want to know him.'

'I'm afraid I did tread on her toes.' Random's voice wasn't hurried, but Grace had the feeling he had interjected a little too quickly. 'We were talking politics. That's always dangerous ground for a newcomer.'

'Always,' said Governor Mackintosh. 'And not just for newcomers.'

'It was good of you to come,' said Grace, wanting to hear nothing of politics today.

'I thought I should,' said Random. 'There are four of us here from Tozabe. A sort of works delegation.'

'Have you settled in yet at the office?'

'Not really. I've hardly seen it. The County Attorney was

questioning me all day yesterday. Had me out where I found the – your husband.'

'What did he question you about?' asked Mackintosh.

'That man Wryman seems to think Mr Random knows all about the murder.' Bonnie spoke for the first time, almost aggressively. She's always been a handful for poor old Hugh, Grace thought, I'm surprised he's so patient with her.

'Do you know all about the murder?' said Mackintosh.

'Haven't a clue,' said the Englishman with that mocking half-smile. 'As the saying goes.'

'How is the investigation going?' Grace said.

'That's how I trod on the toes of Miss Mackintosh. I said I thought a lot of the activity was political window-dressing. She said I shouldn't criticize your system until I understood it.'

Grace saw the quick glance Bonnie threw at Random; could it have been a grateful look? But what would she have to be grateful about to a perfect stranger?

'She's never been a diplomat,' her father said. 'You should have heard some of the things she used to say about the army brass. Including *this* army brass.' He smiled at her, his face cracking: but it was a genuine smile, Grace noticed, full of love for his rebellious daughter. He's changing, she thought, something's happening to him.

Bonnie only half-smiled at her father; she turned to Grace, changed the subject too abruptly. 'I've never seen you in black before. It suits you.'

'I don't feel comfortable in it. I don't think Harry would've wanted to see me in it.'

A shadow passed across Bonnie's face, but before she could say anything a tall, heavily-built man with a shock of silver hair came up behind Grace. 'Grace, I have to leave now. I'm due back in Washington tonight.'

'It was kind of you to come all this way home, Mark. Oh, you don't know Mr Random, the new general manager in our timber division. Senator Mountfield.'

'A pleasure to meet you, Mr Random. You're not from our state I take it. You look as if you might be from the East?'

'Behind that innocent remark there's an insult,' Grace told Random. 'Don't waste your time on him, Mark. He's English, he doesn't have a vote.'

The Senator smiled. 'You forget, I'm not running this time. Split-term elections always allow one half of the Senate to be smug towards anyone up for re-election. How will things go with you, Hugh?'

Mackintosh shrugged. 'Hard to tell, now that Harry's gone. With him or you on the ticket, I'd have been safe. But I hear the other side are now perking up, knowing whoever replaces Harry will have to start from scratch.'

'There was a time when I could carry this state on my own,' said Mountfield without conceit; he smiled at Random. 'It was what you would call my fief.'

'Fiefs have gone out of fashion even in England, Senator.'

'The winds of change, as your Mr Macmillan once called them. The wind has taken a little while to get to our country, but it's blowing, it's blowing. It's your generation who stirred it up, Bonnie.'

'No apologies, Senator,' said Bonnie confidently but politely.

'I think I got out of the army just in time,' said Mackintosh. 'She thinks soldiers should be allowed to grow their hair long and have beards.'

'We have a feller like that in the Senate,' said Mountfield. 'I keep wanting to tell the ushers to throw him out. Can't get used to the idea that the voters sent him there.'

'You men in the Senate need to be dusted off,' said Grace. 'There should be a few more women Senators.'

'If they were as elegant and beautiful as you,' said the old man gallantly, 'none of us men would ever want to retire.'

He said goodbye, made a quick trip round the room to mend any fences he might have overlooked, then was gone. The crowd started to follow him and soon only a very few were left in the big room.

Random came up to Grace. 'The chaps are waiting for me outside. They asked me to pay their respects.'

'Do you think you will be able to work easily with them?'

'I think so. There's a foreman named Chris Peeples who seems to be on my side.'

'If you have any problems, come and see me.'

'I'm not sure of the chain of command. Does that mean I'll have to by-pass Coulson and Shooberg?'

'Probably. But I'm giving you an order – come and see me.'

'You're the boss.' Again she saw the mocking half-smile.

'Does that amuse you?'

The smile turned into one of apology. 'I was thinking of my ex-wife. I used to say that to her.'

'Was she? The boss, I mean.'

The smile changed again: self-mocking this time? 'I don't think so. But one never knows about one's independence. Sometimes it's just a sort of Pyrrhic victory.'

She didn't know what a Pyrrhic victory was, but she would look it up; most of her education had been piecemeal like that. She gave him her hand and once again he raised it to his lips. Out of the corner of her eye she saw Hugh Mackintosh and Bonnie, standing some distance away, look at each other in astonishment. Beyond them the Coulsons and the Shoobergs, the only other people left in the room, stared as if Random had just exposed himself.

'Don't give up doing that,' she said softly and wondered at herself for sounding so intimate.

'I shan't. But it will only be for the boss.'

The mocking smile again: but he turned and left her before she could put him in his place. She went back to join the others and Pet Coulson said, 'I haven't seen that since Charles Boyer retired from the movies.'

'Goddam ridiculous,' said her husband. 'He's not a fag, is he?'

Pet hooted and the other three women also laughed, but more quietly. Grace said, 'I don't think you have to worry about Mr Random.'

'Not so long as he does his job,' said Shooberg. He looked out through the window-wall at the storm rolling away to the east ahead of spears of bright sun. 'We could've done with more rain, that won't have done nothing but make the cattle and horses restless. Well, we better be getting back, Annabelle.'

'Us, too.' Coulson hesitated, then looked at Grace. 'I don't want to rush things, Grace, but when do you want Harry's will read?'

'There's no point in holding it off. Tell Ab Chartwell we'll be in his office tomorrow afternoon at five.'

'Are you coming back to town now?' Mackintosh said. 'Bonnie and I would be happy for you to ride with us.'

'No, I'm staying here tonight. I want to go up to Tozabe in the morning.'

She noticed that both Coulson and Shooberg turned back as if they had run into an invisible door in the archway. 'What are you going up there for?' Coulson said. 'You're only going to run into that goddam Wryman again.'

'I won't *run into* him – I'm going to see him. I want to make sure he is doing everything he can to find out who killed Harry. I don't want him putting on a show just for political window-dressing.'

Bonnie Mackintosh seemed to run into the same invisible door. She looked back quickly at Grace, then she turned and hurried out past her father as he stood holding open the front door for her.

'Don't concern yourself too much with it, Grace,' said the Governor. 'You've been through enough already.'

'Where I come from, you could never leave a thing half-finished,' she said. 'Otherwise you didn't survive.'

3

'Your husband was shot with a Winchester Thirty-Oh Six, a Hot Six. Every second man in the state, maybe even every man, has got one. I've got one myself.'

'Isn't there some way you can trace the bullet from a particular rifle?'

'Yes. But that pre-supposes we've got hold of the particular rifle. If you want to name me anyone you suspect, Mrs Jardine, I'll go talk to him, ask him if he has a Hot Six – '

'I don't suspect anyone, Mr Wryman.'

Wryman accepted the admonition, ducking his sandy head a little. He was a medium-height young man, running a little to fat, with a blond frontier moustache and the confidence of someone who had never lost an election. He had started running for office in high school and he was still out front. He had a long eye and ten, fifteen years ahead he could see Washington, D.C. as plainly as he could see the other side of the street from the window of his present office. Like Grace he had no nostalgia for what lay behind him.

'Where do you come from, Mr Wryman?'

'South of Kremlin, in Hill County.'

'I know it. I come from Kipling.'

'I know, ma'am.'

'What are you thinking, Mr Wryman? That we've both come a long way?'

Wryman smiled, looked around the small office. Like the other county officials he was temporarily housed in this old school building; this had been the principal's office but no air of authority remained in the faded, peeling room. Some dissatisfied students had come back after the building had been vacated by the school and scrawled their opinions on the walls; efforts had been made to scrub out the graffiti, but in one corner three letters of a four-letter word showed faintly, like the obscenity of a rebel who had been a bad speller. The new offices, into which he would move when he was re-elected in November (*defeat* was his own idea of an obscene word), would be much better.

'I think you've come a bit farther than me, Mrs Jardine.'

'Anyone who got out of the honyocker shacks has come a long way. I wasn't meaning to make any comparisons, Mr Wryman.'

She left him, went out and drove down to the Kenneway-Jardine offices. It was a one-storey red-brick building set back from the road behind a small parking lot and a strip of lawn. A tall blue spruce stood on either side of the path leading to the front doors. The sawmill and the lumber yards were further out of town and though she had driven by them countless times she had never been in to inspect them. It came to her again that there was so much she now owned about which she knew virtually nothing.

Random rose from behind his desk as his secretary, a red-haired woman with a prominent bust under a tight bright-green sweater, ushered Grace into his office. 'Mrs Jardine might like some coffee, Beryl.'

'No thanks. I never have anything between meals.'

'I wish I could say the same,' said Beryl Gray. 'I admire people with will-power. Oh, I'd like to say how sorry we all were, Mrs Jardine. You know, the dreadful thing that happened. Just dreadful.'

She went out, closing the door behind her, and Grace said, 'She looks and sounds as if she'd brighten up your day.'

Random smiled. 'She was Wally Fletcher's choice, I gather. He bought her that sweater. I suspect his intentions.'

She smiled, relaxing in the chair opposite him. She was conscious of suddenly being at ease with him. 'Has Wally gone?'

'Left this morning. He's going out of Helena on the afternoon plane.'

'I'll call him at the airport, wish him goodbye.'

'He'd like that, I'm sure. He was an admirer of yours.'

'Of my will-power or my bust?'

'He was never really specific,' he said, still smiling. Then he sat up, leaned forward. 'Are you really going to be the boss?'

'That's why I'm here this morning.' It wasn't. She had come here on the spur of the moment, to see him. Everything about him, at least on the surface, pleased her: his looks, his voice and accent, the quiet, well-bred arrogance that was such a sweet irritation to her. He was a pleasant distraction, if nothing else. 'Just to see how things work. And I'll come up once a week from now on.'

'Have you told Coulson and Shooberg what you intend doing?'

She could feel the atmosphere in the room changing: he was treating her as the boss, not as a woman. She felt a slight disappointment; but she had asked for it. 'Something is worrying you about them.'

He looked down at his hands on the desk in front of him, then he raised his head. 'I don't want to start rocking the boat my first week here – I wasn't sent out here to make trouble. But there's something I don't understand and sooner or later I'm going to have to raise it. I'd rather do it sooner than later.'

'Shoot.' *I sound like a boss.*

He raised an eyebrow, but said nothing. He got up, took a thick, plastic-bound file out of a cabinet and came back to his desk. 'I don't know what you know about operations up here – '

'Nothing at all.'

He glanced at her, as if not quite believing her; then he nodded. 'Then you're coming to it with an open mind.'

'Mr Random, do you usually talk as frankly as this to your boss in London?'

'I'm too far down the ladder ever to be called upon by the boss in London. But if he did, yes, I'd talk to him frankly. That was the way I was brought up.'

She smiled, surrendering. 'I was brought up the same way. Go ahead.'

'Most of the cutting of our timber is done for us by small sub-contractors – it doesn't pay us to have our own crews standing by all the time. There is one bigger outfit, the Jefferson Brothers, who seem to work for us practically year-round. But they bring in these small contractors when there is a big cutting programme and they spread the work around amongst them. None of them are working all at once – or haven't been in the past. But now they are being asked to make themselves available within the next month – *all* of them. If we employ them all, they are either going to be in each other's way, cutting down the same stands, or they're going to strip the valley of trees. Either way, it's something that isn't going to look too good in my report to London.'

'Do you have to report to London direct? That's a bit presumptuous of you, isn't it? You're supposed to be working for Kenneway-Jardine and I'd think that Jim Coulson and Karl Shooberg would want you to pass everything through them. They'll report to me and I'll be in touch with London.'

She hadn't raised or sharpened her voice, but there was no mistaking the reproof she was handing him. She might know nothing about the lumber and pulp business, but she knew already how to be a boss.

'I didn't mean I intended reporting direct to London,' he said, but she wasn't sure that he was telling the truth. *He may talk frankly, but he's no fool.* 'But I assumed everything I wrote would be incorporated in what Coulson and Shooberg would tell London – I mean you.'

'I'll see that it is.'

'There's another thing – ' He hesitated, pushed the file away from him and sat back. 'How much mining went on in the valley before Kenneway-Jardine took it over for timber?'

'I couldn't say. There was mining all through these mountains and valleys back in the old days. Why?'

'There was a mining survey team up here last spring. One of my forestry men was in here this morning – he says they're up here again. He came across them by accident, camped up by some place called Piegan Ridge. He wanted to know what they were doing there, but they just told him to shove off. I'm going up there this afternoon.'

'I'm not sure what you think all this adds up to.'

'I'm not sure myself. But after I've had a few words with this survey team, I'm coming down to Helena to see Coulson and

Shooberg. They are the ones who should be able to put a stop to whatever is going on. If something *is* going on.'

'*I* can put a stop to it, if it's necessary.' She stood up, put out her hand. 'No, don't kiss it. Leave that for out of business hours.'

He smiled. 'I'm never gallant to ladies between eight and five.'

'Not even to your secretary?' She stood with her hand on the doorknob. 'I'm going back to our – my house in Helena today. When will you be coming down to see Jim and Karl?'

'The sooner the better. Tomorrow, I hope.'

'Come and have dinner with me tomorrow evening, seven o'clock. The house is on Harrison – you can't miss it. It has wrought-iron gates and there's a coat-of-arms on them.' She saw his eyebrows go up and she smiled, shaking her head. 'Not ours. The house was built in the nineties by a man who had delusions of grandeur – a lot of them had that disease in those days. Harry bought it from his son. It was his wedding present to me. He thought I had delusions of grandeur, too.'

'I'd heard it was the other way round.'

'Who did you hear that from? Never mind. We all aim a little too high sometimes.'

She went out of his office, closing the door behind her, and Beryl Gray said, 'It's nice to have met you, Mrs Jardine. Come again.'

'I'll be doing that. I hope everyone is making Mr Random welcome. It must be difficult for him, an outlander.'

The bright green bosom bounced like a wave about to break. 'Oh, we all think he's just dandy! The girls, anyway. You don't need to worry about him, Mrs Jardine.'

'I wasn't going to,' said Grace. 'I'm sure he'll be – just dandy.'

4

Abner Chartwell was a man made of dried earth and had a voice coated with dust: if you ran a vacuum cleaner over him, Grace thought, he would disappear. 'Furthermore, the deceased – '

'Do we have to keep calling Harry the deceased?' Grace said. 'We all knew him, Ab.'

Chartwell licked his lips and she waited for mud to form.

'All right, Grace. I guess it won't hurt him if we're informal.

The gist of it all is that, aside from those parcels of shares each to Jim and Karl, you get the whole of the estate.'

'Which is worth how much?'

Chartwell looked at Coulson and Shooberg. 'We don't rightly know, do we?'

'The auditors are still working on it,' said Coulson, and laughed. 'But I don't think you've got to worry, Grace.'

Everyone is telling me not to worry. 'I didn't think I'd need to, Jim. I just like to pay attention to details, that's all. It was a habit I got into when I had to count pennies, stretch them into a dollar.'

'If anything's got to be stretched, we'll do it for you,' said Shooberg. 'That's what we're paid for. Besides, we owe it to Harry.'

She smiled her thanks for his lack of compliment, the smile like a slice of lemon-rind in the beauty of her face, and looked back at Chartwell. 'So there's no other bequest? To any charity, anybody he knew?'

'None. He had no other relatives but you. As for charities – ' The dust of his voice curdled into mud for a moment; she remembered that he also attended to the affairs of several charities. 'None at all.'

'Then I think we'd better give something to a couple of charities. You choose them and we'll give them ten thousand dollars each. In Harry's name.'

'It's not legal.'

'If you announce it, it'll be legal enough. You can hint that there would've been more if Harry had had time to sort out his affairs before he died.'

Chartwell looked at Coulson and Shooberg. Then he sighed, waved a resigned hand at Grace. 'I know why you're doing this, Grace, but I don't know whether Harry would have appreciated it. He didn't believe in charity, you know that. Not unless there was a profit in it.'

'You don't really know why I'm doing it, Ab. I'm doing it for myself as much as Harry. If it's all left to me, everyone is going to say that I got what I set out to get. Harry's money.' She looked around at the three men, smiled the lemon-rind smile again. 'You all think that, too. Right?'

Coulson and Chartwell said nothing, just fidgeted in their

chairs. Shooberg chewed on his holder, then said, 'Right. But at least you're honest about it, Grace.'

'There's just one thing you and everybody else overlooked. When I married Harry I loved him, really loved him. That's hard for you to understand. Because none of you ever did that.'

'Ah Jesus, Grace!' Coulson stiffened with indignant protest; he ran his hand through his hair, as he always did when he was upset, 'Christ Almighty, I thought the world of him –'

'But you didn't love him, Jim. Right, Karl?'

Shooberg chewed on his holder again; then he nodded. 'I respected him. That sometimes lasts longer than love.'

I'm not going to let you get away with that. 'You respected the way he made his money, got his power. We've all got our faults – I mean you, Jim and me. We're going to have to work together from now on, so it's best we all know what's wrong with each other.'

'It didn't have to be today,' murmured Chartwell. 'Not here in my office.'

'Why not?' said Grace. 'It makes our understanding sort of legal.'

Chartwell ventured a personal, not a legal, opinion. 'You sound as if you're going to be as difficult as Harry to deal with.'

'Maybe even more so. You can raise your fees, Ab, if I am.'

Chartwell's face suddenly cracked into gullies of mirth. 'I think I'm going to like working for you. Most women come in here don't know their own minds.'

'I'm sure they do, Ab,' said Grace sweetly. 'It's just that you men can't read them properly.'

Coulson and Shooberg, in a cocoon of mutual silence, quieter than she had ever seen either of them before, followed her out to the street. The offices of Jardine Inc., Harry's (no, hers now) holding company and headquarters, were only two blocks down the street, but the three of them had ridden up here in Coulson's car. Montanans never walked unless it was absolutely necessary, as if they were still haunted by fears that Indians lurked at every corner.

'I'll walk home.'

'Hell, you don't have to do that,' Coulson said. 'We're still friends, aren't we? What was said in there isn't going to alter things –'

'Jim, I'm doing it for exercise, not pique. And I want to think.'

'What about, Grace?' said Shooberg, the pragmatic one who was only interested in the heart of the matter.

'Karl, I want a statement by tomorrow night on everything we own and its present value. Also, I want to know any plans Harry had and any commitments he might have made. Finally, I want a report each Monday on what's gone on during the past week. That will include any complaints or questions put to you by anyone who works for us.'

'Why do you want all that, for Crissake?' Coulson said. 'You don't want to be worried – '

'For one thing, it may give us a lead on who wanted Harry dead.'

'A good reason,' said Shooberg, his face expressionless. 'You got any others?'

'Yes,' she said. 'They're the ones I'm going to think about on my way home.'

She left them and began to walk up the hill towards the West Side. An Indian was standing on a corner, not lurking, just swaying slightly in the breeze that blew up from Last Chance Gulch, the main street. He blinked at her, saddle-brown face as blank as dull leather, then hiccuped loudly.

'Fucking firewater,' he said, suddenly grinned at her and staggered off down the side street.

Unoffended, she looked after him; then felt a welling of pity. She had never been interested in or cared about the Indians; they had lost their war years ago and she had never had any conscience about them. Her pity, what there had been of it, had been reserved for the honyockers like her father and mother and her grandparents, killed by dust and drought, scalped by the banks. But now, all at once, staring after the shambling, rolling figure going down the street, she did feel pity. Though she was hardly aware of it, depths were being opened up in her that had for too long been sealed off. With Harry's death and the inheritance of his fortune, she had been released. She could now splurge on anything she wished, including her feelings.

She walked on up the hill, the slope of what was flatteringly called Mount Helena. This was where the successful ones in the mining boom of the nineties had built their homes, each tycoon trying to out-do his neighbour. In that decade there had been more millionaires per capita in Helena than in any other city in the United States; and very few of them had had much taste. The tree-lined streets on the hill were faced by Gothic mansions that, Grace knew, had in the past housed treasures of vulgarity. But the millionaires and their millions were long gone and the present owners had done their best to sweep out the bad taste without sweeping out or offending the ghosts.

She came to the gates of her own place. It was the biggest house on the hill, a monument to the ambitions of the man who had built it; he lay now in some cemetery in the East, eaten by worms, anonymous in the nation of the dead. But his house survived, built of stone stronger and more enduring than his dreams and fortune, its towers at each corner thrust up in obscene defiance of the fate that had overtaken its owner and builder. A huge portico swept like a frozen wave over the drive that led through to the carriage house at the back. Broughams, victorias and cabriolets had drawn up here with horses prancing and harness jingling; now sedans and convertibles arrived with less noise and very much less *élan*. Balls, and not just the owner's, had been held in this house that had been the talk of Montana. Harry had insisted that all his and Grace's big entertainments should be held out at the ranch, but now, coming in the gates, clanging them to behind her, she determined that, when a suitable time had passed, she would open up the house, throw parties and balls, wake up the ghosts that had slumbered for so long.

She passed under one of the big ponderosa pines that stood on either side of the drive, went up the wide steps under the portico and pulled up sharply as the figure rose from the shadows of the front porch. The thought hit her like a knife: *was she going to be killed, too?*

Then Bonnie Mackintosh said, 'I've been waiting to see you.'

In the deep shadows it was easy to hide her weakening feeling of relief; and her surprise at the girl's being here. 'Let's go inside. I take it you didn't come here just to say hallo.'

They went into the big living room; it had once been called the drawing room, but Harry had had no time for that sort of formality. It was heavy with decoration: carved beamed ceiling, a chandelier like a cluster of stalactites, a big fireplace surrounded by pink Carrara marble: the original owner had in effect nailed his money to the walls. Big French mirrors in gilt frames reflected the room and each other from the four walls: it was the sort of room in which John Singer Sargent had painted his women, wrapping them in the richness of their surrounding possessions. The room sometimes overwhelmed Grace, but she wouldn't change it. It had a solidity, a reassurance that the rooms in the flimsy shack out on the plains had never had.

They exchanged trivia till Lee brought them drinks and had retired. Bonnie took a long swallow from her glass, breathed deeply, then said, 'I wrote Harry some letters. I was hoping you might give them back to me.'

Grace sipped her drink, took her time about replying. She had given up, months ago, trying to keep up with Harry's affairs, thinking she knew which way his tastes lay; it had never occurred to her that he might be laying the Governor's daughter. She looked at Bonnie, wondering if the girl had seen in Harry what she had once seen.

'How long has it been going on?'

'Six months, off and on. We used to fight a lot.'

'They must've been pretty private fights. Harry never really bothered about being discreet.'

'I was the one who insisted on being discreet. I didn't want my father to know.'

'Why did you want me to know? If Harry got rid of your letters, I might never have known.'

'I thought of that. But I wanted to be honest with you. I mean, if you did find the letters, I'd have felt worse – '

'You weren't honest with me while Harry was still alive. It doesn't matter,' she said, putting down her drink; her mouth was dry, but the drink had suddenly lost its taste. 'I fell out of love with Harry a couple of years ago, before you came back home. You were only another one in the queue,' she added cruelly.

Bonnie flinched, put down her own glass. 'You hate me, don't you?'

'I would have two years ago, five years ago, when I was still in love with him. I'd have kicked you out of the house if you had come to me like you have now.'

'You can kick me out now. But please – give me those letters first.'

'If I'd found them, were you afraid I'd have told your father?'

'Yes. I've hurt him enough – '

'Were you in love with Harry?'

'At first, yes. I wouldn't have written those letters if I hadn't been. But then – ' She looked around, as if expecting Harry to come into the room. 'I'd broken it off the day – the day before he was killed.'

'Did you kill him?' It was a brutal question, but she felt she owed Bonnie nothing.

'No!' Bonnie shook her head wildly. 'How can you ask that?'

Grace relented a little. 'I'm sorry.' She stood up, suddenly wanting the girl gone. 'I'll go and look for the letters.'

But she knew they wouldn't be in the house, or anywhere else. Harry had never been one for sentimentality, he had never kept even the letters *she* had written him before they were married. But she went through all the drawers of the desk in the study, looked in the safe, searched his wardrobe and dressing-table in his bedroom; there was nothing that hinted of any of his affairs, except a packet of condoms. She looked at the small box, wondering which of his women had not been on the Pill; probably some Catholic. She slammed the drawer shut and went downstairs.

'They're not here. I'll look for them out at the ranch, but I don't think they'll be there, either. Harry didn't keep things like letters. Not even mine.'

'He kept some of mine, I think. He quoted from them the day we had our last fight. Sarcastically. You know what he could be like.' Bonnie was standing in one of the bow windows that jutted out from the two front corners of the room. Beyond her the view extended down over the city, across the valley to the mountains beyond Canyon Ferry Lake; a fire was burning there in the national forest, the glow reflected from the eastern evening sky like a preview of tomorrow's dawn. As she turned round the line of fire seemed to rest on her shoulder. 'Do you miss him?'

'Of course I miss him. You can't live with a man for ten years, even when you've fallen out of love with him, and not miss him. Do you?'

'I don't know. In a way I'm – sort of relieved. Is that dreadful?'

'It's honest, but I wouldn't go broadcasting it. Who else knew about you and Harry?'

'No one. At least I don't think so. Oh Grace!' She dropped her head, moved slightly; the line of fire rested across her shoulders like a red yoke. She put her hand to her mouth, stifled a sob. 'How the hell could I have done it to you?'

Grace went to her, took her hands. She was not tall enough to have taken the girl in her arms; she felt suddenly tender towards Bonnie, but she was not going to make herself look ridiculous. 'It doesn't matter any more – *believe* me. You're not pregnant or anything, are you?'

Bonnie shook her head, regained her composure. 'No.'

'Why did you break it off?'

Bonnie blew her nose, wiped her eyes. Grace had always thought of her as a girl who would never break down, who had her father's iron control. Somehow she felt kinder towards her, to know that she was vulnerable. 'I got tired of the continual rows. And I could see there was no future in it. He told me he would never leave you.'

'I suppose that's some sort of compliment. He probably figured I was just the right sort of hostess for when he got to Washington.'

'That was exactly what he said.' It was Bonnie's turn to be cruel.

'You can have your barb back,' said Grace, making a pretence of removing the dart from her bosom and holding her hand out flat. Then there was the light clang of the front-door bell, a musical sound as old-fashioned as that of a sleigh bell. 'That'll be Mr Random. He's coming for dinner.'

Bonnie turned quickly away, picked up the fringed shoulder-bag she had been carrying. Grace noticed it was the only hint of how she was so often dressed: casually in slacks and shirt or in the hippy-style kaftans she had brought back from her time in California. This evening she was in a linen suit, shoes instead of her usual sandals, and even stockings: she might have been a secretary applying for a job, except that a professional secretary would have had her seams straight. She turned back and Grace saw that she looked flustered.

'I've stayed too long – I didn't mean to interrupt anything – '

'You're not interrupting anything. Mr Random works for me – it's just a business dinner, to get to know him – ' Is it? she asked herself; and for the first time wondered why she had invited him here to the house. She looked closely at Bonnie. 'Don't you like him?'

'What makes you ask that? I hardly know him – '

Then Lee ushered Random into the room. The latter seemed to pull up sharply when he saw Bonnie, but it was only momentarily; anyone less observant than Grace would have missed it. But he relaxed at once, spread his charming smile on both of them.

'I'm sorry. Perhaps I'm too early?'

'I like punctual people,' said Grace.

'My father beat it into me with a stick. He used to say punctuality was the courtesy of kings.'

'I don't think *our* late king was ever punctual,' said Grace, not looking at Bonnie. 'At least never with me.'

'I must be going.' Bonnie moved awkwardly towards the door. 'Nice meeting you again, Mr Random. 'Night, Grace. And thank you.'

She went out, stiff-legged as if not trusting the high heels she wore, and a moment later they heard the front door close behind her. Lee, white-coated and soft-footed, came back to the living room and moved like a ghost about it, pulling the heavy drapes. He reached the door again and said, 'Supper in half an hour, missus. Annie going to her Bible meeting. A drink, Mr Random?'

'A Scotch,' said Random. 'No water, just ice.'

Lee went out and Grace said, 'You caught me before I could put my face on.'

'I told you I was too early.'

'No. I hadn't expected Bonnie to be here. She had a small problem she wanted me to cope with. Will you give me a few minutes?' She paused at the door. 'You keep mentioning your father. I want you to tell me all about him and your family.'

'Later. There are a few other things I want to tell you.'

Chapter Three

1

Random had paused when he pushed open the gates and looked at the coat-of-arms set into the ironwork. Whoever had designed them had known little about heraldry; or perhaps he had known little about his client. The design was perfunctory; beneath it was a scroll bearing the word *Achievement*. Whether it was a motto or a boast was hard to tell.

When Grace had left his office yesterday he had sat thinking about her. He felt at ease with her; and yet . . . He was still thinking about her when he went out to the company jeep and driver that had been provided for him till he knew his way round the valley.

'We have to go down to the mill first, Tim.'

Tim Yertsen was little more than a boy, with a long sallow face, deep-set eyes behind thick-lensed gold-rimmed glasses, and long lank hair. 'Right, Mr Random. Then we going up the valley?'

'Right.' *Watch it: don't start sounding like a caricature of the natives.*

The town was behind them: they did not have to drive through it to reach the mill, which was half a mile down the main highway. It backed on to the river, set in one of the few cleared areas in the valley. The whine of the saws and the clang of the mechanical log-handlers inside the long galvanized-iron sheds hit Random's ears as he got out of the jeep. A tall old-fashioned tepee burner, a conical tower built of sheet iron where the mill waste was burnt, added its heat to the burning day. Random skirted it, went by the chipper hopper where wood chips were sorted for size for wood pulp, and found Chris Peeples in the long shed where the barking drums were stripping the bark from the logs as they came in on the belts from outside. The noise was deafening, metal and wood clanging and thumping against each other. Some of the men looked at Random, then put their hard-hatted heads together, like conferring mushrooms, and exchanged comments that no one but themselves heard. Random jerked his head at Peeples and the foreman followed him outside.

'If we got to handle all that extra timber they're expecting to cut, I'm going to need another one of those.' Peeples pointed across the big yard to where a mobile log-handler, like a front-end loader with huge claws that Random knew could lift a 90,000-pound load, was picking up giant logs and carrying them across to the belts that took them into the saws.

'Okay, I'll see about it. It's a lot of money for one of those – ' He looked at Peeples, already confident that he could be blunt with the wall-eyed foreman: 'That wasn't the real reason you wanted to see me.'

Peeples grinned, his good eye gleaming. 'I think you and me are going to understand each other pretty good. What do I call you? You want to be Mr Random?'

'Jack.'

'Right, Jack it is. Okay, there *was* something else. I understand you're going up to Piegan Ridge, have a look at them survey buggers. Mind if I come along? I was with Wally when we run out the last lot.'

'You think I'm going to run this lot out?'

'If they're doing what I think they're doing, we *better* run 'em out. We don't want no more mines being opened up in the valley.' His good eye seemed to swivel independently of the other as he looked up towards the rim of the mountains. 'I grew up here. When I kick the bucket, I don't reckon Paradise is going to be any better'n this. I've seen what mines can do, even small ones. We don't want 'em in here, not ever again.'

Random, too, had seen what mining could do. He remembered

his one visit to Queenstown in western Tasmania and the moonscape hills surrounding it; he had not been able to return soon enough to the forested valley in which he had been working. He shuddered to think of these beautiful mountains looking like those ugly Tasmanian hills.

'I don't think there's much chance of that. I can tell you, the London board is only interested in timber and pulp. With paper as short as it is, they're making all the money they're likely to need.'

'The money men, they never settle just for what they *need*. That ain't what capitalism is about.'

'Chris, don't tell me you're a communist?'

The foreman looked sideways at him, the good eye on the far side of the wall-eye. 'No. But I'm an old-fashioned Norman Thomas socialist. Ain't many of us left. My old man was a Wobbly, one of the Industrial Workers of the World, down in Butte. That was before I was born. He blew his arm off, dynamiting some company office down there when the company locked 'em out. It sort of sobered him up and he became a socialist instead of a Marxist. I followed in his footsteps.' He touched his blind eye, grinned. 'I didn't do this blowing up company property. Just got in the way of a trout hook.'

'You and my father have something in common.'

'He's a socialist?'

Random laughed. 'No, he fishes. I don't think he'd know what a Wobbly was, unless he thought it was a new trout fly.'

The short conversation as they walked towards the jeep, almost inconsequential though it had been, had cemented the rapport between the two men. Random felt he could rely on Peeples, that he spoke for the men of the valley.

As they got into the jeep Random noticed the rifle strapped to the back of the front seat. 'Do you go hunting, Tim?'

'Only in the season. But I allus carry it. You never know, y'know.'

Random leaned back. 'What sort is it?'

'Winchester Thirty-Oh Six. A Hot Six, we call it. You go hunting, Mr Random?'

'Occasionally. I've brought a gun with me.'

'What sort?' Tim Yertsen seemed a keen hunter, but it was difficult to imagine him as such. His eyes peered through the thick-lensed glasses as if he was having trouble even in focusing on the road ahead.

'A Holland and Holland Super Thirty Double.' He hadn't been shooting since he had left the army: the last hunt had been for Arabs in Aden. But he would keep that sick little joke to himself. 'It's an English gun, rather ancient now. My father used it to hunt tiger when he was in India before the war. World War Two,' he added, not sure of the calendar of wars in American minds.

Tim Yertsen nodded, impressed, as if Random himself had gone tiger hunting. 'Tiger, eh? You hear that, Chris? That'd be pretty exciting, eh? Better'n shooting goddam elk.'

Random looked back over his shoulder at Peeples, saw the look of sympathy on the foreman's face. 'I guess so, Tim.'

'I ain't got my first elk yet.' The boy blinked through his glasses at Random. 'But it'll come. Just like your first tiger, eh?'

Random nodded, thinking of how badly he missed the two shots he had got off at the one and only tiger he had seen when he was in Assam.

They had left the main road and were on the Juniper Creek road. Then they turned up a narrow gravel road. Wildflowers were scattered like discarded jewels in the sunlit patches among the trees. They passed a narrow cascade tumbling down towards the river; beargrass grew among the rocks, long white-bulbed stalks standing up like sceptres driven into the ground by departed kings. (Had King Harry carried a sceptre? This had been his kingdom). Back in the galleries of the forest chartreuse moss clothed the lower branches, ermine-clad arms stuck out from the thick trunks of the trees. A magpie flew across the road, long iridescent tail flashing like a sweet pain in the eye as it shot through a shaft of sunlight. Random looked out at it all, loving it all, already feeling at home.

Then suddenly he recognized where they were. He looked back, expecting to see the blue Cadillac, the body of the then stranger in the bushes. 'Yeah,' said Chris Peeples, 'I guess it must of been somewhere around here you found him.'

'There they are!' Tim Yertsen pointed up ahead of them. 'Looks like they're packing up.'

Up ahead, among the trees shrouding a narrow-spined ridge, Random saw the station wagon. Yertsen accelerated the jeep and

they went up the gravel road in a storm of dust and swung off into
the trees. For a moment Random thought they were going to hit
the trees, but Tim Yertsen somehow managed to avoid them. He
jerked the jeep to a stop, was already out and walking towards the
three men beside the station wagon before Random and Peeples
had got their doors open.

'This is private property, you know that? You guys ain't got
no right to be up here –'

The three men looked at him, then looked past him at Random
and Peeples. Random saw Yertsen flush angrily; he had been
about to tell the boy to leave the talking to him, but he restrained
himself. But he decided then and there that Tim Yertsen would
not be his regular driver from now on.

'I'm Random, general manager for Kenneway-Jardine,' he
told the three men. 'Who are you?'

'Just three guys up here for some fishing.' The spokesman was
the youngest of the three, a stocky burly man in his late twenties
with black hair, a black beard and an air of truculence that he
made no attempt to hide. He's confident of himself, Random
thought, too confident. 'We're not doing any harm.'

Random looked at the station wagon, saw the fishing rods
conspicuously lying on top of the canvas-covered gear in the back
of the wagon. 'You weren't fishing yesterday afternoon when one
of my men spoke to you. You were using a theodolite. Unless you
take bearings on the fish before you throw them a line?'

Tim Yertsen snickered. The black-bearded man glanced
quickly at his two companions. They were both men in their
forties, hard-muscled and weather-stained; Random had seen
their type in other parts of the world, tough men who knew how
to look after themselves. He didn't expect a physical fight with
the three trespassers, but he knew they were not going to retreat
in any disorder. All three of them had the air of men who were
here with permission, who were not afraid of any consequences
of their trespassing. To be sure, he really didn't know what the
penalties were for such trespassing. He suddenly became cautious,
though he didn't relax his own air of authority.

'We're moving out,' the black-bearded man said. 'So you
don't have to worry. We got no fish anyway. What are you doing?'

'Taking down your licence number. That way I can trace who
you are, perhaps even whom you're working for. Or fishing for,

if you like. I see you have a Wyoming plate. Don't you have good fishing down there?'

The three men glanced at each other again, then Black Beard said, 'We're just doing what we're paid for.'

'A mining survey?' Chris Peeples spoke for the first time.

Black Beard didn't blink. 'I don't think it's any of your business, mac.'

'Jesus!' Tim Yertsen exploded. 'We ought to put a bullet in your tyres. Who the hell you think you are?'

'We'll find that out soon enough, Tim,' said Random; then jerked his thumb at the three strangers. 'Don't come back. If you do, you'll find yourself and your survey gear in the river with the fish.'

Black Beard grinned. 'I wouldn't be too sure about that.'

Random said nothing further, waited with Peeples and Yertsen while the three men got into the station wagon, took their time about getting themselves settled, then drove out from among the trees and down the trail. Random watched them go, suspecting he hadn't seen the last of them, then he turned to Peeples.

'Are there any old mines around here?'

'The old Kinney mine is farther back up this ridge. It ain't been worked in years, not since I was a boy.'

'Let's go and look at it.'

They drove farther up the trail. The gravel was overgrown with grass and wildflowers, but they followed the wheel-tracks that had been made recently. The climb was steep, but at last the ridge flattened out and they came out of the trees into an overgrown clearing beneath the bulging shoulder of a mountain. A mine entrance gaped in the steep slope at the end of the clearing. Rusting equipment lay about and mounds of slag dotted the clearing like slumbering beasts beneath green hides of weeds. Random had seen such disused mines in other corners of the world: they all looked alike, melancholy with the expired dreams of the men who had dug them.

'What did they take out of here?'

'Copper and gold, I think. Mostly gold, I'd reckon. This was never a big mine, as you can see, so they couldn't have taken enough copper out of it to have made a go of it.'

'Was it a rich gold mine?'

Peeples shook his head. 'I never heard of any big fortune that Old Man Kinney made out of it.'

'Who owns it now?'

'Search me. I guess we do, Kenneway-Jardine. I don't know about mineral rights. I'm a timber man.'

Yertsen had been wandering about the clearing. Now he called to Random, and the latter and Peeples went over to join him where he stood on the edge of the steep slope that ran down to the river far below. 'You see, Mr Random? They been down there. You can see where they cut their way through the bushes.'

Random looked back at the mine, then down the slope at the path, rough but clearly discernible, that had been hacked out of the bushes. 'When did you clear this slope?'

'Last fall,' said Peeples. 'I remember it was pretty poor timber. The ground's got a lot of rock in it.'

'Let's go down.'

It took them twenty minutes, slipping and sliding, clutching at bushes to prevent themselves tumbling to the bottom, to reach the point where the slope flattened out to a high bluff above the river. A few fallen trees lay about, rejects that hadn't finished the journey to the mill; a wide track showed where the logs had been skidded out to wherever the trucks had been waiting for them. At the bottom of the slope three yellow iron stakes had been driven into the ground to make a triangle whose sides were about ten feet long.

'What's that for?' said Yertsen.

'I don't know,' said Random. 'But it means they're coming back.'

'Like shit!'

Yertsen grabbed one of the stakes and began to loosen it in the ground. He wrenched it out, swung it high into the air and down into the river far below; then he ran to another stake. Random said nothing; nor did Peeples. The two older men let the boy work out his anger; what he was doing would have been mere petulance if they had done it themselves, but they were prepared to let him substitute for them. Tim Yertsen tossed the last stake far out from the bluff, stood watching it turn end over end until it crashed into the river and disappeared.

'That'll teach the bastards! Right?'

74

'Right,' said Random, but saw his own doubt reflected in the face of Chris Peeples. 'We'd better be getting back.'

'You going to say anything to Karl Shooberg and Jim Coulson?' Peeples said.

'I'll be seeing them tomorrow down in Helena. Perhaps then we'll know what this is all about.'

Tim Yertsen was out of earshot, already clambering back up the slope. Peeples looked at Random, a trick of light suddenly making his wall-eye as shrewd as the other. 'Including why we're letting out all those contracts for cutting?'

Random nodded. 'But in the meantime, if you have any suspicions, keep them to yourself. Remember, I'm still a new boy around here.'

'You'll do all right,' said Peeples.

That had been yesterday; and last night he had gone down to the small public library in Tozabe and borrowed two books. Today he had driven down to Helena and been to see Jim Coulson.

'Karl's down in Butte and won't be back till around five o'clock. He'll be sorry he missed you – we haven't had a real chance to talk.' Coulson waved an expansive hand towards one of the big leather chairs in the big panelled office. 'This used to be Harry Jardine's office. I'm using it temporarily while mine's being redecorated. Well, what's on your mind, Jack? You sounded a mite mysterious when you called up this morning.'

'Not mysterious,' said Random. 'Just puzzled. There's something going on up there in the valley.'

Coulson was still wearing his welcoming smile, but it seemed frozen now on his broad beefy face. 'Yeah? What's worrying you, Jack?'

Random told him about yesterday's encounter with the three surveyors. 'I understand there was another team of them up there in the spring.'

'Who told you that?' The smile had faded and Coulson's voice was sharp.

'I've been going through the files,' Random said smoothly; he had promised Wally Fletcher he would not involve him. 'There was a letter from Fletcher about it. But there wasn't any reply from you or Mr Shooberg.'

'I guess we just overlooked it. We been pretty busy this year,

75

lots of things going on. I wouldn't worry about these guys, whoever they are. We own the whole valley, we're not going to let any outsiders come in and open up that mine – if that's what you're worried about, Jack.'

Jack: he's too damned friendly, Random thought. 'I know we own the valley, Mr Coulson – '

'Jim. Everybody's on first name terms out here.'

'Jim.' *Let's see how friendly you're going to be when I finish what I have to say.* 'We also own all the mineral rights, or what are called *locatable* minerals. Copper, for instance.'

'So?'

For a moment he wanted to draw back; then he took the plunge. 'So I'm puzzled why two survey teams should have been working up in the valley, when whoever is employing them must know they can't go ahead without our company's permission. And I heard no talk in London before I left that the company was thinking of going into mining.'

'Does the London board usually confide in you?' The smile had gone entirely, the beef in the big face hardening.

'No.'

'Unless your father tells you board secrets?'

I shouldn't have put my head on the block, not so soon. But he remembered the concern of Chris Peeples: *the guys are starting to talk, wondering what the hell is going on.* He ignored the crack about his father, knowing he had half-asked for it, and said, 'Mr Coulson, I didn't come down here to rock the boat or poke my nose into something that isn't my business. But I've only been in Tozabe two or three days and already I've had enquiries about what's going on.'

'Who from?' There was no correction to call him *Jim*.

'Several of the men.'

'Like who?'

Random shook his head. 'I'd have to ask their permission to quote them.'

'Jesus H. Christ!' Coulson slapped the desk in front of him. 'Who're you working for? The company or the goddam employees? You're the manager, Random, you're answerable to us!'

'As soon as I get back to Tozabe I'll have them make their enquiries official. I have to work with these men. I'm not going to get very far with them if the word gets around in the first few days that I'm management's man. In the final analysis I *am* your man and I don't plan to be otherwise. But for the time being you have to allow me to use my discretion – that's what middle management is all about. At your level, board level, you don't have to be discreet. At least not in labour relations.'

Coulson sat back, ran his hand slowly through his hair. 'Jesus, you beat everything! Are all you British so goddam cocky?'

Dad should hear this. 'It's a habit we got into when we believed God was an Englishman.'

'What is He now?'

'Judging by the number of prayer meetings one reads about in the White House, we think He might now be an American.'

Coulson suddenly laughed, slapped the desk again but not angrily this time. He was not without humour, though he had never honed it to any subtlety. 'Like I said, you beat everything. Okay, you handle the men your way. If they come to you again, you can tell 'em as far as you know there's nothing going on that's going to endanger their jobs. Kenneway-Jardine has had no approach from anyone to do any mining up in Limbo Valley. And if it had, it would have to be okayed by the joint board. And in case you don't know, London owns fifty-one per cent of the stock. If they're only interested in timber and pulp, they could always veto any mining development. There, that should set your mind at rest. Right?'

Random stood up. He was aware of the wealth and power that this large office suggested; accompanying his father, he had seen offices like it in the City of London. There were differences: instead of the portraits of past chairmen and the occasional Constable landscape or Stubbs horse, this office was hung with paintings of the Old West, by artists such as Russell, Remington and Seltzer whom Random had never heard of till he had begun to read up on Montana. A collection of old long-barrelled rifles hung on one wall, like a satirical reminder of how some early fortunes had been earned in this country; the City privateers were subtler, decorating their walls with old maps of conquered territories. Random paused by the door, ran his hand down the panelling.

'That's beautiful walnut. I didn't think it grew around here.'

'Harry got it in from New York. He bought the office of his

banker and had the whole lot shipped out here and built in, just like you see.'

'What happened to the banker? Is he behind the woodwork?'

Coulson laughed. 'I never thought to ask. We never give a mind to those Eastern fellers. They sucked this state dry – some of 'em still do. It gave Harry a big kick every time he could put 'em down.'

Random looked about the room. 'There's no portrait of him. I thought all bosses had portraits of themselves in their offices.'

'There was one over there where that Charlie Russell painting is. But Mrs Jardine was in here this morning, had us take it down.'

'Whose is going up instead?'

Coulson studied him for a moment, then apparently decided that the question was perfectly straightforward. 'I don't know that anyone's is going to hang there. But it could be Mrs Jardine's. I guess she's the president now. In name anyway.'

Random had left the office, then spent the afternoon looking around the city. There wasn't much of it and one could walk from one end of it to the other in half an hour; it was more a large town than a city, with a few pretensions towards an uncertain future. The Catholic cathedral stood on a hill, a replica of the cathedral in Cologne; its spires suggested no dreaming, only a sort of puzzlement as to what it was doing out here in these sun-burned wastes. On a lower ridge a minaret pointed at the sky like a gold-nailed finger in an Up-you-Jack gesture: it topped what had once been the Masonic temple and was now the Civic Centre; Random couldn't decide whether the city fathers endorsed the Masons' salute to the Catholics. He drove and walked about the city for several hours, was depressed by its drabness and finally was glad when dusk began to soften it and he drove up the hill to the West Side, the most attractive section, where the money was. He was no real lover of cities, but he had been too long accustomed to the beauty of older, less isolated towns.

He rang the doorbell of the Jardine mansion, was shown in by the Chinese houseboy he had seen out at the ranch, walked into the room where Grace and Bonnie Mackintosh stood waiting for him. He pulled up, aware at once that the atmosphere was thick with something more than just social chatter. There were a few moments of banalities, then Bonnie mumbled a farewell and was gone.

He tried to put her out of his mind, to concentrate on the beautiful woman who was asking him to excuse her while she did what he thought were unnecessary things to her beauty. But he knew he had not seen the last of Bonnie Mackintosh.

2

'My folks were what are called honyockers. Harry used to call me his honyocker, when he was drunk. No one is sure what the word means. We think it came from Hunyak, which was what they called the immigrants who came from central Europe. The honyockers had other names – scissorbills, nesters – but honyocker was the one that stuck. I think personally they should've been called suckers, because that was what they all were, every one of them.'

'Including your folks?' He was dropping easily into the local vernacular. The Randoms hadn't been called *folks* since the Middle Ages.

'Them as much as anyone. My grandfather and grandmother came out here in 1910, the first year they opened up the plains for settlement. My father was six years old then. It cost them twelve dollars and fifty cents to come from St Paul, that's Minnesota, by train to Havre, that's out east on the plains. Another fifty dollars to rent a freight car to bring everything they owned with them. The trip took them four days and then they got off the train and the wolves were waiting for them. It cost them nothing to settle a hundred and sixty acres, but the wolves, the locators as they called themselves, charged anything from twenty to fifty dollars just to help the sucker find his piece of land. And when he found it, most of them must've wondered why they'd come. Or if they didn't wonder right then, it wasn't long before they did.'

'What happened?'

'Drought, mostly.' He noticed she pronounced it *drouth*, something he had not heard since poetry lessons at school. 'By the time my grandparents died, the biggest crop on our farm was dust. But my father and mother stuck it out. You never saw such a stubborn pair.' The beautiful eyes misted for a moment.

'Did you? Stick it out, I mean.'

'Only till I'd finished high school. Then I ran away, went

down to Miles City. That was cattle country and there was more money there. I worked in a beauty parlour. Then I met Cliff Pendrick and married him.' She was silent for a moment; then she looked across at him. 'What about you?'

'Well – ' He was surprised that he should want to tell her about himself. 'My family have been on the land for centuries – drought has never worried us.' He grinned. 'But over the years we've lost most of the land and now we have just the house, a damned great pile, and about fifteen or twenty acres. We couldn't afford to live in it if the government didn't help – it's a National Trust house. I don't care two hoots about it – it's a lot of responsibility looking after it and I don't think anyone really thanks you. But my father is the local squire and he takes it all very seriously.'

She shook her head in disappointment. 'All that heritage and you don't seem to care! Why, here we're proud if we can trace back three generations. This house – ' The beautiful eyes looked up and around her. 'It sounds silly, but I guess I've tried to buy what it represents, something from our local history. I didn't want Harry to buy it for me for its size or its location, it's not a status symbol with me. But it was the quickest way of making myself feel part of the history of this state. You don't feel you're that, out in a shack on the plains or in a beauty parlour in Miles City. Or I didn't. I felt nothing, like I was a bit of tumble-weed.'

'What about your first two husbands? Didn't they – ?'

'Neither of them. They were both outlanders, Cliff from Illinois and Oscar from California. Oh, I loved them – ' She smiled, as if he, too, had smiled. 'But Cliff was a railroad engineer then and Oscar was a travelling salesman. It was like being married to a moveable feast.'

'It must have been lonely for you when they were away.'

'It was. I didn't play around. I'm an old-fashioned Puritan in lots of ways. I wasn't carrying on with Oscar while I was still married to Cliff. He came after Cliff and I were divorced. When Oscar was killed there were several men who offered to *look after* me, as they called it. They were married, but they were willing to have me as their mistress.'

'Was Harry one of them?'

'Harry had never been married till he met me. It was a shock to his system when I told him it was marriage or nothing. It was

80

only later that he reverted to type.' She took a sip of water. 'Are you married?'

'Isn't that in my dossier?'

'No.'

'Somebody slipped up there,' he said, gently sarcastic. 'I *was* married. Her family had much more money than mine. Her father had been in the army, but then after the war he went into the City and made a fortune. I was in the Coldstream Guards, following in the footsteps of my father and her father, too – she loved that, she was a great one for continuity. Like you. What she didn't like was that the army had an annoying habit of sending me off to places without her. She couldn't understand why that had to happen in peacetime.' He sipped from his own glass. 'We never really got on, except physically. That's not enough for a marriage.'

She nodded. 'It's a help, but it's not enough on its own. Why did you leave the army?'

He shrugged. 'A lot of reasons. I couldn't afford it, for one thing. My mess bill used to come to more than the army was paying me. The Guards don't recognize poverty – that's for lesser regiments. She wanted her father to stake me – mine couldn't, he couldn't have kept me in the Boy Scouts by then. But her father knew something about another man's pride.'

'What happened to your wife?'

'Oh, she's married again and very happy, too. To a chap in the Grenadiers, with plenty of money.'

'Did you have any children?'

'We never got round to it, thank God.' He looked at her, his question unspoken.

She shook her head. 'I've had two miscarriages. The doctor advised me not to try again. Well . . .' She sat back in her chair, laughed. 'We've really peeled the skin off ourselves, haven't we?'

'Not that deeply.' But he had told her more than he had told anyone in a long, long time, not since he and Jennifer had been in love. Not wanting any more confessions for the moment he said, 'I'd better be going.'

'It's early.' He noticed she didn't look at her watch, and he was flattered: she was measuring the time by her feelings.

'All right. But no more true confessions. I'd rather go home tonight wanting to know more about you.'

She took him round the house, showing it off with pride and enthusiasm. Her bare arms, only slightly tanned, floated about her as she pointed out details; there was a gracefulness to her that he hadn't noticed before, but then he hadn't seen her as relaxed as this. She's beautiful, he thought, feeling suddenly excited: not just sexually excited, but emotionally, too.

'Are you bored? I'm being selfish. But I'd like to show you the attic.'

Puzzled, his hand now in hers, he followed her up a narrow winding staircase to a wide landing backed by double doors. She swung open the doors, switched on a light. 'There!'

It was a ballroom, an attic that could have contained a world of secrets. And probably does, he thought. But it was empty of all but some chairs along the walls and a shrouded grand piano. She led him to the middle of the room, beneath the clouded sunburst of a very dusty chandelier.

'I used to hold big parties when we first came here – fancy ones, with everyone dressed up. I guess I was trying to recapture the old days. President Roosevelt, Teddy, came here once to a ball. But Harry wanted nothing but his goddam barbecues – ' Her face stiffened fleetingly; then she smiled, was relaxed again. 'I'm not one for barbecues. I like a little gracious living.'

He moved across to the piano, pulled back the shroud, tested the keyboard. The keys were stiff; but so were his fingers. He sat down, began to play one of Chopin's simpler pieces. His fingers occasionally stuttered, but it was evident he had a feeling for the piano. The music, played softly, woke echoes in the corners of the big room: ghosts danced, the past was a presence again.

'You play well.'

'Not really. I have a natural ear, but I had lessons only for a year or two when I was a boy. My mother loved music.'

'So do I. I wanted Harry to sponsor visits by some of the symphony orchestras, Cleveland or one of those, but he thought it was a waste of money. That's Chopin, isn't it? What else can you play?'

He suddenly changed the tempo and the period, his fingers confident now. He played *Wild Man Blues*, not well but not badly; then *Lady of the Evening*; and finally *Oh, Didn't He Ramble*. Then he sat back, his fingers already sore, and smiled at her as she shook her head in wonder.

'Where on earth did you learn all those?'

'Listening to records.' He looked around the room. 'That shook the dust a bit.'

'I'd like to shake it all out, open this room up again. I love the idea of people enjoying themselves in beautiful surroundings. I suppose it's a reaction to what I was used to when I was growing up.'

'You're remarkable,' he said quietly.

'How's that?'

He knew she wasn't fishing for compliments; they had arrived at a point where honesty was natural between them. Or a degree of it. He stepped down from the platform, stood beside her.

'If you stopped mentioning it, no one would ever know you came from a shack out – wherever it is. I don't know how much of the world you've seen, but you're a woman of it.'

'A woman of the world?' She tasted the sound of it; then shook her head. 'In a way I suppose I've been waiting years for someone to say that. But it's not true. I'll never be able to forget that shack.'

He was still holding her hand, standing close beside her. He was conscious of the perfume she wore; the warmth of her body seemed to make it stronger. Here beneath the roof of the house the heat of the day was still trapped; he could see air-conditioners set into the windows, but they were not switched on. The air was still and thick, tinged with dust; he could feel the sweat starting under his arms and on his chest. Grace's hand in his began to feel damp and he saw the faint sheen beginning in the hollow between her breasts. She opened her lips, as if she were about to gasp for breath, and he leaned forward and kissed her.

He kept his mouth on hers, waiting for her reaction, aware of the smell and warmth of her. Her lips were soft but there was no response: God, he thought, I've spoiled it all. Then suddenly she opened her mouth, pressed herself against him and her arms went round his neck. They said nothing, remained embracing, mouths still locked; he could hear the tiny ticking of her watch in his ear, but time itself had stopped. At last they drew apart.

'I don't want to stop at that,' she said. 'Not the way I feel now.'

'Not here. Not with the ghost of President Roosevelt looking on.'

'Downstairs.'

He held her as she went to lead him out of the room. 'Not in Harry's bed.'

'*My* bed,' she said. 'Harry and I hadn't slept together for a year.'

'I'm glad of that. There goes the last shred of conscience I had.'

'I'm glad, too. I told you, I'm an old-fashioned Puritan.'

Later in the bedroom on the second floor, in *her* bed, he said, 'You sure that's how an old-fashioned Puritan acts?'

She smiled lazily. 'I have my lapses. You don't know how I've waited for the right one to come along.'

She kissed him, her long dark hair enveloping him in blackness; he felt smothered in the warm, perfumed night of her. For a moment he wanted to escape, suddenly afraid of commitment so soon, but the languid, sensual closeness of her was too much for him.

Some time later, still naked, she sat in front of her dressing-table and pinned up her hair. He watched her, thinking: she is perfection, a woman in her prime.

'How old are you?'

She half-turned, hands still lifted to her hair, breasts raised: one of the great poses of a woman, he thought. 'You've stopped being gallant.'

'No. I was thinking you are in your prime.'

'A man's expression. It sounds like a cattle buyer's quote. I'm thirty-seven, a bit too old for a good market price.' She came across to the bed. He reached for her, but she shook her head. 'Annie will be back from her Bible class pretty soon. She always comes up to turn down my bed.'

'Do you worry about the servants?'

'Yes. Don't you?'

'Can't say I ever gave them a thought. My brother and I were taught to respect them, but I don't think it ever occurred to us to worry about their opinions of what we did.'

'Well, I'd rather not have Annie making comments down in the kitchen to Lee. You see, I was a servant, or a sort of one. When I worked in that beauty parlour in Miles City I can remember how we all gossiped about the women whose hair we were doing. We knew when certain of them came in for a special, a facial and all the rest of it, we knew it wasn't for their husband, it was for the boy-friend.'

'But you're the boss now.'

'I know. But it makes no difference. I don't care how much people gossip about me outside, that never touches me. But in my own house – ' She shook her head. 'I don't want that.'

He got out of bed, went round to the far side of it. 'Come on, I'll help you re-make it.'

Suddenly she laughed, bent across the bed and smoothed the rumpled sheets. Still laughing softly to herself and he occasionally smiling at her, they made the bed, plumping up the pillows, straightening the silk coverlet and replacing the silk cushions. Then they stood back, still naked. and admired their housework.

'Not a trace,' he said. 'Annie will find nothing there to gossip about at her Bible class. Or in the kitchen. Incidentally, where's your butler?'

'Butler? Oh, *Lee.* He's out in the carriage-house at the back, that's where he and Annie live. When he's settled in front of his TV, the place could burn down for all he'd care. He doesn't have much time for me, anyway. He was always Harry's man.'

'Better have your shower,' he said.

She was about to turn away, but paused. 'Why did you say that?'

Already they had reached the point where their ears were attuned to nuances. Like old married people, he thought. 'When I'm standing around you with no clothes on, I don't want your ex-husband's name mentioned. Any of them.'

She stared at him for a moment, the blue-violet eyes suddenly very dark, then she nodded. 'Right.'

She had her shower, then he went into the bathroom, kissing her as he passed her. She put out a hand and held his jaw. 'I'm glad you came to Montana.'

'So am I,' he said truthfully.

He was under the shower when he heard the phone ring in the bedroom. When he at last turned off the water he could hear her still talking; or rather listening, for her part of the conversation was little more than *yes* and *no.* Finally she said, 'I'll think about it. I'll call you in the morning.'

She hung up as he came through into the bedroom. She sat on the bed staring at the phone, seemingly unaware of him. At last she looked across at him.

'Something wrong?' he said gently.

'That was Mark Mountfield. They want me to take Harry' place in the Senate campaign.'

3

In the next week Lord Kenneway came out from London to lay a wreath on Harry's grave and to pay his respects to the widow. He did both with perfunctory grace, as he might have handed a gold watch to some unfamiliar employee who had just completed fifty years' service. Then he came up to Tozabe and did an equally perfunctory tour of the valley.

'Everything looks well, Random. But dry.'

'If I can find some Indians, we'll have a rain dance.'

Kenneway's look was drier than the countryside. 'Not at company expense, not unless they deliver. Anything you want to discuss with me?'

'No,' said Random, one eye on Coulson who had brought Kenneway up to Tozabe. 'Mr Coulson will have put you in the picture.'

'Good luck, then. I'll give your regards to your father.'

And he was gone, on his way back to London and the making of more money. Random did not like the short, aggressive chairman of the board and it was Kenneway's personality as much as anything else that stopped him from mentioning the mining surveys. He would not have been surprised if Kenneway, in front of Coulson, had chopped him down to size and told him to mind only the business he was paid for. Which was delivering timber.

Random did not see Grace for another week. In that time he heard on the radio and television and read in the newspapers that she had decided to accept the nomination to run for the Senate in November. Her dead husband had run unopposed in the primaries and she was flattered and honoured that no one was now opposing her as the Democratic candidate. It was ironic that she should be opposed on the Republican side by her first husband, but she was sure that it would be a clean and fair campaign between herself and Mr Pendrick, whom she had always found a clean and fair husband. On television and in the newspapers she looked beautiful and sincere. But older than thirty-seven, he thought.

The Kiwanis Club put on a luncheon for Governor Mackintosh – 'He's coming up looking for votes, I guess,' said Chris Peeples – and Random was invited. He found himself at the top table, between Bonnie Mackintosh and County Attorney Wryman.

'Is that an old school tie?' said Wryman pleasantly. 'I understand all Englishmen wear old school ties.'

'Only when we visit the ex-colonies. We think it impresses the natives.'

Wryman grinned, looked around the room. The function was being held in the restaurant of the town's largest motel. There were no women other than the waitresses and Bonnie. This was as good a cross-section of the town and county as one could get, if one excluded women as necessary to a cross-section.

'You already made your reputation when you brought in Harry Jardine.'

'Any progress on that?'

'None so far. But I keep telling the press we're hopeful. I'd like to keep the murderer guessing.'

'That means you've eliminated me as a suspect?'

'You were never one of my suspects, Mr Random. It's got to be a local. One of the natives.' He saw Bonnie covertly watching them and he leaned forward, spoke to her across Random. 'We don't see you and the Governor up this way often enough, Miss Mackintosh.'

'Our loss, I'm sure,' said Bonnie, sounding political. 'I didn't realize the valley is as beautiful as it is.'

'I'd be willing to show it to you if I wasn't so busy. Maybe Mr Random would like to discover it with you. He's new here.'

'So I've heard,' said Bonnie. 'Maybe we could do that, Mr Random?'

'My pleasure,' said Random, but was prevented from saying more by the club president rising to say that Governor Mackintosh, my friend and your friend, would say a few words.

Mackintosh said a few words, coining political clichés that rolled off his military tongue like treason; Random, gazing at him, thought he looked even more uncomfortable than his audience. The men grouped at the tables around the room recognized the pap that was being fed them as an extra dessert, but they forgave him. He was still a hero to them and so far he hadn't sullied his image.

'He's been useless as a governor,' Wryman murmured to Random. 'It's taken him all his first term to learn that political life isn't like the army. But I hear he's started to toughen up in the past couple of months.'

'Will he be returned?'

'Oh, he'll get back, sure. He's got no real opposition. But this time the voters will be expecting more of him, a good deal more. And he won't have Harry Jardine to run to for instructions.'

Random looked along the table at the tall straight figure of the war hero and wondered at how such a man could have surrendered. But perhaps, when he had left the army and come back to civilian life, he had not been able to identify the new enemy. Mackintosh glanced in his direction, saw the Englishman, the foreigner, the non-voter, the ex-professional soldier, looking at him and for a moment the cliché of the moment slipped on his tongue. His glance wavered, then he recovered, looked away and went on with his speech.

Random became aware that Bonnie was watching him. 'He wasn't always like that,' she said.

The luncheon finished and Random rose from the table, pulled out Bonnie's chair for her. 'I'd like to talk to you, Mr Random.'

'Are you free now?' He nodded towards her father besieged by Kiwanis.

'He doesn't need me for the next hour.'

They were walking through the town, turning off Main Street and down in the direction of the river, when he asked, 'What exactly do you do for your father?'

'I'm his official hostess. And I'm lousy at it, I know. But I try, I feel sorry for him –'

'Sorry for him?'

'He should never have got himself into this situation. He should've just retired from the army, stayed on our place down in Paradise Valley and spent his time fishing in the Yellowstone.'

'How did you get yourself into *your* situation? I asked you that the day of the funeral, but you got – uptight, I think you call it.'

'You're pretty square, aren't you?'

They had reached a small park that fronted the river. Cottonwoods and quaking aspens grew along the banks and they found a wooden bench beneath the shade of the trees. The fierce sunlight was fragmented on the swiftly flowing river and both of them put on dark glasses against the jagged glare. Behind them, in the middle of the small park, an iron statue of the frontier scout Jim Bridger looked ready to melt in the valley's oven of heat. This was the hottest day by far since Random's arrival and this morning he had looked up the valley's record of forest fires. The last bad fire had been eight years ago when ten square miles of forest had been burned out and seven men had lost their lives. He took off his glasses for a moment to look up and around the rim of the valley, then he put them on again and looked back at her.

'If you mean I don't know all the hip phrases, yes, I suppose I'm a square. But I'd have thought you were too intelligent to judge anyone by such trivia. But then you didn't show much intelligence getting mixed up with Harry Jardine, did you?'

She stared through the trees at the river, saying nothing. At last, when he had begun to lose patience with her silence, she nodded. 'That was what I wanted to talk to you about. To explain.'

She lapsed into silence again and after a while he said, 'I'm listening.'

'I was bored. It was as simple as that, I've decided. All my life I've got myself into some bloody awful messes just because I was bored. But never one like this.' She lifted the dark glasses to her forehead, gave him the frank honesty of an open look. 'If it ever came out that I was involved with Harry, it would hurt my father, really hurt him. Personally and politically. And I've hurt him enough in the past.'

'How?'

She slid the dark glasses down again, looked out towards the river. 'By being such a disappointment to him. I was his favourite. I've got two brothers, but they took off early. Neither of them wanted to be a general's son – not that I blamed them. It must be really rough on a boy, being a hero's son. Ian and Ross didn't want the army as a career – they did their draft service, then they split. Ian's a General Motors engineer in Detroit and Ross is with IBM in Europe. So Dad concentrated on me. Oh, he didn't want me to join the army – '

'You walk like a career soldier – I mean straight-backed, all that.'

'Yeah, I know. It went against me when I dropped out of college and tried being a hippy. I just couldn't *slouch*, you know?' She suddenly laughed, a very musical sound, the first sign of relaxed merriment he had seen in her. Beneath the dark glasses her face softened. 'I left home right after my mother died and went out to California – to Berkeley, you know? The University of California. It was kind of funny – I was looking for the revolution I'd been reading about and when I got there it was already disappearing out of sight. So I dropped out of college and moved into Haight-Asbury, joined a commune. But it didn't work. Maybe it was my fault, maybe I'd been brain-washed as an army brat. I was always trying to *organize* things. It really bugged me to see how unorganized they all were.' She laughed again.

'Were you on drugs?'

'Oh, I smoked pot – who doesn't?' I don't, thought Random, but then I'm square. 'But I was never on the hard stuff. I tried LSD once and it scared the hell out of me. The hallucinations were worse than reality. Maybe it had something to do with guilt, I don't know. Anyhow, about a year ago I came home. That was guilt, too, I guess. Dad and I get on okay. He appreciates I'm trying to help and he turns a blind eye when I sometimes slip up.'

'Would he have turned a blind eye if he had known about you and Harry Jardine?'

'No. But he didn't know. That was one of the reasons I broke it off with Harry. I knew sooner or later we'd be found out by someone and the word would get back to Dad.'

'You were with Mrs Jardine the other night – does she know?'

'Yes, I told her. She took it better than I thought she would.' She smiled cynically. 'Maybe when the man is a son-of-a-bitch like Harry was, the wife and the other women have a certain empathy. You think so?'

He looked at his watch: he didn't want to become involved in any discussion about Grace. 'We'd better be getting back.'

'Are you going to tell Wryman about seeing me with Harry?' She put the question bluntly, pushing her glasses back up on her forehead.

'I haven't so far,' was all he would concede.

'What does that mean?'

'Nothing more than it says. But I like to leave my options open.

I'm beginning to like this valley – and the people in it.'

'What about the people *out* of it, the ones down in Helena?'

'Ask me in a year or so – if I last that long.'

'You like Grace Jardine.'

'I like you, too, when you're minding your own business.'

'Ouch.' But she smiled and again he remarked how soft and feminine she looked when she dropped her stiff, sullen expression. 'Okay, I'll mind my own business. But do me a favour. If you decide you have to tell Wryman about that day, let me know first. I'll come with you.'

'I thought you might. You're your father's daughter.'

She shook her head. 'No, I'm no heroine. If I was, I'd have shot Harry myself.'

4

Next morning Random and Chris Peeples drove out of town and up towards Piegan Ridge again. They left Tim Yertsen behind this time. 'He's a bit too impulsive,' said Random. 'Until we know what's going on with these new chaps you told me about, I want to play it cool. What's the matter?'

Peeples grinned. 'Chaps. I've never heard a feller say that before, except in movies. I thought only David Niven said it.'

'Do you want me to speak American?'

'Hell, no. You talk any way you want. And that goes for when we meet up with these – chaps.' He leaned back in the jeep's seat and laughed aloud.

They had no trouble finding the intruders. Their mobile drilling rig and two jeeps were parked on the high bluff beneath Piegan Ridge, the drilling rig standing where the yellow stakes, torn out and thrown down into the river by Yertsen, had marked out a triangle. The deep hum of the diesel driving the drilling rig prevented the men from hearing the approach of Random and Peeples in their jeep. The four yellow-helmeted heads swung up and around only when the jeep pulled up close by the rig.

Random and Peeples got out and Random shouted, 'Who's in charge here?'

A big bear of a man, stripped to the waist, crystals of sweat glittering on the golden mat of hair that covered his torso, tapped a thick finger against his chest. Random made a polite gesture asking the man to step out of the immediate range of the noise. The man nodded and followed Random down to the edge of the bluff.

Random introduced himself and the man nodded again. 'I heard about you,' he said in a deep rumble. 'My name's Harrison.'

'You're on private property, do you know that?'

'Sure.' Harrison had none of the belligerence of Black Beard, the leader of the survey crew. He seemed amiable enough, but once again Random noticed the confidence, the air of a man who didn't consider himself a trespasser. 'But I understand that's all been taken care of.'

'Whom are you working for?'

'I'm a private contractor.' Harrison hedged a little. The diesel had been stopped and the other three men were lengthening the drilling rod. He looked across at them, then back at Random. 'I don't want any argument with you. I can understand how you feel. But I got a job to do and I've been assured everything's okay. I don't work for shady outfits, I got too good a reputation to spoil it that way.'

'Are you working for a local crowd?'

'No.'

'Mr Harrison,' Random said patiently, 'you can save a lot of ill-feeling between us if you tell me who gave you the contract. You know it can't remain a secret for too long. And there's already resentment building up against you among the people in the valley. How long do you plan to be here?'

'Coupla weeks, maybe less. Depends what we strike.'

'What are you looking for? Gold? Copper? Uranium?'

Harrison shook his head, the yellow helmet wobbling like a loose cranium. 'I can't tell you that, that's between me and the company I'm working for.'

'All right. Are you going to tell me what the company is?'

Harrison pursed his lips, then shrugged. 'Okay. It's a Wyoming company, down in Cheyenne. The Honyocker Mining Company.'

Chapter Four

Grace walked up towards the ranch house from the grave. From behind her came the chip-chip of the Italian stonemason's hammer as he worked on the headstone above Harry's grave. The headstone, a fine piece of green marble, had been erected yesterday, but when Grace had come out to inspect it she had found Harry's name had been mis-spelled. *Harold John Jardin*: she had never known him as Harold or John and the Jardin had made him a total stranger.

The stonemason, squat and broad, his hammer always in his hand like an extension of it, had wanted to take back the headstone, bring another. 'Can't chip an *e* on da end his name, missus. It upset da balance da letters.'

'My husband was always upsetting the balance of things,' said Grace. 'It'll be appropriate.'

'No unnerstand?'

'It doesn't matter, Mr Giuffre. I don't think too many people will be making pilgrimages out here. Just put an *e* on the end there and we'll hope it doesn't disturb my husband too much, having you work on top of him.'

The stonemason shook his head, blessed himself and went to work, marking Harry Jardine properly for posterity. Grace left him and walked back up to the house. She stood for a moment under the blue spruce that shaded the patio and looked down the valley, past the grave and out to the distant mountains. As far as she could see all the land belonged to her now. But there was no feeling of possession, no excitement, and she wondered at herself. Maybe, she thought, I should have buried Harry somewhere else. He's still got his signature on it all: from down the slope came the chip-chip of the hammer and chisel on the marble.

She heard the phone ring in the house, then it stopped: Lee had answered it. She had brought him and Annie out here with her this morning to help close up the place. She did not intend to spend much time at the ranch during the rest of the summer and the house could be opened and aired once a week by the wife of the ranch foreman. From now till November and the elections, the house in Helena would be her base.

Lee came to the door. 'Mr Random on the phone, missus.'

'I'll take it out here, Lee.'

She sat down at one of the patio tables, still under the shade of the big spruce, and Lee brought her the phone and plugged it into the outlet. She waited till he had gone back inside before she spoke. 'Jack?'

'I called you earlier in the week.' There was no reproach in his voice.

'I didn't get any message. I was wondering if you'd had second thoughts.'

'It's a bit late for that. Re-making the bed didn't wipe out what we did in it.'

She laughed and wondered where he was phoning from. 'I hope Beryl isn't listening in on this?'

She heard him chuckle. 'No, I'm ringing from home. Have *you* had second thoughts?'

'I haven't had much time for *any* thoughts. This seems to have been my week for diving off the high board.'

'Do you really want to run for the Senate?'

'Yes.' There was no hesitation about her reply. But there was a silence at his end of the line and she said, 'You don't approve?'

'Grace, what right have I to approve or disapprove?' She said nothing and he went on (she fancied she could hear the self-mocking smile in his voice), 'You see? You've put me in my place.'

'I don't exactly know what your place is,' she said candidly.

Again there was silence for a moment. Then: 'I think we'd

better stick to business for the time being. Grace, what do you know about a company, registered in Wyoming, called Honyocker Mining?'

'Nothing.'

'It has permission to drill for ore samples up here in the valley. The permit was granted by Wintergreen Investments.' It was her turn to be silent and she could feel him waiting on her. Then he said, no question at all in his voice, 'You know something about Wintergreen.'

'Yes.' But she wasn't prepared to tell him what she knew, not yet. Not until she was sure exactly what his place was in her life. 'Leave it to me, Jack.'

'I shouldn't sit on it too long – '

'Don't start telling me what to do!'

Again the line was silent, then there was something that sounded like a sigh. 'All right. We'll forget it – '

'That wasn't what I said.' She wondered if there was a double meaning to his words: *forget what happened between them, too?* 'Jack, tomorrow's Sunday. I'm not going to have too many days off from now on – '

'Your opponent is already at work. Cliff Pendrick has been up here in the valley, shaking hands and meeting people.'

'You can tell me what he's been saying.'

'Do you want me to come into Helena?' The lack of hesitation in his reply comforted her: he was as eager to see her as she was to see him. For a moment she had wondered if she had made herself look too easy, but now she was reassured. She suddenly laughed, feeling like a schoolgirl. 'Why are you laughing? Don't you want me to come?'

'Oh yes. Yes. But no – not to Helena. Let's go for a picnic, somewhere in the valley.' All at once she decided to stay at the ranch tonight. 'Come and pick me up here.'

'What time?'

She heard herself say, 'Come tonight. Don't eat – I'll make supper for us.' She would send Lee and Annie back to Helena. 'After dark. Nine, nine-thirty.'

It was his turn to laugh. 'Don't worry. I'll see your good name isn't sullied, Senator.'

She knew he was only joking, yet the remark hurt. But he had hung up before she could chide him for it. She sat on at the patio table, only half-aware of the heat rising from the flagstones as the sun slid almost unnoticed under the branches of the spruce. She had a feeling of tension, yet it was pleasant tension: she was about to dive off another high tower. She had never dived off an actual high tower in her life; she even entered the pool on the other side of the patio by going down the steps into the water. She didn't know how she had coined the metaphor; but it had been right on the mark. It described the commitment *and* the sensation. I'm talking about being in love, she thought. Not about running for Senator . . .

Jim Coulson and Karl Shooberg came out on to the patio. Coulson, hearing the tapping of the hammer, nodded down towards the stonemason. 'What's the Eyetalian doing?'

'Correcting Harry, something none of us ever managed to do.' Coulson looked puzzled, but she didn't explain. 'It's too hot out here, let's go inside. I didn't know whether you'd come. Isn't Saturday your golf day, Jim?'

'Glad to get out of it on a day like this. Beer, Karl?'

As they came into the living room he walked across to the bar and opened the fridge. It occurred to Grace that he had never made himself quite as at home as this when Harry had been alive and she felt abruptly resentful. But she held in her temper. She was going to need these two men, much as she might dislike both of them.

'What do you do Saturdays, Karl?' *Chew on your goddam cheroot holder just like every other day in the week?*

Shooberg chewed on his holder. 'Swim occasionally. Sit around and read. Just relax, I guess. But you know what Harry was like, he never knew what day of the week it was. If he called — '

'You came running?'

'Not running, Grace.' He didn't smile. 'Harry always knew I had my own pace.'

'Well, we came running when *you* called us, Grace.' Coulson, full of Saturday afternoon bonhomie and the four beers he'd had before he got her call, raised his glass. 'Here's to our new Senator.'

'Thank you,' said Grace graciously. 'Of course if I win, it will mean I'll have to leave practically all the running of things in your hands.'

'Couldn't be better hands. Even if I do say it myself.'

She smiled at him, but turned to Shooberg, who had the real hands. 'Karl, Wintergreen Investments – ?'

'Yes?' He took the empty holder from his mouth, carefully fitted a cheroot into it.

'I know that's one of the subsidiaries – I saw it on that list you gave me. Where is it registered?'

'Down in Cheyenne. Harry wanted it out-of-state.'

'Why?'

He evaded the question, threw one of his own. 'Why the interest in Wintergreen, Grace? It's only small, a nothing company. It was just one of Harry's whims. You know what he was like, spur of the moment things.'

'What about Honyocker Mining? Was that another one of his whims?'

Shooberg carefully lit his cheroot. He shot a quick glance at Coulson, who had suddenly lost all his bonhomie and looked as if he might lose the beer he had drunk. He raised a hand, ran it through his thick hair, then put the hand over his mouth and only half-stifled a belch. Shooberg blew out smoke from the cheroot, spoke round the holder in a voice flatter than normal.

'That one isn't on the list, Grace.'

'I'd have remembered it if it was. Honyocker was a dirty word between me and Harry. Who owns it, Karl?'

He took his time about answering. You bastard, she thought, don't you dare debate whether I'm entitled to an answer. 'It belongs to you,' he said at last.

'Then why isn't it on the list?'

Coulson had abruptly gulped down his beer, got up and moved across to the bar. Grace turned her head unhurriedly and said, 'Don't drink any more just now, Jim. We're talking business.'

Silence was suddenly another presence in the big room, disturbed only by the quiet hum of the air-conditioning. Coulson flushed, made a business of washing his glass in the sink behind the bar, then came back and sat down. Grace noticed that, whether by design or accident, he sat in the big leather chair that had been Harry's.

'You got a burr under your saddle or something, Grace. Karl and I've noticed it this past week. What's eating you?'

'Nothing,' she half-lied. 'In the past week I've become the richest woman in the state – '

'You've been rich for ten years,' said Shooberg. 'Ever since you married Harry.'

'Wrong, Karl. Harry was rich – I was just married to him. Oh, he gave me practically everything I asked for, I'm not complaining about that. But there's a difference for a woman between having her own money and having to ask her husband for it. You ask Pet and Annabelle.'

'Have you joined Women's Lib or something?' said Coulson.

'You know that would lose me too many votes in this state. It's going to give some of the men a hernia anyway to vote for a woman Senator. No, I'm rich in my own right now and that gives me certain rights I didn't feel I had before. One of them is to be able to ask questions about everything I own.'

'When you go to Washington – '

'You seem sure I will, Karl.'

'You will, all right. Hernias or not, the men are going to vote for you, and so are the women. Cliff Pendrick's going to feel he's running up Granite Peak backwards.'

'Will you vote for me?'

'Jesus, why not?' exclaimed Coulson.

But Shooberg said, 'I never tell anyone how I vote, Grace. That's what the curtain is for on the voting booth.'

She smiled, admiring him while she disliked him. 'I'll have to see we have no curtains in the boardroom when we have a vote. Or do I have a veto?'

Again there was an exchanged glance between the two men. Then Shooberg said, 'That was the way Harry had the articles written. He left most everything to us, but he always had the veto if he wanted to knock something back. The articles haven't been changed.'

'Then we'll keep them as they are. Now tell me about Honyocker Mining.'

'We own it,' said Coulson, taking over from Shooberg. He had been sitting restlessly in Harry's chair, but now he settled back as if, having decided that he and Shooberg would have to be totally frank, he had all at once become confident. 'We own another half-dozen that aren't on that list.'

'All of them registered in Wyoming?'

'No, they're spread around. Wyoming, Texas, Delaware, California. All of them are outside Montana.'

'All mining companies?'

'Honyocker is the only one with Mining in its title. But the others can go into mining if they want to.'

'And do I want to go into mining?'

The looks on their faces told her they hadn't missed the *I*. 'That'll depend on you, Grace,' said Shooberg.

'Whereabouts? Up in Limbo Valley or anywhere in the state?'

'Anywhere at all,' said Coulson, then seemed to add reluctantly, 'But right now we're thinking about the valley. Or Harry was,' he further added, as if the dead owner of the chair in which he sat had suddenly goosed him.

'What's up there that interested Harry so much he had to start up all these out-of-state companies? And don't give me anything about his *whims*.'

Coulson ran his hand through his hair again. 'I told Karl you were going to be a tough cookie to deal with.'

'Are you flattering me or paying me a compliment?'

'Jesus!' Coulson abruptly seemed to subside into his chair.

Shooberg had taken the holder out of his mouth, extinguished the cheroot. He leaned forward, elbows resting on his knees. Grace had never seen him so intent.

'Grace, we didn't put those companies on the list till we were absolutely sure what we'd come up with. If we came up with nothing, there was no point in getting you excited about them.'

'Let me worry about my excitement, Karl. Go on.'

'We're still not sure, but up there in the valley we could be on to the biggest copper strike since the good old days. The price of copper has fallen over the past year, but if the strike is as rich as we think, you could wind up one of the richest women in America.'

She felt a flutter, but it was like a tic in some nerve she couldn't place. 'Go on.'

'Jesus!' said Coulson again, but admiringly this time.

'We own the Kinney mine,' said Shooberg. 'We bought that when we bought up the rest of the valley. It's worked out and there's nothing worthwhile in it — we've had it surveyed and it ain't worth a damn. But — ' There was a note of suppressed excitement in his voice, something Grace had never expected to hear. 'But we've picked up an extension of the old vein. There was a fault, some sort of geological disturbance, maybe a million years ago, I don't know. Anyhow, it broke the vein and Old Man Kinney never did pick it up again. But we have – it was an oblique fault and we found it, about fifteen hundred feet away, downwards and sideways. We got a sample out and we couldn't believe it. It showed six per cent copper!'

'That doesn't mean anything to me.'

'Grace, down in Butte, Anaconda is making money out of ore that shows less than one per cent copper. We got a drill up in the valley now and we're tracing the vein. If it runs long enough and wide enough, Christ knows how much you'll be worth!'

He suddenly sat back in his chair, as if the unaccustomed excitement had exhausted him. She had never seen him like this before; even his sallow face was flushed. She looked at Coulson and saw the excitement reflected there, only to a much greater degree.

'Who else knows about this?'

'We've kept it as quiet as possible.' It was Coulson's turn to sit forward. 'The survey team and the drillers know, but we've promised them a bonus to keep their mouths shut. They'll play ball – they know we own all the rights anyway.'

'Who owns them? Me?'

'That's the snag.' Shooberg sat up again and she saw that the excitement had already evaporated. Or been suppressed. He relit the cheroot, put the holder back in his mouth. 'Kenneway-Jardine own the valley and the mine and all the mineral rights. And Kenneway, the British, own fifty-one per cent, the voting majority.'

'Do they know about the copper?'

'No. Harry wasn't sure they'd be interested. And he didn't want to take any risks till we knew the extent of the strike. He figured that right now all they're interested in is paper and pulp. There's a world shortage of paper, the price has never been higher and it's going to get higher, and Kenneway need all the pulp they can get for their mills. We don't think they'd be interested in any mining activity for another ten, fifteen years.'

'Why can't we mine and grow timber at the same time?'

'There's one other snag – it looks as if we'll have to mine deep to get at the vein. That means we'll need power. And that means building a dam, flooding the valley.'

It was her turn to sit back. She had been sitting upright but not stiffly on the leather couch opposite the two men; it was a big couch and, small as she was, she always felt enveloped by it every time she sat on it. But now she leaned back, feeling the need of some support.

'You're talking about wiping out a whole town, Tozabe, a whole community. How many people are there up in the valley?'

'Five thousand at the last census,' said Shooberg, figures at his tongue-tip. 'We haven't gone into it, but naturally we'd try to resettle 'em all. A lot of them would get work in the mine and there'd be ancillary jobs. We'd have to build a rail spur into the valley to bring out the ore – '

'There'd be a reclamation plant,' said Coulson. 'And we'd have to build a new town site. And the dam itself. Nobody working for us now would be out of a job – he'd just be doing a different job. And maybe getting better pay. In the end that's all the ordinary guy thinks about, how much money he takes home.'

Grace wasn't sure of that. Her father had never thought of how much money he brought home; but then he had never had any. 'It's all hypothetical anyway. If Kenneway say no, and you seem to think they will, what's the point of going on?'

'That's the point of these out-of-state companies,' said Shooberg, thoroughly relaxed again. 'Three of them have got British subsidiaries, set up in London. They're working on the quiet, buying up Kenneway stock over there.'

Grace sat quiet, her restless, excited mind a contrast to her composed exterior. She could not bring everything into focus, but already she could see with certainty that the road to riches was going to be something of an obstacle course.

'How will this affect me in the Senate race? Is there going to be any conflict of interest, anything like that?'

'Only if we got involved with Washington, asked for some sort of Federal aid, and we're not going to do that. You don't have to worry, Grace,' said Shooberg. 'We'll put you in the Senate and we'll make you one of the richest women in America in her own right. What more can a woman want?'

Love: but that's something I doubt you'd understand.

The two men left: Coulson in his Mercedes 450, Shooberg in his four-year-old Plymouth. I wonder how much money Karl's got salted away? Grace thought. She knew that Harry had always paid both of them well, that they had stock in certain of the Jardine companies; the king had known how to keep his courtiers happy by never letting their envy grow large enough to turn them into enemies. Jim Coulson always wore his affluence like a badge: the expensive foreign car, custom-made suits and boots, the refurbished old mansion on the West Side: money, with him, was something to be displayed. Karl Shooberg, on the contrary, wore cheap suits bought off the rack at Hennessy's department store, drove the Plymouth, lived on a small ranch out along the road to Great Falls: money, with him, seemed nothing more than a key he kept in his pocket. Grace wondered what door the key would one day unlock for him.

Giuffre, the stonemason, had also left. Grace walked down to the grave again, looked at the headstone. In the blazing heat of the late afternoon the green marble had the cool look of a block of ice; only when she ran her hand over it did she realize how hot it was. *How cold is the grave, Harry?* She shivered at the silent question, as if Harry had reached up and touched her with a dead finger. She looked at his name, now slightly off-centre with the newly-chipped *e*. Mr Giuffre had tried to restore the optical balance by cutting a small decoration at each end of the name, but all he had succeeded in doing was suggesting that Harold John Jardine had been put in brackets for eternity.

She smiled. 'Sorry, Harry.'

When she got back up to the house Lee and Annie were ready to leave for the drive back to Helena. 'You take the Cadillac, Lee. I'm staying out here tonight.'

'We stay too, then,' said Annie. 'No trouble.'

'House too big for you on your own,' said Lee.

In their way Lee and Annie were ghosts of the past. There had been Chinese in Helena during the boom days, running cafés and laundries, but virtually all of them were gone now. Those that still remained were all descendants of those who had worked in the cafés and laundries; the owners, able to afford the fare and with a stake to get them started elsewhere, mostly had followed the money out of town. Lee and Annie, born and raised here, third generation Montanans, were more native than a lot of the whites.

'You just rest up.' Annie was a plump woman, a Chinese who liked Danish pastries and French fries. 'We look after you.'

'You going to be busy starting Monday.' Lee had been born on Water Street in Helena, where his grandfather had run an opium den. But the den was long gone now and with it all the dreams it had supplied. 'You want rest.'

They were a new couple: even their faces seemed to have changed. Why had they suddenly become so solicitous of her? Then she chided herself for her suspicions. In the past all their loyalty had been to Harry, but there was no reason why they should not have changed.

As if aware of her suspicions, Lee said, 'You the boss now, missus. We with Mr Jardine a long time, before you become his missus.'

'You unnerstand?' said Annie.

Grace looked down towards the grave, then back at the Chinese couple. 'You mean he told you I might not be Mrs Jardine for long?'

'He never say that,' said Annie.

'But we know what he was like,' said Lee. 'Mr Jardine good guy in lots of ways. But not all.'

'Do you think I'm going to be a good guy?'

Lee's expression didn't change, but Annie suddenly smiled, eyes almost disappearing in the folds of her cheeks: Grace could not remember ever having seen her smile before. 'You no guy, missus. You all woman. I think it going to be a nice change.' She looked at Lee as if challenging him to contradict her. 'We look after you, we decided. Right?'

Lee nodded, still unsmiling. 'We work for you now, missus.'

Grace impulsively put out her hands to touch theirs. 'Thank you both. But we'll start Monday. Tonight and tomorrow I just want to be on my own. To think. Maybe I should read some Confucius, maybe he could help me.'

'Confucius never help any woman,' said Annie. 'He just Chinese chauvinist. Like American men.'

Like Harry? But only the two women heard the unspoken

question: Grace saw the gleam of amusement in Annie's eyes. 'Drive Mr Jardine's car back, Lee. We'll have to get rid of it, we don't need it any more. And be ready to leave with me Monday morning in my car. You can drive me on the campaign tour.'

It was Lee's turn to smile, at last. 'That be real nice, missus.'

They drove away in the Cadillac and Grace went back into the house and called the ranch foreman, Joe Ullman. 'Joe, I'll be staying up here at the house tonight. I don't want to be disturbed. I have a lot of work to be done – '

Why am I doing all this explaining? Why can't I just be like Jack and ignore the servants? But the old honyocker sense of guilt remained, the subservience to the proprieties.

She had a bath, luxuriating in the water, singing to herself: *Some Enchanted Evening, Love is a Many-Splendoured Thing.* They were all songs from her younger days, pre-Harry, pre-Oscar, pre-Cliff.

She put on a robe, almost ran to the door to answer the bell when Random rang. He took her in his arms and kissed her. She felt his hands under the robe, then she slid her arms up round his neck. She knew she loved him, if so far it was only her body that was telling her so.

He drew back and she said, 'What are you smiling at now?'

'I was thinking of a girl an uncle of mine used to know, back in the twenties. She said she couldn't understand why everyone referred to their private parts. Hers certainly weren't.'

'Get your hands out of there. I was going to take you into bed and feed you later. Now you can wait. I'm afraid it's steak again.'

'Not with an Idaho baked potato, I hope. Don't they raise any other vegetables west of the Mississippi?'

'What do you eat up at Tozabe?'

'Steak and fish and fish and steak. I dream of cold veal-and-ham pie and some English tomatoes.'

'If that's all you dream of, why am I apologizing for steak?'

He helped her prepare the supper. He even found some wine that she didn't know Harry had. He brought in a bottle, looked at the label. 'Chambertin. Did he really know his wines that well? There are a couple of cases of this out in the storeroom.'

'Someone must have given it to him. I never saw him drink a drop of wine in his life. Do you know much about wine?'

'Not much. I only know about Chambertin because we had a chap in our mess who was always telling us it was Napoleon's favourite. He drank it every night on the retreat from Moscow, while his soldiers froze to death or were hacked to pieces by the Cossacks or eaten alive by wolves.'

'And you think that's an appropriate wine for us?'

'I don't know. Depends whether we think we're in retreat.'

'I'm not. I never turn back.'

'Famous words that didn't last. I've uttered a few of them myself.'

'Such as?'

He hesitated, concentrated on pulling the cork from the bottle. 'Till death us do part.'

Later, lying beside him in bed, she said, 'Darling, we can stop this right now if you like. Before it's too late.'

They lay with their limbs entwined, in the comfortable ju-jitsu of lovers whose battle was over. They were both physically exhausted, but she was surprised at how clear and wide-awake her mind was. She noted that she had called him *darling*, a word she hadn't used in almost two years. His head rested on her breast and she looked down at the out-of-perspective planes of his face, like those of a giant fallen idol. She noticed for the first time how thick and long were his eyelashes, almost as luxuriant as her own.

'You've got bedroom eyes.'

'I bring them with me on occasions like this.' He lifted himself, faced her with his chin now resting on her breast; he hadn't shaved too closely, for she could feel the scrape of his beard against her nipple. 'Grace, I love you. Those are famous words that I hope *will* last. But if you have any doubts – '

She stroked his back, feeling the rivulet of sweat in the hollow of it. There was no fat on him and she got a sensual pleasure from the firm muscles she could feel beneath her finger-tips. The physical side of love had always meant a great deal to her and there had been times since she had stopped sleeping with Harry when hunger for sex had been sheer torture. But she had not gone looking for another man, either as revenge or as solace.

But she knew there was more to this relationship than just the pleasure of sex. Jack was gentle and considerate of her; but then so had been Cliff and Oscar; Harry had never been, but she had loved him just the same for other qualities that she now found hard to remember. There were differences in her and Jack's backgrounds that both fascinated and troubled her. He was not the first Englishman she had met; but none of the others had done more than shake her hand and that in a perfunctory way, frightened off by the presence of Harry. Jack *thought* differently from any other man she had met; some of his remarks were so oblique to her that she had difficulty in translating them. His points of reference were all strange to her; he was almost a visitor from another planet. It was not just his *Englishness*, if that was what you could call it, but that he seemed so – detached? – from everything that conditioned her own life and was important to her.

'I wish we'd met some other time. Maybe next year – '

'Why next year? Why not last year?'

'Last year Harry was still alive. Next year I'll be sure of myself – '

'You may be a Senator next year.'

'Will that make any difference to you?' He didn't answer at once, then moved his head from side to side. She slid her breast out from under his chin. 'You're sandpapering my nipple . . . Everything's happening too fast for me. Harry's death, being asked to run for the Senate, falling in love with you – I've never had to readjust to so many things so fast.'

'I've never felt that love was a matter for readjustment.'

'No, it isn't. You're right. We tie up so much with words these days. Readjust, relate to . . . Do you relate to me?'

'I think the answer to that is just coming up.'

'Ah,' she said, wrapping her arms round him, drawing him to her. 'That's a better answer than any words.'

But as he entered her again she knew it was no answer at all, not one to carry them through the time ahead.

3

In the morning, as they were preparing a picnic basket, she said, 'Would you like to go fishing today?'

'I don't have any gear.' But she could see the enthusiasm in his face. 'I've been meaning to buy some – '

'Harry had a collection of rods. And there are several pairs of waders out in the garage.'

'Stepping into his shoes, eh?' He was at once contrite: 'Sorry. I didn't mean that.'

'Never mind.' But she wished he hadn't said it. 'He's going to keep cropping up between us for quite a while, I guess. But how come your wife never does?'

'Oh, she would if we were in England. Thank God we're not.' He kissed her, then stood back from her. 'I never thought I'd admire a woman in jeans, but that's a beautiful arse. Ass.'

'I rarely wear them – I'm not really the outdoor type. But Harry . . . Sorry.'

He smiled, kissed her again. 'We'll drown him in the river for the day.'

They used Random's car – 'It's less conspicuous.'

'Thinking of the servants?'

'No, the voters.'

They drove in the air-conditioned cocoon through the burning-glass heat of the morning. The mountains to the east lay like warped metal under the glittering brilliance of the sky; the shallow valley, yellow-brown, stapled by fences, lay like animal hides stretched out to dry. It was balm to their eyes when the fields gave way to forest.

They smiled at each other, relaxed and comfortable as old lovers. They climbed through Massacre Gap, descended into Limbo Valley, then Random turned off the highway and found a track that followed the river bank. It led them to a short tributary where the water lay with the stillness of a small lake. Trees grew almost to the water's edge along one side and on the other side a lush meadow ran back to the dark bank of forest. Wildflowers grew among the grass, sprinkling the faded green with colour: the yellow of five-fingers, the yellow, red and white of evening star, the white and pink of kinnikinnick. Out on the water a mallard, gliding in, trailed a silver chain behind it. Random pulled the car in beneath the cool shade of the trees.

'It's idyllic!' Grace exclaimed.

'It's all yours. You mean you've never been here before?' He looked at her in surprise, then turned and looked out at the shining stretch of water. A wedge of ducks, like a black arrow-head, plunged in over the trees, then curved away, sketching a flowing line across his vision. 'I think I could stay here forever. Especially since you come with it.'

He donned a pair of waders, took Harry's rod and some flies and went into the water at a point where the tributary swung away from the main stream. She sat on the grass and watched him, lulled by the heat and a consuming feeling of happiness. She idly picked the flowers scattered about her, remembered the daisy chains she had made as a child; she gave up and just lay watching the river and the man in it. No daisy chain would ever bind him to her.

She had bought the rod for Harry as a birthday present, but she had never seen him use it; he had never believed that a woman should be taken along on a fishing or hunting expedition; he had had his own man's world into which she and no other man's wife had ever been admitted. She luxuriated in the sudden knowledge that she now had her own world, this world about her. She felt the first fever of the virus of power, though she did not recognize it.

Random stayed in the water over an hour, she just enjoying the sight of him moving with lazy grace as he swung his arm in a long cast of the fly. At last he came plodding up on to the bank, dropped three plump trout on the grass. 'I'll remember this day.'

She lay on her back, gazing at him with love. 'We should put it under glass, store it away. Why aren't there some of the folk from Tozabe out here?'

'Probably too hot for them. Some of them may come up in the late afternoon. Fishermen. Damn, there's some – ' He stopped, staring across the stretch of water towards the meadow on the other side.

She sat up. 'Some picnickers?'

He gave her his hand to help her to her feet. 'No. The drillers I told you about. The chaps who are working for Honyocker Mining.'

She felt the heat turn prickly; or so it seemed. She put on her dark glasses, stepped further back into the shade. 'Let's have lunch.'

She was aware of his steady stare and silence as she began to lay out the lunch. At last he said, 'Leave it, Grace – the food, I mean. What's going on with Honyocker? You know, don't you?'

On her knees beside the picnic basket she looked up at him,

then sat back on her heels. 'Yes, I do. But it has nothing to do with you and me.'

He laughed, a little harshly, she thought. 'I should hope not. But I can't turn myself on and off. My life, is – *total*, if you like. It's not divided up into compartments. Sunday is your day, Monday is their day – ' He jerked his thumb in the direction of the far meadow.

She was not long-sighted and with the haze above the long grass of the meadow and the black shadows of the trees beyond it she had not yet seen the intruders. But she was not really concerned whether the drillers, whoever they were, were there or not. 'I'm not going to talk about it, Jack. It's something Harry started and I've only just learned about it. And I don't know everything – not yet.' She knew she was half-lying, or anyway being only half-truthful; but she was determined to save the day, in the almost literal sense. 'Now please let's have lunch.'

He looked once more across the water, then he shrugged and sat down beside her. He reached for her hand, kissed it. 'All right. We'll keep wholly ours the Sabbath Day.'

'Words again,' she said, but she was glad of them.

They ate, lay beside each other on the grass, went for a walk through the trees. He pointed out to her the different kinds of trees, what they were good for; he was amazed at her lack of knowledge, that she had lived here so long and knew so little about what she owned. She explained to him that she came from the plains, that trees down there had been regarded by her father and the other farmers as just something that took up good land.

'We have to be careful, that's why we have selective logging,' he told her. 'Do you know how long it takes for a tree to grow to saw-log size?'

She humoured him, playing dumb woman to smart man. 'No, tell me.'

He was smart enough to know she was taking the mickey out of him. He grinned. 'Righto. But you *should* know, now you own it all. It takes 80 years for a Doug fir, anything from 140 to 180 for a ponderosa. So if we just went through the valley, cutting without selecting the mature trees, it would look like a battlefield for God knows how long. All for the sake of a quick quid. Quick buck.'

'Do you think I'd let myself be guilty of that? Anything for a quick buck?'

'No. But to see that it doesn't happen, you'll need to know a lot more than you do.'

'I've only owned it for a couple of weeks. But now I want to know all about everything.'

'Well, for a start we'll go over and see those drillers.'

He wasn't going to let it lie. 'Damn you! Do you want me to start acting as your boss?'

The mocking half-smile: 'Not on Sunday, ma'am.' Then seriously: 'Darling, I think it needs to be looked into. For your sake. You don't know any of the men up here – they're as remote from you as those trees. But I know how they feel. Timber men are the same all over the world, real timber men, that is. They have a feeling for what they work amongst. And you have several of them here in the valley. Chris Peeples, for one. They don't want outsiders horning in here, especially outsiders who won't say why they're here. I have a nose for trouble and from the day I arrived here there's been a smell on the wind.'

'Where did you get your sensitive nose?'

'In the army.'

They were still standing hand in hand, like lovers exchanging compliments. The day, if not lost, was at least spoiled. 'Jack, you're not going to be able to live your whole life in this valley – I mean while you're here in Montana. But if you feel you've got to know, we'll go over and see those drillers. But I can't promise they're going to tell me anything more than they've told you.' She hoped the men, whoever they were, would think of their bonuses and keep their mouths shut. That might save something of the day.

But it disturbed her that already she was committed to concealing things from him. She chatted with him as they packed the picnic basket and the fishing gear back into the car; but later she would not be able to remember one word of what she had said. Guilt had crept through her like a poison fog and her mind knew nothing of the trivia of her tongue. When she got into the car beside him she had the peculiar feeling that she was starting a trip on an unmarked road.

'Look,' he said reassuringly; he had noticed her preoccupation, 'all this may be something you can put a stop to with just a word.

Play the boss and perhaps they'll disappear and we'll have no trouble at all.'

They followed the track along the tributary till it petered out into a narrow creek, crossed the creek by a shallow ford and turned back towards the meadow. The track wound through trees and Random had to drive slowly. But not slowly enough, Grace thought. She began to hope, foolishly and ridiculously, that when they drove out into the meadow the drillers would have gone. Then up ahead, as the trees began to thin, she saw the jeeps and the big drilling rig.

They drove out of the deep shadow of the trees into the bright green glare of the meadow. And the bullet came through the windshield and thudded into the back of the seat right beside her shoulder.

4

Grace fell sideways against the door. Out of the corner of her eye, her gaze as fragmented as the windscreen, she saw Random struggling with the wheel. As shocked as he was, he had instincively swung the car to the left, as if to get out of the line of the bullet that already arrived. The car went off the track, bumping over ruts, ploughing its way through the long grass. But it was only for a moment; he slammed on the brakes, switched off the engine. His binoculars fell off the top of the dashboard, smashed against the door as the car tilted.

'Get out!'

She fumbled for the handle, but he had already reached across her, found it and pushed open the door. She tumbled out, falling on to the grass; he fell beside her, pushed her down. With her face close against the ground she could see nothing, but she could hear the loud throbbing of the rig's diesel not far from them. Then she became aware of shadows above her and she looked up fearfully.

Two men stood there, both of them in yellow hard hats, neither of them with a gun. The bigger of the two men, who looked huge against the sky above her, shouted, 'Are you all right? What happened?'

Random stood up, helped Grace to her feet. He leaned into the car, picked up his smashed binoculars and looked ruefully at them. Then he took a penknife from the glove-box and probed the back of the front seat. He stepped back, held up the bullet.

'That's what happened.' He gestured at the windshield; Grace saw the small hole in the middle of the silvery opaqueness. 'Were any of your chaps shooting?'

The big man gestured to them. Grace and Random followed him and the other man away from the noise of the rig and the diesel. When they were far enough away to converse normally, Random introduced the big man as Harrison. He in turn introduced the second man.

'Fred Olsen. Sure, we all got guns. But we're working, not on a shooting party.' He looked around him. 'Maybe we better all get out of here. Maybe that wasn't an accidental shot.'

Random was staring down the meadow towards the edge of the forest. 'The shot must have come from down there.'

'It must've been an accident,' Grace said. She was still suffering from the shock of what had happened and she could hear the tremor in her voice. Random put his arm round her and she was grateful for his support. 'Why would anyone deliberately try to shoot you?'

'Mrs Jardine,' said Harrison, 'who said they were shooting at *us*?'

'What sort of remark is that?' said Random sharply; Grace felt his arm tighten about her.

Harrison, one eye on the far end of the meadow, said, 'It's not the first bullet that's been fired at someone around here lately. And the first one wasn't meant for us.'

Grace felt a sudden wave of nausea; she wanted to retch. She leaned against Random, saw the meadow go up and down like a green surf. 'You'd better sit down in the shade,' she heard Random say; then he lifted her and carried her across beneath the trees. 'That was pretty bloody brutal, Harrison.'

'I didn't mean to upset the lady.' Harrison sounded genuinely contrite. 'But if that guy, whoever he is, had been shooting at us, he wouldn't have hit your car. You take a look at the line.'

Olsen had gone running across to a jeep as Random had carried Grace into the shade. Now he came back with a canteen of water. 'We don't have no brandy, ma'am. Just some whisky, if you'd like that.'

Grace leaned back against the rough bark of a tree. 'Water

will do, Mr Olsen. I think even a nip of whisky might send me rampaging after that man who shot at us.'

'Are you feeling any better?' Random smiled comfortingly at her. 'You sound it.'

'I'm all right.' But she continued to sit against the tree, still unsure of the loyalty of her legs. She was less confused now as the shock drained out of her, her mind once more beginning to function in its usual clear fashion. She looked up at Harrison and Olsen. 'Can we keep this to ourselves?'

She saw the query in Harrison's eyes, but he was not a man who wore his thoughts too plainly on his face. 'Sure, if that's the way you want it, Mrs Jardine. We'll be gone from here in a couple of days. So long as he don't come back, sure, we'll forget about what just happened.'

'I'd like to go down there to the timber,' said Random. 'May I borrow your gun?'

'No!' Grace struggled to her feet; her legs were stronger than she had expected. 'What do you think you're going to do?'

'I'm not going to have a running battle, if that's what you think. If he's still there – which I doubt. But I'd like to look around down there and I'd like to be prepared, just in case.'

'You don't need a gun,' said Harrison. 'Fred and I'll come along with you. Get the guns, Fred.'

Olsen, a younger man with a freckled sunburned complexion and a continual frown as if he were puzzled by every last remark made to him, blinked his pale blue eyes. 'A shooting party? Jesus, I thought I left all that behind when I come home from 'Nam. Okay, let's go.'

'Jack, I wish you wouldn't – '

Random pressed her arm. 'I think he's buzzed off. Don't worry.'

She moved out of the shade to watch the three men as they walked down the edge of the meadow, keeping close to the trees. The other two men by the rig had switched off the diesel and stood close by one of the jeeps as if ready to dive under it should shooting break out. There was no sound but the singing of the river some distance away and the occasional stutter of wings as ducks took off from the quiet stretch of water behind Grace.

Random, Harrison and Olsen reached the far end of the meadow without incident, disappeared into the trees. Ten minutes later they reappeared and came back towards the rig, out in the open this time and walking close together.

'Did you find anything?' Grace asked when they reached her.

'We found where he'd parked his car. And this.' Random held up an empty shell. 'What sort of gun would it come from?'

'This.' Harrison held up the rifle he carried. 'It could come from several guns, but I'd reckon it was this. A Winchester Hot Six. Everybody has 'em up this way.'

'So I'm told.' Random put the shell away in the pocket of his shirt, looked at Grace. 'You had some questions you wanted to ask Mr Harrison.'

'No.' Her mind was quite clear now; she was putting things into place for future reference. She was still shocked and frightened by the thought that the bullet might have been meant for her; there were other things to be considered than the charade of asking some questions to which she already knew the answers. She felt a sense of betrayal of Jack, but it couldn't be helped. 'Not if Mr Harrison is moving out in two or three days.'

'At the outside,' said Harrison; did he sound relieved that he would not have to answer any questions from her? 'Unless our shooting friend comes back. In that case we'll be gone sooner.'

Random was looking at Grace, his face expressionless; but she could sense his disappointment or annoyance or disgust. *Jack, let me work it out my own way, don't pressure me!* 'Righto,' he said. 'It's finished.'

What did he mean by that? But all she said was, 'I don't want these sort of headlines when I begin my campaign tomorrow. It might give some other nut ideas about taking a shot at me.'

'Good thinking,' said Random, but she recognized the mocking smile. 'So your chaps won't broadcast this, Harrison?'

'You can rely on 'em. In our job we're often paid a little extra to keep our mouth shut.' His big beetlebrowed face was bland as a river rock as he looked at Grace. 'Good luck, Mrs Jardine. I'm told you're home and hosed in the Senate race.'

'Thank you, Mr Harrison. Though you make me sound like a quarter-horse.'

'No, ma'am,' said Harrison and his gallantry had the light touch of a man far different from the one he was, 'I was thinking about a thoroughbred.'

Driving back along the track Random said, 'I think you could charm a male rhino into voting for you.' He had pushed out the broken windshield and the breeze of the car's speed blew coolingly into their faces. 'Though I think Harrison is much shrewder than any rhino.'

'I've got the feeling I mightn't charm you into voting for me.'

'You won't have to trouble. I don't have a vote.'

'You had a vote last night.'

He laughed and nodded, but there was no real humour in his face. She studied him for a while, admiring the symmetry of his features. He *was* handsome, he had the sort of face she had always secretly admired on a man while falling for men with entirely different faces; she knew with certainty that his looks would not coarsen as he got older, as they did with so many men. But she was looking at more than his handsomeness; she sought depths of him, the furies that she knew every man but the dolt had in him. He was intelligent, too intelligent, and he would never be content to accept her purely on her own terms.

'I read once there's no voting booth like the bed.'

'Sounds like something Lloyd George might have said.' She looked blank and he explained: 'He was one of our Prime Ministers who believed there was more than one way of campaigning.'

'I wasn't campaigning last night – despite what I just said.'

'Don't you think I know that?' He looked at her angrily. The wind blew his hair across his forehead and he looked even more savage than she had seen him last night in their love-making. They were out on the main highway now, the landscape rushing past at sixty miles an hour. 'But you're campaigning or something *now*. You started back there when you said you weren't going to ask Harrison any questions. Or before that. When you said you wanted this – ' he took one hand off the wheel, gestured at the empty frame of the windshield – 'kept quiet. I don't think I understand you. That's nothing new for a man – most of us never understand the women we fall in love with. But I'd begun to trust you – '

'Don't you now?' She noticed how his voice had trailed off.

He sighed, let the car slow a little. Unsure of herself again, uncertain of him, she had the feeling that the car was moving in slow motion on currents of heat: they climbed the pass of

Massacre Gap and beyond him she saw the mountains shimmering in the haze as if the earth itself were trembling. He looked out at the landscape, taking his time about it, then back at her.

'I'll trust you to see this valley isn't spoiled.'

Chapter Five

Over the next few weeks there was no break in the heat or the drought. The valley had had no breeze for a week and each day's heat seemed to pile up on that of the day before. Wildflowers began to wilt and die, the grass turned yellow and the trees looked as lifeless as a green petrified forest.

Random, sitting in his air-conditioned office, felt guilty at what the men under him had to endure. He had a conference with Russ Judson, the plant superintendent, and Chris Peeples and during the course of it Peeples said, 'The heat's making everyone bad-tempered. They're questioning things they've never worried about before.'

'Such as?'

'Well, for one thing, they want a statement on the long-range plans of the company.'

'I've been in the valley fifteen years.' Judson was a short bulky man whose muscles had given up the contest against middle-age fat. His hair, too, had retreated and was staging a last-ditch stand at the back of his head. 'People have felt safe here, maybe complacent. It's understandable. Good clean work, good wages. But now . . .'

'All right.' Random tried to sound less reluctant than he felt. He had told Grace he trusted her to see the valley would not be spoiled. The truth was he could not bring himself to trust her fully and he felt angry at her and ashamed of himself. 'I'll draft a letter today to the board.'

When Judson left, Peeples lingered behind. 'Did you know Tim Yertsen has left town? He's been gone a couple of days.'

'Did he draw his card, give any notice?'

'Nope. Thursday he just didn't turn up for work.'

'Where's he gone?'

'Nobody knows. Tim was always a bit of a loner. He come from down around Billings originally, I think. He's a hothead, but he's been a good worker. Ain't like him to go off like this without saying nothing.'

'We'll wait and see if he comes back. Anything else?'

Peeples rubbed his hands over his hard hat as if polishing it. 'I thought you were going to talk to Mrs Jardine about those drillers?'

'I haven't had the chance yet.'

Peeples put his head on one side, lining up his good eye. 'Jack, I saw you and her a week ago last Sunday driving up here to the valley. You passed me and the missus and the kids going down to Lila's folks. I don't know how many other times you seen her, but don't tell me you ain't had the chance to talk to her.'

It was on the tip of Random's tongue to tell him it was none of his business how he spent his Sundays. But he held himself back: he had been glad of the friendship of Chris Peeples and it would be churlish and petty now to start playing general manager and sawmill foreman. He was abruptly frank: 'Righto, I did bring it up. I was told it was none of my business.'

'She told you that?'

He didn't know what reaction he had expected from Peeples, but he hadn't expected him to be incredulous. 'Chris, she *is* the boss.'

Peeples gestured awkwardly, almost dropping his hat. 'I just thought she'd be straighter than Harry was. I don't know why, none of us really know her, I guess, but I thought she'd play everything strictly above board. If something dirty is going on with those drillers, I didn't think she'd want any part of it. Shows you can be wrong about any woman.'

How do I defend her? In love, he took the cowardly way out: 'I'll try again, Chris. But she's out campaigning now. It may take a week or two before I can see her.'

'Yeah.' Peeples sounded unconvinced by the promise. 'Yeah, do that. In the meantime draft that letter to the board, will you?'

He nodded goodbye, opened the door and went out quickly, too quickly. Beryl Gray hung her head and one breast round the edge of the door. 'Chris Peeples in a bad mood or something? He went by me just like I wasn't there.'

'Just the heat, Beryl. We're all suffering from it.'

'Ain't it the truth! I go home at night just pooped, even with the air conditioning. I can't even sleep with my husband, I've made him move into the spare room.'

'We all have to make sacrifices occasionally, Beryl.'

She gave a hoot of laughter, rolled her bosom up as if she were going to throw it at him, and slid back out of view. She slid out of his mind just as abruptly. He had something else to think about. Tim Yertsen . . .

Wednesday evening he had worked late and when he had gone out to get into his car it had been almost dark. Some days he walked to the office and back home in the evening, but Wednesday he had driven to work, knowing he would be needing the car during the day. The smashed windscreen had been repaired without delay – 'You got a stone through it, Mr Random? Yeah, happens a lot up here once you're off the macadam' – and he hadn't bothered to make any comment on it. Wednesday evening it was parked in his usual marked spot in the parking lot to one side of the front lawn.

He was beside the car when he noticed the figure standing in the shadow of one of the tall spruces. 'Who's that?'

Tim Yertsen, glasses glinting as he turned his face up towards the lights on either side of the main entrance, stepped out of the shadows. 'Evening, Mr Random. I – I was waiting for you. I – I been wondering, you going to use me again as your driver? I sure enjoyed being with you.'

'I prefer to drive myself, Tim.' Even in the dim light he was aware of the embarrassed awkwardness of Yertsen; why had the boy been, well, *hiding* in the shadows? 'That's no reflection on your driving.'

'Yeah, I guess so. I mean I understand.' He looked at the car. 'I hear you had an accident.'

'Not really. Just a stone through the windscreen.' He opened the car door, got in, wound down the window. The interior still held the heat of the day; he began to sweat almost at once. He moved uncomfortably in the seat, leaned across to open the opposite window and felt the rough edge of the bullet hole in the vinyl scratch against his arm. He sat back, looked out at Yertsen and said, 'Been doing any shooting, Tim?'

It was a shot in the half-dark; he saw Yertsen's head come up and the light flash on his glasses. 'Shooting? No, Mr Random. No, I – I stick to the season. Why, Mr Random?'

'Nothing, Tim. Just making conversation. Goodnight.'

He backed the car out of the parking lot, drove down the street. In the driving mirror he saw Tim Yertsen come out on to the sidewalk and stand beneath a street lamp, staring after him as he drove away. The boy was still standing there, unmoving, when he lost sight of him in the mirror . . .

That had been Wednesday evening and now Yertsen was gone. Random would never know what had made him ask the boy if he had done any shooting lately. Thinking back, as he had driven away from the startled Yertsen, he knew it had not occurred to him before that the boy might have fired the shot at him and Grace. Even the boy's suspicious behaviour, his almost too casual question about the smashed windshield, had made no connection in Random's mind with the bullet that had lodged in the car's seat. If he had left the bullet where it was the connection might never have been made; but when he had pried it out with his knife he had roughened the edge of the hole. That tiny, almost imperceptible scrape against his bare arm had been like an injection of the question: *Been doing any shooting, Tim?*

But had Yertsen been shooting at him and Grace or at Harrison and his crew? If he had shot at Grace, that compounded the act. Because it meant he must also have shot at Harry Jardine.

He jumped as the phone on his desk rang. 'Phil Wryman here, Mr Random. Could you come up and see me?'

'Now?'

'It's kind of important.'

Despite the heat Random left his car outside the office and walked up through the town. He felt uneasy, still hearing the almost tart briskness of Wryman's voice.

Wryman and Sheriff Gauge were waiting for him and the County Attorney lost no time in coming to the point. 'Mr

Random, we understand someone fired a shot at you a week ago last Sunday?'

Random hesitated, caught unprepared. 'I don't know if they *deliberately* fired at me. It could have been an accident.'

'Did Mrs Jardine think it was an accident?'

'Before we go any further, Mr Wryman,' said Random, keeping his voice even and polite, 'I'd like to know how all this came to your attention. I assume I'm not on any charge or anything.'

'No, Mr Random, you're not,' said Wryman just as evenly, just as politely; but beside him Gauge scowled and tapped his pen up and down on his notebook. 'These are just routine enquiries. Well, maybe not routine. We feel we're getting somewheres now.'

'Somewhere with what?'

Gauge went to answer that, but he wasn't quick enough. Wryman, still with the ball, sidestepped. 'Someone had a few drinks too many. One of the drillers, the guys who've been trespassing up here in the valley the past couple of weeks. He stopped off in town the day they were moving out, spent a little time in a bar and he said too much. What he said took a little time to reach me and the sheriff, but it got to us eventually. He said someone had taken a shot at either them, the drillers, or at you and Mrs Jardine.'

'What he said could have been garbled by the time it got to you.'

'No. We traced the man – it took us a few days. But we got to him eventually, down in Casper, Wyoming. Sheriff Gauge drove down there to see him. Unofficially.'

'He didn't want to talk at first, but I persuaded him.' Gauge looked at his notebook. 'He reckoned the shot was meant for you and Mrs Jardine, all right. He said he'd be glad to swear to that.'

The air-conditioner coughed, wheezed, stopped. Wryman got up, crossed to it, whacked it with his fist and it started up again; but it sounded mournful now, as if he had hurt it. 'I'll be glad to get out of this goddam place. Well, Mr Random, who d'you reckon the shot was meant for?'

Random took his time, treading carefully. 'I still think it could have been an accident. Mrs Jardine thought the same – that was why she asked me not to broadcast it. She didn't want her Senate campaign to start out on a sensational note like that.'

Wryman and Gauge nodded in understanding, both politically sensitive to the season. 'I understand that,' said Wryman. 'Except it leaves her open to another attempt on her life.'

'Do you really think that's likely?' Random had considered the possibility, but it had been too disturbing to contemplate for long. 'Why should anyone want to kill her?'

'We don't know why anyone would want to kill her husband, but he did.' The air-conditioner stopped again, but Wryman ignored it this time. 'Did Tim Yertsen ever make any comment to you about either Harry Jardine or Mrs Jardine?'

'What's Tim Yertsen got to do with this?' He hoped he sounded ignorant and surprised.

'He's disappeared, left town without telling anyone,' said Gauge. 'I thought you'd know that, Mr Random. He works for you.'

'I learned about it less than an hour ago. Are you connecting him with the shooting? Both shootings?'

'The bullet had been dug out of the seat of your car,' said Gauge. 'One of my deputies had a look at it this morning.'

'You might have done me the courtesy of asking me first.'

'He didn't want to trouble you. The car windows were open – I guess we all leave 'em like that in weather like this. What sort of bullet did you find, Mr Random?'

Reluctantly, feeling he was helping to snap handcuffs on Tim Yertsen, he said, 'I was told it was the sort they use in a Hot Six.'

Wryman nodded, satisfied. 'Yertsen has a Hot Six. He never tried to hide it.'

'With his eyesight I wonder that he could hit anything at more than fifty feet.' Random wondered why he was defending Yertsen; unless, for some reason he could not yet fathom, he was defending Grace. 'Whoever fired the shot that hit my car was at least a hundred and fifty yards away.'

'He could of used a 'scope,' said Gauge. 'Decent hunters up around here don't use 'em, but some do.'

Random surrendered: it was not his place to defend Yertsen. 'Perhaps so. Have you picked him up yet?'

'We'll get him,' said Gauge confidently and snapped his note-book shut. 'We'll let you know when we want you again, Mr Random.'

Random looked at him carefully, disliking him intensely all of a sudden. You sod, he thought, you're trying to make me sound like an accomplice before or after the fact, aiding and abetting or whatever the legal term is in this state. 'What does that mean, sheriff?'

Gauge looked surprised, then suspicious. He screwed up one side of his face, snapped, 'It means if you're going to come in here, a goddam foreigner, we want you to co-operate with us more, that's what it means.'

The goddam foreigner looked at Wryman as the latter calmly said, 'It means, Mr Random, that when we bring Yertsen in, we'll need you as a possible witness.'

'And Mrs Jardine, too?'

The two men opposite him looked at each other: suddenly Gauge's suspicion was reflected in Wryman's face. 'What does *that* mean, Mr Random?'

'We could go on asking each other that question all afternoon.' Random still felt uneasy, apprehensive; but it was a small consolation to know that Wryman and Gauge also felt the same way. 'All I'm trying to do, gentlemen, is keep my boss's name out of the newspapers in connection with this shooting – the shooting last Sunday week. You are politicians, I understand you'll be wearing two hats from now until November. I also understand that you are both on the same ticket as Mrs Jardine.'

'You've learned our customs very quickly, Mr Random.' There was a tinge of admiration to Wryman's voice; Gauge had just screwed up his face again, doubly suspicious now. 'There is just one flaw. Sheriff Gauge and I are honest law officers. Right, Bill?'

'Right,' said Gauge.

'The shooting is our minor concern. If we bring in Yertsen – *when* we bring him in – we'll be questioning him first about the murder of Harry Jardine. If he confesses to that, then the shooting at you and Mrs Jardine won't matter a damn.'

'Not a pinch of shit,' said Gauge, adding his authority for what it was worth.

'So if we call Mrs Jardine as a witness, it will only be in connection with her husband's murder. And I don't think that will hurt her politically, Mr Random. Not the way our voters, especially the women, think.'

'It won't hurt you and Sheriff Gauge, either.'

'That's the way our system works, we get votes on results. Isn't it that way in England?'

'Scotland Yard doesn't get any votes,' He was about to add, *you know that*. Wryman, he recognized, was more than a small town law officer: he was well aware of the outside world. He decided he couldn't win against the County Attorney, not on his home ground. Grace, he further decided, would have to look after herself. He stood up, dismissing himself: he was not going to allow them the privilege of telling him he could go. He had been here in the valley less than a month and already he was having to adopt attitudes he would rather have avoided. He was not aware of it, but some of the old Random arrogance came back. 'When you bring in Yertsen, call me. We'll see then how much evidence you want from me.'

2

'I wish we had something like the Guards regiments in our army,' said Governor Mackintosh. 'Of course, our damned egalitarian outlook wouldn't stand for it. But a little elitism helps.'

'Father is the last of the mid-Victorians,' said Bonnie. 'More wine, Mr Random?'

'Do you like the better things of life?' said Mackintosh. 'I mean food, wine, all that?'

'Is that a political question, sir?'

Mackintosh laughed, winked at his daughter. He was much more relaxed than on the other occasions Random had seen him, much less the ramrod military type. 'No, it's one of the reasons I got Bonnie to ask you here this evening. I wanted someone at my table who wasn't a voter or a lobbyist.'

Random had accepted the invitation, not only because one did not refuse a call from the Governor (the old Guards etiquette was still there in him) but because it afforded an escape from his house in Tozabe. Each night he waited on a phone call from Grace and none came.

'Have you seen Mrs Jardine lately?'

It was an unexpected question, but Random could see nothing in the Governor's face to suggest it was loaded. 'I understand she is off campaigning somewhere.' Better to sound casual; but he was aware of Bonnie studying him. 'I suppose you'll be going off again soon. It must be tiring.'

'I don't enjoy it,' said Mackintosh.

'Dad would like all the voters drawn up in ranks, so's he could give them an order of the day, take the salute and then tell the Secretary of State to dismiss them. Sometimes, when I'm with him, I think it wouldn't be a bad idea.' Bonnie looked fondly at her father; they were in accord tonight. Then she looked at Random, said too innocently, 'I wonder how Mrs Jardine likes campaigning?'

Grace had begun her campaign gradually. Her first major appearance had been as one of the guests of honour at the Last Chance Stampede in Helena, where she had created more excitement than any of the bucking broncs. The newspapers had begun to feature her, but so far she had said nothing controversial, espoused no causes that would offend the majority. She was acting like a safe candidate running for a safe seat. Random, seeing her on television and reading about her in the newspapers, hating himself for his objectivity, had wondered what such bland, superficial non-commitment could contribute to the government of a country as great as the United States.

'I wouldn't know.'

'Didn't you see her on TV Monday night? She was down in Billings. She is drawing bigger crowds than anyone since Custer at Little Bighorn.'

'That's a bit sick,' said her father mildly. 'I don't think anyone is going to massacre Grace. The reverse will be the case, I think, with her poor ex-husband. The first one,' he added hastily, as if he had just made a sick joke himself.

'Do Governors and Senators work together much?' Random asked.

'Depends on the personalities and whether they're from the same party. I think Grace and I will work well together.'

'Better than you would have with Harry,' said Bonnie.

Random noticed the bitterness in her voice. If her father remarked it, he made no comment. 'Harry was not the easiest man to get on with. Perhaps you were lucky, Jack. I mean – ' For the first time Random saw him awkward and embarrassed; Random guessed that he tried to keep his gaffes to a minimum. 'Well, you know – '

'Everyone keeps telling me that.'

It was just a casual reply by Random, meant to get the Governor off his embarrassment hook; but Mackintosh sat up straight, looked as if he had just been handed an unexpected despatch from the battlefield. 'Really? You mean there's no real regret that he was – murdered?' It was a word that didn't come easily to his military tongue; legal killing, the art of the soldier, was one thing, but murder was another. 'I knew he had a few enemies, of course. He used to boast about them – '

Random was watching Bonnie out of the corner of his eye; she was tracing patterns on the tablecloth. In the last few minutes the mood at the table had changed; or so he felt. As if the good meal had suddenly brought on food poisoning. He began to wonder if he *had* been brought here for purely social, non-political reasons.

'I just get the occasional comment, that's all. Some of the men from the company. I don't think the County Attorney would want to arrest anyone on what's been said.'

'No. No, I guess not. There's always gossip – ' Mackintosh sat back; the despatch had contained no real intelligence. 'I suppose he'll be forgotten in a year or so. Especially if Grace proves a success in Washington.'

'She will,' said Bonnie; she had stopped her tracing and her hand was tightened into a fist. 'With her looks and that nice cold intelligence she's got she's going to have all those old fogies who run the Senate committees eating out of her hand. Don't you think so, Jack?'

'I don't know. I've never had a woman offer me a handful of fodder. Do women do it often in this country?'

Mackintosh laughed and Bonnie smiled, loosening her fist and turning it into an acknowledging wave. 'I asked for that. But we'll win in the end, you know.'

'The women of America?'

'No, just women. You wait and see.'

Then Mackintosh excused himself, saying he had some papers that had to be attended to. He thanked Random for coming, shook his hand firmly and warmly. 'I'll call you again, Jack. We'll have a meal and a talk, just the two of us. I need an outside point of view, just to remind me there's a sane world outside the one I live in now.'

'The military world?' said Bonnie. 'You're kidding, Dad.'

'Jack knows what I mean,' said Mackintosh; but Random wasn't sure that he did. 'Goodnight. Keep your powder dry.'

A maid came in to clear the table and Bonnie led Random out on to a terrace that looked down over the city. The air had cooled a little with the altitude (Random had to keep reminding himself that Helena was 4000 feet above sea level), but it remained still and stale. The lights below glowed yellowly, like tiny dull suns, and even the stars had a yellow tinge to them, as if they had been scorched by the heat of the day. The night was quiet: he imagined that everyone lay exhausted, breathless, in their houses, waiting out the heat as the earlier settlers had waited out the blizzards. I still have those to come, he thought, the blizzards.

Down the valley a train whistle wailed, mournful as a cry for the long ago. 'I remember that,' he said. 'I used to love it when I'd hear it in old films, American films. English train whistles never sound like that. They're always rather shrill, like harridans screaming.'

'You've got quite an ear. I can't ever remember hearing a harridan – though I may grow into one. I guess it can happen to the best of us. I wonder if Grace Jardine will become one?'

'I don't think it's at all likely,' he said evenly. 'Why do you keep on about her?'

'Maybe I'm jealous.' He looked at her sharply and suddenly she was flustered. 'I don't mean about you – '

'I'm glad to hear it.' The thought was a conceited one, but was she becoming interested in him? God, he hoped not. 'What *do* you mean?'

'Well, she has everything, hasn't she?' But her argument was too weak; she was more intelligent than that.

'You wouldn't want most of what she has. Not if what you told me the other day is true.'

She stared at him, then abruptly turned away. 'Why do I always have to spoil everything?'

He dared not touch her. He knew the worst was true, that she had become interested in him. All he could hope was that it was a mild infatuation, that she was focusing her intense attention on him because there was no one else. Perhaps she had got herself involved with Harry Jardine in the same way: but that was a thought he wouldn't pursue.

'Bonnie, you've spoiled nothing. You do get a bit carried away – '

'Don't patronize me! I'm not some bloody schoolgirl!'

He sighed, keeping cool. 'Americans never seem able to say *bloody* without making it sound like a foreign word.'

'You're still being bloody patronizing.'

'I think we'd better call it a night, don't you? When it gets a little cooler – '

'When what gets cooler?' But then she seemed to appreciate that this sort of conversation was non-productive of anything but more heat and that she was the one who was getting heated. She faced away from him; she had slumped a little; but now he noticed her straighten her back again. When she looked back at him she, miraculously, managed her young, charming smile again. 'I'm sorry, Jack. I get scratchy like this with Dad, too.'

He took the risk of lifting her hand and kissing it. 'Don't grow into a harridan. You have more to offer than that.'

'Such as?'

Damn, he thought: they never miss a slip of the tongue. Was she really so starved of compliments? 'I'll tell you next time you invite me to dinner.'

'You could invite me. Though if you're as fond of food as Dad is . . . He tells me there isn't a decent restaurant in the whole of Montana. But I can cook – if you invite me up to Tozabe.'

He laughed, deciding compromise was the quickest means of escape. 'You don't beat about the bush. Righto, I'll call you and we'll make a date.'

She was still smiling. 'I'll bring a bottle of Dad's French wine.'

He wanted to say, *Don't be too eager*. But the joking between them was their compromise and he didn't want to spoil it. 'A bottle of white and one of red, if you can manage it.'

At the front door she took his hand. They were standing close together, each aware of the warmth and smell of the other's body. No, he thought, this is a minefield: to kiss her would be to take a dangerous step. But she leaned forward, kissed him softly on the cheek.

'Don't worry, Jack. I'm used to disappointment.'

Then she closed the door and he was outside in the hot night, feeling cowardly and ashamed but relieved. He went down the steps, got into his car and switched on the air-conditioning. He was sweating (from the heat? From relief?) and it took some minutes for the air-conditioner to cool him down. By then he was almost down to the highway, ready to head north to Tozabe. Then abruptly he swung left, drove up towards the West Side. He turned into Harrison, drove two blocks and pulled up behind half a dozen cars parked on the opposite side of the street from Grace's house. There were a dozen or more cars parked on her side of the street and another half a dozen in the driveway of the house. The house itself was ablaze with light: it seemed to him that only the attic-ballroom on the third floor was in darkness. He switched off the engine and his lights, sat in the darkness, felt the dry heat beginning to seep into the car again.

'I'm like a bloody schoolboy,' he told himself. 'Or a bloody private eye.'

He had never done this when he was young, never had had to. The girls of his youth had always welcomed him, never kept him at arm's or leg's length while they busied themselves with other people or other boys. But he guessed there were men all over the world, callow youths and men of his own age, even the middle-aged and the elderly, sitting or standing in the shadows watching the houses of the girls or women they loved. Some were doing it out of suspicion, some because of shyness: he wasn't quite sure why he was here. He had never been like this before, doing something on the spur of the moment for no apparent reason. Though he had never been dedicated absolutely to any purpose, not even to the army, he had always avoided being aimless. Yet this detour up here tonight seemed aimless, unless he had expected Grace to be standing on the front steps, having just by chance come out of her air-conditioned house for a breath of hot dry air. Which was the sort of fortunate chance that lovesick youths looked for . . .

'Why, Mr Random! You coming in to salute the queen?'

A car had drawn up behind him, but he had taken no notice of it. He had heard the car door slam and taken it for granted that its driver and whoever was with him would just cross the road and go into the Jardine house. But Petula Coulson, even though her eyes were martini-fogged, was not one to miss a lone male sitting in a car parked outside Grace Jardine's house. Chauffeurs were rare animals in Helena, unless they were driving official cars, and she knew this was not an official one. She leaned on the door and peered in at Random, her breath suggesting she would now be in jail if any policeman had stopped her on her way up here.

'No, I don't think so, Mrs Coulson. I was to see Mrs Jardine on business – ' He was becoming a glib liar. He supposed all lovers became liars in the end, particularly to each other: truth could be the death of true love. But lying to an outsider was honourable: 'I guess she must have forgotten.'

'Grace forget anything? You're kidding, Mr Random.' She pulled open the car door, grasped him by the arm. 'Come on, we'll go in and remind her she mustn't ignore business for politics.'

He followed her, only half-reluctant. He did want to see Grace and Pet Coulson could be his camouflage; with her, his presence would be unremarkable among the political crowd. They crossed the street, went up the steps under the arch of the portico and into the house.

Random had never witnessed an Election Night in America, but he guessed this would be a good preview. No one seemed depressed or exhausted by the heat; there was an air of gaiety and excitement as if victory had already been won. No one stood around in groups; people milled and moved in a joyous surf. The rooms were drenched in a spray of euphoria and it was hard to realize that voting was still almost three months away.

He had seen the same crowd at Harry Jardine's funeral. They were in the entrance hall, the dining room, the living room: in the latter they were multiplied countless times in the facing mirrors, a multitude hailing the new monarch. The king is dead, long live the queen . . . Random looked for some *memento mori* among the gaiety, but Harry was forgotten tonight.

'I tell you, she was great, just great!' A bald-headed man was moving his arms up and down like a cheer-leader. 'She's got charisma, Christ, has she got it!'

'She's also got nice boobs,' said Pet Coulson. 'They're great vote-catchers, don't you reckon, Mr Random?'

Random gave her a careful smile. He began to wonder if Grace had any friends among the women in Helena. 'Not on male politicians.'

'We'll be a shoo-in!' A pretty girl took off her steamed-up glasses, opened her eyes wide as if she had seen a vision. 'Down in Custer County she'll take seventy-five per cent of the vote – and that's Cliff Pendrick's home territory!'

'She should take him back into her bed,' said Pet Coulson. 'That'd guarantee her one hundred per cent.'

'She's got to widen her platform, though,' said a young man with a high-pitched voice. 'Equal rights for women isn't enough.'

'How'd he get in here?' said Pet Coulson. 'He's the only fag in Helena. I'm told he won't last past the next hunting season.'

'Hallo, honey.' Jim Coulson appeared out of the crowd, gave his wife a perfunctory kiss, took a deep sniff of her breath. 'I take it you don't want another drink.'

'You take it wrong, lover. I not only want one, I *need* one. A woman should have some support against the crap that's flying around tonight. Who's that hanging on your manly tit?' She made a pretence of peering at the big button, featuring a picture of Grace, stuck on his shirt front. 'Minnehaha? Germaine Greer? Heavens to Betsy, it's not our own dear queen?'

'I'll get you some soda water.'

'You do that, lover. I'll give three burps to Queen Grace. Where is she, anyway? Giving private audiences? She's got to – got to – ' Suddenly she was very precise in her speech: it was a habit Random had noticed with some drunks, as if they suddenly turned a corner and decided, a little late, to sound respectable and sober. 'She has got to give an audience to my good friend Mr Random. Business.'

'Business?' Coulson looked suspiciously at Random. 'Ten-thirty on Saturday night?'

'Actually, I'm just gate-crashing. It was your wife who gave me the excuse.'

'Did I?' Pet Coulson blinked drunkenly; then abruptly her gaze focused as she looked over Random's shoulder. 'Grace, you look divine! Just divine – as we hypocrites say. Not a mark on you.'

Random turned and felt the excitement take hold of him; but it was a different excitement from what was gripping the rest of the crowd. *They* weren't in love; though he could not be sure that at least some of the men didn't feel that way about Grace. Especially the way she looked now. Dressed in pale pink, something light and soft: whatever it was, it suited her, was reflected as a soft glow on her arms, her throat and her cheeks. She looked cool, clear-eyed and radiant: it was impossible to imagine that she had just come back from two weeks' hard slog on the hustings in heat that, so the newspapers said, was driving even cattle to their knees. If all queens looked like this, he thought, every man would be a monarchist.

'Pet, I love an honest hypocrite – there are so few of them left. But you must be pleased I've brought Jim home to you. There is not a mark on him, either.'

'None that I can see,' said Pet, not even glancing at her husband. 'But it's so long since I've seen him without his clothes, I wouldn't know.'

'Goddam it,' said Coulson, 'shut your bitchy mouth!'

'Mr Random,' said Grace, giving him her hand, 'how nice to see you again.'

Random all at once felt confident and careless of the crowd around them: he raised her hand to his lips. 'And you, too, Mrs Jardine.'

'I just love that!' Pet Coulson shoved her hand under Random's nose. 'Have a smack at that size seven-and-a-half.'

'For Crissake,' said Coulson, 'come and I'll get you a drink.'

'Now you're talking, sweetheart.' Then she looked at Grace, seemed to concentrate on her gaze and her voice: 'No hard feelings, Grace.'

Grace put her hand on Pet's arm. 'I told you before, Pet. Us sincere ones have got to stick together.'

'You bet,' said Pet Coulson and allowed herself to be dragged away by her angry husband, telling him as they went, 'Easy on my arm, for God's sake! You're not on the old college team tonight –'

'I wish Jim was as nice as she is,' said Grace. 'She made the mistake so many of us make, she fell in love with the wrong man.'

'I hope that doesn't include me.'

For a moment they were in a lagoon of their own among the surging sea around them: they loved each other with their eyes. 'I missed you, Jack. Really.'

Then Senator Mountfield, silver hair standing out like a helmet that had been split open from the back by a blunt axe, descended on them. 'Grace, they tell me you've got the voters eating out of your hand.'

The voters of Montana seemed a hungry lot, thought Random.

But he was watching Grace's reaction to the Senator's compliment. Her eyes lit up with enthusiasm – no, excitement. It was a reflection of what he saw on most of the other faces in the house.

'I didn't think it would be so – so *easy*, Mark. Everywhere I've been they've *welcomed* me. I was ready for some sort of antagonism, but it hasn't been like that at all.'

'That'll come after you're elected,' said the veteran; but Random could see no scars on him. 'Come over and meet Jake Quiller, he's just arrived. He's on the national committee, he came in specially from Washington to meet you – '

Grace threw Random a glance – 'Excuse me, Jack' – and left him standing in the middle of the room. He stiffened with anger; maybe it was petulant anger, but she did not have to desert him like that. He had the feeling he was sliding down the totem pole; the top of the pole was occupied by politicians. Well, serve him right for gate-crashing a political shindig.

He turned to leave, but stopped as he saw Shooberg, moving unusually quickly, come into the room and go up to Grace. The men around them stopped talking and crowded closer. Random, still prickled, sensed at once the change of mood in that corner of the room. The stillness of the group spread out; people seemed to freeze in mid-sentence, heads turned. The chatter died abruptly, like the volume knob being turned down on a television set.

Then Jim Coulson, on a word from Shooberg, broke away from the group and moved quickly towards the door. Random followed him on an impulse, going round the outskirts of the room, pushing through the crowd who had come in from the rest of the house as if the quietness in the main room had been a magnet. He caught up with Coulson as the latter was going out the front door.

'Something wrong?'

Coulson hesitated, then jerked his head towards the front steps: 'You better come with me. They picked up a guy, going to charge him with Harry's murder. Guy named Yertsen, works for us up in the valley.'

'What are we supposed to do when we get there?' Random said.

He had left his car in the street outside Grace's house and joined Coulson in the Mercedes. He noticed that, despite the way he had hurried out of the house and down the steps into his car, Coulson did not drive fast. He wondered why the big man had such a powerful car if he always drove it at such a sedate pace.

'We look after Mrs Jardine's interests,' said Coulson.

Random asked no further questions, not quite sure how intimately Coulson placed him in Mrs Jardine's interests. They drove in silence for a while; the edges of the city slipped away behind them. But Coulson was the sort of man uncomfortable in silences, as if he suspected they worked against him.

'We find out why he killed Harry and if it has anything to do with Grace, we try to get him to keep her name out of it.'

'Do you know Tim Yertsen?'

'Maybe I met him, maybe I didn't. I don't know every guy works for us. What's he like?'

'Young chap, a bit quick-tempered. Has poor eyesight, judging by the glasses he wears. If he shot Harry Jardine, I think he'd have been right on top of him.'

'That's what the coroner said, he was shot from close range.'

Random said nothing while the long slice of road slid at them down the ramp of the headlights. Had Grace told Coulson and Shooberg, told *anyone*, of what had happened last Sunday week? If she hadn't, then it was almost certain that Wryman was going to tell Coulson within the next hour.

'I think I'd better tell you,' he said just as Coulson was about to chew at the silence again, 'Grace – Mrs Jardine and I were shot at, the Sunday before last. The bullet smashed the windscreen of my car, went right between us.'

Coulson's reaction was delayed, as if he couldn't believe what he had heard. Then the car wavered on the road and he lifted his foot from the accelerator. He got the car straight again, took it back up to its steady fifty miles an hour. It was his turn to be silent.

At last he said, 'Where did it happen?'

'Up in the valley. We were going out to talk to those drillers I told you about.'

'You mean you went over my head to tell her about them?'

'No.' *How much of the truth do I tell?* But if Tim Yertsen had killed Harry Jardine and had fired the shot that Sunday, then the truth would soon be out anyway. 'We were out on a picnic together when we saw the drillers at work.'

'Out on a picnic with her? With Grace?' The car slowed again; Coulson's emotions seemed to react through his foot. 'You mean you been socializing with her?'

'If you want to put it that way.'

Coulson continued to drive the car at the slower pace: they seemed to crawl through the dark night. 'Jesus H. Christ, you're sure some mover, ain't you? You been here – what? Three, four weeks? – the boss ain't cold in his grave and you're taking out his missus. You didn't waste any time. And you try to tell me you didn't go over my head, for Crissake!'

Random gazed ahead at the brightly-lit corridor of road; walls of trees slid by on either side. A deer stood mesmerized for a moment in the glare of the lights, then jumped to one side and, still blinded, crashed into a tree. The car's air-conditioner had a rasping hum, as if its fan was rusty: it did nothing to cool the atmosphere between the two men. Random, cool himself, could feel the heat of Coulson's fury.

'What the hell you think you're trying to do? You some sort of fifth column or something? Did London put you up to this?'

It was the funniest thing he had heard since landing in America: he laughed with genuine amusement. 'Coulson – I take it you'd rather not be on a first name basis just now? No? Look, Coulson – my relationship with Mrs Jardine outside of office hours is purely a personal one. London knows nothing about it, it's none of their business. And if I may say so, it's none of yours. If it were, I think Mrs Jardine herself would have told you.'

Coulson's foot stamped hard on the accelerator: the car shot forward like a fist punched at the air. Random's head jerked back, but that was his only reaction: he was not going to shout at Coulson to be careful. A curve in the road hurtled at them, white-railed fence bending away above a black void: Random guessed they must now be in Massacre Gap. They went round the curve in the middle of the road, tyres screaming; then abruptly Coulson slowed, forced himself back in his seat. In the glow from the dashboard Random saw the sweat suddenly start on the big man's face.

Their speed dropped, Coulson driving stiffly and decorously now. 'Sorry.' Random was surprised by the apology; but he nodded his acceptance of it. 'My old man was killed in an automobile accident. I was with him, I was just a kid, ten years old. He was driving too fast.'

'Is that why you don't drive fast?'

'You noticed? Everything else, I push myself, go the limit. But not when I get into a car. The wife drives faster'n I do. She's going to kill herself some day, I tell her.' The friction, the anger, of a few moments ago seemed forgotten. But then he looked sideways at Random. 'Don't get Grace talked about, you understand?'

'I'm always the gentleman,' said Random drily; but tasted the cold of irony on his tongue. 'But if Yertsen talks, then everyone is going to be talking about her. Neither you nor I are going to be able to stop that.'

'Okay, then we better say you and her were out on business that day. Say you'd gone up to find out what those drillers were doing.'

'And if anyone asks, what shall I say we learned?'

Despite Random's soft-voiced query, Coulson caught the acid in it. Suspicious and antagonistic again, he looked at the Englishman. 'You learned nothing. Just say Mrs Jardine talked to 'em.'

They said nothing the rest of the way into Tozabe, Coulson evidently as afraid now of talk as of silence. They pulled up outside the old junior high school, Coulson having some trouble finding a space among the cars parked there. Despite the lateness of the hour a small crowd stood around the bottom of the steps: some older people, a dozen or so teenagers. Some of the men nodded to Coulson and Random, but only the latter acknowledged them. They went up the steps together and Random stood aside with sardonic deference to let Coulson enter first; but the big man missed the mockery and slammed his way through the doors. Random, catching a door just before it bounced back in his face, followed him.

Chris Peeples, good eye looking worried, joined them as they went down the corridor to Wryman's office. The corridor seemed full of people: deputies, Highway Patrol officers, reporters and

photographers. Camera lights flashed like an electrical storm.
'How did the press get here so quickly?' Random asked.

'Tim was picked up near Kalispell by the Highway Patrol,'
said Peeples. 'The newspaper guys came back with Bill Gauge
when he went up to collect him.'

They went into Wryman's office, the crowd outside the door
parting to let them through. Peeples slipped in after Coulson and
Random, stood just to one side of the door. In the room were
Wryman, Gauge, two deputies, a Highway Patrol officer and a
young black-haired man who looked Indian and wore brass-
studded denim jacket and trousers. And Tim Yertsen, slumped in
a chair, long hair hanging forward over his down-turned face,
manacled hands pressed between his knees.

Wryman stood up, but Random noticed that was the only hint
of deference he gave Coulson. 'I heard you were on your way up,
Mr Coulson. I don't think there's anything you can do at this
stage.'

'I'm here to represent Mrs Jardine.' Coulson was not going
to be put down by any ambitious County Attorney, not one as
young and brash as Wryman. 'This the guy who did it?'

'We haven't established he did anything yet,' said Wryman
evenly. He might be political, but he was also legal; he's ambitious, Random thought, but he's also honest. 'We're still interro-
gating him.'

'You getting anywhere?'

Random, standing to one side, aware of everyone in the room
but Yertsen watching the encounter between Coulson and the
County Attorney, took a step back as he saw Peeples lean towards
him.

'He's a hothead, Jack,' Peeples whispered, 'but he didn't
kill Harry Jardine. Do something for the poor bugger.'

What, for instance? He was the stranger in town and now they
wanted him to play counsel for the defence. He saw that Wryman,
ignoring Coulson, had suddenly stopped to look directly at him.

'You want to say something, Mr Random?'

Random said the first thing that fell into his mind: 'Does
Tim Yertsen have a lawyer?'

Yertsen's head had come up sharply when Random's name was
mentioned. He put up his manacled hands and brushed the lank
hair away from his face. He was not wearing his glasses and he

blinked and peered at Random as if he were being hit in the face by spray. There was a dark bruise on his bony cheek and a cut across the bridge of his nose. He had the look of misery and utter defeat that Random had seen on the faces of the homeless in the streets of Calcutta. There were born losers everywhere . . .

'Tom Cloud is acting for him.' Wryman gestured to the black-haired young man in the denims.

'I ain't got no money for a lawyer,' croaked Yertsen, sullen and afraid. He cleared his throat, still looking at Random. 'Mr Random, I didn't shoot Mr Jardine. I – I put that bullet into your car, I already told 'em that – '

'Don't admit anything yet.' The young Indian lawyer pressed his client's shoulder. 'Keep it cool, Tim.'

'No, I'll admit that bit. Jesus, that's better'n being charged with – with *murder!* I hit your car, Mr Random – I'm sorry about that. I was sick all that night, thinking I might of killed you and – '

'Why did you take the shot at me?' Random interrupted quickly.

Yertsen stared at him as if he couldn't see him, puzzled-looking as if Random had suddenly disappeared from in front of him. Then he looked around, at no one in particular. 'Where's my glasses? Can I have my glasses?'

Sheriff Gauge took them out of his shirt pocket, dangled them on a thick finger. 'They're broke. You broke 'em when you resisted arrest, remember?'

'Resisted?' Yertsen shook his head, as if he didn't quite understand what the word meant; then he began to weep, the tears rolling down his thin bony face. 'Oh Christ, what's happened? How did I – ?'

Random stepped forward, put his hand on the boy's shoulder. Tom Cloud was still standing with his hand on Yertsen's other shoulder: it struck Random that they must look like some sort of tableau. One in which, like Tim Yertsen, he wasn't quite sure how he had arrived.

'Why did you take the shot at me?' he repeated and tried to make his tone kinder.

Yertsen sniffed, found a grubby handkerchief and wiped his eyes. He looked up at Random past the curtain of his hair. 'I didn't shoot at *you*, Mr Random. Jesus, why would I want to do that? I fired at them drillers, all I wanted to do was scare 'em out of the valley, that's all. I'm a lousy shot – ' He gulped, as if it hurt him, the dreamer of tiger hunting, to admit it. 'I aimed just to the right of 'em – I always pull to the right. Then you come out of the timber – ' He retched as if he were going to be sick and Random pressed his shoulder comfortingly. 'I keep waking up nights sweating, thinking I might of killed you or – '

'Or wounded me?' said Random quickly again. *Why am I trying to keep Grace's name from being mentioned?* It was inevitable that her name must come out sooner or later. But later would be better than now: he could see the reporters and photographers, microphones and cameras aimed like grenades, poised ready to charge in from the corridor outside. 'Tim, it was an accident, I'll accept that. If Mr Wryman will – ?'

'We're considering other charges.' But Wryman seemed to have lost his confidence. Or his enthusiasm, thought Random: he has one weakness a political ambitious prosecutor should never have, pity for the prisoner.

Coulson walked to the door and before those outside in the corridor realized what he was about to do, shut it in their faces. He looked at Sheriff Gauge and the latter, a little slow on the uptake, then nodded to one of his deputies. The deputy moved to the door, locked it and stood with his back to it. Fists pounded on the door, voices yelled. 'The company may own the valley, Coulson!' someone shouted. 'It don't own the law!'

Coulson stood waiting for the pounding and shouting to die down. It went on for a minute or so, then it faded away abruptly. Coulson nodded to the deputy. The deputy unlocked the door and swung it open; three men, bent in listening attitudes, almost fell into the room. Wryman, as if choosing the law over politics, glanced at Gauge.

'Take 'em all outside, Bill. We'll issue a statement in half an hour.'

'That'll be too late to make the morning edition,' complained one of the reporters. 'The goddam TV guys will get it all – '

'Fifteen minutes then,' said Wryman, retreating; newspaper support was still useful in an election. 'Now don't hold us up, fellers. Outside, please!'

The reporters, slightly mollified, backed out into the corridor again, herded by the second deputy. Wryman looked at Peeples 'You, too, Chris.'

'I'd like him to stay,' said Random.

'Why?'

'He's a friend of the court.' Random nodded at Yertsen. He felt slightly alarmed at his out-of-character impulsiveness, as if he had stepped on to some treadmill over which he had no control. 'Is that what you call it in this country?'

Yertsen roused himself enough to say, 'I'd like Chris to stay, Mr Wryman.'

Wryman shrugged and the deputy shut the door on the crowd outside. The air-conditioner, as if weighed down by the total atmosphere, climatic and emotional, had stopped; Bill Gauge, standing near it, gave it a thump and it started up again. Coulson decided to take over the meeting.

'You said you were thinking of other charges – '

'We want to hold him a while,' Wryman said. 'He still hasn't told us where he was the day Harry Jardine was shot.'

'I told you I don't remember!' Yertsen whimpered; he looked like a badly scared schoolboy. 'It was a work-day, wasn't it, Chris? The office would know where I was – '

Random could see that the boy was so badly frightened he could not remember where he had been only yesterday. He had interrogated Arabs who had been picked up in Aden: the innocent ones had been recognizable after a few minutes. In Yertsen he saw the same fear and confusion that turned a man's mind into an incoherent mess incapable of putting even the simplest facts into any sequence.

'Tim, take it easy. You're not alone here – some of us are trying to help you.' He didn't look at Wryman or Coulson, but he saw Tom Cloud nod agreement. 'If you just try to think back, you'll remember where you were that day. Where were you when you heard that Mr Jardine had been shot?'

Yertsen gulped, tried to concentrate. Then his face cleared and he opened his eyes wide, as if his eyesight had been miraculously cured. 'I was down in Helena! I took some books, ledgers or something, down to head office. Mr Judson sent me – '

Random looked at Wryman and the latter said, 'We can check on that. But I want to know when he left here, when he got to Helena, when he got back here.'

'Before you ask all those questions,' said Tom Cloud, 'I want some time alone with my client.'

'Okay.' Wryman looked relieved at the respite, as if he might want some time alone with himself.

The door was open and Cloud, Peeples and the deputy, running interference, took Yertsen through the press of people and disappeared down the corridor. One or two of the older reporters, knowing where the real source of their news still lay, lingered by the door, but Sheriff Gauge, with a gruff apology, closed it on them again.

The four men left in the room looked at each other: Coulson, Random and the two law men faced with an election in a couple of months. Random had been puzzled by the extra element he had felt ever since he had come into the room. Now he knew what it was: politics.

Coulson said, 'You're both on our ticket. If you're going to charge him with Harry Jardine's murder, you got to be sure it don't come unstuck. Otherwise everybody's going to say it was political, you did it hoping for a conviction. It could bounce back on us if the grand jury goes against you.'

'You said too much up there at Kalispell,' Wryman accused Gauge.

The sheriff bridled, but his protest was weak: 'You said yourself, before I left, he was the guy we wanted.'

'I didn't say it for publication, for Pete's sake.'

'He still could have done it,' Gauge said, persevering without much hope. 'He's still got to account for them hours he was away from Tozabe.'

'What would have been his motive for shooting Mr Jardine?' Random asked.

The three men looked at him and Wryman said, 'Why are you so interested in Yertsen? You're the outlander here.'

Random could hear the silent echo of the question from the other two. He threw the ball at Coulson: 'I was asked to come up here by Mr Coulson. I assumed it was because I could contribute something.'

'You haven't contributed much so far.' Coulson sounded as if he wished he had left Random behind in Helena.

'Yertsen might think he has,' said Wryman grudgingly. 'But

I think maybe you're being over-charitable to him, Mr Random. He takes a shot at you and Mrs Jardine – '

'I don't believe he did. I think he was doing what he said, trying to scare off those drillers – ' Then Random abruptly gave up. All at once he recognized that Wryman had lost confidence, that the County Attorney knew he was trying to pin far too much on Yertsen.

'Do you want to lay charges against him?' Wryman said.

Random didn't look at Coulson, but he was aware of the big man watching him. 'No. I've talked to Mrs Jardine and she feels the same way – we think it was an accident.'

'You could get the drillers to lay charges,' said Gauge, but he didn't sound as if he wanted to press his suggestion.

'They wouldn't want to come back here to give evidence. They'd lose money being away from work.' The air-conditioner coughed, spluttered. Wryman hit it, but more in frustration at his own position than to get it working again. He looked at Coulson. 'Unless the company that's employing them would want to pay their expenses?'

'I don't think that's likely,' said Coulson, poker-faced.

'Okay, then.' Wryman sounded resigned, defeated. 'What do we do?'

'You keep him overnight, let him go in the morning after the newspaper guys have given up and gone home. Say you checked his story and there wasn't enough evidence to lay charges.'

'It's not going to look good,' said Gauge, peeved but also resigned.

'It'll look a goddam sight worse if you try to take it further,' said Coulson, suddenly angry and impatient again. 'Jesus, why didn't you get in touch with us before you started going off half-cocked? We could have kept it all quiet – '

'Like one of the guys outside there said, Mr Coulson – Kenneway-Jardine doesn't own the law up here in the valley.' Wryman had lost a battle, but he hadn't lost his self-respect. 'Okay, we didn't handle it well. But when we get the guy who *did* murder Harry Jardine, I'm not going to ask your permission to charge him. I'm on the same ticket as Mrs Jardine, sure, just like Sheriff Gauge is. But that doesn't say we don't do our job the way it should be done.'

He looked at Gauge and the sheriff, after a moment's painful hesitation, nodded agreement. 'We got to live with the people up here, Mr Coulson. Some of 'em don't love the company as much as you think. Not with what's been going on lately, the drillers and all.'

Coulson didn't ask Gauge to elaborate on that. 'Okay, you let him go in the morning. I'll see that Indian lawyer is paid for his time. But don't let any of the reporters near him – Yertsen, I mean.'

'Once we let him go he's a free man,' Wryman pointed out, a little sarcastically, Random thought.

'You better look after him then,' Coulson told Random. 'Get Chris Peeples to take charge of him, get him out of the way for a few days. The reporters will soon give up, they ain't going to hang around here indefinitely.'

'There's the local radio station,' Wryman said. 'They'll be looking for news.'

'We own that,' said Coulson, and that was that.

When Coulson and Random got out into the corridor there were still three or four men waiting there, including a grey-haired man who said he was from the *Independent Record*. 'Any comment, Mr Coulson?'

'Not at this stage,' said Coulson, sounding unexpectedly pompous. 'Every man is innocent till he's proved guilty.'

Random wanted to throw up and the reporter looked as if he felt the same way. 'I hadn't heard that before, Mr Coulson. May I quote you?'

'Get fucked,' said Coulson, less pompously.

He pushed past the reporter and stalked off down the corridor. The reporter looked at Random. 'I'm told you're the new general manager here. You got any comment?'

'Just that I'm glad to be in your wonderful country,' said Random, winked at the reporter and followed Coulson out of the building.

Coulson was down by the Mercedes, surrounded by the other reporters and photographers. He fended them off with some non-committal remarks, jerked his head at Random and got into the car. Random got in on the other side, having to push through the crowd to do so. Coulson pushed a button and the windows slid up. They sat in a four-wheeled goldfish bowl, the reporters staring in at them. Random hoped that, if Coulson was going to say something important to him, there were no lip-readers among the spectators.

'You get back inside, stay with Yertsen,' said Coulson.

'Yes, sir.'

'None of that *sir* crap. You're too goddam independent. You seem to forget – we're both up here to look after Grace.'

'I don't think it's as simple as that.' Random saw the row of faces over Coulson's shoulder; the goldfish bowl was suddenly illuminated by a flash. 'But this is no place to discuss it.'

'I'll talk to you tomorrow. In the meantime stay away from Grace.'

Another flash, this time behind Random, lit up the interior of the car. It seemed to lay Coulson bare: Christ Almighty, Random thought, he's jealous of me! Is he in love with her, too?

'Isn't that for her to decide?'

'No,' said Coulson and confirmed what Random had just suspected. 'I'm telling you, stay away from her!'

Chapter Six

Grace lay in the huge bed staring at the room without really seeing it. It had been a very empty bed, mocking in its size, for far too long. Except for that night with Jack just – how long ago was it? She had lost track of time: she had begun a new life in which the clocks had a different face.

She had been apprehensive when she had started out a week ago last Monday. Though she was always outwardly composed, there were still moments when, as her grandmother had once described them, she was fit for the vapours. Self-confidence was one of her gifts; but her soul was not all concrete ego. When she had left Kipling nineteen years ago for Miles City she had gone with a bold face and a doubting heart; she had not turned back only because that would have been harder to do than to keep going. It had been that way ever since.

Ab Chartwell, a state committeeman, had taken time out from his law practice to go along with her. He rode with her in her car; Lee drove and Kerry O'Toole, Grace's brand-new secretary, sat beside him. Two other campaign cars, two press cars and a television van completed the convoy.

'Just be yourself,' said Chartwell, veteran of a dozen campaigns but never a candidate. He enjoyed the hurly-burly every two years and looked on it as his vacation for that year; but he was always glad to get back to his law office. There, you might be abused by some dissatisfied client but you could always send him a bill for the privilege. A candidate, successful or otherwise, could never send a bill to an abusive voter. 'The voters can always recognize a phony front.'

'I thought that was the essence of politics,' said Grace. 'The phony front.'

She saw Kerry O'Toole, twenty-two and new to the game, look sharply over her shoulder. Chartwell saw the girl's reaction. 'Pretend you never heard that, Miss O'Toole. You pretend you never said it, Grace.'

'So I'm putting up a phony front right away.' But she smiled, put a hand on his bony knee. 'I'll be myself, Ab, don't worry. And don't you be too disillusioned with me, Kerry.'

The secretary, petite and quick-moving, attractive Irish face wide-eyed on the world through her gold-rimmed spectacles, nodded. This was her first political job and she knew she had a lot to learn; but she had been bred to it. 'My Uncle Phil couldn't be himself even when he went to the bathroom. But he was re-elected five times. How do you explain that, Mr Chartwell?'

'Your Uncle Phil had so many relatives, he couldn't lose.'

'Having a Bishop for a brother also helped,' said Grace. 'Half the voters feared excommunication if they voted for anyone but your uncle.'

'I can talk to my uncle the Bishop, if you like,' Kerry volunteered.

'Only as a last resort. I don't think he's going to make the Sign of the Cross over a lapsed Lutheran.'

'We'll get your Uncle Mick to look after the Catholics,' said Chartwell. 'Every Sunday he's outside the Cathedral, holding court like the Archbishop himself. Come to think of it, I've never seen him go inside.'

'He never does,' said Kerry. 'He just looks as if he's heard more masses than anyone else.'

This trip was just exploratory: the candidate and the voters and the party workers looking each other over. Cliff Pendrick was already off and running, but Grace had been advised to build her race quietly, let the public gradually get used to the fact that Harry Jardine was dead and that his widow, fighting her grief and shock, had stepped into his shoes.

'You are running as a public duty,' Ab Chartwell told her. He appeared to have shed his dry, desiccated image, though his humour was still dry. Grace felt herself warming to him, was glad he had come with her. 'You were reluctant to take the nomination, but we persuaded you. That's what we been telling the press. You're going to get a friendly welcome. This is man's country out here, Marlboro Country, like the commercials say. But it's been this state, and Wyoming, that's always given women a place in politics. Wyoming gave women the vote back in 1869, even before we'd stopped killing the Indians. They were the first ones ever to elect a woman governor, Nellie Tayloe Ross, back in 1925. You weren't born then, but that was the year back East when they had the Scopes trial, tried a feller for teaching the Darwin theory about Man. And when Montana sent Jeannette Rankin to Congress in 1917, she was the first woman ever elected there. They had to put in a special washroom for her – the plumbers had never been told a woman was likely to be elected. We're not so backward out here, despite what those smart-Alecks in the East think. You got a lot going for you, Grace, being a woman. Being Harry's widow is going to help, too.'

On the Friday of the second week the campaign caravan was in Havre, the county seat of Hill County. The temperature was 105, a dry baking heat that turned the landscape into a shimmering yellow sea in which farmhouses stood like burnt-out hulks, their shadows lying about them like floating ashes.

'I want to make a little side trip,' Grace said.

'Sure,' said Ab Chartwell. 'We'll go anywhere you like. I'll tell the pressmen.'

'No.' She was tired of the company of men, especially of the pressmen who, unaccustomed to a woman candidate, not as aware of history as Ab Chartwell was, still treated her with suspicion, as if she might be capable of some sort of treason against their male world. 'I'd rather go alone.'

But in the end she took Kerry with her. They sat in the back of the Lincoln and Lee drove them out of Havre and down Route 2 to Kipling. There, on Grace's direction, he turned south and they drove another ten miles along a dirt road through the flat countryside. The sun was a blood-red world sitting on the horizon; shadows were strips of dark purple mourning crêpe laid on the dead earth. The crops, dry as withered sticks, were ready to be flattened by the first strong wind that might blow. People sat on the shady side of their houses, watched the big car as it went by trailing its train of dust; none of them was energetic or interested enough to stand up and see where the car was heading. The car rattled its way across a wooden bridge spanning a dry creek bed; beneath them a cow nosed at a cracked pool of dried mud. Crows went home, cawing death cries on the heavy dry air that seemed to make flying difficult for them.

'Here,' said Grace, and Lee pulled the car into the side of the road. She got out and looked back at Kerry. 'It's like a furnace. You better stay in the car.'

'No, I'd like to come,' said Kerry bravely. 'I mean, if you don't mind?'

Grace pushed open the rickety wooden gate; its remaining hinge gave way and it fell over, raising a small explosion of dust. They walked up the narrow path, overgrown with dry yellow weeds, between the stunted brittle sorghum. The house, or what was left of it, had the crop growing up to within a couple of feet of its walls.

'Why on earth didn't they knock the place down?' Kerry said. 'Why plough around it?'

'When my folks died it was the only thing they had to leave me. I sold it to the man who owns the land on either side. But I stipulated he was never to pull down the house, unless it fell down itself. He understood, because his folks and his grandfolks had been honyockers, too.'

She walked round the house while Kerry, still young enough not to need the yardstick of memory, stood on the roofless verandah and wondered why so many people wanted to go back to memories best forgotten. The house, most of its roof gone, its windows and doorways just gaping holes, had none of the simple dignity and defiance of a log cabin; you could not imagine any pioneer family holed up in this shack and fighting off Indians with nothing but courage and a couple of long-barrelled rifles. The fight, that had gone on forever, had been against nature, the crop market and the banks. The US Cavalry had never ridden to the rescue here.

Grace touched parts of the house, as if trying to grasp the past: a piece of rotten clapboard broke off in her hand, some tar-paper insulation crumbled like ash in her fingers. She stepped through the gaping back doorway, careless of the dust and debris on her expensive shoes. All the furniture had gone, but there was still some rotting linoleum left on what remained of the floorboards. Some rusted hinges hung in an empty frame in the floor: that had been the trapdoor to the tiny cellar, dug out of the hard earth, that had been her grandparents' cool chamber. Her own parents had been lucky enough to own a second-hand refrigerator.

She walked through the shell of the house, treading carefully, as much cautious of disturbing too much of the past as of falling through the floorboards. She pushed back the door of what had been her bedroom; the room was open to the sky and as she stepped into it a bird suddenly took off and went out between the roof beams. Startled, she pulled up: she was expecting ghosts but had forgotten the house was probably occupied by other creatures. She looked around the room, trying to remember what she had dreamed of when she had lain here in the dark twenty, twenty-five, thirty years ago. But none of the dreams came back: long-ago dreams were like long-ago pain, almost impossible to recall.

Two faded rotogravure pictures were pasted to the back of the door: Cary Grant and Marlon Brando smiled at her, the loves of her girlhood. Old and grey, one of them now; double-chinned and thinning-haired, the other. *O lost, and by this movie fan grieved, ghosts, come back again.* She hoped Thomas Wolfe would forgive her for paraphrasing him.

She stepped out on to the rickety verandah where Kerry waited patiently. 'Did you read Thomas Wolfe at school?'

'Just skimmed through him,' said Kerry, who put anyone before Salinger in Ancient Lit. 'He was considered old-hat, sort of. Did you read him when you, er, lived here?'

'I read *everything* when I lived here.' She looked out on the flat landscape stretching away to the edge of forever: that was the way she had thought of it as a girl: dreams lay just beyond it, Cathay, Camelot, Hollywood. The sun had gone down but it had taken none of its heat with it; the sky was smeared above the western horizon, like a faded shroud pulled away from a bleeding world. The last of the colour, yellow and brown, was draining out of the fields; towards the east they were already bluish-grey, the horizon there smudged by the darkening sky. The Lincoln, dark and solid, stood in the roadway, the symbol of the present.

'There wasn't much else to do. We had a radio, but we didn't have TV.'

Kerry, too, looked out at the landscape. She took off her glasses, wiped them, put them back on again. 'It's a sort of desert, I guess. I mean, it must've been to a teenager.'

'Summer *and* winter. A winter down here – ' She shivered, despite the heat. '*Kissin-ey-oo-way*'-*o*. That's Cree, Indian, for *It blows cold*. God, does it blow cold! The year my grandfather died it fell to 40 below. He had a heart attack out there somewhere – ' She nodded at the flat burnt landscape; one couldn't imagine it blanketed by snow. 'My father brought his body in and they kept it in a snowdrift for a month out back of the house. The ground was frozen too hard for them to dig a grave.'

'Is he buried out there now?'

'No, I had him and Grandma dug up and taken into town, buried alongside my mother and father. They'd had enough of this place while they were alive.'

There was silence for a long moment. The house creaked, as if protesting their presence. A long way off a dog barked desultorily, but it seemed only a faint whisper in the vast silence of the dying day. At last Kerry said, a little uncertainly, 'I think I understand why you came here today.'

'Remember it, Kerry. So you'll understand anything I may do in the future.'

They got back into the car and Lee swung it round and they went back up the long dusty road. Kerry turned and looked through the rear window. The house, grey and stark, was dissolving into the dusk. She looked at Grace, sitting gazing straight ahead.

'Aren't you going to look back?'

'I've been doing that for almost twenty years,' Grace said.

2

There was a knock on the door of the motel bedroom. Grace, lying on the bed in the dark, decided to ignore it. It was probably Ab Chartwell or one of the other men wanting to ask her to have dinner with him; but she wanted to be alone tonight, or at least not have the company of men. Except, of course, Jack: she had been lying here for the past half-hour wondering whether to call him. He would not be able to get down to Havre in time to have dinner with her; and she could not expect him to drive a 500-mile round trip to spend a couple of hours with her and have to go to bed in a separate room. Propriety was part of politics; at least till you were elected. But she would call Jack anyway, talk to him, tell him how much she was missing him; and hope that the motel operator would not eavesdrop on the call. So she would ignore the knock on the door and hope that whoever it was would go away.

There was another knock, louder this time. 'Grace? It's Jim – Jim Coulson.'

Jim Coulson? What was he doing down here? He was not part of her political campaign team; it had been decided that none of her business associates should have anything public to do with her campaign. She got up, switched on the lights, looked at herself in the mirror and switched the main light off. She was not interested in making an impression on Jim, but a woman was entitled to her small vanities. She looked tired, a little dishevelled and several years older than thirty-seven.

She opened the door. 'Jim? Is there something wrong? What are you – ?'

He followed her into the room. 'Wrong? Hell, no! You think I'd drive all the way down here to tell you something was wrong?'

She didn't follow his logic, but she was too tired to query it. 'Okay, so everything is all right.'

'Sit down, Grace. You're going to feel weak in the knees after what I got to tell you.' She had seen him excited before, but never like this. 'Grace, we got the report today from the guys who surveyed the valley. You are going to be one of the richest women in America!'

She was too tired to feel any immediate reaction. 'Go on.'

'Jesus, I got to admire you – you're so goddam cool!' Then abruptly he tried to cool himself, as if it had occurred to him that she was making him look young and foolish. He became businesslike. 'Grace, they've come up with a deposit that is 6 per cent copper – '

'You already told me that at the ranch.'

'Yeah, but we didn't know the extent of the strike then. The vein looks like it could be anything between 20 and 30 feet wide, it's over 4000 feet long and just over a thousand deep. It could have broken off and start up again farther along, but so far, so good.'

'Put it in money terms,' she said and realized at once how mercenary she must sound.

But Coulson was deaf to such nuances. 'We'll get rid of the bad news first. Copper is down, but they don't think it's going to get much lower. It's a mineral that's always going to be in demand, sometimes more, sometimes less. Over the last ten, twelve years, the price has fluctuated between 42 and 84 cents a pound. One per cent copper, that's a pretty normal return these days, brings 20 pounds to the ton of ore. Six per cent means 120 pounds to the ton. Let's average the price out at 60 cents a pound. That means 72 dollars a ton, right?'

'Right.' She had always been good at mental arithmetic.

'Okay. Now if this deposit is no more than what we say, and we told 'em to be conservative, they estimate we'll take six million tons of ore out of it. Six million times 72 – '

Her mental arithmetic was not *that* good: it was difficult to hold all those zeros in her mind. Even Coulson had to refer to a slip of paper he took from his pocket.

'It's four hundred and thirty-two million dollars. If the price goes up to 80 cents again, it's five hundred and fifty-six million.' He said the words slowly. 'That's without all the side products, the silver, lead, zinc, gold. They tell me the silver and gold return alone would carry the costs of the whole project. Everything else would be clear profit! Jesus H. Christ!' He leaned back on the bed, laughed at her; he was like a big, grey-haired schoolboy who had just been told he had been nominated All-American tackle or whatever while he was still in high school. 'With everything else you own, if that don't make you the richest woman, I'd like to meet the one who is!'

'You forget I own only half of whatever comes out of the valley. Forty-nine per cent, to be exact.'

'We're trying to fix that. And even forty-nine per cent of five hundred and fifty-six is still a lot of money. On top of what you already got. Grace, you will be really rich, believe me!'

'Is that all you're interested in, Jim? How much I'm worth?'

It was an idle, bantering question: her tired mind was a step or two behind her tongue. But at once, as soon as she saw him sit up on the bed, she knew she had said the wrong thing.

'No, Grace. I'd be interested in you if you didn't have a dime.'
All at once she was aware that she was treading on eggshells.
'Jim, I was joking – '

'I wasn't.' He was no longer a schoolboy; there was no mistaking the look on his face. 'I've been in love with you, Grace, ever since Harry brought you up to Helena. I never gave you even a hint while he was alive. I know you and a lot of other people, including Pet, think I'm a pretty simple soul, you can all read me like a book. But you're all wrong. I only let you know what I want you to know about me.'

'I wish you hadn't let me know *this*.' She stood up, switched on the lights: the one bedside lamp suggested an intimacy that she didn't want in this particular scene. To give herself something to do while she collected her thoughts, tried to stir up her sluggish mind, she stood in front of the mirror and brushed her hair. Then realized it was a wrong move: it suggested she was trying to make herself presentable to him. She threw down the brush, turned to face him. 'Jim, I don't thank you for telling me how you feel. I'm not flattered by it and I don't think you're being very fair to Pet.'

'I don't care a damn about Pet!' He bounced off the bed and for a moment she thought he was going to attack her. 'Jesus, do you know what it's like being married to a – a souse? That's what I call her, you know? My faithful souse. That's the only thing you can say for her – she's faithful. Which was more than you could say for your Harry, the son-of-a-bitch. You think it didn't get me in the gut every time, seeing him whoring around with every bitch that'd lay down for him? There were times when I could have killed the bastard – '

'Did you?' She was as surprised by the question as he appeared to be.

He blinked at her, then slowly raised his hand and ran it through his hair. 'Jesus, is that what you think of me?'

'I don't know what to think of you. You're full of surprises. You've admitted that. Did you shoot Harry?'

'I don't think that even deserves an answer.' He sounded ridiculously pompous; but she couldn't laugh at him. 'I hated the son-of-a-bitch, but I'm not going to admit even that to anyone but you. Even Karl don't know it.'

'Does Karl know about the extent of the copper strike?' She

went off at a tangent, trying to get him back on their original topic.

'Of course he does. We're working in this together for you, ain't we?' He stared at her quizzically, looking slightly comic. 'You're changing the subject, right?'

'I didn't think it was so obvious.' She smiled, deciding to try for the light note; it had been a successful defence with other unwanted suitors, before Harry had come along. 'Jim, don't get involved with *two* women. We could turn you greyer than you are now.'

He recognized he was being brushed-off. She expected an angry reaction, but once more he surprised her: he wasn't without a sense of dignity. He shrugged, made a gesture of surrender. 'Okay, you win. But it don't change my feelings about you. J love you, Grace, and that's the truth.'

For a moment she softened towards him. To be loved was not to be degraded or humiliated; for all she knew, he might love her more than Harry ever had. 'Jim – I'm sorry – '

'Forget it.' He was making an attempt at being dignified; and doing much better than she had expected. 'I ought to have known better . . . Well, I came down here to give you some good news. Let's get back to that.'

The atmosphere was full of loose ends, they would keep fluttering between them from now on. But she knew of no way to resolve the situation, at least not right now. She tried for a crisp note, the president of the board: 'What is Karl doing about Honyocker?'

'Nothing about Honyocker – that's okay. He's been on the phone most of the day, talking to London.'

'To London? You mean he's told the English board about the survey?'

'Hell, no! They're the last ones we're going to tell. We got to keep it quiet as we can, not even give them a hint anything's going on. We cancelled some contracts we'd let out for stripping the timber – we'd figured we might as well make as much as we could out of the timber before we flooded the valley. But now it don't matter. We'll make so much out of the strike, we can forget the timber. And they might've started asking some questions. Some of the workers up in the valley were already getting too nosey. Random, for instance.'

'I know,' she said, but didn't elaborate; though Coulson looked as if he might have a question or two of his own on what Random had said to her. 'Who has Karl been talking to in London?'

'Brokers. Monday he wants them to start buying more Kenneway-Jardine stock. He'll have brokers in New York doing the same thing. We'll buy quietly through the companies we got registered in the other states, buy enough till we got a majority of the stock, along with what you already own. Then we present them with, like they say, a *fait accompli*.' His French was not as good as his mathematics: it came out as all one word, *fatecomply*. 'You'll have the majority vote in Kenneway-Jardine and you'll decide we'll get out of timber and into mining.'

'Is that what I'll decide?'

He frowned slightly and his face seemed to harden. 'Grace, we've been a long time on this, Karl and me. Oh sure, it was Harry's idea, but we did all the donkey work. Still are doing it. We'll make you rich, much richer than you already are, but there's got to be something in it for me and Karl, too. Maybe we didn't tell you that, but we didn't mean to hide it from you. We got stock in all those out-of-state companies and we got stock in every company that's got the Jardine name on it. We worked over twenty years for Harry and we didn't do it for love or a pat on the back from him.'

'What *did* you do it for? Respect, like Karl said?'

'Bullshit. We pulled a lot of dirty tricks for him, but we never pulled one on him. But all those years Karl and I, we were working for ourselves as much as Harry, and now's the time for the pay-off. So don't spoil things, Grace. You'll make the decisions, okay, but don't forget we were working for Harry long before you came along. You owe us, Grace. You owe us plenty.'

The angry lover had disappeared, to be replaced by the cold hard businessman. She wanted to make some sardonic comment on the turnabout, but that way lay danger. Better to keep everything on a business footing.

'I don't owe you anything, Jim. Maybe Harry owed you something, but I'm not paying his debts. You'll be looked after, both of you. You'll go on doing the donkey work, as you call it, and you'll get more than a fair return for it. But I'm the boss and I'll make the decisions. Goodnight, Jim. Thanks for coming down all this way with the good news.'

'And what about the bad news? You and me.' For a moment the angry rejected lover was back. 'What about that?'

'Goodnight, Jim. Give my love to Pet.'

The crash of the door as he slammed it after him must have been heard in every other room in the motel wing. Grace, trembling a little, her control relaxing now she was alone, sat down heavily on the bed. All at once she felt lonely, wanted someone to talk to. She reached for the phone, but paused with her hand on the instrument. The two pieces of news she had received tonight were not items she could confide to him.

3

So she didn't call Jack Friday night and late Saturday afternoon she returned to Helena. She called him then, wanting to confide in him nothing more than that she loved him; but there was no answer, either from his home in Tozabe or the office. She felt unreasonably put out, as if he should have been standing by waiting for her call. She was experiencing what had happened to her when she had first fallen in love with Cliff, then Oscar, then Harry: the petty selfishness that demanded the man she loved should always be there when she wanted him. She despised herself for the feeling, but she knew that love was not all generosity and there was nothing she could do about it but try to hide it.

Sunday morning Shooberg called. 'By tomorrow noon I hope to hear from London how much stock they've been able to buy.'

'Are you buying in large lots?'

'We got to take it carefully. We got to spread it, but we can't afford to take too long. That's why we're buying in both New York and London.'

'How much money do we have to lay out?'

'About three million dollars. That's going to be our problem – putting that much money into one stock all at one time. We got to do all our buying before London wakes up to what's happening. When we've done it, you should have 52 per cent of the stock.'

'Do we have that much money on hand?'

'We've sold stock in some of the other companies and we're good for a million at the banks. It's no problem, the money.'

She was only just becoming accustomed to the idea of how rich she was. Harry had denied her nothing and after marrying him it had taken her only a year or so to take for granted that she was a rich man's wife. But, as she had said to Karl and Jim, there was a difference between being the wife of a rich man and being rich oneself. It was the difference between having the luxuries of power and of having power itself. But it struck her that, considering the money involved, she was placing great trust in the two men who had worked for Harry, one of whom had hated him and the other who had said he had no more than just respected him. She had already decided to be cautious of Coulson from now on. But what of Karl Shooberg: was unloving respect for Harry enough to keep him honest in his dealings with Harry's widow?

'I hope it's no problem, Karl. I'm placing a great deal of trust in you and Jim.'

He had the sharpest ear of any man she had ever met. 'That sounds like you have some doubts about us.'

'No-o, Karl.'

Her voice, she hoped, dragged just enough to keep him wondering. Ever since she had left Kipling, with forty-two dollars in her purse and a wardrobe that could be packed into one large suitcase, life had not been simple for her. There had always been stratagems she had had to adopt in the war with men. There had been the armistices with Cliff and Oscar and Harry; but even with Cliff and Oscar, the two most harmless, there had been times when total honesty from her would have been a victory for them. With Harry, over the last two years, their whole relationship had been one in which the truth had always been hidden behind the smokescreen of malicious banter, the echoes of which she heard in the conversations of Jim and Pet Coulson. Only she knew how much she had been wounded, how she had longed for the impossible, that the truth could not hurt.

But now she was in another league, not of love but of high finance and politics. The men in this game would be more ruthless than the men she had been in love with: the husband or the lover at least accepted you as a woman. But she felt confident, was surprised at the exhilaration she felt. She was discovering a whole new reef of pleasure and excitement and interest: running far better than six per cent to the ton.

'I'll see you tomorrow at ten, Karl.'

When Jack arrived she was still pondering the feelings that were creeping up on her. But as soon as Lee brought him into the living room she forgot all suspicion of men; it took all her control not to rush to him while Lee was still in the room. She waited till the butler had gone, then she clutched at Jack, kissed him so passionately that she hurt her lips, pressed her body so close to him that in a few moments she could feel him standing hard against her.

'I'd like to go to bed *now*!'

'I thought I was only coming for lunch.'

'Like hell you did.' She pulled away from him reluctantly, straightened the silk shirt she wore, looked at herself in the French mirror over the fireplace. Her mouth looked as if she had been eating blood-red plums. 'I better go up and repair this. You need cleaning up, too.'

She took out her handkerchief, wiped his mouth clean. He glanced over her shoulder into the mirror. 'We're both out of practice at kissing.'

'It's like swimming – you never lose the knack. There, now you're respectable-looking again.'

'Fit to parade in front of the servants, eh?'

'You live your way, I'll live mine.'

'When I came up the street I noticed a few curtains fluttering. My car's been parked outside your house all night, did you know that?'

'How did you get down here?'

'One of the trucks was going down to the mill at Townsend. He dropped me off at Cedar Street and I walked up.'

'You should've been saving your strength for better things.'

'You're sex mad, I'm glad to say.'

Later, over lunch of lobster salad and a bottle of California white wine that, she noticed, he seemed to appreciate, he said, 'You should have met my grandfather. He thought all servants were blind and deaf. Periodically he would get drunk, usually after weekend house parties when all the guests had gone home, and he would wander stark naked round the house shouting, "Who wants to shake hands with the one-eyed demon?" My grandmother would just ignore him, walk right by him as if he were just one of the suits of armour we have around the house. They were a couple of real eccentrics. They are a dying breed, I'm afraid. The eccentrics today are just a lot of conscious exhibitionists.'

'Maybe they treat their servants with more respect than your grandfather did.'

'I doubt it. It's hard to explain, I suppose, but my grandfather and his servants respected each other. I don't think any of them ever left his service. But it was another era, another way of thinking.'

'Would you have wanted to belong to it? I mean, lived then?'

'No.' He smiled at her: half-mocking again. 'At heart I think I'm more a democrat than you are.'

After lunch, when Lee and Annie had taken themselves off to visit some of Annie's Bible class friends out of town, Grace took him up to bed. She had to touch him before he was fully undressed and they coupled like lovers who hadn't seen each other for two years instead of two weeks.

'The second thing I did,' he said, 'was take my pack off.'

'What's that?'

'An old army saying. A soldier from the wars returning . . .' He sat up, took off his shirt and socks, the last of his clothing. 'That must be one of the most ridiculous sights in the world, chap making love with his socks on.'

'I didn't notice.'

He looked at the shoulders and collar of his shirt sketched with lipstick. 'I wonder what Cheryl is going to think when she sends my laundry out tomorrow?' Cheryl was his part-time housekeeper, Beryl Gray's quieter but equally physically imposing twin sister.

'There, you see? You are worried about the servants.'

'I'm only worried that Cheryl or Beryl will think I'm fair game and jump into bed with me. How would you like that?'

He had lain down beside her again. She stroked his chest and belly, a tactile pleasure in her fingers as they brushed skin and hair, felt muscle and the hidden bone. She felt sensually relaxed, but she knew he could stir her again whenever he wanted to. 'Do you think I'm the jealous type?'

'Yes.'

'That's a blunt answer.' But it didn't disturb her. 'Yes, I am. That's how I know I love you, that it isn't just sex I feel about you.'

He kissed her. 'I've never wanted anyone as much as I've wanted you these past couple of weeks. It was partly sex, but it was more than that. When I saw you last night I wanted everyone else in the room to drop dead all of a sudden. That was the quickest way I could think of getting rid of them. It wasn't what the one-eyed demon felt for you down here – ' He tapped his genitals. Then he lifted her hand and put it on his chest. 'It was what I felt in here, too. I wanted you alone, not to share you with anyone.'

The articulate lover: what a change he was from Harry who, in bed, had been capable only of grunts and obscenities. They continued to talk, learning more and more about each other, facets that came unexpectedly to light under the microscope of loving and being loved. They made love again, at first gently, then wildly with the passion just this side of murder. Then she got up, put on a gown, went downstairs and got them drinks. When she came back he was in his shorts, sitting in the window seat looking out on the big side lawn. She went and sat beside him, gave him his drink.

'A penny for them.'

'It'll cost you more.'

'You mean you, too, are after my money?' She put on mock dignity.

'If it comes with you – of course. We English, above a certain level of class, have never had any false pride about marrying for money. Our family has done it for generations. It's only the middle classes who are snobbish about money.'

'Some time, when we're back in bed, you must tell me what class I belong to.' She sipped her drink, looked at him seriously. 'What were you thinking about?'

'Wondering what you thought last night when they told you Tim Yertsen had been arrested for the murder of your husband.'

'I don't know what I thought. I've never wanted Harry – *revenged*, if that's what you mean. Harry himself would've wanted that, but I don't believe in revenge – I don't think it accomplishes anything. When Jim Coulson called and said they were going to let – Yertsen? – go, I was, well, *relieved*. I wouldn't want anyone charged if they weren't sure, perfectly sure, that he had murdered Harry.'

'Do you really want to know who killed him?'

She was startled; the drink splashed in her hand. 'You mean you know?''

'No, no. I meant would you be happier if you never found out who killed him?'

She put down her glass, wiped the splashed liquid from her hand. It was the sort of physical action one did while one's mind changed gears. She had become practised at it over the past two weeks, the cover defence of the politician. But she was not playing politician now. The question, she realized, was far too personal.

He waited patiently (like a prosecutor? she wondered) and at last she said, 'I wouldn't be disappointed if I never found out. Don't you think that's often the best thing? I mean, not to know?'

'No,' he said, and she suddenly recognized that he might have a greater capacity for the pain of truth than she herself had. 'That would be dangerous.'

Chapter Seven

1

August burned itself out and September came in; but only the calendar seemed to note the change. There were two electrical storms in which lightning ripped the sky with threatening fury and the fire crews stood by; but there were no fires and, worse, there was no rain. There were no freshening fall winds; the pines and firs stood like green rock pinnacles in the dry hot air. The leaves of the aspens and alders and cottonwoods had not yet begun to fall but they looked and felt as brittle as charred paper. The fall colours were muted, the yellows and reds and browns faded like a palette left too long in the sun. Random, a man for the changing of the seasons, had looked forward to his first North American autumn, but was deeply disappointed.

'It's bad,' said Russ Judson. 'The wife tells me I keep sniffing in my sleep, as if I'm trying to smell smoke.'

Random took off his hard hat, ran his hand over his hair. 'I keep expecting my hair to fall out, it's so dry.'

Judson took off his own helmet, grinned and tapped his balding skull. 'You wouldn't believe I used to have thick curly hair. Then I came up here and the altitude and the summers, it started to go straight. I don't know if that's the reason I started to go bald, but I'm thinking of suing the company. Just like the miners sue for silicosis.'

'How wide are you cutting the strip?'

'Two hundred yards. I figured it would give us a good fire-break as well. I'm taking out all the trees, young and old. It's going to scar the ridge, but it can't be helped. Maybe we should have cut more fire-breaks. If lightning strikes, Christ knows what's going to happen.'

The teams were working on a stand of spruce that was destined for the pulp mills over in Missoula. The area was on one side of a cutting between two ridges called Horsethief Gap; the river glittered below like a sword that had severed the spine of a giant green beast. The terrain here was too steep for mechanical harvesters and the morning was loud and savage on the ear with the whine and buzz of power saws. Trees crashed with the roar of exploding shells, preceded by the snap of rifle-fire as branches were broken off during the fall; the earth shuddered and brush and dust flew up in small explosions. The air was heavy with the smell of crushed leaves, of newly-cut timber: the scent that for Random could never be equalled by the *parfumiers* of Grasse or anywhere else. He picked up a spruce cone, already chestnut brown, delighting in the feel of its papery softness in his fingers. This was his ambience, his climate: no matter what opportunities for promotion lay ahead, he knew he could never entirely desert field work. This was food and drink to whatever soul he claimed to possess.

'Any more word on those mining guys?' Judson asked.

Random shook his head. 'I sent off that letter you suggested, asking for a statement on what's going to happen here. So far they haven't even acknowledged it.'

'You mean Shooberg and Coulson or London?'

'Neither.' He had not sent a copy of his letter to London; first, he wanted some sort of answer from Shooberg and Coulson. And from Grace. He had not sent her a copy, but he knew she would know of it. He had been tempted to call his father, explain unofficially what was going on, but had decided against it. He disliked nepotism, in whichever direction it ran. 'I'm hoping things have settled down, Russ. That whoever was interested in the valley changed their minds when they got the feel of the mood up here.'

'You don't know this part of the country yet, Jack. If some mining company thinks it can make a buck or two, it don't worry about anyone's mood. I've never met a mining man yet who cared two cents about what's above ground. I wasn't born here, I came out from West Virginia. You ought to see what the mining companies have done to the Appalachians.'

'But that's coal, isn't it? There wouldn't be any coal around here.'

'Don't make no difference. If they dig it up and it's going to make them money, it don't matter whether it's coal, gold, copper or crap.' He looked out over the valley below them, then back at Random. 'There's been some rumours, Jack. About Tim Yertsen.'

'What sort of rumours?'

'That he took a shot at you and Mrs Jardine about a month or so ago.'

Random took his time about replying. Fifty yards below him he had recognized Yertsen, working a small bulldozer that was clearing the slash, the residue left after the trees had been trimmed, from the break cut in the forest. 'I think you'd better squash that rumour, Russ. He didn't take a shot at us. It was just an accident. He was a bit careless with a gun, but I gather that's a national habit, isn't it?'

He realized at once that that was the wrong thing to say. Judson said stiffly, 'Not necessarily. Most of us around here know how to handle our guns.'

'Sorry.' He tried to make his tone more conciliatory: 'I think people are making too much of that night the sheriff hauled him in for questioning. They were talking that night of charging him with Harry Jardine's murder, but that was ridiculous. They knew they had nothing on him. I think Tim's just a born loser and he's always going to be making mistakes that will start up rumours.'

'Yeah, I guess so.' But Judson sounded unconvinced.

'How's he making out here? Chris Peeples told me he'd been moved out from the mill.'

'He's a good worker, tries hard. But he's accident-prone, that's why they got him working down there on the 'dozer, clearing the slash. He's less likely to get in the way. Personally, I'd fire him, but Chris tells me I'm too hard on the kid. But he's got a chip on his shoulder against the company, if you'll pardon the expression.'

Random grinned. 'I've been avoiding that expression ever since I got into the timber game.'

He left Judson and went down the hill towards the track where his car was parked. He had to pass Yertsen and he waved to the boy. Yertsen waved back, peered at him, then jerked the bulldozer to a halt and cut its motor. He jumped down, fell over, picked himself up and came stumbling over the rough ground and crushed undergrowth.

'Geez, Mr Random, I didn't recognize you! How's it going, eh?' He took off his hat, wiped the sweat from his face. His glasses were steamed up and he took them off, eyes blinking and half-shut as he peered at Random. 'I – I didn't get a chance to thank you for, you know, what you done for me. I mean that night, you know, down with the County Attorney. I mean, I really appreciate it, Mr Random. That your car down there? I'll walk down with you.'

He put on his glasses and hat, fell in, with his stumbling flat-footed walk, beside Random. 'How do you like it out here, Tim?'

'Great, just great! I keep hoping they'll promote me, put me on one of the saws – ' He stopped, looked to where a man was high on a tree, taking off the crown. 'That's what I'd like, up there tipping 'em off. Jesus, you know, you could think of yourself as sort of, you know, king of the forest.' He glanced at Random, wiped sweat and embarrassment from his face, said hesitantly, 'You know what I mean?'

'I know, Tim. I think any real timber man would know exactly what you mean.'

Yertsen beamed, as if he had just been blessed; or crowned king of the forest. He looked up at the man on top of the tree, then his face clouded and he shook his head. 'I ain't ever going to make it. These goddam eyes of mine – '

'Well,' Random said inadequately, 'at least you're working in timber.'

Yertsen nodded, said nothing more till they had reached the track where Random's car was parked with the cars and pick-ups of the workers. Abruptly he left Random, disappeared among the cars and trucks. Random, surprised but guessing that the boy was overcome at the confession of another of his dreams, got into his car and started it. He was about to pull out on to the track when

Yertsen came back with three trout hung on a piece of wire.

'I camped out here last night. I got up early this morning and caught these down in the river. I'd like for you to have 'em, Mr Random.'

'Tim – ' Random felt a thickening in his throat at the boy's gesture. He stood there beside the car, the tiger hunter, the king of the forest, the dreamer who would always be too blind to see the dream. Random reached out and took the fish. 'Thanks, Tim.'

'You're welcome, Mr Random. That's a fact.'

Random drove back to town, went to his office for an hour, then went home for lunch, carrying the three trout which Beryl had put in the office refrigerator for him. When he stepped up on to the verandah of his house Cheryl Lyons was just coming out of the front door. Her resemblance to her sister was extraordinary, but she seemed to have more control over her prominent bosom than Beryl had over its twin. She was married to a driver of one of the logging trucks, a hulking giant who, Random guessed, kept Cheryl on her back most of the time he was home.

'Why, they're just wonderful, Mr Random! You want me to stay and cook 'em for your lunch? I'd be just happy to do that for you – '

'I'll cook them for you.'

Random turned. Bonnie Mackintosh, dressed in a featherweight kaftan, her blonde hair tied back with a ribbon, looking more like a guru's girl friend than a governor's daughter, stood at the bottom of the steps. Random looked back at Cheryl.

'It was kind of you, Mrs Lyons. But Miss Mackintosh – '

'Sure.' Cheryl, unlike Beryl, had only one expression; it was impossible to tell what she was thinking, or if she was thinking at all. 'Well, enjoy the fish. I'll be here tomorrow.'

She went off and Random, the fish still hanging from his hand, was left with Bonnie. 'We'd better go in before these fish start humming. You look cooler than they do.'

'I think that's the first compliment you've paid me.'

They went into the house. He noticed she had an easy confidence about her today; she had forgotten, or put out of her mind, the friction of their last meeting. She took the fish from him, asked where the kitchen was and went out to it. He excused himself, had a shower, took his time about changing into fresh clothes while he pondered why she had come up here to Tozabe. Whether by design or by accident, she looked remarkably attractive today; he just wished her bra-less breasts were not so evident under the thin kaftan. He had an eye for bosoms, but he was determined he would not show any sign of having noticed hers.

When he went out to the kitchen the fish were ready. 'I set the table in your dining room,' she said. 'Do you have some white wine to go with this?'

'I don't drink in the middle of the day, it makes me sleepy. But if you'd like some – ?'

'It does the same with me. I didn't come up here to sleep.'

'I'm glad to hear it.' Then he regretted what he had said: he wanted no hint of the bedroom. 'Why did you come?'

She toyed with her fish, looked around the dining room. 'You have a pretty comfortable set-up here. But don't you get lonely?'

The house was too large for him with its eight rooms, but he wasn't going to waste time explaining to her that he had grown up in a surplus of rooms. The house was a typical company house, furnished in solid, no-frills Grand Rapids, without character but not without comfort. If he felt lonely in it, it was none of her business.

'Why did you come? You're not on official business for your father, not dressed like that.'

'No-o. It's just the coolest thing I own, that's all. A relic from my days at Berkeley . . . Jack, someone else knows about me and Harry. I mean besides you and Grace.'

'Who?'

'I don't know. In yesterday's mail I got a package. It had some of the letters I'd written to Harry in it. There was a note with it, printed in block letters, like whoever it was didn't want me to recognize his handwriting. It just said: *You ought to be more careful.*'

'Why did you come all the way up here to tell me?'

She threw down her fork: it hit the plate with a clang, bounced on to the floor. 'Who else have I got to tell? Jesus, why are you such a heartless bastard? I thought you'd understand – '

He stayed in his chair. 'Bonnie – ' He waited till she had

regained control of herself. She searched for a handkerchief, but her handbag was out in the kitchen. He tossed her the fresh one he had picked up when he had changed. She dried her eyes, blew her nose, kept the handkerchief. 'Bonnie, I'm not heartless – at least I don't think I am. But ever since I drove over the mountains at the top of this valley – I don't know, I just don't seem to have any control over my own circumstances. I find a murdered man, a stranger – well, he was when I found him, though now I seem to have known him for years. I find him and ever since people have been involving me in things I'd rather not know about.'

'Including Grace?'

It was his turn to throw down his fork; but with less force than she had. 'Look – '

'I'm sorry.' She picked up her fork from the floor, tried to squeeze herself back into some semblance of composure. 'I came up to see you because whoever sent those letters could be the murderer. Which means he would have seen you and me together down there on that road before – before he killed Harry.'

It was his turn to apologize. 'I'm stupid and thoughtless – I'm sorry. You did the right thing coming up to see me. I'm really in it now, up to my neck. Oh, I'm angry, all right,' he said as she looked up at him, 'but being angry is pretty futile, at least in this particular mess. Whom do I thump, kick up the behind? The way it's going, soon I'll be taking on the whole of Montana. Still – ' He picked up his fork, listlessly ate a piece of fish. It tasted like soggy cardboard and he pushed his plate away from him. 'Have you any idea, any idea at all, who it might be?'

She shook her head, at the same time pushing her own plate away. He noticed for the first time the strain on her face, the tiredness in her eyes. 'The package was posted down in Butte. But that doesn't mean anything – anyone could drive down there and mail it. If I turned the wrapping paper, with the lettering on it, my name and address, over to the police for – what do you call it?'

'Forensic science, I think.'

'Yeah, that's it. If I did that, I'd have to tell them about Harry and me. And I'm not going to do that.'

'What puzzles me is, why did he send you the letters? Unless he's some crank. And if he is – ' He stopped.

'Go on. If he is, then you and I could be – could be on his list. I've thought of that.'

He was quiet for a while, then he said, 'I think you should tell your father.'

'No way.' She shook her head emphatically. 'I'm scared – I admit that. But I got myself into this mess and I'm not going to ask Dad to take on any of the worry of it. Not now. He's got enough on his mind.'

He leaned back in his chair, stared at her across the table. 'Who looks after you, then? You can't go running around on your own. You took a risk coming up here today, especially to see me. What if this chap, whoever he is, had followed you?'

'It needn't necessarily be a – chap. It could be a woman.'

'Who, for instance?' But he saw her tongue had slipped on her once again. 'Grace? Forget her. She didn't kill Harry.'

'I know that.' She nodded, shamefaced. 'I'm sorry. She's a tough bitch, but she's not a murderess.'

'I don't think she's a tough bitch, either,' he said, angry at her for the description. 'But I'm not going to argue with you about her. The only thing we have to consider is your safety. You'd better go back to Helena and from now on stick as close to your father as you can. At least the aides he has around him should give you some protection, even if they don't know it. I'd better find someone to go back to Helena with you today. There are some lonely stretches on that road.'

'I'll be all right – ' But she was scared, had begun to appreciate that she might be in danger. 'Are you coming down to Helena today?'

'Not today. Tomorrow. I have to go down for the weekly meeting at head office.'

'Then I'll stay here tonight! I can call Dad – he's down in Billings anyway for the night – '

'It would be better if you went back home. If we put you into a motel, you're still going to be unprotected – '

'Why can't I stay here? You've got plenty of room. Oh, don't worry – I shan't knock on your door, ask can I come into bed with you – '

'Look, haven't you any sense of position?' Look who's talking, he told himself. Where was the chap who never worried about the servants? 'You're the Governor's daughter. You don't go around sleeping in strange men's houses – not in a town this size, anyway. It would be all over the state tomorrow morning before you'd washed the sleep out of your eyes. It wouldn't help your father.'

She nodded, disappointed but intelligent enough to see his point. 'Bloody conventions! Why can't people trust people?'

'You should ask a politician that question. He'd give you a better answer than I can.' There was a knock at the front door. 'Excuse me. That's probably someone from the office.'

But it wasn't: it was Wryman. 'This is a bit unusual, me calling on you. Can – ?'

'Come in.' Random took him into the living room. There was the sound of clattering dishes from the dining room and Wryman cocked an eyebrow. 'It's all right. Miss Mackintosh, the Governor's daughter, has been having lunch with me.'

'Oh – then I better go – ' Wryman looked suddenly awkward, as if he had committed some sort of political gaffe. 'I'll see you later. Up at my office, if you don't mind – ?'

Random knew that the County Attorney had not dropped by on a social call. He had something on his mind, something that concerned Random himself. 'Let's hear it now, Mr Wryman. I gather you have something you want to ask me?'

Wryman hesitated, then nodded. He was a man who preferred not to defer any task, as if he could afford no delays in his race towards the realization of his ambitions. He glanced towards the door that led to the dining room, then looked back at Random. The clatter of dishes had now receded to the kitchen.

'The Governor's daughter does the washing-up, too? I envy you, Mr Random. That's the sort of political influence we'd all like.' Then he did something Random didn't think he was capable of: he blushed. 'Sorry. I didn't mean that the way it sounded.'

Random liked the young prosecutor. 'Believe me, I have no influence with Miss Mackintosh, political or otherwise. If I were not Kenneway-Jardine's general manager, I doubt if anyone in the Governor's family or on his staff would take any notice of me.'

'Oh, you'd be noticed, all right. Harry Jardine would've taken care of that. Unwittingly, of course. That's why I'm here. Mr Random – ' his voice took on an official note – 'was there a gun in Jardine's car when you found him?'

'No. Why do you ask?'

'He had quite an arsenal. Expensive guns, cheap ones – he used to buy them the way other men buy ties or socks. He had two Winchester Hot Sixes. One of them can't be found.'

'I went right through his car looking for something to identify him with. There wasn't even the registration tag.'

'We found that. It was on the floor, under one of the mats. Did you look in the trunk?'

'The boot? No. I only went through the glove-box and the door pockets. But I'm sure there was no gun, not a rifle anyway, in the car. Are you suggesting the murderer could have killed Jardine with his own gun?'

'I don't know. I'm not suggesting anything, after the foul-up with Tim Yertsen,' he said candidly. 'But it opens up the possibility that the murder wasn't premeditated. Maybe Harry Jardine got his gun to either frighten, maybe even shoot whoever was blocking the road. And the guy took it away from him and shot him instead. What I mean is, it could've been someone from out-of-state, an absolute stranger who had no intention of killing Jardine, didn't even know who he was.'

No: whoever had killed Jardine had sent the letters to Bonnie. And he would not have had time to search the car for them; Random remembered that the killer's car had raced off almost immediately after he had heard the shot. The letters had been found by someone who knew Jardine, who had access to Jardine's hiding places. 'Would it help you if that was the case?'

There was no sound now from the back of the house, but Wryman seemed unaware of the silence. 'It might,' he said, but he did not commit himself any more than that. 'But I'm not letting up. I don't work for Kenneway-Jardine.'

'I'm sure everyone at Kenneway-Jardine would want you to find the murderer, stranger or not.' Spoken like a true general manager, Random thought: in his own ears he sounded as if he had read from a prepared statement.

'Yeah,' said Wryman and there was no mistaking what he thought about such a statement. 'Well, I better be getting along. Give my regards to Miss Mackintosh.'

'I'll accept them personally,' said Bonnie, coming in from the dining room. 'You must come down and visit with us some time, Mr Wryman.'

'I'm due to do that some time next month,' said Wryman,

looking at her closely, wondering how much she had heard. 'Your father is holding a reception for everyone in the state on the party ticket.'

'I'll look forward to that,' said Bonnie, as if she had never seen such a gathering. 'I believe the back-scratching is like an epidemic of hives.'

'Just like a hippy commune,' said Wryman. 'Only we're better dressed.'

Their smiles showed every tooth in their heads: political rictus? Random wondered. Wryman left and Random came back into the living room.

'I take it you heard every word that was said?'

'Most of them.'

'I like an honest eavesdropper. What do you think?'

'I don't think a stranger killed Harry. Politically, I suppose it would be better for everyone in the state, Democrats *and* Republicans – just in case it was a Republican who shot him – if they could say it was a stranger and they could close the case. But it wasn't. It wasn't a stranger who sent those letters – he wouldn't have known who I was. They were on plain notepaper, I was careful about that, and I never signed them with my name, just my initial, *B*. Harry could have been sleeping with half a dozen *B*'s, for all I know, but I got my own letters back.'

'Well, we have to get you back to Helena.' He pondered a moment, running over in his mind what he had to do in the office this afternoon. 'Look, I'll come down with you, I'll stay in Helena overnight. I'll be about an hour up at the office, then we can leave. You'll be all right here.' From outside had come the harsh buzz of a lawn-mower. 'That's the company gardener. He'll be here for at least two hours. Nobody's going to worry you while he's around.'

'I feel it's all slightly ridiculous,' she said. 'But to be honest, I am a bit scared.'

'You just have to be careful, that's all,' he said and wondered how careful he should be himself.

It was an hour and a half before he could get away from the office. He took his briefcase, went back to the house and packed an overnight bag, got into his car and followed her in hers as she took the road south to Helena. She drove fast, as he guessed she might, and, keeping up with her, he could not relax and settle down to some sustained thinking as he had hoped to do.

He left her outside the Governor's mansion. She got out of her car and came back to him. 'Thanks for bringing me home. Where will you stay tonight?'

'I'll find a place.'

'You could stay here. The staff will chaperone us. We often have overnight visitors, not all of them honourable if I gave them half the chance to be otherwise.' She looked less uncertain now, as if she had done some thinking on the way down and decided there was really nothing to be scared about. 'Or at least stay for dinner.'

He patted the briefcase on the seat beside him. 'I have too much work to do. I did you a favour coming down with you.'

At once she was contrite: he wished she would not be so eager not to upset him. 'Of course! God, I'm sorry – I really am a selfish bitch –'

He pressed her hand resting on the car door. 'I'll ring you tomorrow. In the meantime give a thought to who might have sent you those letters.'

He drove away, turned right at the bottom of the hill and headed along to the Colonial Inn on the edge of town. It was a sprawling motor hotel, the sort of inn that was only just beginning to appear in Britain and Europe; it stood like a better-class fort on the eastern slope of the city, looking down across the valley. Colonial it was called, but no pioneer or Indian would have recognized it. Random checked in, walked through the lobby past the trickling fountain, excused his way through a long line of Daughters of the Pioneers registering their names for their convention, and went down a long corridor to his room.

He threw his briefcase on the bed, looked at it conscientiously for a moment or two, then picked up the phone and called Grace's home.

Lee answered. 'Missus out . . . Oh, that you, Mr Random? Missus down at TV station. I got to pick her up in half-hour. I tell her you come by?'

He hesitated, then said, 'No, Lee. Ask her to call me. I'm at the Colonial Inn.'

He hung up, wondering why he was leaving it to her to call him. He was like some damned schoolboy playing hard to get. But no: that implied confidence in oneself. And he no longer felt as confident as he had, at least not about himself and her. He opened the briefcase, tried to concentrate on the papers he had brought with him for tomorrow's meeting, but they could have been written in Sanskrit for all that he took in of them. He put them away and switched on the television set, hoping he might catch Grace being interviewed live. But evidently they were taping her, probably to go on air in the evening. Live, he got a Daughter of the Pioneers, in a frontier outfit of silk and cashmere and a string of pearls that looked like a lariat, telling the story of how her great-grandmother had survived the Starvation Winter of 1883–4; when pressed by the interviewer she was vague about the details and one got the impression great-Grandma might have survived by eating great-Grandpa. He switched off the set and the Daughter, went out to the lobby and bought a paper and some magazines.

Back in his room he skimmed through the magazines. Both *Time* and *Newsweek* had long pieces on Britain, the sinking ship of Europe; he didn't read those stories, knowing the hurt and anger he would feel at how his country was almost complacently committing suicide. He threw *Time* down on the bed, it fell open at the United States pages and Grace, beautiful as any star on the Cinema pages, smiled up at him.

The story on her might have been written by a Democrat and a lover. In a column and a half the only implied criticism of her seemed to be that she had once been married to Harry Jardine. It was assumed that her election was a matter of course and that, barring an affair with the President or some Communist, the Senate seat would be hers for as long as she wished. When one finished the story one might have thought that Dolley Madison, Germaine de Staël and Cleopatra were descending on Washington in the person of Grace Jardine, the sure-to-be Senator-elect from Montana.

The phone rang. 'Jack – '

'I've just been reading about you. Someone on *Time* loves you.'

'I'll never live up to what he says about me. The phone's been ringing all day down at headquarters. They want me to go to New York to go on *Meet the Press* and half a dozen other shows.'

'Are you going?'

'Of course. But only after I've seen you. Can you come over for dinner?'

'What's on?'

She sighed, then laughed: he loved her laugh, liquid and deep in her throat. 'I'll have Annie prepare something Chinese. Is that all right?'

'So long as it doesn't have an Idaho potato, Cantonese style.'

'Don't you ever cross over into Idaho. They'll shoot you down at the border.'

Both of them recognized the banter for what it was, a smoke-screen. There were things each of them had to say to the other, but neither had yet thought them out. They were on new terrain and Random, the ex-soldier, had the feeling that forces were building up against him, that, whether Grace willingly enlisted those forces or not, he was going to be outnumbered. But he was not going to be another General Burgoyne and surrender.

'I'll come over now. And to hell with what the servants think.'

'I have an idea they know what's going on. And I think they approve.'

2

After supper, when Lee and Annie had retired to their rooms in the carriage-house, she took him up to her bedroom. But she would not allow him to stay the night.

'No, I think I have to be a *little* discreet.' But she held him tightly, as if she needed him. 'Oh darling, I hate to let you go!'

'I'll stay, then.'

She leaned over him, her black hair enveloping them in a darkness of their own. The warm smooth closeness of her, the rich musky smell . . . He had been wrong about the smell of newly sawn timber and crushed leaves. She offered the best perfume there was . . .

'I'll stay,' he repeated.

'You won't.' She kissed him, lay back beside him. 'I wish you could. Now, I mean. You give me more pleasure – oh, I don't mean just the sex bit, though that's wonderful. But you give me a sense of – ease. Of just being content.'

'We've had a few arguments. Or near-arguments.'

She raised her head, looked at him sideways, brushing a lock of hair out of one eye. 'Are we going to have one now?'

He smiled, rolling his head on the pillow. 'No. I'm too –

content.' For the moment anyway, he thought. But he had no sense of ease, not about themselves once they got out of this bed. 'That's why I think I'll stay.'

'No. Out!' She swung out of bed, stopped in front of the long wardrobe mirror as she passed it. 'I think I'm losing weight.'

'I hadn't noticed it. I thought you'd put on a little, the areas I handled tonight.'

She made a face at him in the mirror, then looked at herself again. She stretched lazily as she gazed at her smeared mouth and her rumpled hair. He felt the stirring of excitement again, marvelled at her beauty and the fact that she was his. Or nearly so.

'*Time* should run a picture of you like that. You'd get the vote of every red-blooded male in the state. Perhaps even the queers, too. If a red-blooded state like Montana admits there are some here.'

She looked at herself a moment longer, but he could see the expression on her face changing in the mirror. Without turning she said, 'Will you come to Washington with me?'

'When?'

'When I have to go. When I'm elected.'

He noticed she said it without any hesitation; or conceit, either. She was stating a fact she had already accepted.

'What as?'

The perversity of the sated lover: he hated himself for what he heard himself say. But it had happened before, with Jennifer and other women, the malice, and at worst the cruelty, that was always there beneath the skin of love.

There was just a flicker of recognition in her eyes: she had experienced it before. She countered with, 'That would be up to you.'

I'm expected to ask her to marry me. And he wanted to. But – 'Don't you think we should wait till after the elections? If we moved to Washington – ' He sat up, swung his legs over the side of the bed, began to pull on his shorts. 'Frankly, I haven't really thought about Washington. Perhaps I've been afraid to. It would mean a whole new life for me.'

'It would for me, too.'

'Only partly. You'd still have your own identity.'

She was making no attempt to dress or even to put on a robe.

He wished she would put on something: he felt at a disadvantage again, the traitor in his crotch.

'I can't imagine you ever losing your identity. Are you trying to tell me you don't want me to run for Senator?'

'Darling – ' One should not have serious discussions while getting dressed. Shirt buttons and trousers zips got in the way, were an unwanted punctuation. 'Look, I'm not a male chauvinist. Or I try not to be. You said Harry was – '.

'He was. But I don't think I said so.'

No, that was a slip: it had been Bonnie who had said that. 'Well, you implied it or I inferred it, one or the other. I shouldn't want to be Number One, as he obviously tried to be – I mean in your relationship. But I shouldn't want to be Number Two, either. If we went to Washington I'd have to find something to do. *Be* something, other than just the chap hanging about outside the Senate waiting for you to knock off. That's what I have to think about. It isn't going to be easy, darling. It has nothing to do with male pride. Well, perhaps it has – '

'I'm glad you're honest.' She opened the wardrobe, took out a robe and put it on.

He began to put on his shoes and socks. 'You can't expect me to do a complete turnabout, not after I've lived in a male world all my life. School, the army, the jobs I've had since I got out of the army. Sitting on my bum in Washington will take a bit of getting used to. If you're honest, you'll have to admit that.'

He had made the last remark without any intention of malice; but he saw her mouth tighten. She picked up a comb, ran it through her hair, facing away from him again into the mirror.

'I love you, Jack,' she said, her voice low and steady. 'But every time we get out of bed we seem to spoil everything that's gone before.'

He finished tying his shoelaces, stood up. 'The course of true love never runs smooth ... We must be truly in love. I know I am and I think you are, too. But that – ' he waved a hand at the bed – 'we can't spend all our time in there. If we could, perhaps we could wear ourselves out and die young and happy. All I'm asking is that you give me time to think about what I can do when I'm not in bed with you. If you were staying here in Helena, I could go on doing what I'm doing now. It might raise a few problems with Coulson and Shooberg, the general manager being married to the boss, but we could cope with them. But if we go to Washington – ' He shook his head doubtfully. 'Please let me think about it.'

She suddenly smiled, moved to him and kissed him. 'I've got a dozen advisers in my campaign team. But none of them is an expert in personal problems.'

He returned her kiss: they were the sort of kisses husband and wife exchanged when the husband was going off to the office. 'I wouldn't listen to him, anyway. They've all probably got the male chauvinist point of view.'

'You're so right. But I can handle *them*.' She kissed him again, passionately this time, as if he might not be returning. 'You're the one I can't.'

He went back to the Colonial Inn. Some of the Daughters of the Pioneers sat about in the lobby, worn out by their long day of convention argument and gossip; some of them were revived by the sight of the good-looking Englishman as he passed them by, but none of them wanted to start more gossip by getting up and following him. One woman, a pioneer spirit, smiled at him and Random smiled back, but the response from each of them was automatic. He wondered what the talk would be if the Daughters knew he had just come from the bed of the virtual Senator-elect for their state. That would beat the Starvation Winter of whenever-it-was as a topic.

He went to bed but sleep came hard. It seemed that every door in his mind was wide open and thoughts blew through them like tumbleweed. When he at last fell asleep he dreamed of Arabia and the Empty Quarter, a trackless region he had once traversed on a patrol from Aden to the Trucial Oman coast. When he woke, mouth dry, face feeling as if it were coated with Saran-Wrap, he was too exhausted to try to trace any connection between the Empty Quarter and life in Washington as a Senator's husband. The obvious connection seemed too obvious.

At ten o'clock in the morning, feeling a little fresher, he was at the offices of Jardine Inc. Grace, Coulson and Shooberg were already in the big walnut-panelled office when he arrived. With them was an egg-shaped man with rimless glasses and what looked like an auburn toupee: he was introduced as Colin Lidcombe, the company secretary. Seated to one side was a mousy, middle-aged stenographer who blushed when she was introduced as Carlotta, as if she had just been charged with false pretences.

'I'm sorry I'm late. My watch must be slow – '

'No, you're on time.' Grace sat in the big chair, Harry's chair, behind the desk, with Coulson and Shooberg at either end of it. Random sat opposite them on a chair between those of Lidcombe and the stenographer. The image in his mind was that of a Soviet-style court of enquiry rather than a company meeting. 'Karl and Jim and I had an earlier date. Well, shall we get started?'

The points for discussion this week were only routine. There was still a demand for timber and pulp; the world still wanted to choke itself on paper; even bankruptcies had to be recorded extravagantly. Random knew there would be countless copies made of the notes of this morning's meeting.

At the end of forty-five minutes Grace said, 'Well, anything further?'

'A semi-social note,' said Shooberg. 'Business, too, in a way. Do we hold Harry's annual hunting party this year? I've already had several enquiries, guys who've never missed it.'

'Do we have to?' Grace said. 'I don't want to be there.'

'You don't have to be. Like I said, it's business. A company thing, public relations. We've held it now for ten years.'

'I think we ought to hold it,' said Coulson. 'Just to show there's continuity, that the company's still alive even though Harry's dead. It could now be a sort of memorial to Harry.'

'All right,' said Grace. 'But you organize it – I don't want to have to do anything about it. And *don't* let it be a memorial to Harry. It's to be public relations for the company, nothing else.'

'Whatever you say, Grace.'

'Where is it held?' Random asked.

'Up in the valley,' Shooberg said. 'The last weekend in October. You'll be expected to turn out. Do you shoot?'

'I've done some,' said Random and heard himself further say: 'Tiger, mostly.'

Lidcombe and Carlotta looked impressed. Grace raised an eyebrow, but he couldn't tell whether it was at his unexpected schoolboy's boasting or at the exotic prey he had hunted.

Shooberg and Coulson looked at each other. Then Coulson, as if deliberately trying to sound unimpressed, said, 'We better get on with what we were discussing before. That'll be all.' He nodded to Lidcombe and Carlotta; then he looked directly at Random, his face stiff and unfriendly. 'Glad to hear things are okay up in the valley. We'll let you know if there's going to be a meeting next week.'

Random, at the door, waited till the secretary and the stenographer had gone out; then he turned back, though he did not go all the way back to his chair. He had been dismissed by Coulson, but, resentful of the big man, he was not going to let him have the last word.

'You might like to know Wryman has been questioning me again. Seems Mr Jardine had two Winchester Hot Sixes and one of them is missing.'

Both Coulson and Shooberg looked sharply at Grace, but Random was watching only Coulson. The big man raised a hand towards his head, then abruptly dropped it behind the edge of the desk, as if trying to hide it. Grace looked straight at Random.

'You didn't tell me that when I saw you last night.'

Random, in the instant before he looked at Grace, saw the sudden jerk of Coulson's mouth, as if he had bitten on a raw nerve. 'I was trying to spare your feelings. I don't think you should be continually reminded of how your husband died.'

'Mr Wryman is continually reminding me. He came to me for permission to check Harry's collection of guns.'

'You knew one of the Hot Sixes was missing?' Shooberg said. 'Yes.'

There was a tap on the door and Lidcombe looked into the room. 'Mr Chartwell just called. He suggested you turn on the TV. Cliff Pendrick is on right now, holding a press conference.'

Coulson crossed quickly to the big cabinet in a corner, swung back the doors and switched on the set. Grace said sharply, 'Why didn't someone warn me he was having a press conference this morning?'

'It wasn't on his schedule,' Shooberg said, 'This is something he's called in a hurry.'

Cliff Pendrick came up on the screen, green and confident. 'He looks like an Irish comic,' said Grace, but nobody laughed. Nobody but Random, and he felt the odd-man-out.

Coulson adjusted the set and Pendrick, in his true colours, said, 'All I can say in answer to that question is what I said before.

The Jardine Corporation, of which the Democratic candidate is the chairperson, is planning a mining venture which will threaten the whole ecology of Limbo Valley.'

'Jesus H. Christ! Where did he get hold of that?'

'At this point in time – '

Pendrick went on talking, but Random had stopped listening to him. Instead he was watching Grace, Coulson and Shooberg. The two men, even the usually unflappable Shooberg, looked stunned. But Grace was gazing at her opponent on the television screen with the resigned look of a patient wife who had heard everything her husband was telling her and was wondering why he was going on at such length.

'Turn it off,' she said; and Coulson, acting on reflex as if to stop his pain, switched off the set. 'Get me a transcript of everything he said at that press conference. Within half an hour, Col.'

'Right, Mrs Jardine. Within half an hour.'

Lidcombe disappeared. Random turned to follow him, but Grace said, 'You better stay a while, Jack.'

Coulson glared at Random. 'You know anything about this?'

'Only what I heard Pendrick say,' said Random coolly.

'You know goddam well what I mean! Do you know how he got that information?'

'Take it easy, Jim.' Grace was still sitting at the desk, still, on the surface, unruffled. 'Jack hasn't known everything that's been going on. He might have suspected something. You did, didn't you?'

'A little.' It was strictly boss and employee this morning. It seemed to him that she could slip in and out of the relationship more easily than he could. 'But nothing as much as what Pendrick just said. Is it true?'

'Of course it's true!' For the first time she showed some reaction; but she sounded only irritated, not angry. She looked at Shooberg; he now seemed as calm as usual. 'You better ask Cliff if he and I can meet privately.'

'Maybe then we can find out who doublecrossed us,' said Coulson. 'I've got a couple of questions I want to ask him – '

'It'll just be Cliff and me,' said Grace, not even looking at Coulson but still talking to Shooberg. 'Tell him I don't want to make any deals. I just want to talk to him, nobody else to be there but him and me.'

'Do you think that's wise?' Shooberg said.

'I don't know. It won't be if Cliff puts out word that I'm looking for a private word with him. But I don't think he'd play that dirty.'

'He's playing dirty now, for Crissake.' Coulson was smarting from having been put in his place by Grace. 'Just like you said he'd warned you he would.'

'He's not stirring up real muck – you know that. He's found out something about us and he's making political capital out of it. I don't think that's dirty, Jim. Not by some of the standards in this state in the past. What I want to find out is whether he has something worse he'll use on us.'

'Do you think he'll tell you if he has?'

'I hope he might. Cliff and I were divorced, but we never hated each other. There's still a little respect left.'

'In politics,' said Shooberg, 'you need more than that.'

He left the room, never a man to waste time about a task that had to be done. Random, Grace and Coulson were left alone, with Random still feeling the odd-man-out. The feeling of last night between himself and Grace had completely evaporated; or had been put in cold storage. They exchanged glances and for a moment her expression softened. Then immediately she was the Senator-elect again.

Or would she be the Senator-elect now? 'Will this affect your vote?' he asked.

'It depends on how much support Cliff drums up.'

'I don't think it's your worry,' Coulson said to Random. He smoothed down his hair, closed the doors of the television cabinet, began to put everything back in its place. Including me, thought Random. 'You'll have enough to handle up in the valley, company-wise.'

'What policy do I adopt?' Random asked the question of both of them. 'Company-wise?'

'You stall 'em. We'll have to talk to London first, now the cat's out of the bag.' Random noticed that Coulson's hands were trembling; he closed them into fists. 'And we don't want you talking to your old man, either.'

Random's own fist tightened on the briefcase. 'If he calls me, I'll tell him I've been instructed by one of the American directors not to talk to any of the London directors. He'll make something of that, I'm sure.'

'You're fired! You can pack your bags and get – '

'That's enough, Jim!' Grace snapped; but her voice still was not raised. 'Leave me alone with Jack for a few minutes.'

'Grace, this isn't something for you to handle on your own! Look, this son-of-a-bitch isn't working for us – '

'I said that's enough. Wait outside.'

'Jesus!'

Coulson looked ready to explode; he leaned forward as if to pound the desk in front of Grace. Then abruptly he whirled, shoved out a hand as if to push Random aside, and went out the door, slamming it behind him.

Random put down his briefcase, sat down in one of the chairs across the desk from Grace. He noticed that there was still no portrait of her on the walls, not even a photograph; the Charles Russell painting still covered the spot where Harry Jardine's portrait had hung. But Grace didn't need pictures of herself to tell her who and what she was.

'Jack, I think you had better get used to the idea that Jim and Karl run this company for me. I can't keep pushing them out of the way just to please you.' The intercom on her desk flashed its light and she flicked the switch. 'I don't want to be interrupted, Carlotta.'

'It's Mr Chartwell on the phone – '

'Tell him I'll call him back.' She flicked the switch, sat back in her chair. He saw that she sat very straight-backed, succeeding in not being reduced by the size of the chair. 'Jack, all this had got started before Harry was killed. I didn't initiate it, I don't know that I would have if the decision had been mine at the start. But I'm going along with it now. You might as well know that.'

The Russell painting was of a band of Indians waiting to ambush a lone Conestoga wagon coming across the prairie towards a dry gulch: vague and distant in the summer haze, the wagon was already doomed. 'I'd like to know more before I pass an opinion. If I'm going to be asked for an opinion.'

'You may not be.' She closed her hand into a fist, tapped it gently on the leather top of the desk, sat gazing at it for a moment or two. Then she looked up at him, a frown between the beautiful eyes. 'Don't you think I wish this situation hadn't arisen? I'm committed, darling. There's no way I can get out of it.'

'You still haven't told me more than I heard from Pendrick on TV.'

She sighed, relaxed her hand. 'We now own the controlling interest in Kenneway-Jardine. Harry had set up some companies and this week they succeeded in buying up enough stock to give us 52 per cent. There is an equal number of American and British directors on the joint board. Lord Kenneway is the chairman and he has the deciding vote if there should be a deadlock. We have enough stock now to appoint our own chairman. Or chairperson, if you like.'

'Meaning you.'

'Meaning me. If I wanted the job. Which I don't – not if I'm going to Washington. But since I'm the principal stockholder, by a long way, I can appoint my own chairman, if I wish. I could appoint you, for instance.'

If his smile was mocking, he was unaware of it. 'You couldn't buy me that way, my love.'

'I'm not trying to buy you!'

'Righto, I take that back. You still haven't explained to me what's going to happen up in the valley. The men will be down at my house this evening asking. What do I tell them?'

'You stall them, just like Jim said. You say you don't know.'

'And you're willing to leave me out on a limb like that?'

She stared at him, her eyes suddenly dark; then she sighed and shook her head. She relaxed her back, seemed to shrink in the chair. 'Darling, why the hell must we fight? I can't turn this thing back now. It's gone too far, cost too much. And no one's going to lose by it – '

He wasn't sure, but he sensed a lack of conviction in her. 'Who's going to gain by it?'

'I am, I suppose. And Kenneway-Jardine – the company, I mean.' She sat up, leaned forward. 'And so will Montana. There is copper up there, the richest strike anywhere in the country, I mean the whole United States, since the days when millions of dollars went out of this state to the banks and finance men back East. This time the money will stay in Montana – hundreds of millions of dollars!'

'Including the Kenneway 48 per cent?'

'You don't miss a trick, do you?' She sat back, relaxed again, looked at him shrewdly. 'You wouldn't make a bad chairman – if you were on my side.' He said nothing about whose side he was on and he knew she hadn't missed the point of his silence. After a moment she went on, her voice cooler: 'We'll strip the valley of all the millable timber. That can be going on while they are building the dam – '

'There's going to be a dam?'

She nodded. 'And a reclamation plant, a power plant, a whole new town, new roads – '

'Why a new town?'

'The dam will flood the top half of the valley. Tozabe will be right in the middle of it.'

'Where's the dam to be? Massacre Gap?'

She clenched her fist again, thumped the desk. But she didn't hurl abuse at him or scream at him: he couldn't remember when he had last seen such control and he had to admire her for it. At the same time he began to dislike, even hate, this side of her that he had never seen.

'That's uncalled for. We're not massacring anyone. I promise not a single person will lose their job – '

He shook his head, sick at heart, not really wanting to argue any further. 'Don't make promises like that. You haven't gone into any detail yet, I can see that. You have no real idea of what the consequences will be.' He stood up. 'Will you make one promise you *can* keep?'

'What's that?'

'That you'll make a statement not later than tomorrow, just so the people up in the valley will know exactly what their future is to be.'

'I'll do that,' she said readily and he believed her. 'And when they've heard what we propose, I don't think there'll be anywhere near as much opposition as you think.'

'I shouldn't bet on it. We still don't know why your husband, the chap who started all this, was killed.' Then he nodded at the Russell painting. 'I'd get rid of that. In the circumstances I don't think it projects the right image. Company-wise, that is.'

3

Grace issued a statement that evening, in time to catch the television news. It also gave the editorial writers for the following morning's newspapers time to dream up not-too-critical phrases for a golden idol who had turned out to have, if not feet of clay, a pedestal of high-grade copper. The statement, Random thought, had all the pious self-righteousness of a papal encyclical. Limbo Valley, it seemed, was the only Promised Land that would be better off for being flooded.

When Random got to his office in the morning Peeples and two other men were waiting for him. 'We're an official delegation,' said Peeples. 'We held a meeting last night and Ted, Clint and me were delegated to come and see you.'

'That was quick. The meeting, I mean.'

'We were ready for it, Mr Random.' Chris Peeples was being formal this morning. 'When we heard what Cliff Pendrick said on TV yesterday morning we figured we had to do something.'

'It couldn't have been much of a meeting. I didn't hear anything of it.'

'We called you, but you weren't home. We understand you were down in Helena.' There was no mistaking that Chris Peeples guessed where Random had been. 'The meeting was big enough, don't worry about that. Believe me, we represent all the workers in the valley. Right, fellers?'

'Not just the workers.' Ted Zeeland was a logger, squat and muscular, with a long flat-topped head and a face blotched by sun cancers. He had been born in the valley and lived all his forty years there. 'There's retired folk, like my old man and lady.'

'And people like me, guys in business.' Clint Hauger owned a general store and motel on the edge of town. He was a thin pole of a man with an irascible nature that he tried to hide behind a public smile that he put on each morning with his clean shirt and string tie. 'We got a lot to lose, Mr Random. Everybody has.'

'We listened to that bullshit Mrs Jardine put out last night,' said Peeples. 'It didn't fool any of us. Okay, so maybe some of us will get work in the new set-up, maybe even earn more money. But nobody's asked us if we want to be miners. I sure as hell don't. And who pays us while the change-over is going on? You don't just have a timber company one day and, hey presto, next day you got a fully working mine company. Somebody's going to suffer and you can bet your balls it won't be Mrs Jardine.'

All the antagonism, Random noticed, was directed at Grace. He wondered if that was a deliberate tactic on Peeples's part, aimed to make him feel uncomfortable because of his relationship with Grace.

'I can't tell you any more than was in that statement. I was down at the weekly meeting yesterday when we heard what Pendrick said at his press conference. To tell you the truth – off the record – ' he glanced at Peeples but only the wall-eye was turned towards him and he could read nothing in it – 'I don't think Shooberg and Coulson have worked up any plans for what's going to happen up here. They were caught with their pants down by Pendrick's announcement. They've been so busy buying up the controlling interest in Kenneway-Jardine.'

'There was nothing about that in her statement.'

'Well, it's true. London is the minor side now.'

'Will you British try to fight 'em?'

'I don't know. We British have only tried twice to take on you Americans on your home ground and we lost both times. 1776 and 1812.'

'Don't bullshit us, Jack,' said Peeples, in no mood for humour this morning.

Random held back a sigh. 'Chris, I'm not here representing the London board. Though it seems to look that way, judging by some of the remarks I've had directed at me. I'm working for the company as a whole. If they turn this valley over to mining, I'll be one of the first to go. They won't have any use for a general manager who doesn't know, and doesn't want to know, a thing about mining.'

'Okay, will you fight 'em?'

He hesitated, acutely aware that he was about to step off a cliff. 'All right. But I don't know how much help I'll be.'

'Mr Random – ' Zeeland was a type Random thought had disappeared: he rolled his own cigarettes. His stubby fingers made a surprisingly smooth, thin tube; he ran his tongue along it to seal it. But he was looking at Random all the time. 'Mr Random, I got the feeling you'd rather be somewheres else but here.'

'I would,' said Random candidly, avoiding Peeples's good, accusing eye.

'You could help keep things cool,' said Hauger. 'There are some hotheads in this valley and things could get out of hand. I tell you, Mr Random, things are pretty strong.'

Random looked at the three men in turn, then said, 'Would you two chaps mind if I talked to Chris alone?'

Zeeland and Hauger glanced at each other, then both moved towards the door. 'We trust Chris, Mr Random. We hope we can do the same with you.'

When the door had closed behind them Random said, 'Who are the hotheads, Chris? You and who else?'

Peeples had been standing ever since he had come into the office, but now he sat down, spread his legs out in front of him. 'You think all socialists are hotheads, don't you, Jack? I'm not. I'm not going to run away from a fight if we got to have one, but I believe in negotiation. It was my old man who was a hothead and for the rest of his life he had only one arm to remind him of it. But there are some guys who don't have any patience for negotiation. Someone killed Harry Jardine and we still don't know why. It could have been because they knew what he was cooking up.'

'I put that proposition to Mrs Jardine yesterday.'

'What she say?'

'Nothing. She doesn't scare easily, Chris.'

'Yeah, I guessed she wouldn't. She's a real tough cookie.' He looked warily at Random. 'Am I treading on your toes saying that? People are talking about you two, you know that.'

On reflection Random knew he should not be surprised. In a community as small as Helena a woman as prominent as Grace could not flout the conventions and hope not to be noticed. It was a wonder that *Time*, which liked its gossip as much as any small-town newspaper, had not mentioned her relationship with one of her employees.

'Is that why you want me to be your negotiator? You think I may have some influence with her?' He shook his head, opened a chink of confidence to the wall-eyed man across the desk from him: 'Chris, when it comes to talking business I have no more influence with her than you or anyone else in the valley. As you say, she's a real tough cookie.'

To his surprise, Peeples nodded sympathetically. 'That's tough for you, then. A woman who's got a split personality in and out of bed.'

'Chris, don't let's get too personal about her,' he said stiffly; he was not accustomed to defending a woman's honour or whatever it was called these days. 'We'll stick to the business side.'

'Sorry.' Peeples stood up. 'Yeah, well, see what you can do. We've invited Cliff Pendrick up here to talk to us. You can tell her we'd like for her to talk to us, too. If she ain't interested in doing that, she could find a lot of the voters out working for Cliff Pendrick. She might finish up richer than she is, but she could also wind up not being sent to Washington. Depends which she wants most.'

4

Cliff Pendrick, obviously a man who didn't believe a hot issue should be allowed to cool off, came up to the valley that afternoon. He seemed to be gaining in subtlety as his confidence increased; he didn't call for one big meeting but went around talking to people in groups, testing his toe in the hot water of his topic. Beryl Gray came in to tell Random that Pendrick was in the district.

'Chris Peeples is with him. He's taken him up to Horsethief Gap. That's where they think the dam might be.'

'How do you feel about all this, Beryl?'

'Disgusted!' Then she blushed and her bosom quivered. 'I'm sorry. I shouldn't have said that, Mr Random.'

'Beryl, you're entitled to your opinion.' But Random rose at once, careful not to open the conversation too wide. 'I'm going up to the Gap.'

'I'm glad you're on our side. Looks like we're going to need all the support we can get.'

'I'm an outlander. That limits me.'

She didn't blush this time nor did the bosom quiver. 'Not with the influence you've got, Mr Random.'

She went out of the office before he could think of an answer to that. When he passed through the outer office she had gone.

He drove fast, too fast for his thoughts. When he parked the car below Horsethief Gap, he still had not formulated any approach to Pendrick. Sweating and uneasy, he walked up through the new slash towards the group of men sitting in the shade half-way up the ridge. There was no sound other than the occasional call of a bird and, somewhere on the other side of the river, the growl of a truck as it climbed a gradient on the highway. The power saws and the bulldozers were silent and the trees, still standing and living, at least for the moment, made no sound. The whole valley seemed to be listening to the deep voice of Cliff Pendrick.

Whatever he had to say to the assembled men, he was at the end of it when Random came up. 'Ah, Mr Random.' He had become more expansive, blown up on the politician's diet of bonhomie. 'I'm taking up the company's time, I'm afraid. But I'm sure Kenneway-Jardine can afford a small drop in production. A few trees lost – '

'May I have a few words with you, Mr Pendrick?'

'As spokesman for the company?' Pendrick looked jovially around him. 'Or for your fellow-workers?'

Random felt all the stares impaling him to the tree behind his back. 'As an outlander, Mr Pendrick. Just like you used to be.'

Pendrick nodded, acknowledging a good political answer. He looked around him again. 'Excuse us, fellers. If I can get him to become a citizen, he may even vote for me.'

Random noticed that some of the men, including Peeples, looked cynically disillusioned. They wanted a better bargain than rhetoric and cheap jokes.

But Pendrick was not dumb. As he and Random walked down the slope he said, 'They're not going to be put off by easy words. Mine or your company's.'

'What about Mrs Jardine's?'

'She'll have to say something better than she put out last night.' For a moment he was the ex-husband. 'Grace used to be pretty straightforward.'

'Where did you get your information on their plans?'

'I'm not telling. I think you'd be surprised. I wish I could've seen Grace's face when she heard what I had to say.'

'You'd have been disappointed. You didn't put a hair out of place on her head. But you upset Coulson and Shooberg.'

'That's some satisfaction then.' He chuckled, nodded amiably. 'No, I can see Grace just sitting there, not turning a hair. She's a goddam marvel, you know.' He looked sideways. 'You do know, don't you, from what I hear?'

'I've only known her a couple of months,' said Random cautiously.

'Maybe you won't learn any more than you know now. I don't know that I did, all the time I was married to her.'

'Did you see her yesterday for that private talk?'

'No. It wouldn't have been wise, not with all those newsmen hanging around me like sucker fish. I'm probably the first man ever said no to her. Except Harry Jardine, of course. She doesn't have much luck with her husbands, does she? You better be warned.'

Chapter Eight

I

'When will Lord Kenneway be arriving?' asked Kerry O'Toole.

Grace, her thoughts on another Englishman, looked up. 'What? Oh, some time tomorrow afternoon. He's on the Polar flight from London today, but he's staying in Seattle overnight. I gather he's very careful about the effects of jet lag, especially if he has to have any serious discussions. Our plane is to pick him up in Seattle at noon and the pilot will radio ahead when he's due, so we can go out and be the welcoming committee.'

'Will there be anyone else there to welcome him? Demonstrators, I mean.'

'We haven't announced he is coming, so no demonstrators should know about it.'

'Is he coming alone?'

'He's bringing another director with him. Sir Nigel Random.'

'Mr Random's father, up at Tozabe? He's very attractive – Mr Random, I mean. I was looking at him that night here when we got back from our first trip. He admires you, I think.'

The girl's face was blandly innocent. I have enough on my mind, Grace decided, without looking for any more enemies. So, just as blandly, she said, 'He *is* attractive. We'll have a small dinner party one night soon so you can meet him properly. When things quieten down a bit.'

'That Cliff Pendrick, he's really stirred things up. Frankly, I didn't think he had it in him to go in for that sort of in-fighting. He seemed too nice a man.'

'He is nice, Kerry. He just wants to get to Washington awfully bad, that's all.'

'You're too kind to him.' Kerry was a true ward boss's daughter: you showed kindness only to a dead opponent and then only when he was buried.

'Not really. I just happen to know Cliff better than most candidates know the men who are running against them.'

But she had been surprised when Cliff had refused to talk with her when she had sent the message asking for a private meeting. Maybe she did not know him so well after all; maybe the Cliff of seventeen, eighteen years ago had not been infected by ambition. She wryly remarked to herself that it had been a long time since any man had refused a request from her. And the last one had also been a husband, Harry.

She had been thinking of a possible fourth husband when Kerry had interrupted her thoughts. The word *fourth* had rasped in her mind like an echo of gossip; she knew that to some people she would look like some sort of political Zsa Zsa Gabor. It would be useless to tell them that, puritanically, she preferred marriage to affairs; even Jack had worn that half-mocking smile when she had tried to explain herself. But she had been thinking seriously of marriage again and to Jack.

She loved him: there was no question in her mind about that. It seemed to her that the hours she had spent with him (were they really so few? Clocks and calendars meant nothing: love was a season in itself) were a dream in the hard reality of the past two years; yet, paradoxically, they seemed at the same time the only reality. She felt a contentment when with him that she had felt with none of the others, not even with Cliff in their first year. That was what she told herself, though deep in her secret heart she wondered if she were capable of true contentment: the dreams of the honyocker years had had their own acid, had scoured a hole in her that might never be filled. They argued (and the arguments hurt, more than Jack realized), but never about their love for each other. She had argued with Cliff, with Oscar, with Harry. Some of the arguments had been fierce, especially with Harry; but they had not fought with her in the first few months of their relationships. But then there had not been the outside pressures that were now coming between her and Jack. Yet she knew she could not turn her back on those pressures; they were part of the life that had suddenly become hers. Suddenly: or so it seemed. Yet she knew this life had begun in the dreams back in the flimsy house on the plains south of Kipling.

'Mr Shooberg has just driven up,' said Kerry, interrupting her thought again. She stood at the window of the study and Grace, looking at her, thought how quickly the girl had become part of her own scene. Her scene was becoming crowded with personnel who told her and convinced her that they were necessary. Kerry, one of the most necessary, turned and said, 'I'll let him in. I'll be in the office if you want me.'

Harry's study, redecorated to give it a more feminine atmosphere and less suggestion that she was, after all, only Harry's replacement in business and politics, was too small for both Grace and Kerry to work in. The small music room in the opposite wing had been converted into an office and reception room and Kerry, with a part-time typist who came up from campaign headquarters, had settled in there as if she had lived in this house as long as Grace herself.

Karl Shooberg, another necessity in her new life, greeted Grace with even less warmth than usual. The formality of a friendly greeting was a waste of time, though he avoided being boorish about it. He plunged straight into the reason for his visit, as if Grace should take the preliminaries for granted.

'I can go up to Seattle with our pilot tomorrow morning, if you like. Sound out Kenneway on the way back. You don't want to go into a meeting with him cold tomorrow, not knowing how he thinks about what we've done.'

'I don't think anyone likes something being done behind his back.'

'He's a businessman, Grace. I know his record. He's scalped more competitors than the Indians ever did around here. Mind if I smoke?'

'I'd rather you didn't.'

It was not just that she did not like the smell of cigarettes and even less the smell of his cheroots: it was a way of telling him she was boss. A petty way, she acknowledged to herself, but Karl had begun to assert himself a little too much in the past week. With the taking over of control of Kenneway-Jardine he had begun to take over a little of her.

He showed no reaction, but put away the pack of cheroots and stuck the empty holder back in his mouth. 'I've prepared a projection of what we can expect in earnings over the next five years, once we're into mining. We'll show him that tomorrow at the meeting. These British like to act like amateurs, but they can read a balance sheet better'n anyone I know.'

'Better than you?' She smiled, but there was some lemon at the corners.

'No.' There was no conceit. He took the holder out of his mouth, put it away in his pocket. He sat with his elbows on the arms of his chair, his bony hands locked together, the forefingers raised in a steeple. There was a new air about him, the authority of a financial cardinal. 'I made Harry's fortune for him, Grace.'

'I wonder what he would think of that, if he could hear you.'

'He knew it, but he'd never have admitted it. Harry was the ideas man and he was the one with the money to take the gamble. But I always worked out the odds for him. Without me, Grace, he wouldn't have been as rich as he was. Neither would you.'

'I'm truly grateful.' She made a little mock bow with her head. 'What do I owe you?'

'In money terms, nothing. I just stay with you from now on, that's all. With the base you got now, you're going to go a lot farther than Harry ever would have. I think you got more on the ball than he had. You've developed in the last couple of months, Grace, really come on.'

'You sound almost admiring, Karl. I didn't think you liked women very much.'

'I do admire you. But not because you're a woman – that's only incidental. You got a mind that would do credit to any man.'

She had to laugh; she couldn't help herself. It was a real laugh, right from her belly; it sounded more like the deep mirth of a much bigger woman. 'Karl – ' She shook her head, the laugh dying away in a ripple of chuckles. 'Does Annabelle ever threaten to hit you over the head?'

Abruptly he smiled widely, matching her mirth but silently: it was as surprising as an obscene joke on the lips of a nun. She was at once suspicious, then she saw the laughter in his eyes and knew he was enjoying the joke as much as herself. Something had happened to Karl in the past week. He was becoming extravagant, spending himself in humour.

'What you and I have got is nothing like what there is between me and Belle.'

She wanted to ask what there was between him and his wife, but she had always respected the secrets of other people's relationships. Instead she asked, 'What about Jim? The way you're talking about you and me . . .'

'He won't be doublecrossed. He's part of the team. But he's not the brains. You and I are that.'

She was silent for a while before she said quietly, 'Does he ever resent you, Karl? Do the two of you ever fight about anything?'

He took his own time about replying, unlocking his hands and taking the holder out of his pocket and putting it back between his teeth. 'Jim fights with everyone. It's his nature.'

'Did he ever fight with Harry?'

'Several times. About three months ago Harry almost fired him. I talked Harry out of it. It all blew over in a couple of days. Both of 'em were like that and that was what I told Harry, that they'd both regret it soon's they cooled down.'

'You haven't said whether he fights with you.'

'He would if I let him. I just don't fight with anyone, that's all.'

'No, I guess you don't.' She knew it wasn't cowardice on his part; he would just know other ways of getting what he wanted. 'But I think I'd trust you more, Karl, if you fought with me occasionally.'

'There's nothing to fight about right now. Anyhow, we'll have a fight on our hands with Kenneway.' He stood up, picked up his hat. It seemed to Grace that he had been wearing the same hat ever since she had first met him, an old fawn Stetson with a brim just wide enough to suggest that he came from cattle country but not wide enough to be too obvious when he was talking business in city offices. He saw her looking at it and he rolled it round in his hands. 'Might get myself a new 'un. Belle has been at me for years to throw this one away.'

'Don't let our success go to your head, Karl.'

He grinned at the joke: he really seemed to be turning human. 'I don't think that's likely to happen to either of us. Oh, one more thing. Old Silver tells me the national committee has been making nice noises about you. I think you ought to make a sizeable donation towards their funds.'

'How sizeable?'

'Maybe a hundred thousand for starters. Nothing public. Those who know about it will appreciate it and those that don't won't be troubled.'

'I'll think about it.' She would do it, she knew, but she wasn't going to fall in at once with every suggestion he put to her.

He stood looking at her, still spinning the old hat, the past, in his hands. 'Grace, you've only just started. You play your cards right and eight, ten years from now you'll have more power in Washington, in the country, than old Silver Mountfield has ever had.'

'Was that what Harry was planning?'

'Yes. But you got more going for you than Harry ever did.'

Suddenly suspicious of him again, she said, 'Don't bother to go up to Seattle.' She didn't want him alone with Kenneway, not before she had seen the Englishman. 'We'll play it by ear when he gets here.'

The hat stopped spinning in his hands. But all he said was, 'Whatever you say, Grace. You're the boss.'

Then he nodded and abruptly left: farewells, too, were a waste of time. Grace sat staring at the empty doorway through which he had disappeared. She could feel herself trembling inside; she looked at her hands, but they were steady and she knew the trembling was too deep for any exterior sign. It was as if she were a sea and hidden beneath her surface a great wave had begun to surge; it frightened and at the same time excited her. The wave, she knew with a sort of joyful dread, could carry her on to the end of the dreams.

Kerry appeared in the doorway, materializing in Grace's stare. 'Governor Mackintosh's secretary called. The Governor would like to see you at four-thirty, if it's convenient.'

She was puzzled and resentful: she had never expected Hugh Mackintosh to summon her like this. 'Any hint why he wants to see me?'

Kerry shook her head. 'I tried to sound out his secretary, but she's an old hand. Oh, Inger is here, too.'

Inger was Grace's masseuse, a cheerful Swedish woman with a

talkative tongue and, Grace suspected, a streak of sadism. She worked on Grace, slapping, pummelling and stroking, talking all the time. When Grace could get a word in she said, 'How do people feel about what's been in the papers?'

'You mean that thing about Limbo Valley?' She gave Grace two extra hearty slaps, but they were not a remonstrance. 'People I talk to around here, they could'nt care less. Nobody in Helena worries about it. I personally myself don't care. If it's going to bring money to Montana, like you said, well and good. Most people got wallets in their heads. The more money is here, the more to go around, right?' She thumped Grace's behind, like a mother spanking a child. 'You putting a bit on there.'

'Just leave me enough to sit on,' said Grace, wincing. 'So you don't think the Limbo Valley project is a bad thing?'

'Like you said, money's what counts. You can't spend a tree at the supermarket, right? Trees are nice to sit under, but what do they feed? Squirrels, birds. They don't feed your kids. Leastways not mine. I don't go up to Tozabe, nobody up there wants a massage. But I'd tell 'em, if they asked me, you got to take the broad view. If it's going to do Montana a power of good, what's a few trees?' She finished with four thumps that Grace was sure had bruised her. 'There, that make you feel better?'

'A little,' said Grace, thinking of the conversation rather than the pummelling.

'Just watch your fanny. A good fanny is worth a lot of votes, so my Lars tells me.'

Assured of Lars Lindquist's vote, Grace got off the table. 'You better come again Thursday. I think I'm going to have a long tiring day tomorrow.'

'I never thought I'd be saying this to you, Mrs Jardine. But you got to relax more. You didn't use to be like this. Tense, I mean. But I could feel it in you today. Relax. You got nothing to worry about, really. Right?'

'Right,' said Grace, but wondered.

Punctually at four-thirty she was in the Capitol building, walking down the long echoing corridor towards the Governor's office. The word must have got around that she was coming: the corridor was full of clerks and typists going nowhere with files and sheets of blank paper. They all smiled at her in welcome, but their eyes were bursting with curiosity.

Miss Gimble, the Governor's secretary, was a middle-aged woman with horn-rimmed glasses and a brisk manner that suggested she could just as easily have guarded the Pentagon as the governor's office.

'The Governor is expecting you, Mrs Jardine. You're right on time.' She said it as if she were pinning a medal on Grace.

'Punctuality is the courtesy of kings,' said Grace, echoing Random.

'And of queens,' said the Governor from the doorway of the inner office. 'Come in, Grace. We're not to be disturbed, Doris. No phone calls, either.' He closed the door and looked at Grace. 'You're more beautiful than ever. Politics must agree with you.'

'It's all cosmetics, Hugh.' She sat down, arranging herself neatly and easily. There was a style and ease about her that seemed to reverse the authority of their respective positions. She looked up at the governor, who suddenly appeared ill at ease. 'What's on your mind, Hugh? I'm not used to being asked to call on men, not even governors.'

He went to sit down on the couch next to her chair, changed his mind and moved round to sit behind his desk. He's acting the governor part, she thought, and began to feel the tension in herself that Inger had remarked upon.

'Grace –' There was a forced crispness to his voice; he sounded like a military commander about to lead his men on a suicide mission. 'Grace, you and I have always been friends. I think we can talk straight to each other.'

'I hope so.'

Straight talking was evidently going to come hard for him. He looked around his office as if he wasn't quite sure that he should be here. It was not a particularly big room, not designed to equate space with the occupant's self-importance, and the panelled walls and red carpet seemed to suggest it was more cramped than it really was; it struck her that Harry's office, *her* office, at Jardine was at least half as big again as this room. A United States flag and a Montana State flag hung limply from standards behind the Governor's chair; they looked as if they had never been stirred by the breeze of politics that had blown through the office. A Russell painting faced the desk and there were several small pieces of sculpture by Russell and Remington on tables about the room. Grace made up her mind then that in her room in the Senate building, when she reached it, there would be works by other artists: the ubiquitous Russells had become almost like religious pictures in Italy, hung on every available indoor wall. On the desk was a family photograph, taken when the governor's wife was alive, and on one wall was a photograph of Mackintosh, in uniform, having a medal pinned on him by President Johnson. He looked happier in both pictures than he did now.

'Grace, are you determined to go ahead with this business up in Limbo Valley?'

'Yes.' She made up her mind she was not going to make it easier for him. She was beginning to resent being called here like some defaulting taxpayer or, with one eye on the photograph on the wall, a soldier accused of some dereliction of duty.

'Then – ' he seemed to take a deep breath – 'I'm going to have to go against you, Grace. They have already been to see me – '

'Who's they?'

'Some men from the valley, one or two of whom work for your company. Two ecology groups have been here and I've had letters – ' He gestured towards the only papers on his desk, an inch-high pile of letters neatly stacked and held down by a brass paperweight in the shape of a bison. 'The opposition to your scheme is strong and growing. One of the Assemblymen has already promised to put a bill before the House committee.'

'Where does he come from? Around here?'

'No, down on the Plains. That's the point, Grace. With the coal mining development already going on down on the Plains, we can't just go on chewing up this state to make more money.'

'This isn't a wealthy state, Hugh – as Governor you should know that better than anyone. My project will bring in millions and the money will stay here. Can you say that about the coal developers?'

'Not all of it, no. Some of it will go out of the state. But what sort of place will this be to live in if we go on ruining all our beauty spots? The coal people already want to flood my home place, Paradise Valley, down past Livingstone. I'm trying to stop that, but I don't know if I can. But I think I can stop your project.'

'If you do that, Hugh, you're going to have us on the same ticket but on opposite sides of the fence.'

'I hope that won't get you into any unladylike contortion.'

This seemed to be the day for humour from unexpected sources. 'Why do you have to cause the split? Does the state committee know how you feel?'

'Yes, and some of them are backing me. You seem to forget, Grace, that as Governor I'm more responsible for this state than you will be as Senator. I hate to say it, but you seem to be thinking just like Harry did.'

'What do you mean by that?'

He hesitated, then seemed to think better of what he had just said. 'Nothing. Harry's dead, so we'll leave him out of this. So . . .' He stared at her across the desk. He looked composed, but she could see the stiffness in the fingers of the hands resting on the desk. 'Now you know how I feel, that I'll do everything I can to stop the project, will you give it a second thought?'

'No.' She stood up. 'I think you'll find it more difficult than you anticipate to stop me. The valley is privately owned by our company.'

'Not the township.'

'Most of that, too. We'll build a better town, a planned one, with better houses than there are in Tozabe now.' She was improvising; up till now she had not given much thought to what should be done for the townspeople. She did not believe they would suffer and was determined they should not, but she had not given any consideration to details. She would get Karl and Jim to put someone on to planning such details at once. It was obvious that she was going to be faced with arguments such as Hugh Mackintosh's from now on. 'I'm not going to be one of the old style copper kings, Hugh. Or copper queens. Give me some credit for humanity.'

He surprised her by shaking his head. 'I'll reserve judgement, Grace. In the meantime I'll be speaking against your project.'

'You don't think it will do harm to your campaign?'

'I don't know. But I'm my own man now and the voters may appreciate that. For too long I was Harry's man. I wouldn't want them to think I'd been bequeathed to his widow.'

She kept her temper, but only just: her bones seemed to turn to iron rods in her limbs. 'Goodbye, Hugh.'

She called Jack that evening. She hesitated about doing it. Twice that day her relationship with two men had changed; she was afraid what might happen the third time, with the man who meant most to her. But the desire to speak to him, to see him if it was possible, was too much.

'Are we speaking? I've been waiting for you to call me.' *Why did I have to say that?*

'I wasn't sure where I stood. Employees usually don't call up their bosses except to talk business. We didn't have any business to talk about, not after your statement.'

Is this Jack I'm talking to, the man I'm in love with and who is in love with me? 'Shall I hang up and call you back and we'll start all over again?'

She could imagine his smile: but would it be half-mocking? 'Okay, you win. I've missed you, darling.'

'Do you want to meet me at the ranch? I can be there in an hour.'

'I'll be there.'

'Just one condition – we don't talk business.'

There was just the faintest silence on the line before he said, 'No business. We'll talk about anything else you like, but not business.'

She packed a small overnight bag, got on the house phone to Annie. 'I'm going out to the ranch. If anyone calls, tell them you don't know where I am. If it's important, tell them I'll call them back, then call me.'

'You want me or Lee to come with you? Awful lonely out there.'

'I don't think I'll feel lonely.' *Make what you want of that,* she thought. But, as she had told Jack, she had given up worrying about the servants. 'I'll be back first thing in the morning.'

She drove out to the ranch through the dark-blue night. Over in the Big Belt mountains a fire was burning, staining the sky: she idly wondered if it was the same fire that had been burning, it seemed, for the past two months. When she arrived at the ranch she phoned the ranch manager's wife to say she was there and did not want to be disturbed. There was a difference between what the servants might think you were doing and being caught by them in – what was it called? – flagrante delictus or something. She must learn a few Latin phrases: Silver Mountfield was always tossing them into his speeches in the Senate. Though flagrante delictus (o? um?) was not one you could lightly put into a Senate speech.

She looked into the mirror of her dressing-table, was pleased at the flushed, expectant face she saw there. She looked *young*; or anyway younger than she had felt all day. And, so far, there had been no sex. Even the *thought* of Jack was now an elixir.

She was in the best of humour when he arrived and she went into his arms without a word. He smiled and said, 'Let's get down to business.'

'You said – ' She stiffened in his arms; then she saw his smile widening and she kissed him again. 'Let's.'

They didn't lie in bed afterwards: it was as if they had silently agreed that their arguments always began in the rumpled, cooling bed of love. He put on his shorts and she gave him one of her terry-towel robes; it was tight under the arms and didn't close across his chest. He looked slightly ridiculous and their laughter helped their mood: but it was also a protection, a shell. She was aware of the brittleness of the atmosphere and she was afraid for the rest of the night.

They watched television, sitting side by side on a couch like an old married couple. It was another re-run, the chewed-over diet of the Late Movie watcher: *Mrs Miniver* once more fought her private war against the Germans.

'Is England really like that?'

'From what I've heard, that's the back lot of M-G-M in Hollywood.'

'No, I mean, do people really touch their forelock and say Yes, mum, and No, guv?'

'They used to do that to my mother and father. I don't think they still do. The forelock touch has now been replaced by the jerked thumb. Except to really beautiful women.' He kissed her.

'Could you see me at Random Hall?' But at once she knew she should not have asked the question: she could not see herself there.

'No.'

God, she thought, he reads me better than any of the others

ever did. Even Harry, after ten years, had always had to have her spell herself out to him.

'You'd be wanting to come back here after six months. Or to Washington. You'd be the – the outlander there and I don't think you'd like that.' He seemed to sense that they were getting close to dangerous ground again. He smiled, got up and switched off the television set, chopping Greer Garson off in mid-sentence as she read from *Alice in Wonderland: and find a pleasure in all their simple joys.* 'Let's do as Mrs Miniver suggests. Let's go back to bed.'

Exhausted from their love-making they overslept the next morning. They had only orange juice and coffee and were coming out of the front door of the house when they saw the silver-blue Mercedes coming up the long avenue of cottonwoods. Random looked at Grace and she said, 'What the hell is he doing out here?'

Coulson brought his car round in a wide sweep, as if he were making some sort of entrance. He got out and came across to them, walking flat-footed, heavily deliberate.

'I didn't expect to be intruding.' His voice, too, was flat; he glanced at the overnight bag Grace was carrying. 'I wouldn't have come, otherwise.'

'What are you doing here?' Grace's voice was sharp, too sharp for her own comfort.

'The idea was that Kenneway and Random would stay the night here when they come. The other Random, that is,' he added with heavy sarcasm. 'We talked about it the other day.'

She had completely forgotten. 'And you came out here just to make sure everything was okay?'

'Yes.'

She wanted to call him a liar, but that would be too much. Maybe he *had* come out here for that reason, but she doubted it; it was not the sort of minor job he would usually have done. No, Annie or Lee must have slipped up and told him where she was and he had followed her out here. Whether he had expected to find her here with Jack was something she couldn't tell.

'Well, now you're here I'll leave it all to you. Mrs Ullman can bring someone up from the ranch to look after them.'

Coulson spoke directly to Random. 'Are you going out to the airport?'

'I wasn't going to.' Random looked at Grace. 'Unless you want me to?'

'I think it would be better if you didn't,' she said. 'I'll tell your father you'll come down and see him here tonight, all right?'

He nodded, opened the door of her car for her. 'I think it would be better still if he came up to Tozabe to see me. Tomorrow or the next day, whenever he can manage it.'

'Why?' said Coulson.

Random looked at him coolly. 'Because I'm trying to sit on the fence for the time being. I can do it better if I stay in my own bailiwick. Up there I have reminders all round me that I'm working for the company as a whole.' He closed the car door, looked in at Grace, grinned and touched his forelock. 'I'll ring you this evening, mum.'

She smiled, trusting him and loving him till it hurt. She wanted to lean out to kiss him, but that would be too much like waving a red rag at the bull standing watching them. She looked at Coulson, nodded goodbye without speaking. Then she took the Lincoln down the avenue, the house soon disappearing from view behind her. At the end of the avenue, just inside the front gates, she pulled up the car and cut the engine. She slid the windows down and sat back in the seat. The morning air was still fresh and comparatively cool and she could smell the scent of new-mown hay coming from somewhere beyond the cottonwoods on her right. She sat watching the long open tunnel of the avenue stretching away in the driving mirror.

It was ten minutes before Random came barrelling down the avenue, a whirling drogue of dust trailing him. He was almost on her car before he saw it in the shade of the trees; he skidded to a stop and pulled in in front of her. She got out of her car and ran forward through the enveloping dust. He opened his door and slid out as she reached him. The dust settled, coating both of them, then she saw the cut on his swollen upper lip and the smear of blood on his chin.

'What – Did you two have a fight?' He nodded, touching his lip tenderly. 'What about?'

'Several things.'

She wanted to hit him, to hit anything: she punched her fist against the roof of his car. 'Good God, what's the matter with you?'

'Nothing's the matter with me,' he said calmly; but touched his lip again. 'Except this.'

'Are you going to tell me about it?' She took a handkerchief from the pocket of her skirt, wet it with her tongue and wiped the smear of blood from his chin. 'Or are you going to be stupid and tell me it's men's business?'

'Yes, it's men's business.'

'I should bust your other lip, wipe off that damned smile. Was it over me?'

He thought for a moment, as if deciding how much he should tell her. Then he nodded. 'Partly. I'm not usually given to alarmist talk, but I think Coulson is dangerous.'

'To you?'

Again the slight hesitation; then: 'No, to you.'

She frowned, became conscious of the dust on her face and wiped it off with her handkerchief. She had put on no make-up this morning other than lipstick, but the dust still stuck to her clear skin. She gave up, leaving her face smeared and older-looking. She caught a glimpse of herself in the side mirror of the car and frowned again. Where had the young, in-love face of last night's mirror gone?

'I can handle him,' she said. 'But I don't want you involved.'

His soft harsh laugh was hidden behind his hand as he still felt his lip. 'It's a little late to be saying that. But don't worry, I can look after myself. The point is, can you look after *yourself*? He's in love with you, you know that?'

'Yes.' She looked back up the avenue, but there was no sign of the Mercedes. She did not want another confrontation, not this morning. 'It's a problem and I hate the thought of it – mainly because of his wife. But once I got to Washington –'

'That's going to be our problem then,' he said, but didn't give her an opportunity to reply. 'I think we'd better disappear. He'll be coming down here soon. I'm not afraid of another fight, but I don't want it to happen in front of you.'

He took her back to her car, put her in it. She reached out and put a finger on his lip, smiled lovingly at him. 'I shouldn't ask – but who won?'

'I hate to tell you – *he* did.' He held her hand, kissed it in the old half-mocking gesture. 'But that was only the first round.'

She drove away, still loving him so much that there was almost a physical feeling of sweet pain; but she was troubled, by his fight with Jim Coulson and by his remark about Washington. She began to wonder if she had acquired, gradually and only half-voluntarily, some sort of Pandora's box. She remembered she had read the story as a child and how scared she had been by it. Something had been left in the box, but for the life of her she could not remember whether it had been good or evil.

She went out to the Helena airport at three o'clock, going alone in the Lincoln with Lee driving her. Shooberg and Coulson were already there. Shooberg smiled at her and took off the new Stetson he wore.

'Same size as the old one.' You couldn't apply the word chirpy to him, but he was close to it.

'Let's hope it lasts as long as the old one.'

'That's what I told Belle.'

She looked at Coulson, searched his face for a bruise or cut but there was none. 'Did you get everything fixed up out at the ranch?'

'Just about everything.'

He was looking hard at her, but she wasn't going to give him the satisfaction of searching for double meanings. 'Then let's hope Lord Kenneway and Sir Random appreciate it.'

'You call him Sir Nigel,' said Shooberg. 'I looked it up.'

You would, she thought; but was grateful to him. 'I'll take them in my car. We'll go to the house, have the meeting there instead of the office. There are no reporters here, are there?'

The small airport lounge was crowded with people, travellers and farewelling friends waiting for the afternoon plane going south. All of them were gazing at Grace; behind the chatter of farewells there was the whisper of gossip. Several were taking surreptitious photos of her, but they were all amateurs. The press was not present.

'They don't know Kenneway and Random are coming,' said Shooberg. 'But they'll know ten minutes after they arrive. One of the airport staff is sure to call them.'

'If they haven't already,' said Coulson, pointing to a girl in one of the car rental booths who, staring at Grace, was dialling the phone on her desk. 'Let's get out of here.'

'Our plane's coming in now,' said Shooberg, nodding through

the glass doors at the Beechcraft just touching down on the run-way.

They got Kenneway and Nigel Random away from the airport before the newsmen arrived. Grace rode in the back of the car with Lord Kenneway and Sir Nigel rode up front with Lee. She was aware of the glances he kept sneaking over his shoulder at her and she wondered if Jack had told him anything of what was going on between them.

Kenneway was like Karl Shooberg: he didn't believe in small talk. He was a short man, broad-shouldered and -chested, with thick black hair flecked with grey and a face that reminded her of a square wooden mask she had once seen on a trip to Mexico. He didn't look English, except for the cut of his clothes, which were expensive and discreet. He was not a man you would have picked out first in a crowd, but once you had focused on him everybody else would be just part of the background. Grace, sitting next to him, looking at him now for the first time as an adversary and not just as a business acquaintance of her late husband, felt the presence of a man of power. But was not frightened by him: rather something in her responded, she felt the excitement of her own power.

'I'll be frank, Mrs Jardine. I'm not accustomed to dealing with women. Women don't rise to the top in England, very few of them. In politics, yes, but not in business. So you'll forgive me if I talk man to man.'

'I'd sooner it was person to person.'

'Makes it sound rather like a telephone trunk call,' said Nigel Random, turning round and smiling at Grace. 'But she has a point, Ian. We're not back home in the City, y'know.'

It seemed to Grace that Kenneway permitted himself a smile. 'All right. Person to person. No holds barred.'

'Within the bounds of decorum,' said Grace. 'Just now and again I want to remember I'm a woman.'

Nigel Random chuckled, looked at her admiringly, then turned to face forward again. He was a leaner version of his son, but with a more restless air, a man dissatisfied with the less-than-orderly way the world was run. His grey hair was brushed close to his scalp, with small wings sticking out above his ears, and his trim military moustache was almost white. His clothes, Grace noted with her usual eye for dress, were good but they seemed to have been worn much longer than Lord Kenneway's. He looked slightly frayed around the edges, as if he could no longer afford the proper upkeep of himself. She remembered Jack had said it was a struggle for his father to keep up Random Hall. He was wearing what she now knew was a Guards tie and she also now knew it was something that would always distinguish him, in some British eyes, from Lord Kenneway. She was beginning to learn some of the small distinctions, the tribal snobberies, that marked the wider society into which she was moving. She wondered what distinctions she would notice among the tribes in Washington.

Kenneway took no interest in their passing surroundings; he was no tourist and he had been here before. But Nigel Random was looking at everything with an interested and curious eye, particularly the West Side when they drove up through it. When they pulled into the driveway of the house on Harrison he looked up at it and nodded appreciatively.

'Jolly nice. Something to be said for the older things, y'know.'

'You wouldn't have been happy in the Middle Ages or whenever it was your family got started,' said Kenneway. 'Things were a damn sight worse run then than they are now.'

Coulson and Shooberg, each in his own car, pulled into the driveway behind them. When they all went up into the house Colin Lidcombe was waiting for them, notebook in hand. He could take shorthand and it had been decided that Carlotta or any of the other stenographers was not wanted. The less tongues to spread the details of what might go on in the coming in-fighting, the better.

Kenneway looked at the four Americans. 'Looks as if we're outnumbered, Nigel.'

'It wasn't meant to be tactical,' said Grace. 'It's just a question of – is demography the word I want?'

'I doubt it,' said Kenneway, person to person. And put Grace at an instant disadvantage, showing she was trying to appear more educated than she was. 'Well, shall we start?'

3

The meeting lasted two and a half hours. At one point Grace suggested a break for tea, but Kenneway asked her why.

'I thought all Englishmen stopped for tea.'

'Most of them do, the ones who get left behind by the rest of the world. This one doesn't. You don't want any, do you, Nigel?'

Nigel Random smiled faintly beneath his white moustache; he obviously liked his tea, whether the world left him behind or not. He had said very little during the meeting and Grace had begun to feel disappointed in him, wondering why he had come. If he was a sample of the London directors, she didn't think much of them. But the smile now reminded her of Jack's, half-mocking. Maybe there was more to the older Random than his silence suggested.

'One can always look forward to a whisky at the finish. Keep going, Ian.'

Grace had been allowed to sit in on only one of Harry's business meetings and she had been a little shocked but at the same time impressed by his tough approach. He had been rude and arrogant, but he had got what he had wanted and had chopped out what he called the waffling, one of the few British terms he ever indulged in. But Kenneway was even tougher, just as arrogant and, though slightly more refined, just as rude. He was a man of obvious subtlety; or subtle obviousness: either way, you always got his point. Coulson and Shooberg, especially the latter, had come prepared with all their arguments; but, before they had gone very far, it was obvious that the battle they had prepared for was going to develop into a long war. Their tactics were good, but they didn't have the overall command of strategy that Kenneway had.

'We can delay you, if not indefinitely, then certainly for a year or two. We have already lodged a complaint with the Securities and Exchange Commission and I'm told they are six to nine months behind on their hearings. They will be interested to know how you bought up all your controlling shares.'

'We did it legally,' said Shooberg.

'I'm sure you did,' said Kenneway in a voice that could have meant just the opposite. 'But we can make you wait six to nine months while you prove it. We've also got one of your State Assemblymen bringing in an environmental protection bill – '

'*You* did that?' Grace said. 'How?'

'I'm afraid that's a trade secret.'

'Is Governor Mackintosh working for you, too?'

'That's for you to find out. There's another factor you've overlooked – '

'What's that?' said Coulson. Grace was aware that Coulson and Shooberg were beginning to sound like men with their backs to the wall, but she could feel the adrenalin beginning to course through her. She was studying Kenneway intently, though she still had her outward calm: she had had battles with men, but she had never been to war with a man before, not even Harry.

Kenneway looked at her and for the first time treated her as a woman, a recent widow. 'I don't like bringing this up, Mrs Jardine, but it was not I who started all this. Your husband was murdered and so far no motive has been established. Two months after he was murdered, a business partnership in which he was perfectly happy suddenly turns into a take-over engineered by his wife and two of the American directors of the company.'

Nigel Random said, 'I say, Ian, isn't that going a bit too far?'

Coulson clutched his hair, stood up abruptly and swore. 'Jesus H. Christ, I ought to bust your – '

'Sit down, Jim.' Grace was surprised at how calm her voice sounded. She was seething inside now, hating this squat, well-dressed man, like a sleek gorilla, sitting opposite her. 'Lord Kenneway, Harry himself originated this take-over. He had put it in motion before he was killed.'

'I know that. I've checked back when the first buying of shares started. But I'll ask your police, or the FBI, to check that as a possible motive. It may come to nothing. But it won't help your Senate campaign, Mrs Jardine. I understand that after Watergate, Americans want all their political candidates to be as pure as the driven snow.'

'You play pretty dirty,' said Coulson.

'As you say in this country, that's the name of the game.'

Kenneway didn't look at Coulson. He and Grace were gazing steadily at each other. Each of them had the taste of power in his mouth; but Grace knew hers was a suddenly acquired one. Kenneway's was natural: she guessed he had asserted it in his nursery. His, too, was a ruthless power and she knew she could never go as far as he in the use of it. Or hoped she would not.

'You were right, Lord Kenneway, you are only used to dealing man to man. I think you'd cut the balls off any man who got in your way.'

'I don't admire crudity in a woman,' said Kenneway almost primly.

'I don't admire it myself. It's a measure of what I think of your dirty tricks. Somehow I had always thought the English were different.'

'Some of us are,' said Nigel Random mildly. 'I'm sorry, Ian, but I divorce myself from your remarks.'

'That's your privilege,' said Kenneway. 'I don't expect all my directors to be yes men. But don't tell me you endorse what Mrs Jardine and her colleagues have done. I shan't believe you're *that* gentlemanly.'

'I don't.' Nigel Random was not the most intelligent of men, but he was honourable to an out-of-date degree. 'I'll back you all the way against what they have done. But I shan't tread through any muck to do it.'

The argument and in-fighting went on, but when the meeting finally broke up the two sides were still at a stand-off.

'I'll be here for two more days,' said Kenneway. 'Think about what I've said, Mrs Jardine. I think it would be a pity if the Senate were deprived of your beauty and talents.'

'Thank you,' said Grace with a cool smile. 'I didn't think you were capable of compliments.'

'Only when the minutes of the meeting are closed,' said Kenneway with a glance at Lidcombe, who had put away his notebook. 'I'll be in touch tomorrow afternoon.'

'Are you going up to the valley?' asked Coulson.

'Naturally. Well, now you can have your whisky, Nigel. The battle is over for today.'

But when Shooberg took Kenneway and Nigel Random out to his car to drive them up to the ranch, Grace knew that the truce was only a blind while both sides reviewed their tactics for tomorrow's battle. She went back into the house after saying goodbye and Coulson, pouring himself another drink from the tray on the side table, said, 'The son-of-a-bitch is going to make it as tough as he can.'

'Did you expect him to be otherwise?'

'I don't know. He's one guy I can't anticipate.'

'What did you think of Sir Nigel?'

'A lightweight.' He spoke from behind his glass and his hand: 'But he's got his son working for him.'

'Come out and say it – working on me, you mean. Right? You're making trouble for yourself, Jim.' She did not mention that she knew of this morning's fight: it might look as if Random had come running to her with the news of it. 'What Jack and I do together is none of your business.'

'You going to marry him?'

'That, for a start, is none of your business.'

'He's dangerous.'

'To you?'

'No, to you.'

This was an echo from this morning. 'No more than you are. Maybe less. You're overstepping your mark, Jim. If you keep it up, you're out. Understand – *out*!'

'You can't do that.' His voice was quiet and steady, but the hand holding his glass shook. 'I own stock – '

'I'll buy your stock or you can keep it – it doesn't really matter. But you'll be off the board, you'll have no say in the company – '

He slammed the glass down on the tray, splashing the drink. 'You think I'm going to let you brush me off like that? I worked twenty years for Harry, slaved my guts out for him. You think I'm going to let you push me out after all that, all because that Englishman has got your ear in bed? You got another think coming, Grace – '

She turned on her heel, said as she went out of the room, 'Find your own way out.'

As she went up the stairs she caught a glimpse of Kerry standing just inside the doorway of her office. She was on the landing when Coulson hurried out, slamming the front door savagely behind him. There was a tinkle of glass as a small pane fell out of the ornamental transom above it. Grace stopped, looked down as Kerry came out into the hall.

'Send Mr Coulson a bill for the damage, Kerry. Tell him I'd like prompt payment.'

'Yes, Mrs Jardine.' Kerry looked ready to smile, but she knew when to be discreet. During the campaign she had come to hate some of the male chauvinists who surrounded her boss; Jim Coulson was one of the worst. Anything that put him in his place had her full approval. 'Oh, while you were in conference, Miss Mackintosh called. I said you'd call her back.'

Grace went on up to her room, closed the door and lay down on the bed. She looked at the familiar surroundings, all at once glad of them; she was in a rosewood womb, safe for the moment. She had closed the door against pressures that seemed to be multiplying like strangling seaweed; but she knew her bedroom was no real haven. Even the love-making with Jack in this bed had ended with the phone call from Silver Mountfield asking her to run for the Senate.

And now Bonnie Mackintosh was calling her. She sighed, picked up the phone and dialled the Governor's mansion. When Bonnie came on the line she said without any preliminaries, 'Grace, can I come and see you?'

'What's it about?' She did not want to be involved in any discussion with Bonnie about Hugh Mackintosh.

'Those letters I mentioned.'

Grace hesitated a moment: another pressure was being added. God, she thought, why can't I just tell her I'm not interested? But she was caught in the seaweed. 'Can you come over now?'

'Ten minutes. And thanks, Grace.' Bonnie sounded genuinely grateful.

Grace hung up, sat up and was surprised to find she had a headache, something she rarely experienced. She went into the bathroom, took some aspirin, washed her face and neck, put on some cologne, repaired her make-up and went downstairs. Kerry, briefcase under her arm, was just coming out of her office.

'The newspaper and TV reporters have been on the phone again. I didn't put them through – ' She looked solicitously at Grace. 'They wanted to know if you or Lord Kenneway was going to make a statement. But I thought you'd want a rest from all that for a while.'

'We'll put out another statement just before Lord Kenneway goes home. Are you off now?'

'Unless you want me to stay? I have a date – '

'Is he in politics?'

'No, he's a lecturer at Carroll. English and American Lit. He lives in a little world all his own. He's not interested in politics or making money or the environment, none of the things that count.'

'Is he interested in you?'

Kerry blushed a little. 'I hope so.'

'That's all that counts, Kerry.'

But as Kerry went out of the house Grace wondered if the girl believed her.

Bonnie Mackintosh arrived in ten minutes as she had promised. Her MG thrum-thrummed its way into the drive and Grace, on an impulse, went out to meet her. The early evening was warm but not as unpleasantly hot as the past weeks had been; there was still no sign of rain, but summer was at last heading south. Lee brought them a jug of lemonade and the two women sat at a white cast-iron table on the lawn in the shadow of one of the big ponderosa pines.

'It's so quiet and pleasant here,' said Bonnie. 'You could be miles from anywhere.'

'It's an illusion.' Grace offered her a glass of lemonade. 'Or do you want something stronger? You look a bit worried.'

'No, lemonade is just fine. Grace – ' She looked at the older woman and Grace recognized that she was being treated as a friend. 'I got those letters back. Someone sent them to me through the mail. About three weeks ago.'

'Why didn't you tell me?'

'I didn't want to worry you. I figured it was my problem, not yours.'

'It's my problem if someone else knows about them.' More pressure: she felt the headache come back. Inside the house she heard the phone ring, but she had told Lee she was not to be disturbed. Unless it was Jack . . . She looked expectantly towards the house, but Lee did not appear. The ringing phone, she guessed, had just been the sound of another pressure.

'I figured that since I'd got all the letters back, who else would know but you and me and whoever sent me the letters? If he'd tried to do anything – blackmail, for instance – he'd have had no evidence to back him up. At least that was what I thought up till this morning.'

The western sky had reddened alarmingly: the ponderosa was black, charred, against a cloud of fire. 'What happened this morning?'

'I got another two of my letters in the mail. With the same note as I got last time. *You ought to be more careful.*'

'How many letters did you write Harry?'

'That's it – I don't know. You don't keep carbons of love letters. I don't even keep a diary. The stupid things you do when you think you're in love!' She put a fist to her mouth, looked away. 'And when I think about it now, it never even resembled love!'

'Are you weeping?' Grace said. Bonnie turned her face towards her and nodded; a shaft of red sunlight stabbed her face and her eyes shone with pink tears. 'That's self-pity. You're capable of better than that.'

Bonnie sniffled, wiped away the tears with a grubby handkerchief. She was dressed this evening in jeans and a madras shirt; there was no attempt to impress as there had been on her first visit here. Whatever did Harry see in her? Grace wondered. Harry, who had always wanted *her* to look as if she had stepped straight out of a *Vogue* advertisement.

'Did you bring the note with you? Let me see it.'

Bonnie took the piece of notepaper from the pocket of her shirt. 'It was in a brown-paper envelope, but the postmark was different than on the first packet of letters. It wasn't Butte this time, it was Great Falls.'

Grace looked at the scrawled capital letters on the thin sheet. 'He's certainly tried to disguise his hand.' She turned the sheet up to the shaft of sunlight, held it against it. 'Whoever he was, he's been faithful to the company. That's a Kenneway-Jardine watermark.'

Bonnie leaned forward. 'Do you think we could trace whoever did it?'

'What would be the point? We couldn't prosecute them. They've done nothing illegal – so far.'

Bonnie bit her lip, then said carefully, 'I've wondered if whoever sent the letters, killed Harry.'

I'm exhausted, Grace thought, why didn't I think of that? But knew that it was not exhaustion that had kept the thought from her mind. She was afraid to think about Harry's murderer: better to let the murder, like its victim, lie buried on the hill out at the ranch. She had her own increasingly complicated life to live; she felt a stab of conscience, but she knew selfishness would win out. Justice was County Attorney Wryman's business, not hers.

'Do you want me to tell Mr Wryman?' she said, guessing what Bonnie's answer would be.

'No,' said Bonnie reluctantly and tugged at the Indian beads round her neck. 'But I worry – what if he should want to kill you or me?'

The sun dropped away beyond the slope of the mountain: the dusk was suddenly like a grey chill. 'Why should he want to do that? He killed Harry because of something between *them*.'

Bonnie sat back, nodding her head and staring at the patches of night gathering under the trees and bushes. 'You're right. It's just – I don't know.' She looked suddenly young and vulnerable. 'Life gets so bloody complicated, doesn't it? I thought I was running around in circles out in California. But it's worse here.' She bit her lip. 'I know about you and Dad falling out.'

'That's one of the worst things,' said Grace sincerely. 'But I hope it won't affect you and me.'

'It won't.' She was all awkwardness; she couldn't handle honest sentiment. 'You're the only woman since my mother died who I can talk to. Even though I don't do it very well,' she added with blunt self-candour.

'We're beginning to understand each other. That's something to go on with. I just wish your father understood me better.'

'Don't be bitter towards him. He really likes you, I know that. As a woman, I mean.'

'I like him, too. As a man.'

They walked across the lawn towards the MG. The air was still and sounds slid along it, bumping against the ear: music playing somewhere in a house across the street, the note of a car engine changing as it turned up a steep grade, a woman calling a child in to supper. The ordinary sounds of an ordinary day against which Bonnie said, 'Be careful, Grace. Just in case whoever killed Harry is against you, too.'

'I'll be careful. But I don't really think I have anything to worry about. Not in that way.'

But when Bonnie had driven away she went inside and put through a call to Colin Lidcombe at his home. 'Col, who cleaned out Harry's office after he was killed?'

'I don't know, Grace. Someone in the office, I guess. I could ask Carlotta, it might've been her.'

'No, never mind. I'll ask her. What's her home number?'

He gave it to her. 'Is it something important, Grace? Do you want me to help?'

'No, it's all right, Col. It's just something personal – a memento I can't find. I'll call Carlotta.'

Carlotta answered the phone almost too quickly, as if she had been sitting beside it waiting for someone to call. For a moment Grace felt pity for the middle-aged spinster, for whom life must stop each day when she left the office. 'Yes? Oh, Mrs Jardine! This is a nice surprise! Can I help you at all?'

'Carlotta, when Mr Jardine was – when he died – ' *Killed* was too harsh a word for Carlotta's ears. But then Grace wondered why she should be so solicitous of the other woman's sensibilities. Carlotta had been Harry's secretary for fifteen years and her sensibilities had probably developed thick calluses. 'Who cleaned out his office? His desk and safe?'

'Was something missing, Mrs Jardine? I saw that it was all packed in two cartons and sent them over to your house.'

'So you cleaned out the office?'

'Well, not exactly. I'm sorry if something is missing – '

Grace tried to sound patient. 'Just some letters I wrote Mr Jardine, personal ones. I thought he may have kept them in his desk.'

'He did keep things in his desk, personal things I mean. There was one drawer he always kept locked.'

'Did you find any letters in there when you finally opened it?'

'Just business notes, that was all. Some of them were a bit, well, *harsh* on some people. Mr Coulson had me burn them, he thought it was best we do that.'

'Mr Coulson?'

'Yes. He took over Mr Jardine's office while his own was being redecorated. He was the one who cleaned out Mr Jardine's desk.'

Chapter Nine

1

Lord Kenneway and Nigel Random came up to Limbo Valley
on the afternoon of the following day. Random shook his father's
hand warmly and Nigel returned the firm grip.

'You're looking remarkably fit, old chap. Nasty cut on your
lip, though.'

'A flying chip, that's all.'

'From someone's shoulder?' said Kenneway, but said it as if
he expected no one to laugh.

Random introduced them to the office staff, remarking his
father's courtly if gruff charm and Kenneway's perfunctory
courtesy; then he took them on a tour of the town and the valley.
He drove them up to Horsethief Gap, pointed out where the dam,
if the Jardine side of Kenneway-Jardine got its way, would be
built.

'From here back to the end of the valley will be water, with
something like seventy square miles of best timber buried under
it. That's speaking purely in economic terms.'

'Those are the terms we're dealing in,' said Kenneway. 'For
the time being, anyway. I don't want to get myself involved in
any ecological argument in someone else's country.'

'We have the ecologists on our side,' Random pointed out
mildly. He could see the men working further up the Gap were

watching them and he hoped none of them came closer. He had the feeling that Kenneway might not prove too popular with them. 'At least so far.'

'We'll use them if we need them.' Kenneway dismissed the ecologists from the conversation. He picked up some dead leaves, crushed them in his hand. 'Conditions are very dry. What are your fire precautions like?'

'Inadequate if the whole valley went up. If a solitary fire should break out, I think we could localize it.'

'Do you think the whole valley could be set on fire?'

Random raised his eyebrows and his father said, 'Good God, Ian, are you suggesting Mrs Jardine and her crowd would stoop to something like that?'

'I'm not suggesting who would do it. But if this valley were suddenly all burnt out, we'd be glad to settle for a copper mine, wouldn't we? I try to think of all the possibilities. And when I do I never give the opposition any credit for ethics or morality.'

'I don't think anyone is going to set the whole valley on fire,' said Random. 'I know Mrs Jardine would never countenance it, anything like it. And if it were to happen, I think she'd renege on the whole mining project.'

'You're naïve if you believe that,' said Kenneway. 'Or in love with the woman.'

Random saw his father cast a quick, sharp glance at him; he hoped he showed no reaction to Kenneway's remark. Kenneway, for his part, did not press either alternative. He said, 'If the valley were burnt out, what would be the point of her cancelling her plans? The damage would have been done, with or without her consent. She'd be a fool if she didn't profit by it. That woman is as interested in money and power as her late husband ever was. She may not have been once, but she's got the bug now.'

You'd know, Random thought; but hoped Kenneway was wrong.

They drove back to Tozabe. When Random drove into the parking lot outside the office he saw that his space was occupied by Coulson's Mercedes. He felt a flash of irritation, but at once squashed it; his reaction was as petty as Coulson's action in taking the marked space. There were several other vacant spaces and he drove his car into one of them.

Coulson and Shooberg were waiting in Random's office.

Random, again feeling petty, was pleased to see that Coulson had not occupied his chair behind the desk. Beryl Gray brought in two extra chairs, then Random gestured to the seat behind his desk. 'Yours, Lord Kenneway.'

Kenneway showed the only note of graciousness since his arrival; or, with extraordinary perception, he sensed what was going on between Random and Coulson. 'It's your desk,' he said and sat down on one of the hardback chairs that had just been brought in.

Coulson was perceptive, too: he caught the point of Kenneway's gesture. 'Well,' he said aggressively, 'did you see anything to help you change your minds?'

'That's something I'll tell you at another board meeting,' said Kenneway. Confronted by Coulson's aggressiveness he seemed suddenly to have become quieter, less aggressive himself. 'You have your problems.'

'Such as?' Shooberg took the ball away from Coulson, not trusting the big man's game.

'You have four or five thousand people in the valley whom you have to get on your side. That's one problem to start with.'

'We'll educate them,' said Shooberg. 'Give people better homes than they got now, better civic amenities, more money in their pockets, they're going to be satisfied.'

'Agreed,' said Kenneway, surprising both Shooberg and Coulson. 'The majority of people want only those things. But majorities don't run this world, you know that. Not even a democracy like America. You have only to see the influence and power of the lobbies in Washington to appreciate it. Random here tells me there is a powerful lobby building up in this valley.'

'Outsiders,' snapped Coulson.

Kenneway looked at Random and the latter shook his head. 'No, men who work for the company.'

'Who's leading them?' demanded Coulson. 'Have you been encouraging some of the hotheads?'

Random could feel that Coulson's antagonism had increased even since they had last met; he wondered if there had been some sort of scene between him and Grace. He had tried to call her last night but her phone had been interminably busy and in the end he had gone to bed without talking to her. The cut on his lip suddenly seemed to throb and he had to restrain himself from touching it. He became London's man.

'Be sensible, Coulson,' he said coolly, and the big man's face darkened. He was aware of his father and Kenneway watching him closely. 'I'm not an agitator.'

'There could be a difference of opinion on that,' said Coulson.

'You had better explain that remark,' said Kenneway quietly.

But then Random's intercom crackled and Beryl said softly and urgently, 'Mr Random, could you please step outside a moment?'

Random excused himself, went out to the outer office, closing the door behind him. Beryl, one hand on her bosom, was standing at the front windows of the office. 'There, Mr Random. I thought you ought to know.'

Across the street, in the gathering dusk, a crowd of about fifty men were grouped, most of them still wearing their hard hats. Even as Random looked at them a street light went on directly above them, like a stage illumination: all at once the silent men took on an air of menace, their faces shadowed beneath the gleaming yellow helmets. Random had a sudden sharp memory of another crowd, hatless, standing exactly like the one across the road in exactly the same lighting: Arab demonstrators poised in out-of-character silence for a moment before they broke into the storm of riot.

'I've never seen the men in that mood before.' Beryl was frowning, looking far more serious than Random had ever seen her. 'They look like pictures of the miners when they went on strike down in Butte, back in the old days. They were terrible days then. Men killed and hurt.'

'Nothing like that is going to happen,' Random reassured her and hoped he sounded convincing. 'I'll go out and have a word with them.'

'Be careful, please.'

Her concern for him was touching: I'm the valley's man, too, he thought. 'I'll be all right, Beryl. I hope I have one or two friends out there.'

One of his friends was standing right at the front of the crowd. Random crossed the road, walked up to him and said, 'What's going on, Chris? Lord Kenneway said he would see a few of you, not a mob.'

Peeples shrugged. 'You think I could keep 'em away? How is he, Jack? He on our side or not?'

'I think he's on your – our side. But it's hard to tell, he plays his cards so close to his chest. All I can tell you is, he's not letting anyone push him around. Least of all Shooberg and Coulson.'

'What about our lady friend?'

Random was aware of the men behind Peeples crowding closer. Their ears seemed to enlarge and stand out on their heads like those of the fennec, the desert fox he had seen in Arabia. (Why were images of that dangerous time coming back?) Then he saw that the giant ears were hands cupped to the side of the head to catch every word that was being said between their representative and the company's man. The men were not letting politeness stand in their way.

'I don't know how that meeting went,' said Random and was grateful that he did not have to lie or hedge.

There was a stir in the crowd and heads turned to look up the street. A moment later two sheriff's cars, sirens growling, as if Bill Gauge was reluctant to come barging in full-throated, slid into the kerb on the opposite side of the road. Sheriff Gauge and four deputies got out, hitching their belts so that their holsters came forward on their hips. The deputies stood in a line beside the cars and Bill Gauge, arms swinging awkwardly, came lumbering across the roadway.

'What's going on here, Mr Random?'

'A company meeting,' said Random; but behind him someone sniggered and spoiled the effect of his calm reply. He glanced over his shoulder and saw Tim Yertsen smirking at the sheriff. 'Nothing is wrong, sheriff.'

'We had a complaint,' said Gauge.

'Who from?'

'Mr Coulson.'

Random looked across the road. The lights had been switched on in the offices of Kenneway-Jardine and Kenneway, Nigel Random, Shooberg and Coulson were silhouetted against them as they stood at the window of the front office. You stupid bloody clot, thought Random, staring at the bulky outline of Coulson.

'Does that mean nobody's going to talk to us?' demanded Peeples, and at once an angry murmur ran through the crowd. Random heard a swishing sound behind him and he turned. The crowd, like magicians producing cards out of the air, had swung up several banners and placards: THE VALLEY IS OURS. NO MINES IN LIMBO. The faces of the men beneath the banners had suddenly turned ugly.

'Who's your delegation?' Random said.

'Same as came to see you,' said Peeples. 'Me, Ted Zeeland and Clint Hauger.'

'Let's go over and see Lord Kenneway.'

But as they crossed the road Random saw that the four silhouettes had disappeared from the office windows. He slowed his step, but then kept walking. As they went up the path between the blue spruces Kenneway and the other three men came out of the front doors. At once there was a shout from the other side of the road, a yell from Sheriff Gauge, then the crowd came surging across the road. They pulled up at an invisible line, as if there were a rope between the spruces, leaving the eight men, the negotiators, to meet in the open space between the trees and the office building.

'What the hell you think you're doing?' Coulson glared at Random. 'You trying to start a riot or something?'

'He's not doing anything, Mr Coulson,' said Peeples.

'Shut up – I wasn't talking to you –'

'Did you want to see me or Mr Coulson?' Kenneway interposed; and Coulson was left with his mouth open, as if he were choking on the anger and abuse he couldn't expend. 'My name's Kenneway.'

'Sorry to meet you like this, Lord Kenneway.' Peeples, Zeeland and Hauger, without actually moving, managed to give the impression that they had turned their backs completely on Coulson. 'But we couldn't keep the guys away. Like you can see, feeling is running pretty high about this business of what's going to happen to the valley.'

'At present nothing is going to happen to the valley,' said Kenneway.

'At present? What's that supposed to mean? How long's *at present*?'

'I can't tell you. I should think it would mean six months at least.' There was an angry growling in the crowd and Kenneway, with arrogant patience, waited for it to subside. 'The people who want to change conditions here have the controlling interest in our company. That's the legal situation. But I'm doing my best to stop them going ahead – '

Peeples turned away from Kenneway and looked at Coulson and Shooberg. Random, watching Kenneway, saw the chairman's face stiffen; he wasn't used to being treated as just one of a panel up for questioning. Random guessed that no stockholder at a Kenneway annual general meeting in London would ever have got away with such brusque treatment of the chairman. But no annual general meeting in London would have contained the anger that this meeting had. No stockholder from Tunbridge Wells or Reigate or Cheltenham would be defending his job, his home and his town against destruction.

Sheriff Gauge had pushed through the crowd and now stood to one side of the front door of the building, one hand resting on the heavy Magnum pistol in his holster. The four deputies had split up and were posted in pairs on either side of the crowd, just beyond the spruces. The still night air had a static to it that had little to do with the dryness of the atmosphere.

Random was not a stranger to violence and he felt a growing fear. He had stepped away from Peeples and up on to the bottom step of the front entrance; he was trying to preserve some sort of neutrality for himself, but he knew it was futile. He looked out over the heads of the crowd and saw the other, less cohesive crowd drifting in like a dark tide behind and around them. It seemed to him that the whole town was coming down to the Kenneway-Jardine offices: women, children, teenagers, elderly people: bringing a silent fury with them that, if it congealed all its parts into the one storm, none of them would be able to control. Again he remembered the Arab crowd in the back street of Aden and the one sudden screaming voice, a sound of lightning, that had sparked off the riot. Fourteen Arabs and three of his own men had died before the armoured cars had come rumbling down the street and the demonstrators had fled. There would be no armoured cars here, just Sheriff Gauge and four deputies, all of them looking uneasy, their hands too obviously close to their guns.

'What have you got to say, Mr Shooberg?' said Chris Peeples. 'And you, too, Mr Coulson?'

'We got nothing to say right now.' Shooberg looked calm and cold, as if the silent threat of the crowd meant nothing to him.

'We're preparing a statement which will explain everything to you. It will take a little time, that's all.'

'To hell with time!' someone shouted from the side of the crowd; Random looked in that direction and saw the flash of Tim Yertsen's glasses in the lights from the office windows. 'We want to know about our jobs *now*!'

'You don't have to worry about your jobs!' Coulson shouted, voice roaring. Shooberg looked with pained disgust at his partner: you didn't deal with a crowd by shouting at every interjector on its outskirts. But Coulson, anger bursting out of him, was in no mood for conciliation. 'You'll all have jobs – you'll all make more money – '

'Lies! Bullshit!' Yertsen's voice had been joined by others. 'What about our town?'

'We'll build you another town – a better one – '

'We're happy with this one!'

The crowd's fury was mounting: it pressed like something tangible against the men in front of the company entrance. People at the back had begun to chant and yell: the chorus gathered, rolled forward and burst against the wall of the building in a giant deafening wave: the banners waved like storm-wracked sails. Then suddenly the crowd began to move, swaying like a black surf ready to break. A section of it broke off and next moment there was the sound of breaking glass.

'Stop them, sheriff!' Coulson bellowed. 'For Crissake, they're wrecking my car!'

Random looked towards the parking lot. A score of men were rocking Coulson's Mercedes; Tim Yertsen was smashing at the already broken windscreen, using his helmet as a hammer. The rocking of the car increased, then abruptly, with a yell of warning and of triumph, the men jumped back and the car crashed over on its side. Then Sheriff Gauge drew his gun and fired a shot into the air.

The crowd froze, turned and looked at the sheriff almost in disbelief. What had they done that merited shooting off a gun? The noise abruptly stilled; a last piece of glass fell out of the car's broken windshield with the light tinkle of a toy being broken. Random, standing close to Gauge, could hear the sheriff's heavy breathing.

'That's it! Ever – ' Gauge's voice stuck, as if he had shocked himself by what he had done; he cleared his throat, shouted louder. 'Everybody go home now!'

The crowd stood irresolute, most of them knowing they had gone too far too soon: the talking hadn't finished yet. But it had been interrupted and Kenneway, a man who knew the value of moments as well as of money, grabbed the moment of hesitation.

'We'll talk tomorrow,' he said to Chris Peeples. 'Down in Helena. But get all these people home while you can.'

Peeples's blind side was towards Random: the latter couldn't tell his reaction to the sudden turn of events. For a moment it seemed that the wall-eyed foreman was going to refuse Kenneway's advice; then he turned, held up his arms and shouted for everyone to go home. 'They'll talk to us tomorrow! Break it up, everybody – go home before there's real trouble! We don't want that – not yet!'

The crowd, muttering but no longer immediately threatening, began to drift away. Sheriff Gauge, relief and sweat suddenly breaking out to smear his face, put away his gun. His deputies, who had drawn their own guns, now slipped them back into their holsters, began to move the crowd on its way like friendly ushers at a ball game.

'They're reasonable folk,' said Gauge, nodding his head and smiling like a candidate who had just been returned to office. 'They'll listen to reason, you talk to 'em.'

Reason was a gunshot? Random wondered. But Coulson, swearing a froth of obscenities, had run across to his car and now came stalking back.

'Jesus H. Christ, you going to let 'em get away with that, sheriff? They wrecked my car – *wrecked* it, you hear? That guy Yertsen, he was smashing the windshield – '

'I didn't see nobody, Mr Coulson,' said Gauge. 'I mean nobody in particular. There was a lot of guys around your car – '

'I tell you, Yertsen was the leader of 'em! I saw him! You saw him, Random!'

'I saw a lot of chaps turning your car over,' said Random. 'But I shouldn't want to go into court and swear to identify any particular one.'

'Who's talking about going into court?'

'What do you want me to do then, Mr Coulson?' Sheriff Gauge had already caught the scent of the wind: he knew which way the votes were going to go in a few weeks' time. 'I think you better forget it, Mr Coulson. I'll back up your insurance claim, if you want.'

'Better do what the sheriff suggests, Jim,' said Shooberg. He looked shaken, the bone in his face as evident as that of a skull; he was carrying his new hat and his hand had crumpled it as if it were paper. He had not really appreciated the mood of the crowd, he had not expected its sudden fury. He *is* capable of emotion, Random thought, or anyway fear. 'We better get out of town, just in case some of those hotheads have second thoughts and come back. Can you give us a lift back to the ranch, Lord Kenneway? We can take one of the pick-ups from there back to Helena.'

'Of course,' said Kenneway, but didn't sound enthusiastic; chivalry towards his enemies was not one of his principles. 'You ready, Nigel?'

'I think I'll spend the night with Jack.' Nigel Random looked at his son, who nodded. 'I'll be down at the ranch by eight in the morning. Jack will have someone drive me down. I'll get my hat from the car.'

The two Englishmen and Shooberg walked across to the station wagon that, driven by one of the ranch hands, had brought Kenneway and Nigel Random up from the ranch. Sheriff Gauge, ignored, hesitated a moment, then lumbered off towards his own car on the opposite side of the street. Random and Coulson were left alone in the harsh pool of light on the front steps.

'You organized that demonstration,' said Coulson, voice grating.

'Balls,' said Random wearily. 'Go home, Coulson.'

'I'll knock your teeth in – '

'You'll try it once too often. Cool down and go home. This is more than something personal between you and me, Coulson. Before this is over there could be more men killed than just Harry Jardine. Go home and think about it.'

He was tensed, poised on the balls of his feet, ready to dodge the punch he expected Coulson to throw. But the big man, at the mention of Harry Jardine, seemed to slacken his body, as if the muscle that had made him so threatening was no more than anger that now suddenly drained out of him. He stared at

228

Random and the latter had the curious feeling that Coulson couldn't see him.

Then Coulson walked out of the pool of light, stiff-legged and heavy-footed, and crossed towards the parking lot. He walked towards his overturned car, had stepped into the frost of glass lying about it, his boots crunching it, before he heard Shooberg call his name. He turned and, like a man suddenly coming awake, moved across to the station wagon.

2

'What on earth is precipitation? I just heard it on your wireless.

'Rain,' said Random. 'Everywhere else in the world they have rain, but here in America they have precipitation. Just as we have the wireless and everyone else has the radio.'

'At least we don't use four or five syllables when one or two will do. Seems to be part of their national habit for over-production.'

Random and his father were beginning the meal that Random had cooked for them: steak, salad, no Idaho baked potato and a bottle of burgundy. Nigel Random picked up the bottle of wine, looked at the label and raised his eyebrows in surprise.

'Chambertin '61. You didn't get that at the local supermarket, I take it?'

Random smiled. His father was a wine snob, but his snobbery was mostly academic: he didn't have the money to indulge it. 'I save it for special occasions. Someone gave Harry Jardine two cases of it, but I gather he liked harder stuff. Grace Jardine gave them to me.'

Nigel Random was having trouble controlling his distinguished-looking eyebrows. 'General managers in England don't get that sort of bonus, unless they work for someone like Rothschilds. Must have been for some other sort of services rendered, was it?'

'Services rendered is an unfortunate choice of phrase. I'm in love with the woman and she is with me. How's your steak?'

'Jolly good, actually. Not as good as English beef, of course. Well, here's your health.' Nigel Random raised his glass. 'And the lady's.'

'Aren't you going to ask me about her?'

'You know me better than that. You should, y'know. But if

you want to tell me . . . Rather good salad, this. Much more palatable than those they serve at White's. Or anywhere else in London, for that matter.'

'They bring the lettuces up from California. We fell in love rather quickly, I'm afraid.'

'The best way. Pass the salt.'

'You probably don't know, but she and Jardine hadn't been man and wife, in the accepted sense, for two years or more.'

'Glad to hear that. Wouldn't have thought much of you crawling into a widow's warm bed before the husband was cold. Thanks, I shall. Glad we got rid of Kenneway. Been a pity to waste stuff as good as this on him. Pretends he knows wines, but doesn't really, y'know. You thinking of marrying the gel?'

'If you mean have I asked her – no. I should like to.'

'But there are hurdles, eh? Understand that, especially the way things stand now. Damned unfortunate, all this. Those men tonight, felt sorry for them. Don't think I should want *my* home buried under tons of water. What d'you think of Kenneway?'

'Son to father or employee to board director?'

'My dear boy – ' Nigel Random looked hurt, but only for a moment; he was as afraid of the showing of love as of love itself. But Random saw the quick pain in his father's face and was sorry he had asked the question.

'Righto, just between us. I can't say I like him, but I don't think that would worry him. What's worse, I don't know whether I could trust him. You've heard the old joke about the Hungarian businessman and the revolving door. I think Kenneway would bring his own revolving door with him.'

Nigel Random sipped his wine, but this time there was no look of appreciation on his face. 'Unfortunately, I think you may be right. He's not going to see those men tomorrow, y'know. We go down to Butte first thing, he wants to talk to some chaps from the Anaconda Company, then we fly out of there for Seattle and home.'

'The son-of-a-bitch!'

'Very expressive term, that. The Americans can coin descriptions such as that, then spoil the language with words like precipitation. Extraordinary people, really. They have another expression I rather like. Put one out on a limb.'

'The next one I was about to use. The son-of-a-bitch has put me out on a limb with Peeples, the wall-eyed chap, and those other two delegates. I think they would have asked me to go down to the ranch or Helena with them in the morning. I'm on their side, y'know.'

'I gathered that. Don't blame you. Would be the same if I were your age.'

'But not now?' Random looked across the table at his father, suddenly apprehensive.

Nigel Random gazed at the glass of wine in his hand. Red: the colour of the blood he once would have shed in the cause of duty without question or regret. 'Dreadful thing for a soldier to say, Jack, but I'm afraid I'm neutral in this. Can't afford to be otherwise. I need the job and the money, dear chap.'

'Christ,' said Random, not at all angry but terribly sad. All at once, for the first time in his life, he found himself loving his father. 'I never thought I'd hear you say that.'

'Nor I. The taste of it is ruining this.' He held up the glass, then drank the last of the wine in it. 'Sorry to disappoint you, Jack. In more ways than one. Let me know how things go with you and Mrs Jardine. Beautiful gel, y'know. Haven't seen a beauty like her in years.'

'Not since Mother died?' said Random gently.

'No,' said his father and closed his eyes for a moment against the pain of memory.

It precipitated during the night. Random, troubled in a sleep where his mother and father, as young as he remembered them from his childhood, walked like smiling, kindly ghosts, came awake as the rain beat heavily on the roof. He got up, shut his bedroom window and stood looking out at the golden lances falling against the glow of the street lamp opposite. The air had turned cold and he shivered, but he continued to stand there watching the pools of water growing on the path and the almost grassless lawn. He said a prayer of thanks that one problem, at least, was being washed away. If it rained like this for the next twelve or twenty-four hours he should not have to worry too much about fire up in the forests.

It was still raining, though not so heavily, when he got up at six. He made breakfast for his father and himself, then went out, turning his face up like a child to the benison of the rain, and got out his car.

'I'll drive you down to the ranch,' he told his father.

Nigel Random did not protest, but looked grateful. 'Was afraid that wall-eyed chap or one of his friends might be my driver. Rather not have that.' Then as they drove down the valley and climbed up through Massacre Gap he looked out at the rain and the mist blurring the trees and the mountain tops. 'Be a pity to spoil all this.'

'Are you coming back soon?'

'Possibly. Depends on Kenneway. Shooberg mentioned a shoot here in a couple of weeks, gather it's an annual thing. Be splendid if we could come back for that. We might shoot together.'

'If I'm invited,' said Random with a half-sour grin.

He deposited his father at the ranch, said goodbye to him and Kenneway and turned the car round. He wanted to tell Kenneway what he thought of him for his broken promise to the men of Limbo Valley, but he knew it would have no effect on the chairman. Kenneway was harder than any of the trees that grew in his forests.

When Random got back to Tozabe he put through a call to Grace. He would not have been surprised if Lee had come on the line to tell him she had gone to Missoula or Washington or even Europe; he was beginning to see that if he asked her to marry him, she would be a peripatetic wife, always off on some junket. When she came on the line he said, 'I was thinking how peripatetic you are.'

'What a nasty thing to say to a girl.'

'I thought you might be in Washington.'

'How did you know? I'm going East for a few days, New York and Washington. A sort of introduction what to expect after next month.'

'They're taking it for granted you're going to whip Cliff Pendrick?'

'Don't you think I will?'

'I'm no psephologist.'

'You're talking terribly dirty today. Can you come down and see me? I need a little morale boosting.'

'Who's talking dirty now?'

He went down to Helena in the late afternoon. The rain had stopped and when he came down out of Massacre Gap into the shallow valley that led to the capital the countryside glistened like yellow silk.

He pulled into the driveway of Grace's house and at once recognized the car parked there. He had no desire to see Shooberg just now, but it was too late to back his own car out of the driveway. Lee, in white coat, was coming down from the servants' quarters in the carriage-house.

'Missus say you coming for supper.'

'Is Mr Shooberg here for supper, too?'

'Don't think so. He never come here for supper, not even when Mr Jardine alive. Missus don't like him, I don't think.'

The Chinese were among the world's best, or worst, gossips: he could remember his father, who had spent a year in Hong Kong, telling him that. He wondered what gossip about himself and Grace went on in the carriage-house when Lee and Annie had knocked off work in the big house. It was comforting to know that Grace did not like Shooberg. But that did not mean she would not take his business advice.

But Grace and Shooberg were not talking about Limbo Valley when Random was admitted by Lee. At least not about the valley's future as a mining complex.

'Karl is organizing Harry's annual hunting party. Or it used to be Harry's. I guess it's mine now, since I'll be footing the bill. That's one thing I don't want, Karl. I'll pick up the tab, but I don't want it called Grace Jardine's party or whatever. I'm against killing animals for sport.'

Why have the party then? Random thought. But didn't say it. Shooberg said, 'We won't call it anything, Grace. Everyone will still think of it as Harry's. It was his for so many years.'

'I'd just as soon forget it.'

Shooberg shook his head. 'Wouldn't be wise. All the important men in the state come to it, even some Republicans. They look forward to it, Grace. Gives them the best chance all year to get together.'

Random spoke directly to Grace. 'I suppose Karl has told you about what happened last night up at Tozabe? The feeling is pretty high. Do you think it's wise to put on a hunting party at a time like this?'

It didn't escape him that Grace looked at Shooberg for the

answer. *She may not like him, but she is letting him run the business and political side of her life.*

'It won't make that much difference. You don't understand people around here, Jack – not yet, anyway. Hunting's a way of life here, it ain't just a rich man's sport. The people up at Tozabe will accept it, they been doing it for years. Lot of 'em look forward to it, especially the motel owners and the store-keepers. There's going to be fifty, sixty men come into the town for four days, bringing a lot of money with them. Grace'll pick up the tab for their accommodation, but they buy their own meals and liquor, their ammunition, all that. Adds up to quite a bit. The townsfolk won't say no to that. We ain't class-conscious out here, not like in England.'

I wasn't thinking about class-consciousness and you know it. 'Will Lord Kenneway be coming back for it?'

Shooberg looked at him warily. 'Could be. I understand he don't shoot much – except his opposition.' He evidently felt confident enough to make jokes; he was a different man, no matter how slightly so, from the one Random had met on his first day in Montana. 'Mebbe that's the reason he'll come back. He's going to find we got all the ammunition, though. Right, Grace?'

'Right,' said Grace, smiling at Shooberg and, it seemed to Random, studiously avoiding looking at *him.*

Shooberg, after wishing Grace a good trip to the East – 'Watch out for 'em there. Even you, they might think they got a hick they can put down' – went out to his car and drove away. As soon as the front door closed behind him, Grace went into Random's arms and kissed him hungrily.

He winced and drew back. 'Watch the lip. Find somewhere else to kiss.'

'I will later. Not down here.'

'I hope you don't have those sort of thoughts on the floor of the Senate.'

'You were supposed to call me. I was expecting to hear from you last night and the night before.'

'You'd better get a private line in, just for you and me. Trying to get you is like trying to get on to the queen.'

'The queen? Oh, you mean *your* queen. Ah no, I'm more available than that. To you, anyway.' She kissed him on the cheek, then gently disengaged herself from his arms. 'Was it bad last night?'

'The demonstration? It was ugly enough. It could have got worse.'

'It's only a minority.'

'That's what everyone keeps saying. It's like saying snake-bite isn't as bad as having your head blown off. It can still be pretty fatal, though.'

'Who's the ringleader?'

'There are several, not all of them company workers. Their spokesman is Chris Peeples, the sawmill foreman.'

'Can't you fire him?'

He looked at her steadily. 'I'll forget you said that.'

'I'm sorry. I don't know what made me say it.'

'I do. You're suffering from your own form of snake-bite, Grace. You're starting to think like a real boss. Go on the way you are and you could have held your own with Clark, Daly and Heinze.'

She looked at him as steadily as he had looked at her. 'I'll forget *you* said *that*. Let's go in to supper.'

They had dinner, sitting close to each other at one end of the long table. They both did their best to forget the sour note that had come between them out in the living room and gradually the mood warmed again between them. Lee served them, his impassive face occasionally split by what looked like a benevolent smile.

'He approves of you,' Grace said. 'The best silver, the candles. So does Annie. She went out of her way tonight when she knew who was coming for supper. Beef Stroganoff. Not steak, you notice?'

'I thought it looked different. Very good, too.' It wasn't, but he gave Annie marks for trying. And for approving of him. He couldn't afford to look any gift friends in the mouth just now.

They had coffee at the dinner table. Leaning forward, her elbows on the table, her head close to his, the candlelight soft on her face, she said, 'Bonnie Mackintosh has been to see me again.'

He was surprised at her remark. He had been savouring the intimacy of the moment, the lover's haven of candlelight. He didn't straighten up, but his spoon seemed to pause of its own accord in its stirring of his coffee. 'Why?'

'Maybe I shouldn't tell you this. She was having an affair with Harry.'

He finished stirring his coffee, put the spoon down gently in the saucer. 'I know.'

'When did you see her?'

He caught the slight rasp of jealousy in her voice, and he smiled. 'Don't be like that. I'm just her Dutch uncle.'

'I'll bet. I mean, I bet she doesn't see herself as your Dutch niece. Go on.'

He grinned, pressed her hand. Then he told her everything he had seen on the day of his arrival in the valley, of Bonnie coming to tell him she had received her letters in the mail, of how he had done his best to keep her name out of the investigation.

'Now I come to think about it, I suppose I did it as much out of regard for her father as anything else. No, I amend that. I did it out of regard for him, because I like and respect him. But I did it more for you. I could imagine what they would have said if it had come out that Harry had been having an affair with the Governor's daughter.'

'It could still come out. She got two more letters in the mail on Monday. And I think I know who's sending them to her.'

'Who?'

There was a ring at the front-door bell. She sat up, frowning in annoyance, took her hand away from his. 'Damn! I was hoping we wouldn't be disturbed tonight.'

He sat back, equally annoyed but resigned. 'Another bloody committeeman, I suppose.'

She smiled placatingly at him, pressed his hand again. 'Don't be like that, darling, please. If it is, I'll send him away.'

Then Lee came to the doorway. 'A visitor, missus. I took her into the living room. Mrs Coulson.'

3

'I'll stay here,' he said. 'Lee can bring me another Drambuie.'

'I shan't be long.' She was back within two minutes. 'I think you better come in, darling.'

He followed her without a word across the hall into the living room. Pet Coulson sat in a chair, knees close together, her hands clutched like entangled dead birds in her lap. Her shoulders were hunched, as if she were shivering, and at first he thought she was drunk. Then he saw that she was sober, the first time he had seen her completely so.

She looked up at him, sighed, then straightened up. 'I told Grace I didn't mind if you heard what I had to say. I know how things are between you and her.'

'Jim has left her,' said Grace.

Random said nothing, just nodded. Pet Coulson abruptly stood up, her body and limbs stiff as if her joints had suddenly rusted, and began to move about the room. Random was not sure how old she was, probably in her early forties, but this evening she looked aged, the hollows of her neck already shadowed by the years ahead.

'He's moved into the Montana Club. It'll be all over town by breakfast time tomorrow. You know what it's like in this place. Gossip is the principal crop.' A hint of the old dry humour remained.

'Why has he left you?' Random asked. 'That is, if you want to tell us.'

'Oh, I've already told Grace. Because of her. He told me he's in love with her, has been for years. Did you know that?'

Random felt his lip, 'I'd guessed it.'

'You fought over her, didn't you?'

'How did you know that?' He glanced at Grace, but she shook her head, as puzzled as he was. 'He didn't tell you, did he?'

'No, I put two and two together. I was never very good at maths, but I can add two and two.' Her voice was thin, with a brittle edge to it; she sounded on the verge of hysteria. 'He said something about you, I can't remember what it was. Then I saw the big bruise on his ribs.'

'I must have got in one good blow,' said Random with satisfaction.

'You must've hit him real hard. I'm glad. You should've broken the bastard's jaw.' She clenched her hands into fists, as if she wished she could have added to the blows. 'I asked him about it and he told me he'd had a fight with you. Then I asked him if it was over Grace.'

'It might have been better if you hadn't,' said Grace quietly. 'He might still be at home with you, if you hadn't.'

'I don't want him home!' Then she shut her eyes and sat down suddenly; it seemed fortunate that there was a chair right behind her because she gave no indication that she knew it was there. 'Yes, I do. Oh Grace!'

Grace moved to her, put her arms round her and gently stroked the blonde head. The two women were beneath a wall-bracket light and Random could see the grey in Pet's fair hair: the night was being cruel to her, stripping her in every way. He looked at Grace and marvelled at the tenderness in her beautiful face as she comforted the other woman; yet an hour ago she had suggested he fire Chris Peeples, someone else whose secure life was threatened. A part of his mind wondered if he would ever fully understand her.

'Cry it out of you, honey, if it helps.' Grace had another voice: rougher, warmer, gentler, younger. Random was not to know it, but it was the voice of the honyocker girl who had comforted her despairing mother. 'It don't harm you. Go on, honey, weep all you want.'

But there was still some strength left in Pet Coulson. She dried her eyes, blew her nose, looked up at Grace, pressed the latter's hand. 'I should hate you, Grace. But I know for a fact you never gave Jim any encouragement. You never really liked him, did you? Oh, don't be embarrassed. I know lots of people don't like him, can't stand him. It was the same with Harry, if you don't mind the truth. I couldn't stand *him*.'

'I don't mind at all. Not tonight, just between us.'

Pet nodded. 'But we loved them, didn't we? Jack wouldn't understand that, probably. Men never do, unless they're the bastards we love. Then they take it for granted. You loved Harry for a long time, even though he was a son-of-a-bitch. I still love Jim – ' For a moment it seemed that she was going to break down again; but she sniffed hard and kept her chin up. 'And he's a son-of-a-bitch, too.'

'What are you going to do?'

'I don't know. Stay in the house, I guess. Fortunately the kids have gone back to school.' Random knew that the Coulsons had two children, a girl who was at school somewhere in Colorado and a boy who was a freshman at, of all places, Harvard. Pet looked at Grace. 'What we have to do is keep your name out of it.'

'I'd like it if we could. But that's unimportant beside what's happened between you and Jim. I wish I could do something to help, but I guess it would be better if I did nothing.'

'You'll have to go on seeing him. I mean in business. Especially with all that's going on now.' She looked at Random. 'You fought about that, too, didn't you?'

'He appears to have let his hair down to you. To tell you the truth, I don't really know if there was any specific reason for our fighting. Perhaps he just thought the English were trying to take Washington again.'

'That'd be too subtle for Jim.' Pet looked at Grace and managed a smile.

'He just doesn't like me,' Random said. 'And, for your sake, I'm sorry to say the feeling is mutual.'

'Well – ' Pet Coulson looked about her, as if she were all at once wondering why she had come. 'Well, I better go. You know why I came, don't you, Grace? I just wanted you to know I don't blame you. And I wanted you to know it before you started hearing gossip from other quarters. I don't suppose anyone would believe we could be friends.'

'Could be?'

Pet was looking into one of the French mirrors, repairing her face. She paused for a moment, as if she had seen a stranger there. Then, not looking at all reassured, she spoke to Grace again. 'We've never been real friends, Grace. You're easy to meet, but hard to know. Isn't that right, Jack?'

Random took refuge in his half-smile, one eye on Grace, who was silently demanding an answer. 'Right.'

'I don't hold it against you, Grace. I don't believe in easy friendships any more than you do. The world is full of those, none of them adding up to anything. But we could be closer – '

'We will be,' said Grace; and looked at Random and gave her own half-smile. 'Even Jack will admit we're a little closer than when we first met.'

Pet laughed: it was a trifle strained, but there was some humour in it. 'I'll bet. And you look better for it. Both of you.'

She said goodbye to Random and Grace took her to the door. The two women had something further to say to each other; it was two or three minutes before Grace came back to the living room. The doors to the dining room had been closed, but they could hear the faint clink of plates as Lee and Annie cleared the table.

'Do you want more coffee?'

'After that, I think I'd rather have a Scotch.'

'Help yourself. Well, what do you think of her news? I suppose the writing's been on the wall for some time, for a long time. But I thought it would be over her drinking, not over me. The damned fool!'

'Don't get too upset. It's their problem, not yours. He's not going to come up here demanding you choose him or me. He's stupid in some ways, but he's not *that* stupid.'

'I don't know. He's either very clever or very stupid. He's the one who sent Bonnie those letters of hers.'

He raised an eyebrow, took a sip of his drink. 'That was something that hadn't occurred to me. About him, I mean.'

'Why would he do it? He's not trying to blackmail her or anything. Not so far.'

'Have you any proof he sent them?'

'No. Nothing I could confront him with. But he was the one who cleaned out Harry's desk – and I bet that was where Harry kept the letters. It's Jim, right enough. What's worse – '

She paused and he finished for her: 'You think he murdered Harry? I've thought so for some time. He had plenty of motive.'

'You mean me? I asked him about it down in Havre, it was just something that popped into my mind. He denied it – ' Then she frowned. 'No, I don't think he did deny it. He just sort of avoided it. He's got the temper to have done it. I don't know whether he would do it in cold blood.' She shuddered, as if her own blood had run cold.

'Wryman thinks the murder may not have been done in cold blood. They think Harry was shot with his own gun. So there could have been a fight – Harry might even have been trying to shoot *him* – '

'Oh God.' She laid her head against his chest. They stood in the centre of the room, the French mirrors reflecting them into an infinity of love and what looked like despair. 'What are we going to do?'

It was the first time he had ever heard her confess any kind of defeat. 'Are you afraid of him?'

She lifted her head. 'No.' She sounded surprised that he had asked the question. 'If you mean that he'll try to kill – No, of course I'm not. He won't kill anyone else. But he shouldn't be allowed to get away with killing Harry. But how can we go to Wryman, tell him what we suspect? What we *know*. There's Bonnie to consider. And Hugh and Pet – '

'That's the bugger of it,' he said, talking to himself as much as to her. 'If nobody else was involved – But it can't go on like this indefinitely. Sooner or later we're going to have to give Wryman some sort of hint.'

'After the election.' She drew away from him; in the mirrors he saw dozens of them come apart. 'I don't want any of it to come out before then.'

4

He did not stay the night. With Shooberg's car in the driveway when he had arrived, he had not brought his overnight bag into the house. So she did not know he had come prepared to stay the night, did not press him when he said he had to be at the upper end of Limbo Valley by seven in the morning to check on a new cut. They did go to bed, but it was unsatisfactory and both of them knew it, though neither of them commented on it. But at least their love-making did not end in the acrimony that both of them had begun to fear.

The grandfather clock in the hall was striking eleven when he kissed her goodnight, still careful of his cut lip. Once, during their love-making, she had forgotten and crushed her mouth against his and he had had to stop himself from crying out. It was still sore and his kiss was like that of a tentative schoolboy saying goodnight to his first date.

'When will you get back from the East?'

'Tuesday night, I hope. I'll be at the Pierre in New York and with the Mountfields in Georgetown. That's Washington.'

'You'd be surprised how much I know about Washington.'

'Since when?'

'Since Mountfield asked you that night to run for the Senate.'

'You're a deep one. But I'm glad. It means I can go on discovering new things about you right into our old age.'

'Likewise, as the natives say.'

Chapter Ten

I

Grace liked Washington, fell in love with Georgetown. Congress was not in session and she felt the charge of it only by osmosis: the sense of government that hung in the air like the electric currents of two hundred years, the sharp, heady taste of power that permeated the Senate committee rooms like the after-effects of a drug. But it was enough. The corridors and chambers, almost empty when Silver Mountfield took her through them, were more evocative to her, because she could see them clearly, could stand back from them even while in them, than if they had been filled with talking, bargaining, gossiping members. Before she left Washington she knew, for the first time, how much she wanted to belong to it.

Constance Mountfield, a veteran of thirty years in Washington, showed her Embassy Row, Chevy Chase, Georgetown, took her through the various districts and showed her the houses of the influential and the famous.

'It'll be a whole new world for you, sweetie.' Everyone was *sweetie* to Connie Mountfield; unlike her husband, she hadn't an enemy in the world. She had called six Presidents *sweetie* and only strict herd-riding by her husband had prevented her from calling the Shah of Persia, Emperor Hirohito and Queen Elizabeth the same. 'But you'll be all right. We'll look after you,

Mark and me. God willing, that is. We're both getting on and we never know which election is going to be the last. That's the Vice-President's little house, as his sweetie calls it. I went to school in a house smaller than that.' Then later she said, 'Now that house there – do you like it?'

'Oh, I just love it!' It was a house of character, standing in about an acre of land, big without being too big, *rich*-looking: but rich in the Eastern way, restrained, dignified. Suddenly Grace thought about the house back on Harrison and was ashamed for what she all at once felt about it.

'Well, sweetie, I know it's going to be put on the market. It belongs to a Senator from New England who's not going to be re-elected. He'll go back home and he's going to need the money he'll get for that place. He wants half a million, but he'll take four-fifty. I'd buy it, sweetie. Make an offer for it while you're here.'

'It's an awful lot of money, Connie.'

'You've *got* an awful lot of money, if you'll forgive me being rude. And Mark tells me you're going to have an awful lot more. If you want, Grace, you're going to be in this town a long, long time. My advice is, if you can afford it, live in comfort and style. The voters never give you extra votes for trying to live like them.'

'Won't it be, well, ostentatious, buying a house like that as soon as I arrive in Washington?'

'Sweetie, in this town, with your looks and your money, which everyone is going to envy, if the worst they say about you is that you were ostentatious, you'll be lucky. In any case, they *expect* us 'uns from the West to be ostentatious if we've got any money at all. Anyone from the East, though, they come down here and spend money to buy themselves a house like that, that's all right. That's not being ostentatious, it's just transferring their life style. Thumb your nose at them, in a ladylike way, of course, grow old gracefully and in time to come they'll point you out with pride to the tourists, like they do my Mark. The shine wears off ostentation, sweetie, and then they start calling it the glory of the past. It's like that, been like it, throughout history. I'd like to know what the neighbours said when that Egyptian king, whatever his name was, built the Pyramids. It's like that back home in Helena, on the West Side, only in a smaller way.'

Before she left Washington Grace offered four hundred and twenty-five thousand dollars for the house, had it accepted and paid a deposit. She called Random twice, told him she missed him and loved him, asked about Jim and Pet Coulson, said she hoped he could come down to Helena Tuesday night when she got back. But she did not tell him about the house and she was not sure why.

She went to New York and went on *Meet the Press*, the Mike Wallace show and *Today*. Johnny Carson did not want her when he learned she was going on the other shows, but said he would be glad to have her when she came to Washington as a Senator. Her appearances were noted in the television columns where several critics, all male, said she looked the most beautiful politician since Cleopatra, had wit and poise and she showed the political ability, like that of a veteran, to sound intelligent while talking but saying nothing. On both *Meet the Press* and the Mike Wallace show she was asked about the growing opposition to her project in the Limbo Valley and how she felt about the opinion polls which were showing surprising gains for her opponent, her ex-husband Cliff Pendrick. She was asked what interest, if any, she had in foreign affairs; what she thought about the future place of women in national affairs; and if it was true that she had once said that in America, a man's country, beauty was no handicap to a candidate, so long as the candidate wasn't a man. She answered all the questions, as the critics said the next morning, with wit and poise and, on the deeper questions a refreshing lack of clichés if nothing else.

Monday afternoon she left the Pierre, went to Bergdorf-Goodman's and bought herself an entire new winter wardrobe. For two hours she forgot Washington, Helena, Limbo Valley and even Jack; she indulged herself as a woman, buying with herself and other women, and not a single man, in mind. She bought nothing *ostentatious*: she chose suits, dresses, gowns, coats that were elegantly severe, confident that she had enough beauty to carry them off. The looks of approval from the sales women told her she was right in her choice. She would show the snobbish hostesses of Washington a thing or two in taste.

Then she went down to Abercrombie and Fitch and bought Jack a pair of binoculars to replace the pair that had been smashed when that crazy boy Yertsen had almost killed them.

'These are the best we have,' said the sales clerk. 'Leitz. They are five hundred and twenty dollars.'

'I'll take them.'

'Does your husband hunt? Perhaps you would like to see our collection of guns?'

She shuddered inwardly. 'No, just the glasses will do. I'll pay by credit card.'

The clerk looked at the name on the card, then at her. 'Of course, Mrs Jardine. I should have recognized you. I saw you on TV. Would you care to open an account with us?'

'Yes,' she said on the spur of the moment: as Connie Mountfield had said, she could be here in the East a long, long time. 'It may be useful.'

She went out of the store on to Madison Avenue feeling like a young girl who had just been asked for three dances in a row before the band had even struck up: that is, she told herself, if young girls these days were *asked* for a dance. It was one thing to be recognized in Helena – but here in *New York*! She walked up Madison in the shining October air, her simple egotistical pleasure showing in her face, feeling like all the young girls she had once read about in a story by Irwin Shaw. Men, New York men, tired, jaundiced, slowed their hurrying strides to look back at her, wondering to themselves why all women, particularly their wives, couldn't look like *that*.

Tuesday she flew back to Helena, taking the binoculars with her and leaving the new clothes to be air-freighted to her within the week. Kerry O'Toole and Lee met her at the airport in the Lincoln and drove her to the house. There had been a three-inch fall of snow at the weekend; the surrounding mountains were already set white for winter and patches of snow lay like white shadows in hollows beside the road. The air was crisp and crystal-clear after the air in the East and the sun was dying as a silver blaze behind the Divide. She was glad to be back, was eager to see Jack again. And yet, for the first time ever on returning here, there was a feeling of let-down.

'Mr Shooberg and Coulson and Chartwell are waiting at the house for you.' Kerry was looking at her cautiously, respectfully appraising her. 'You look, I don't know, *different*. Did you enjoy it? I mean, *everything*?'

'Everything. I think I'm going to like Washington very much. I hope you will, too. And Lee.'

'I know I'll love it,' said Kerry. 'Does that mean you want me to stay on with you?'

'Of course. I thought you understood that.' There had been no reaction from Lee and she leaned slightly to one side to catch his face in the driving mirror. 'You haven't said anything, Lee. Don't tell me you and Annie haven't discussed the thought of going to Washington?'

'Oh, we talked about it, missus. Annie, she say she be happy anywhere, long's the comfort's like she got here.'

'I promise her all the comfort in the world there. But what about you?'

Lee seemed to have to concentrate on negotiating the traffic in an almost traffic-less street. 'It comf'table here.'

But Grace knew at once what he meant: it was safe here. She had no idea how old he was, forty-five, fifty-five; but he was not young enough to want to start a new life in a new town. He would probably meet many more Chinese in Washington than he ever met here in Helena, but they would make him feel no more secure. Here he had arrived at an acceptance of being a minority and knew the boundaries of other people's prejudices.

'Well, we'll talk about it some more,' she said lamely.

Coulson, Shooberg and Ab Chartwell were in her study. All of them had been smoking and the air was thick and acrid. She said hallo, then went to the windows and pushed them wide open.

'Better put your coats on if you're going to feel the fresh air.' She was wearing a mink coat, but she took it off, handed it to Kerry. 'Put it up in my bedroom, please. There's a pink cardigan in my sweater closet – would you bring it down? It's going to be a little chilly in here for a while.'

She winked at Kerry and saw the answering gleam in the girl's eyes. Both knew there would always be mild skirmishes in the war of the sexes, even among those on the same political ticket. Kerry, straight-faced, said, 'Shall I bring in the Fresh-Air spray?'

'Never mind. I see Mr Chartwell is already doing his anti-pollution job.'

Kerry left the room and Ab Chartwell, shaking his head, was slapping at the smoke with a newspaper. 'You're going to have to get used to this, Grace. Don't you know politics are born in a smoke-filled room?'

'Not my rooms, Ab. From now on there'll be no smoking in any room where I have to sit and confer with you men.'

246

'What did they do to you in Washington? Offer you a chance to run for President or something?'

'I may do just that in ten years' time, Ab. Now what's been happening while I've been away?'

'Well, the temperature dropped about twenty degrees,' said Coulson, unconsciously humourous. 'Jesus H. Christ, let's shut the windows!'

'A few more minutes won't hurt you.' Kerry returned with the pink cashmere cardigan. Grace slipped it on and waited till the girl had gone across to her own office. Then she looked at Chartwell and Shooberg ignoring Coulson. 'I read the polls. The temperature is not the only thing that's dropped. So has my popularity.'

'Nothing to really worry about,' said Shooberg, his empty holder, an empty gesture of defiance, still stuck in his teeth. He was sitting closest to the window, but if he was feeling the cold he did not show it. 'You still got about ten points on him.'

'I hear the ecology people are still making a lot of noise.' Grace looked at Chartwell, still avoiding looking at Coulson. 'What are we going to do about it?'

'Ignore it,' said Chartwell, wriggling his bony shoulders as if feeling the cold. 'You got to start spelling out how much money is going to come into the state. Tell 'em you are going to suggest to Hugh Mackintosh that the state corporation taxes should be increased – not much, but a little. That'll raise a howl from Anaconda and the Power Company and some of the others, but it should help take care of the charge that you're going to be the one who'll benefit most. People in this state have never loved the bosses, but you'll be the first who ever voluntarily suggested you should be taxed more.'

Chartwell, obviously chilled, didn't stay long. When he had gone Grace turned to Shooberg, Coulson and the problem of Limbo Valley. 'Any word from Lord Kenneway?'

'He and Sir Nigel are coming on Friday. Can we shut the window now?'

Grace smiled: it was almost as if she had discovered a weakness at last in Shooberg. 'Go ahead.'

But it was Coulson who jumped up and slammed down the windows. So far he had said nothing, but Grace was determined that she was not going to show that she had noticed his sullen mood.

She had arrived back as airborne by euphoria as she had been by the plane that had brought her home. But now the feeling of let-down that had hit her as she had stepped off the plane had increased; she had glimpsed the fruits of victory, but the battles still had to be fought. She pulled her cardigan a little tighter about her, though she did not feel the cold. She only half-listened to the further reports Shooberg had; but she was aware that Coulson, too, seemed to be only half-attentive to what was being said. At last Shooberg stood up.

'That's it, Grace. You coming, Jim?'

Coulson shifted awkwardly in his chair. 'I got a few things to discuss with Grace – about the hunt party. I'll see you tomorrow.'

'Yeah.' Shooberg's face was expressionless. 'Sure.'

He left with an abrupt goodbye, his hat already on his bald head before he had got out of the room. Coulson took a pack of cigarettes out of his pocket, looked at his hand as if he had only just recognized what was in it, and put the pack away again. He got up, went to the drink cabinet in one corner, then again seemed to realize he had done something automatically, something that might not be condoned. He looked over his shoulder at Grace.

'I could do with a drink.'

She squeezed out a little pity for him. 'Me, too. A small Scotch.'

'That's not your usual.'

'I don't feel usual this evening.'

He brought her the drink, sat down opposite her and took a long swallow from his own stiff bourbon. He sucked in a deep breath, then said, 'Pet came to see you last week. She told you about us.'

'Have you gone back to her?'

'Nope.' His quiet, sullen mood had reduced his usual garrulity; he sounded like one of the hands out at the ranch. 'Nor planning to.'

'It's your problem, Jim. But I think you're being stupid.'

'You think it's just my problem?' He looked down at the glass cupped in his two big hands. 'What about you?'

She shook her head, keeping her patience. The room, either the emotional atmosphere or the central heating, seemed suddenly oppressive and she had to stop herself from getting up and flinging open the windows again. She looked at him, wondering what had been in his mind when he had killed Harry. It was still an act that she found difficult to imagine, yet she had convinced herself it had actually happened. She marvelled that she could sit here opposite him, knowing what he had done, and yet not be afraid of him. But she could not let it remain as it was: she would have to tell County Attorney Wryman, let him close the case and take Jim Coulson out of her life. But not till after the election.

Coulson said, slowly becoming garrulous again as the bourbon loosed him and his tongue, 'I didn't want to feel this way about you – '

(As if being in love, she thought, was a matter of wanting or not wanting. She listened to his selfish conceit, wondering how many men knew what real love was all about).

'It only started – properly, I mean – when I saw you and Harry weren't hitting it off any more. Before that, well, it was just, you know, like any guy feels for a good-looking woman.'

'You thought I'd be a good lay?'

'Well, yeah, I guess that was it. No offence. It was a compliment in a way.'

'Women love compliments like that. They're lying down all over the world, legs spread wide apart in gratitude.' She put her drink down on her desk. She noticed that the desk didn't look as if it had been dusted while she'd been away. She'd have a word with Annie about that. 'I don't know how I've got the self-control to sit here and listen to you, Jim. Maybe it's because I feel so damn sorry for Pet, I'm doing it as a favour to her. Or maybe it's just that I'm so tired of you I can't even shout at you. Just go, Jim. Go back to Pet, go to the Montana Club or just go to hell. But don't ever open your mouth to me again about how you feel for me. You and I are finished – as friends and as business associates. I'll give you a week to make up your mind what you tell Karl. He'll probably guess why you're resigning, but what you tell him will do as your public statement. You can talk with Karl about what it will cost me to get rid of you. Whatever it is, it will be worth it. Goodbye, Jim.'

She hadn't meant to say as much as she had, but it was done now. Coulson stood up, put his glass down deliberately on the small side table. She waited for the explosion of fury, but it did not come. He looked at her steadily (and sadly? The image came to her mind of a man staring in farewell at his dead love. And she shuddered), then he went unhurriedly out of the room and a moment later she heard him close the front door gently behind him. At least he went with dignity, she thought, surprised.

Kerry came to the door. 'Can I get you something? You look peaked.'

Grace held up her almost untouched Scotch. 'Just turn out the lights, Kerry. I'd like to sit in the dark for a while. After a certain age there are times when darkness is a kindness.'

'Not always,' said Kerry. 'I know a lot of old people who are afraid of the dark, they think of it as part of dying. I was a social worker for a year.' But she turned off the lights. 'That better?'

'At least I don't feel as if I'm dying.' She heard the girl's tiny gasp and she looked towards the silhouette against the light in the hall outside. 'I'm sorry, Kerry. I shouldn't burden you with my mood.'

'We all have them. You don't have to be a certain age – ' Then she giggled in embarrassment. 'Sorry.'

'Go home, Kerry,' said Grace with good humour. 'Before you start behaving like a social worker towards me.'

After Kerry had gone she sat in the dark for almost half an hour. It was the longest time she had spent alone with her thoughts in weeks; even the flight back from Washington had had its distractions, other passengers recognizing her and wanting to talk to her, that had stopped her mind from being entirely her own. But the discipline of darkness and quiet brought no clear pattern to her thinking. Her thoughts blew like leaves through a forest where every tree, close to, was familiar but the forest itself was strange and she had no sense of direction. The metaphor of the leaves and trees crossed her mind and she wondered why. A honyocker girl from the Great Plains shouldn't think of forests, except as havens from the heat and drought. But Limbo Valley was no haven . . . Her head jerked and she sat up. She had begun to doze, dying for a while in the darkness, just like people of a certain age.

She got up, switched on all the lights, scouring the room with illumination. She picked up the phone, called Jack. 'I want to see you, darling. *Now.* I'll be at the ranch in half an hour.'

She rang for Lee, told him where she was going. 'I'll be there with Mr Random, Lee.' It no longer mattered what the servants thought. 'Call me only if it's important, but don't tell anyone where I am.'

'You want me to drive you out, missus? Could be some ice on the road.'

'I'll be careful, Lee. I'm in a very careful mood tonight.'

She did drive with care, taking her time, but even so she was at the ranch half an hour before Random arrived. She kissed him and said, 'I was beginning to worry. That you might've gone off the road or something.'

'I was waiting on a call from my father. He rang today while I was out and said he'd ring back at eight o'clock. He's bringing his guns out for the shoot. How was Washington?'

'I loved it.'

He changed the subject; or perhaps he thought she had said all there was to be said about it. 'I've eaten. Have you?'

'No. I'll cook myself some bacon and eggs. Mrs Ullman keeps the freezer stocked.' She led him into the kitchen. 'Is your father going to stay with you for the hunt?'

'He wants to. I gather you and Kenneway are going to be talking while we're out shooting.'

He sounded constrained, but she skirted round his mood; it seemed this was a night for moods. She gave him the binoculars. He looked at them, then looked at them again more closely. Then he shook his head.

'You shouldn't give me presents like this. These are about the best there are.'

'The best for the best. Or should I sing that?'

He put them to his eyes, looked around the kitchen, directed them straight at her. 'You're just a blur. A beautiful blur.'

'Are you cross with me? I just felt so good yesterday in New York. I splurged on myself, a whole new winter wardrobe. Then I thought it was only fair to splurge on the man I love.'

He put the binoculars back in their expensive case, kissed her gently on the mouth. 'Only because I love you. But never again, right?'

'Right.' But she wished now she had chosen something else,

something more in keeping with his own pocket. The house in Washington suddenly began to look – ostentatious?

She cooked herself supper and he sat opposite her in the big kitchen and drank coffee, saying little but looking at her with what she recognized, and was thankful for, was love. Whatever was troubling him, and tonight she was afraid to ask him what it was, he still loved her.

They went to bed like a married couple, taking their time about undressing, cleaning their teeth, turning down the central heating: winding up the day as they wound up their watches. Random even glanced at one of the books on the table on his side of the bed.

'Do you want to read for a while?' The book was one by Will James, the cowboy author: it had been a favourite of Harry's, when he bothered to read at all.

'Not unless you do.'

She looked at the books on her table: more political education, given her by Ab Chartwell. 'No.'

It was almost as if they were putting off the act of love. But then she lay back on her pillow, turned towards him. 'We're going to have to stop doing this. For a while, anyway.'

'The servants?'

'No, the voters.' She smiled; but held his exploring hand. 'People know about us. Helena is a small town and it likes to think of itself as respectable. They'd like its first woman Senator to be thought of as respectable, too.'

His hand rested on her hip, a safe respectable spot. 'Till after the election then?'

Unless you want to marry me now. But she couldn't bring herself to propose. More than just their love was here in bed with them, there were too many other pressures. 'We'll celebrate on Election Night.'

He smiled, but his face was too close to hers and she could not tell whether it was the old half-mocking smile. 'I'll get the last vote.'

'Leave the light on. I like to look at you.'

'Love in the dark,' he said, 'is for the old and the ugly.'

It was a cruel thing to say and so unlike him. But she said nothing, just yielded herself to him. She knew from experience how much cruelty was spoken in bed, including *this* bed.

In the middle of the night she got up, put on her gown and went out to the living room. She stood at the window wall and looked out on the blue-pewter night. The Big Belt mountains were a white frieze to the blue, sequined curtain of the sky; ponds of snow lay in pockets all down the valley floor. Snow rimmed Harry's grave like a border of kinnikinnick; it struck her that not once since he had died had she put flowers on his grave. He had never been a sentimentalist and he would not have wanted them; but it would not have hurt her to have made the gesture. But she knew it would have been hypocritical, done to impress the people on the ranch, the servants; but hypocrisy, she hoped, had never been one of her failings. Or so Harry had told her, with that harsh booming laugh that she had come to detest. She looked around the big room, at the trophies ghostly in its gloom, and all at once felt his presence again. But didn't miss him, was glad, without being malicious, that he was gone.

Harry, just don't laugh at me, that's all I ask. But knew that the son-of-a-bitch, if he was capable of it where he was, would be doing just that.

2

The hunters began arriving on Friday morning, coming early, like refugees anxious to escape whatever plagued them in the outside, workaday world. Grace was coming up in the afternoon to greet them, but most of them were making their own welcome by midday, aided and abetted by the grateful liquor-store owners.

Random's father arrived just before lunch, driven up by one of the ranch hands from the Lazy J.

'Kenneway's down at the ranch with Mrs Jardine,' he said as he got out of the pick-up, taking his bags and his gun out of the back of it. 'Just the two of them. Sort of summit meeting, I suppose. Felt I wasn't wanted, so I came on up here.'

Later he sat at the dining-room table, newspapers spread out on it as protection, and worked on the guns, his own and Random's, with loving care.

'You needn't have done that,' Random said. 'I was going to do it this evening.'

'It gives me pleasure. Sort of takes me back to the time I

spent in India, though I had a servant to do it in those days.'
He paused for a moment, looking across the years, continents and
oceans. 'I was never really happy there, y'know. The Indian
Army chaps always looked on us fellows on secondment as outsiders. Suppose you sometimes feel like that here?'

'Sort of. Though I don't think I could compare Coulson and
company to Indian Army wallahs.'

'No, I suppose not. How's Mrs Jardine? Looked jolly pretty
today. Absolutely beautiful gel. Everything that's happening to
her seems to be doing wonders for her.'

'Everything?'

'Well, you for a start, I suppose.' Nigel Random looked carefully down the barrel of the Royal ejector; he was not accustomed
to discussing his sons' women with them. 'Then the certainty of
going to Washington, to the Senate. Must be rather like going to
the Lords – though I wouldn't fancy *that*, m'self. Better paid, of
course – the Senate, I mean. Though she shouldn't need any of
it. She's a rich woman now, I gather, but she's going to be
awfully rich pretty soon.'

'You talk as if it's a foregone conclusion.'

'That's up to Ian Kenneway. But he's told me how much money
may come out of this scheme. Mind boggles, I'm afraid. Your
lady, for her part, could be worth something like three hundred
million dollars, just out of this valley alone.' He peered up the
barrel of the gun again, then set the gun down on the newspapers.
'I see your mind boggles, too.'

'I had no idea it would run to that much – '

'It's true, I'm afraid. Ian has done his homework, always does.
Had those talks with the chaps down in Butte, y'know. That
much money would put the bloom on any woman, I suppose.
Sorry. Didn't mean to sound like that.'

Random had never really concerned himself with any specific
thoughts about Grace's wealth. He had been annoyed that she
had spent so much on him when she had bought him the Leitz
binoculars, but that had only been because he would never be
able even remotely to afford a reciprocal gift. He was no stranger
to the climate of wealth; it was just that he and his parents had
arrived at the tail-end of the Random fortune. At school and in
his army days and during his marriage he had been surrounded
by money; one took for granted that some people were fortunate

254

enough to have it and one let it go at that. He had never been interested in being rich and he had never envied anyone their wealth; and being like that, it had never occurred to him to measure anyone else's money. Least of all Grace's.

But now he was confronted with riches that he could not ignore, that he could not take for granted. That he could barely *comprehend*. That, he suspected, he would never comprehend. And so would never be comfortable with.

'I am beginning to think we may be naïve,' said his father, almost as if reading his thoughts.

But before he could ask his father to elaborate on that, there was a knock on the front door. Random got up and went to it. Bonnie and Governor Mackintosh stood there, the latter with two guns slung over his shoulder and a large valise on the verandah floor beside him.

'They tell me I'm billeted with you,' said Mackintosh, smiling, but regrettably sounding like a soldier in an occupied area. 'Couldn't be happier.'

Random looked at Bonnie. 'Is your corporal billeted with me, too?'

She flapped a reassuring hand, making a face at him. 'Relax. I'm staying with Mr Judson and his wife. I couldn't intrude on this all-male weekend. I just drove Dad up here, that was all.'

'In her MG,' said Mackintosh. 'Hair-raising.'

Random took them into the house and introduced them to his father. The two older men hit it off at once and Nigel Random looked appreciatively at Bonnie, who was dressed in a bright red sweater and plaid slacks and had her hair drawn back in a chignon.

'Last Governor's daughter I met was in Hong Kong years ago. Looked rather like his horse. If she'd looked like you, m'dear, I think I might have applied to be his ADC.'

Something's happened to the old man, Random thought, or I never really knew him. But Bonnie flashed her most brilliant smile. 'Sir Nigel, you could teach your son a thing or two. He's the slowest man with a compliment I've ever met.'

'Used to be that way m'self,' said Nigel Random with a glance at his son. 'Left it too late, I'm afraid.'

Random caught the note of real regret in his father's voice; and thought of his mother who had died too early for the compliments. Bonnie, too, seemed to sense that the older Random's remark had suddenly touched a sad memory; she turned away and said something to her father, leaving the Randoms to paper over their secret regret, whatever it was. Random picked up Mackintosh's valise and led the Governor out to one of the spare bedrooms.

'I understand Lord Kenneway is closeted down at the Lazy J with Grace.' Mackintosh noticed Random's look of surprise and he smiled. 'I have my intelligence corps. How's it going between them?'

'I have no idea.'

'I thought your father might have given you a hint.'

Random shook his head. Then, one ally to another, he said, 'Hugh, do you know how much money this mining project could be worth?'

Mackintosh nodded, chewed on his lip. 'You've heard, too? Money really does talk, doesn't it? In the last few days I've had more people leaning on me – ' He threw up his hands in a half-despairing gesture, one that looked out of character in him. 'The ecology people are starting to sound like a very faint voice in their own wilderness.' He grinned in embarrassment. 'My speech writer dreamed that one up. So far I haven't used it on anyone but you.'

'Are you going to use it elsewhere?'

Mackintosh sighed, looked troubled. 'I'm beginning to feel like I did in Vietnam. You don't know how fortunate you British were to have stayed out of that war.'

'We're in Ulster. I think we have as much hope of winning that as you had in Vietnam.' Random studied the worried-looking ex-general. 'Are politics getting in your way here, too?'

'Not just politics. Money.' He stood staring down at the bed on which lay his two guns in their long pouches; then he looked up and shook his head. 'You don't know the pressures there are, Jack. And I'm not going to ruin your weekend telling you about them.' He felt the bed. 'Good and hard, the way I like it.'

'At least it's not one of nails.'

They went out of the bedroom and Random excused himself and went out back of the house to gather more wood for the fire he had going in the living room. The house was centrally-heated by oil, but there was a big stone fireplace in the living room and Random had set a fire in it. He was stacking small logs into the wood basket when Bonnie came out of the house.

'I had four more letters in the mail today. I didn't know I'd written so many! There was a note this time. And they were posted in Helena. He's getting confident, mailing them close to home now. Or he's planning something.'

'Has Coulson been to see your father again this week?'

'Not so far as I know. Why?'

'Nothing. What about Karl Shooberg?'

'Yes. He's been to see Dad twice, both times at the house. The second time, yesterday, he was with Ab Chartwell and a couple of state committee men. I – '

'What?' he said as she stopped.

It was her turn to say, 'Nothing. You want some more wood?'

'No, this'll be enough. Bonnie – ' She paused on the back steps of the house, looked over her shoulder at him. 'I think we're losing the war.'

'I know we are,' she said and went ahead of him into the house.

Nigel Random and Mackintosh were standing at the front of the living room looking out towards the street. 'You have some visitors.'

Random went to the front door and opened it. The silver-blue Mercedes, not a dent or a scratch showing on it, repaired to look as good as new, was in the driveway behind Bonnie's MG. Coulson and Shooberg were getting out of it. Random, his mind over the past week or two working in a pattern of intermittent memories, saw a flashback to the first day he had met these two men. They had arrived together, got out of the car together, came towards him.

But they had been much more friendly on that first day; or better actors. Today Coulson just looked right through him and Shooberg, cheroot holder in mouth, just said, 'The Governor inside?'

Random took them into the living room, offered them a drink and a chair, both of which they declined. Shooberg said, 'We're not staying. We're just making sure all our guests are comfortable.'

Mackintosh had retreated from the window and now sat in an arm-chair, a drink in his hand.

'Just fine. You couldn't have provided me with better company. Who's my partner tomorrow?'

Shooberg looked at Coulson and the latter said, 'I am, Governor.'

Mackintosh didn't move, but Random saw the stiffness spread through him. 'How's that?'

'My partner's just phoned through, he can't make it here till Sunday. You didn't make up your mind till yesterday, Governor, whether you were going to come. By that time 'most everyone had his partner. So it's you and me, I guess. If it's okay with you?'

'Sure,' said Mackintosh, but he still looked stiff and unrelaxed and as if all the pleasure of his weekend had already disappeared.

Shooberg looked at a map-board he was carrying. 'Each pair has got an area that's all theirs – that's the way we always work it on the first day. You and your father, Jack, have got the area from Piegan Ridge down to the B-2 fire-break. Jim and the Governor will be east of you, on your right.'

Random nodded, wondering which of them had chosen to send him and his father into the area where he had found Harry Jardine's body.

Nigel Random asked, 'Is it good country? I mean, for game?'

'The best side of the valley,' said Coulson. 'There's been four or five elk sighted up there in the last couple of days. Jack knows it well.'

He glanced at Random and the latter, half-smiling, said, 'If we get lost we can always get our bearings from the mining survey pegs.'

'Don't forget,' said Shooberg, ignoring Random's remark, 'you're limited to one elk apiece. We don't want any bad publicity with someone breaking the law.'

'Heaven forbid!' said Bonnie, fluttering her eyelashes and putting a spread hand on her bosom. 'That might upset the elks.'

'Elks are men,' said her father, as if deciding to make the best of a bad weekend and not to allow his daughter to spoil it further with her anti-blood sports attitude, 'they are members of a civic organization. The collective name for the animal is elk, whether it's one or twenty.'

'Never understood it, m'self,' said Nigel Random. 'But it's right, of course. One doesn't go hunting elephants or tigers.'

'Men go hunting women, don't they?' said Bonnie.

Random grinned and his father, not sure whether his leg was being pulled, said, 'That's different, I suppose. Never gone in for that sort of hunting, m'self.'

The atmosphere had lost a little of its chill. Even Coulson and Shooberg smiled; and decided this was the moment to depart. They went out of the house and Random followed them as a matter of courtesy.

'You got my message about no volunteers?' he said.

'Yes,' said Shooberg. 'What happened?'

'I asked Russ Judson to spread the word that we'd like some men to stand by, on overtime rates, in case of emergency. An accident, anything like that. Or someone getting lost up there in the timber. Russ came back and said they'd told him we could stuff the hunt as far as they were concerned.'

'Who told him that?' said Coulson. 'That goddam Commie, Peeples?'

'I didn't enquire. But I gather the sentiment was pretty general.' They had reached the Mercedes. 'I think we're lucky they're not being more obstructive. At least, so far they've just been negative that way.'

Then Bonnie came out of the house and across the lawn towards them. She strode up to them, stopped with her feet apart, her hands on her hips, glared at Coulson challengingly.

'Jim, if you have any more of my letters, don't bother sending them. Just burn them or hand them out to the newspapers. But don't waste any more postage on them.'

All three men looked at her as if they had not quite understood what she had said. Random was shocked by her bluntness and wondered what had made her suddenly and recklessly confront Coulson like this.

Coulson recovered first, but only partly: he was overblown with bluster: 'I don't know what the hell you're talking about! Go back inside, Bonnie. You give me a pain in the ass!'

'The feeling's mutual! How your wife's stood you for so long – how *anyone's* put up with you – '

'Take her back inside, Random, before I shut her mouth!'

'I shouldn't try to do that, if I were you.' Random took his own reckless plunge: suddenly he wanted everything out in the open. Well, almost everything: he couldn't accuse Coulson and

Shooberg of murder, not yet. 'I know about the letters, Coulson. And so does Grace. It was a bloody petty thing to do, unless you are planning to tell the press about Bonnie's affair with Jardine. Or are you going to tell her father, put the pressure on him?'

'He's not going to do either,' said Shooberg, taking over from Coulson. The big man seemed to retreat into the background without actually taking a step backwards. 'I knew nothing about all this, Bonnie, till I found out about them by accident. Jim and I've had a talk about the letters. *I* sent you that last batch – that's the last of them. I didn't read 'em, take my word for it.'

Bonnie had had the tables turned on her. She had come out here looking for a fight of some kind, hurling her challenge at Coulson, and the challenge had been folded up and put aside like an unwanted circular by the cool, rasp-voiced Shooberg.

'Jim is resigning from our corporation. The announcement will be made Tuesday, after the hunt is finished and everyone's gone home. All you're asked to do is keep it quiet till then.'

'If she doesn't?' said Random.

'Put it another way,' said Shooberg. 'If you two say nothing about Jim's resignation, we'll say nothing about her and Harry. We'll just let bygones be bygones.'

He got into the Mercedes. He waited a moment, then leaned out and said patiently, 'Time to go, Jim. We still got all the other guests to call on. We got to get 'em into that motel for Grace to say hallo to.'

Coulson had been standing by the car, stiff and unmoving, his big broad face set and mottled like frozen beef. He moved his lips as if to say something, but the sound he made was no more than a muffled moan. Then he turned, stumbled, recovered and walked round to the driver's side and got into the car. He took it out of the driveway in reverse at speed, braked sharply when he reached the road, swung it round and went up the street with a screech of tyres, driving as if he no longer cared if he died in an accident as his father had.

Random turned to Bonnie. 'Well, that looks like one battle won.'

'You think so?'

But he hedged on that question, the cautious soldier who knew no battles were really won till the war was over. He said, 'What prompted you to face up to him like that?'

'My father knows about Harry and me. He's known about it all along. He told me so on the way up here, but he wouldn't tell me who'd told *him*. I don't know – when Jim Coulson arrived up here, I just blew up inside. You're lucky I didn't shoot my mouth off in front of your father.'

Over her shoulder Random saw that Hugh Mackintosh had come out on to the verandah of the house, was gazing at the two of them.

'I'm glad you got it off your chest,' he said to Bonnie. 'But I wonder what's happened that they are kicking Coulson out?'

'You could ask Grace,' said Bonnie and nodded at the Lincoln Continental as it swung slowly into the driveway.

3

'I'm a realist,' Lord Kenneway said as he and Grace, sitting wide apart in the back seat behind Lee, climbed the winding road above Massacre Gap. 'My decision is going to be unpopular in some quarters, but making money will always be unpopular in some quarters.'

'I'm glad we're going to remain friendly partners.' Grace was wearing one of the suits she had bought at Bergdorf-Goodman and felt elegant and comfortable in it. Even rich and successful, she told herself, and was a little ashamed of her conceit. 'I'm sorry we had to go about it the way we did. But Harry started it and I had no option but to finish it the way he'd planned it.'

'No hard feelings. That's always been my motto in business – on the rare occasion or two when I've lost.' He smiled, but with no false modesty. 'Do you want me to remain as chairman?'

'We'll see. The SEC may insist on us restructuring the company, now the American side is the major stockholder.'

'Meaning you don't trust me.'

'Let's say I have great respect for your ruthlessness.'

Suddenly he laughed, not a warm laugh but still full-bellied. He said nothing further, but she had the feeling she could now trust him. He had met his match and, as he had said, he was a realist.

They were on the edge of Tozabe when he next spoke. He had been gazing out at the timber stands as they drove past them. They were not trees to him, a living, growing part of the earth to be admired and treasured: they were symbols on a balance sheet.

'This will all be under water, I take it?'

'All of it.'

She was surprised at the sudden regret she felt as she said it. She knew they would build a better town, but it always hurt to see something of the past wiped out, something built by the sweat and labour of men. She remembered the honyockers' sod houses and flimsy shacks that had been knocked down, ploughed under, when the big farmers had moved in down on the Plains. She had saved her family's shack, but you couldn't preserve anything under a hundred or two hundred feet of water.

'We'll buy other forests from the profits – from *London's* profits, that is,' said Kenneway. 'Some here in Montana – there is a good tract up for sale over on the western slopes of the Divide. It'll be good public relations. Those that don't want to work in mining can transfer.'

Lee swung the car into the driveway of the general manager's house and she saw Jack, Bonnie and Hugh Mackintosh standing as if waiting for them.

'Will you transfer Jack Random?'

He glanced at her, for once was not the chairman of the board. 'I'll leave him to you. He's your problem, I think.'

They got out and Random came towards her, took her hand and raised it to his lips. 'Afternoon, ma'am. This is an honour.'

'In your eye,' she said, smiling at him, loving him but wondering how he was going to take Kenneway's news. 'I've come up to say my party piece as hostess to these hunters of yours.'

'Not mine. They're all your ex-husband's, I gather. Or Coulson's and Shooberg's.'

Something's happened. But she turned aside and said hallo to Bonnie.

Bonnie's voice was tight. 'You look stunning.'

'Something I bought in New York. Have you met Lord Kenneway?'

Kenneway had been standing in the background, out of character, a spectator. But now he came forward, took Bonnie's hand and shook it. 'I'm afraid I'm no hand-kisser, Miss Mackintosh.'

'I understand you're also no ass-kisser,' said Bonnie.

'Bonnie!' Mackintosh had come across the lawn and up behind her.

Oh Bonnie, thought Grace, why do you always try so hard? But she had seen the girl's look when Jack had kissed her hand, had recognized the sudden pain of jealousy. She knew it herself, from the inside, and she knew what it could do to the tongue that could not be controlled. And Bonnie had always had a reckless tongue.

Kenneway dropped Bonnie's hand as if it had burnt him and as quickly dropped his awkward attempt at charm. 'You and I speak a different language, Miss Mackintosh.' He turned away from her, dropping her off the edge of his world. 'Is your father inside, Jack?'

Bonnie stared at them all, looking last at her father, embarrassment and anger at herself plain on her face. Then she spun round and almost ran to her car. She had clambered into it before Mackintosh moved. Then he ran across the lawn after her, scrambled in beside her, saying something that the others couldn't hear. Bonnie swung the MG up on to the lawn on the far side of the drive and reversed it past the Lincoln and out on to the road. Then she was gone, staring straight ahead, seemingly heedless of her pleading father sitting in the bucket seat beside her.

'I'm sorry for her father,' said Kenneway. 'Is she always like that?'

'Only half the time,' said Random.

'No,' said Grace. 'You were unlucky, Ian. She is normally one of the nicest, warmest-hearted girls you could meet.'

She saw Random's sharp glance at her when she called Kenneway *Ian*. He missed nothing, she thought. But he made no comment, led them across the lawn and up into the house, standing aside for her and Kenneway to enter. She walked in ahead of Kenneway, took one quick look around and took in everything. This was a man's house, the home of a man who needed no possessions to tell him who or what he was. He is satisfied with *this*, she thought; and wondered again how she was going to tell him about the house in Washington. But that was a problem for another time, when they were alone.

Kenneway wasted no time. 'I'm going back to London tomorrow, Nigel. I've come to a decision. We're not going to fight Grace. We'll accept our 48 per cent of the mining project.'

The two Randoms looked at each other, then the elder said, 'What made you change your mind?'

'Facts and figures. I had the Anaconda people check the estimates Shooberg gave us. We'll make more money out of that copper deposit in a shorter time than we ever would out of timber and pulp. You and I will recommend to the London board that we should accept, that we are going to diversify. The shareholders in London will thank us.'

'Of course,' said Nigel Random flatly.

Grace had been watching the other Random. 'Are you surprised, Jack?'

'Not really.' His voice was as flat as his father's, a rasp almost as harsh as Shooberg's. 'Money always wins in the end, doesn't it?'

'Don't say something you'll be sorry for,' Kenneway warned. 'Your father is accepting the situation. You'd do well to do the same.'

'My situation is a little different from my father's.' He touched his forelock to Grace, gave her the old half-mocking smile. 'Excuse me, ma'am.'

He turned and before Grace could stop him he was closing the front door behind him. She looked at Kenneway and Nigel Random, feeling suddenly hurt, angry and small. The two men looked embarrassed and Nigel Random was also angry.

'Damned rude of him. I apologize for him.'

'Don't,' she said, putting her composure together again. 'I'd rather have it from him. May I have a drink, Nigel? In a few minutes I have to go up to the Happy Hunter Motel and make welcoming noises. Do you want to come?'

'I'll stay here. Just in case Jack comes back.'

'I'll stay, too,' said Kenneway.

'Just remember,' she said. 'He's *my* problem.'

Five minutes later Grace went out to her car and Lee drove her uptown to the Happy Hunter Motel. There were cars parked in front of every unit of the motel and the parking lot to one side was full. There were also cars parked on both sides of the street and a small crowd had congregated on the sidewalk. Lee took the Lincoln in off the street and pulled up at the entrance to the restaurant, where the reception was being held.

'I won't be long, Lee. Stay close by.'

'Will we be going straight back to Helena, missus?'

'I don't know yet.' That would depend on whether she saw Jack before it was time to leave.

Ab Chartwell and Karl Shooberg were waiting for her in the lobby. Behind them, in the restaurant, she could hear the gravel-rumble of men's voices and the occasional donkey's laugh that told her the drinking had begun early. Well, at least she wasn't picking up the tab for *that* part of the weekend.

'Where's Jim?'

'He's disappeared,' said Shooberg. 'We had a few words.'

She looked at him, but he wasn't going to tell her any more right now and she didn't push him. She took a deep breath, patted her hair. 'Okay, let's get it over with.'

'Remember, Grace,' said Chartwell. 'Practically all the influence in the state is in that room. You don't need them to win the election, but you might need some of 'em in the future.'

'Are you going on the hunt tomorrow, Ab?'

'Can't shoot. I'm short-sighted.'

'You're kidding,' she said.

She spent less than half an hour playing hostess. She was the only woman in the restaurant but for the waitresses spread around the walls like moveable furniture.

'Where's a vestal virgin? I want another drink!' A man looked around, waving his glass, and one of the waitresses, after a glance at her sister vestal virgins, pushed through the throng towards him. 'Bourbon, honey, and don't spare the bottle!'

The tables had been stacked in one corner and the room was a milling mass of masculinity, a phrase that came to Grace's mind and brought on a sour giggle behind the political smile. But the men, all of them flattered by her charm, did not see behind the phony front: it's working overtime tonight, she told herself. She moved from group to group, escorted by Chartwell and Shooberg, always looking for Jack but not really expecting to find him here.

The men towered over her so that at times she had the feeling she was drowning in a surf of the male sex. That might have appealed to some women, but not to her. She passed a middle-aged waitress leaning against a wall, arms folded, a non-virgin who looked as if she were wondering why such an evil as men

265

were necessary. She looked sourly at Grace, but the latter was not going to allow herself to be mistaken for the enemy: I'm not the camp follower here, she thought. She looked directly at the waitress, then she winked. The woman, plain-faced, tired, stared back at her. Then she returned the wink, but with no other expression on her face, and Grace passed on, feeling better. The noise of the men around her was giving her a headache; but all the shouting, the laughing, the bonhomie, was just wind. The lords of the earth would never know that they'd lost the war of the sexes when Eve said hallo to the serpent.

At last, and it seemed to her that she had been there for three hours instead of thirty minutes, she made her exit, all the men shouting a loud farewell as if she were a stripper with a touch of class who had given them all a free pass to her next show.

She walked out into the lobby with Chartwell and Shooberg, breathed deeply of the comparatively fresh air. 'I feel as if I've been pack-raped.'

'All in a good cause,' said Chartwell.

'Ah, when I retire from politics I'm going to have you hung by the neck from the top of the Capitol building.'

'I'll be long dead by then. And I'm going to be non-political in the next life.'

Shooberg had been staring out through the glass doors of the lobby. 'I think you better stay in here a while, Grace. I'll get the sheriff to move that crowd out there.'

'Not if they're voters,' Chartwell protested.

'They're not voters. Not the sort we want, anyway. Look who's up front of 'em.'

Grace looked out through the doors. There were fifty or sixty men there, faces hard and angry. At their head were Chris Peeples and Random.

'Go back inside, Grace,' said Shooberg. 'I'll call you when we've got rid of this mob.'

'No,' she said, looking out through the glass at Random. 'I've got to face them some time. Let's do it now.'

'Karl's right,' said Chartwell. 'Don't be foolhardy, Grace – '

But she had already pushed open the doors, stepped out on to the concrete apron that fronted them. The apron gave her a few extra inches of height: she was able to look straight into Random's eyes. 'You wanted to see me?'

'Not him,' said Chris Peeples. 'Us, Mrs Jardine. Us!'

There was a growl, just below an angry shout, from the crowd. The men glared at her, some of their faces contorted into what, she realized with shock, was hatred. There was no bonhomie here, none of these men was going to be flattered by her charm, taken in by the phony front.

'I told them of Kenneway's decision,' said Random. The crowd had stilled and his voice, though quiet, was clear and distinct. 'I thought they should know the truth now. Not have to wait till after the elections.'

Oh Jack, why must we always fight? 'You wouldn't have had to wait till after the elections. Lord Kenneway and I intended issuing a statement as soon as he got back to London and talked to his board of directors there.'

She waited for the half-mocking smile, but he surprised her: there seemed as much pain in his eyes as she knew must be in her own. They were trapped: the circumstances, his idealism, her ambition, *something*, had proved too much for them.

She looked at Peeples. 'You have to believe me – you are all going to gain from this!'

There was a yell of derision from the crowd and Peeples said, 'Not as much as you are! We're happy like we are, can't you understand that? Sure, we'd all like more money – ' the crowd roared its support for that ' – but what we're concerned about is this town – our town! And the valley, *our* valley! We don't want it spoiled, we want to go on working in timber – '

'You can go on working in timber. You can transfer, all of those who want to. We'll see you lose nothing by it – ' She was disconcerted by Peeples's wall-eye: it seemed to remain fixed on her. 'We're buying other tracts on the other side of the Divide, there will be jobs there for everyone who wants them – '

'We can't take the valley with us!'

She looked at Random and he said, 'That's the one thing you don't seem able to understand. And I don't think you ever will. Especially when you get to Washington.'

There was the whine of sirens and three cars, led by Sheriff Gauge's, swung into the driveway. As Gauge got out of his car, the lobby doors behind Grace swung open and Shooberg and Chartwell came out. Behind them were a dozen or more of the hunting party, attracted by the sound of the sirens.

Gauge came lumbering up, a mixture of aggression and reluctance, the would-be neutral stigmatized by his badge. 'What's going on here?' He sounded almost plaintive.

'Go home, sheriff,' someone in the crowd called out. 'We don't need you.'

'Lock 'em up,' said a drunken voice from behind Grace.

She swung round, but the crowd behind her had grown bigger; the lobby was filled with hunters trying to get out to watch the fun. She had the sudden frightening idea that they were already on the hunt, for trouble.

'Shut up, you!' A boy with lank hair and thick glasses was standing just behind Random; he blinked angrily at Grace and her supporters, the battalion she didn't want. 'Get back inside! This's got nothing to do with you!'

Grace tried to gain control of the situation, but she knew it had already slipped away from her. She looked at Peeples, hoping he might listen to her if Jack wouldn't. 'Come down to Helena and see me Monday.'

'No, Mrs Jardine.' Chris Peeples recognized a lost cause; he had too much dignity to talk surrender terms. 'Enjoy your money!'

'That's all you bastards think about!' shouted the lank-haired boy, face contorted; Grace wondered who he was that he could hate her so much. Then the sun flashed on his thick-lensed glasses and all at once she remembered Jack's description of the boy who had accidentally almost shot them. 'You're all the same – goddam money, that's all you care about!'

'Who's that goddam Red?' There were angry shouts from behind Grace.

She swung round to silence them, afraid of the sudden tension in the air. But she was too late to prevent what happened next; and she was never sure exactly what did happen next. She caught a glimpse of something, a stone, a piece of wood, hurtling over her head. There was a loud crash and the glass wall of the lobby seemed to disintegrate; big shards fell out of the upper framing like broad, transparent spears and several of the hunting party had to leap aside. There was a roar of anger and shock from the hunters and they surged forward. At the same time the company workers bunched together and advanced, pushing Random and Peeples, who were shouting in vain for the men to hold back, ahead of them. Drink and bitterness, one ingredient from each side, brewed the storm. Sheriff Gauge fired off a shot, but no one took any notice of it. The riot blew up like an explosion.

Grace, suddenly terrified, saw the angry faces coming towards her like so many cannonballs. Someone hit her in the back, hurtling her forward. It was sheer chance that she fell into Random's arms; she felt him clutch her to him. He lifted her up, staggered as he almost lost his footing; they were caught in a wild surf of raging men. Fists were thrown like rocks, hands clawed, feet flailed; she saw rather than heard Random gasp with pain as someone hit him in the back. She saw nothing clearly: everything was fragmented like the glass wall of the lobby. Yells beat at her ears; no one actually hit her, but shoulders and hips thumped against her. Random was holding her with one arm and trying to beat his way out of the ruck with the other. The mêlée was a whirlpool now: there were no drawn lines and the two sides had merged into the one big brawl. Random hacked savagely, careless of whom he hit, fighting an individual battle now; Grace, breathless from the constriction of his arm about her, felt his fury as much as she felt that of the men still crushing them. Then suddenly they fell out of the mob, both of them falling to the ground as, abruptly, there was no pressure of bodies to support them.

Random dragged her to her feet, pulled her away. Sheriff Gauge was still firing his gun into the air and his deputies were skirting the brawling mob, wielding their batons but having little effect.

Random picked her up, carried her across the strip of lawn towards the parking lot. She protested that she was all right and, after a glance at her, he put her down on her feet. As he did so she looked past him, saw Jim Coulson standing some distance away between two cars. The big man stared at her and even at the distance she sensed there was something wrong with him; but then abruptly he turned and disappeared and just as abruptly she forgot him as Jack put his arm round her. He led her towards her car.

Lee, his usually expressionless face cracked with worry, opened the back door and Random helped her into the car. Feeling a sudden mixed reaction of shock and relief, she closed her eyes and lay back in the seat. But she opened them at once when she heard Hugh Mackintosh say, 'We better get her out of here.'

The Governor was standing beside Random, peering in at her, his face as concerned as those of her chauffeur and the man she loved. She put out a hand to Random and he took it. He pressed it and she felt his love in the pressure. Then he looked at Mackintosh.

'Take her down to my place. I'll be there in a few minutes.'

'Where are you going?' She sat up, afraid for him.

'Don't worry.' Across in front of the motel the brawl seemed to be subsiding; Sheriff Gauge was no longer firing off his gun, there was only the occasional yell fading away. 'But I think I'm needed over there. Look after her, Governor.'

Then he left them, running across the parking lot. She watched him go, still afraid for him; then she moved over in the seat as Hugh Mackintosh got in beside her. Lee got in behind the wheel and took the car out of the lot. A crowd, attracted by the noise, had flooded the street outside the motel; Lee had to ease the car through the swirl of people. Some looked in at Grace, mouthing abuse, but the windows were up and she heard none of it. A few fists thudded on the car, but they were only token gestures. The car rolled through, Lee speeded up and they went down towards the edge of town.

'You were lucky,' said Mackintosh. 'Are you hurt?'

'A few bruises. And my feelings.' The sleeve of her suit jacket was ripped at the shoulder and she had lost one of her shoes; her hair was dishevelled and there were dustmarks on her face like the imprint of fingers. But as Hugh had said: she was lucky. 'If it hadn't been for Jack . . .'

'Yes.'

She looked directly at him for the first time. His voice was flat, listless. His face was lined, there was lipstick on his chin; he looked anything but a general and a governor. She handed him the handkerchief with which she had been about to wipe her own face.

'There's lipstick on your chin. Bonnie's, I hope.'

'Yes.' He rubbed his chin, gave her back the handkerchief. 'She sends you her apologies. Sincere ones.' He sighed, then looked at her cautiously, as if not sure of her. 'Maybe this is not the time – Grace, could I talk to you?'

They had reached the entrance to Random's driveway. Grace touched Lee on the shoulder. 'Don't turn in, Lee. Pull up here. Leave us for a few minutes.'

Lee pulled the car into the side of the road, got out and moved up to stand some distance away. Grace turned to Mackintosh.

'If it's about Bonnie, I'm willing to help. I can take her to Washington, find a job for her there.'

'I don't think she'd work for you, Grace.'

'I wasn't thinking of her working for me. I'm not dense, Hugh. Nor insensitive, I hope.' *Or am I?* Maybe Jack would tell her otherwise. 'But Mark Mountfield and I, between us, could find something worthwhile for her.'

'Thank you. No, she's going back to our place down in Paradise Valley. So am I.'

She looked at him, all at once aware of how – *slumped* he was in the corner of the seat. Something had happened to take the ramrod out of his back. 'I guess I *am* dense now. What are you trying to say?'

He sat up, his strong profile outlined against the slanting sunlight outside the car. She waited on him, suddenly uneasy. Was he, like Jim Coulson, going to tell her he was in love with her? The conceit shamed her, and she determined that she would be kinder to him than she had been to Jim.

'I hoped I'd never have to tell you this, Grace. But I guess it's against the whole grain of my nature not to.' He turned to face her. 'I killed Harry.'

'I don't believe it!' But she knew she would have to believe it: the truth was there in his face.

'It was an accident, Grace.'

'I hope so.' Her voice was faint, taut, even in her own ears. 'I can't see you as a – a murderer.'

He stared out past her and she could see the pain, like scars, in his face. He was a decent, honest man and she knew how he must have felt to have carried this secret for so long.

'Harry called me some time the beginning of July. I went out to see him at the ranch. There were just the two of us and he told me there was copper up in Limbo Valley and he was going to develop it. He told me if the strike was as big as he hoped, the valley might have to be dammed and flooded and he didn't want any opposition from me.'

'What did you say?'

'I think I surprised him. I told him I thought the state had enough projects going that were ruining its beauty. I said I'd veto any bill that came before me asking for permission to flood the valley.'

'What happened then?'

'You know what he was like. He flew off the handle, told me he'd have me off next week's ticket before I could make my first campaign speech. I knew he could do it – and he knew that I knew. So – ' He paused, shook his head. 'I hate politics, Grace. But I've enjoyed being Governor. Call it vanity, if you like. Holding a position like that, having power, even if I sometimes had to ask Harry's permission to use it – it all infects you.'

'I suppose so,' she said, but admitted no more.

'So I backtracked. I said I'd have a look at the valley. It was a couple of weeks before I could get up here alone. I called Harry and asked him to meet me up at the Kinney mine. I drove up there and waited for him, but he was late. You know what he was like, he would keep you waiting if he wanted to put you in your place. After an hour I got angry. I drove back down the road and then I saw – I saw Bonnie and Harry down on the other road. That was the first time I'd ever seen them together. I had no idea they were having an affair.'

'Neither did I.'

'I saw him hit her and – I'll be honest, I'd have killed him right then. Only I didn't have a gun. I stayed where I'd pulled up and a few minutes later he came up the road, heading for the mine. My car was blocking the way and he stopped, but didn't get out. Then he must have noticed that I could see down to the main road, that I'd have seen him and Bonnie. He got out of his car, foaming at the mouth about me spying on him. He had his gun, the Hot Six. I don't know what he intended doing with it – I don't think he intended shooting me, not with Bonnie still down there on the road. But he was as furious as I was. He came at me – it was a case of both of us being blind with anger. I grappled with him and the next moment the gun went off. I pushed him away from me, at first I didn't realize he'd been hit, and he fell backwards down the slope – '

'Don't go on – '

'I panicked, Grace. A terrible thing for a soldier to do. I had

Harry's gun in my hand – I threw it into my car, turned round and drove back up the road. There's a timber track that leads down the other side of Piegan Ridge. I took that and I was back in Helena when they phoned through to say what had happened to Harry.'

She pressed his hand. 'I believe all you've told me, Hugh.'

'It's been agony these last few months. If they'd indicted that young feller, Yertsen, I'd have confessed. I'll tell the truth to Wryman now, if you want me to.'

'Does Bonnie know?'

'No. Only you.'

'Then she would be hurt.' She saw the silver-blue car coming up the road, but she took no notice of it other than to wonder about Jim Coulson and to think how wrong she had been about him. But Jim was already destroying himself for other reasons, and she would never be able to offer him a reconciliation. 'I'd like time to think, Hugh.'

'I'll take my name off the ticket. We'll say my health has suddenly gone, or something.'

'It's too late for you to draw out now – '

She saw the Mercedes slow, then stop opposite them on the other side of the road. Hugh Mackintosh's back was to Coulson and he did not see Coulson aiming the rifle at him. Grace snatched at the door on her side, tumbled out to run round the back of the car towards Coulson. She screamed, 'Don't, Jim!' but her shout was lost in the crack of the rifle. Through the back window of the car she saw Mackintosh lurch forward. He fell out of the open door and she knew he was dead even before she reached him.

4

Random, coming down the street, saw Coulson's Mercedes pull up opposite the Lincoln. He saw Coulson's rifle barrel laid on the car door and he began running. But he was still thirty yards away when Coulson fired, then the Mercedes, engine roaring, was coming straight at him and he had to jump aside. He caught a glimpse of Coulson as the latter looked at him; then, amazingly, there was a screech of brakes and the Mercedes skidded to a stop. Random pulled up, torn between going after Coulson and going on to help Grace as she bent over the Governor. Then he ran on, shouting to his father as he saw him come out of the house.

'Call a doctor!'

But one look told him it was too late for a doctor. He grabbed Grace, pulled her away from the body sprawled in the dust. Lee had come running up and he helped Random support Grace as she looked ready to faint.

'Let's get her into the house – quick!'

Random glanced over his shoulder as, carrying Grace between them, he and Lee went up the path to the house. Coulson had the door of the Mercedes open and was sitting half-in, half-out of the car, staring back at Random.

'Why?' Grace was on the verge of hysteria. 'Why kill Hugh?'

'It wasn't meant for him.' Random had a flash of insight. 'He thought it was me in the car with you – Take her, Lee!'

He shoved Grace into Lee's arms, bounded up the steps and into the house. His father and Lord Kenneway, the latter at the phone, spun round as he raced in the front door.

'Never mind the doctor – get the sheriff! Tell him Jim Coulson's just shot the Governor!'

His rifle still lay on the dining-room table. He grabbed it, swept up a box of cartridges, and turned for the front door again as Lee brought Grace into the house. He heard her cry and the shout of his father, but he didn't stop, went out the door on the run. He was half-way down the driveway when he saw the Mercedes shoot away with a shriek of tyres. He raced across the road, jumped into the Lincoln, started it up and swung it round. He had no clear idea what he was going to do, just knew that he was not going to let Coulson get away.

The Mercedes had at least two hundred yards start on him and he guessed it was faster than the Lincoln. One block up the main street Coulson swung left, going round in a wide skid. Random followed him, struggling to hold the big Lincoln on the road. Again Coulson swung left and Random followed him, narrowly missing a boy on a bicycle. Coulson swung left a third time, then right and he was back on the main street, heading out of town. So far he had gained nothing on the Lincoln, but that was due more to his wild, bad driving than any comparison between the two cars. But on the straight out of town he opened up the Mercedes and Random, driving a car with which he was unfamiliar, acutely conscious of its weight and its roll on the bends, soon lost sight of Coulson. He kept driving till he came to a long straight stretch where he could look ahead up to the road as it wound up through Massacre Gap. He slowed, peered ahead, watched for the flash of silver-blue as the Mercedes sped up through the Gap. But there was nothing, just two cars and a truck coming from the direction of Helena.

He swung the Lincoln round, went back down the highway. He passed the road that led up to Piegan Ridge; he halted, then backed up. He saw the skid marks on the macadam of the highway, the tell-tale black burns as the Mercedes had been swung sharply off into the side road. He turned the Lincoln into the narrow road and, as watchful as he had ever been on armoured car patrol in Aden, drove cautiously up through the trees. He passed the spot where he had found Harry Jardine; he would not have been surprised to see the Mercedes parked among the trees, but there was no sign of it. He continued climbing, wondering if he should turn back, go down to the highway and wait for the sheriff and his deputies.

Then the road, a track now, ran out. And among the trees, just below the old Kinney mine, he saw the Mercedes. He pulled the Lincoln off the track, cut the engine. He loaded his rifle and slipped the box of cartridges into his pocket. Then, carefully, ready to fall flat as the first bullet was fired at him, he got out of the car and slipped into the timber. Reassured by the trees around him, feeling less exposed, he let out a shout.

'Coulson!'

There was a crashing in the timber to his right and he spun round, bringing up his gun. Then he saw the four dark shapes, two large and two smaller ones, moving with a lurching run through the trees and across a small clearing. As the grizzlies came into the clearing the sun struck across them, sheening their dark coats, then they had disappeared into the timber on the other side and in a moment the sound of their progress had died away.

Then Random looked down at the rifle in his hands, held at the ready position to whip it to his shoulder and fire. Was he really going to shoot at Coulson when he at last caught up with the big man? This wasn't Aden or the dangerous hills behind it; he wasn't in the army now hunting terrorists. True, Coulson was a murderer, a double murderer: he had killed Harry Jardine, Random was sure of that now, and he had killed Hugh Mackintosh: he had as much blood on his hands as any terrorist in Aden. But this was a civilized country, not a dying outpost of a dying empire; there were laws here to deal with murderers and one did not take the law into one's own hands. Or shouldn't.

He would not shoot unless there was absolutely no alternative; but as he moved on he continued to hold the rifle at the ready. He did not shout Coulson's name again: if the big man was in the vicinity he would have heard the challenge. He moved up through the timber towards the mine, moving carefully from shadow to shadow. The sun was dropping and he knew he had to find Coulson, or be out of here, before dusk set in.

Then he heard the bull elk bugle. The deep whistle, mounting to a high note, came clearly on the still air, thrilling music to any hunter's ear: Random remembered the sambar stag he had stalked in Assam. Ear sensitive to the direction from which the bugling had come, he looked up to his right. The bull was standing on the top of a ridge, the six-pointed antlers raised high as he bugled again, the sun shining on the dark-brown, almost black, head and the yellow-grey sides and back. Random thrilled at the sight of him. Then, downwind from the elk, he saw Coulson.

He was sitting in the clearing above the entrance to the mine, his back to a rusted piece of mine equipment, his grey head catching the sun as distinctly as the hide of the elk above him. He had his rifle across his lap and he was staring out across to the slope on the other side of the river.

Random stepped out of the timber and shouted once more. There was no response at all from Coulson, who did not even move his head; but up on the ridge the elk raised its antlers, then suddenly was gone down the other side of the crest. Random, gun at the ready, began to walk cautiously up through the snow-pocked long grass towards the mine and Coulson.

He stumbled as his foot sank into a deep trough of snow and he took his eyes off Coulson as he tried to stay on his feet. Then the bullet hit the ground close to him, he heard the crack of the shot, and he flung himself into the trough of snow.

'Coulson! Hold it – '

The answer was another shot that took splinters off the small log behind which Random had luckily fallen. He could feel the coldness of the snow in which he lay already seeping into his thighs and belly. Head close to the ground, his chin in the snow, he stared up the clearing towards the mine. But his eye-level was too low and he could not see Coulson.

He raised his head cautiously, waiting for another shot. But there was none, only silence except for the rustle of wind high in the trees. Coulson was still sitting where Random had first seen him. His usually neat grey hair hung down over his forehead and ears. He raised a hand and ran it through his hair in his characteristic gesture, but didn't push it back from his face. As Random watched him he lifted a flask to his mouth, drank from it, then up-ended it. Disgusted with its emptiness he tossed it away. Then he reloaded his rifle, taking his time. He appeared to be making no effort to conceal himself, was sitting like a hunter in a hide who had all the time in the world to kill his prey.

Random, seeing Coulson intent on loading his gun, stood up and in a crouching run went as fast as he could up the edge of the clearing. He dropped down behind a mound of slag as Coulson fired at him again.

The sound of the shot died away and he shouted, 'Coulson! Let up!'

Another bullet sent dust into his face, then he heard the yell, almost a berserk scream: 'I'll get you, Harry!'

Random frowned: he knew he had heard the name right. 'Coulson! It's not Harry – it's Random! Jack Random!'

But Coulson was not prepared to listen; or was not capable of it. There were two more quick shots, both of them fired from much closer. Random knew he had to get out of here as quickly as he could. Or kill Coulson.

'I don't want to shoot at you, Coulson!'

Two more shots: one of them ricocheted off some metal half-buried in the slag and whined away. A splinter of metal hit Random above the eye and he spun away, clapping his hand to the wound and taking it away with blood on it. He had to get out of here, get back down to the highway and wait for the sheriff and his men. He knew now that he could not shoot down Coulson, a man who was obviously out of his mind, who was shooting at a ghost.

But as, blood dripping down past his eye, he looked back the way he had come he saw that Coulson had suddenly come down behind him. He scrambled to his feet and, half-blinded, not really sure where he was heading, ran towards a thin line of trees up ahead. Coulson fired at him again, but this time the bullet was high over his head. He was sweating heavily, gasping for breath, and blood was still running down into his eye. He was running through drifts of snow, some of them a foot deep, and the muscles were burning in his legs. He had no idea where he was running to: just to get away from Coulson, not to have to turn and kill or, at best, wound the crazed man.

He ran into the timber and almost before he knew it was out on the other side. He ran out into the narrow clearing before he realized that it ended in a cliff. He pulled himself up just in time, saw the glint of the river far below, then swung round as he heard Coulson crashing through the timber behind him. He jerked up his rifle, ready to shoot now as an instinctive urge to survive; then out of the corner of his clear eye saw the narrow path running down round the edge of the cliff. It skirted a huge boulder: at once his soldier's memory saw the possibilities. He plunged down the path, not daring to look at the sheer drop on one side of him, running hard with only one eye to guide him down a path no more than three feet wide. Two bullets hit the ground close to him before he reached the boulder; then he was safely behind it, once more had his gun ready. Coulson could get to him no other way but down the path, had to come round the boulder and into his sights.

He wiped the blood from his eye; waited, but Coulson did not appear. He glanced quickly behind him; then, still watching the bend in the path, he backed up and slid down between two smaller boulders. He looked up and over his shoulder; Coulson couldn't come at him from above. He wiped the blood from his eye again, drew a deep breath, tried to steady the pounding in his chest. Then he looked back at the path, waited for Coulson to come round the big curve of rock.

He could hear the wind sighing in the trees and at the edge of his gaze he could see an eagle riding the air currents high above the river. The sun was low now, had gone from this side of the valley, and the air was suddenly cold. He eased back the catch on his gun, his mind detached, wondering if he would actually shoot when Coulson came into his sights.

The big man came round the edge of the boulder, his gun held loosely in his hand. 'Drop your gun, Coulson!'

He turned his head, looked towards Random but did not seem to see him. He was close enough now for Random to see him clearly: the unkempt hair, the bloodshot vacant eyes, the loose gasping mouth.

'Drop your gun, Jim. I don't want to have to shoot you.'

Coulson continued to stare at the boulders, but Random knew now that the big man could not see him. Then Coulson dropped his gun on the path, said, 'You son-of-a-bitch, Harry,' turned round and walked off the edge of the cliff and dropped from sight.

Chapter Eleven

The sheriff's men found Coulson's body two miles downstream. It was so smashed it was almost unrecognizable and at the coroner's examination Pet Coulson, hurriedly brought up from Helena, collapsed when she had to identify it. Grace took her and Bonnie back to Helena with her and the hunters went home without having fired a shot between them but talking, as they would talk for months ahead, of the shot that had been fired and had killed Hugh Mackintosh, one of the finest men the state had ever produced.

Jim Coulson was buried on the Tuesday, the day his resignation from Jardine-Kenneway and the other Jardine companies was to have been announced. But no announcement was made and he was buried without eulogies. The funeral was private, attended only by his wife, his two children, Karl and Annabelle Shooberg. And Grace, a mistake she regretted only when she got to the grave: she brought the photographers. Their presence upset Pet Coulson and Grace, losing her temper for once, angrily ordered them away.

On the Wednesday Hugh Mackintosh was buried, with all honours and long eulogies from which Mackintosh, a man of few words, would have been glad to escape. The crowd filled the cemetery, stamping their feet to keep warm and cursing, while the minister prayed, the cold wind that blew down from the north. Grace stood with Bonnie and her two brothers and their wives; no one studying her would have known that she was attending the funeral of the man who had killed her husband. She looked down at the coffin as it was lowered into the grave, thinking, without resentment, of Hugh and the accident that had brought about the circumstances of the past few months. She wondered what she would be doing now if Harry were still alive. Then she looked up and saw Jack Random at the back of the crowd on the far side of the grave. Sudden tears came to her eyes, tears that were misinterpreted by those close to her.

'She thought the world of the Governor,' someone whispered, and heads nodded. 'They'd have made a good team.'

The first sod was thrown in on Hugh Mackintosh, the crowd began to break up and Random pushed his way through the crowd to Bonnie. The two of them were alone for a moment as Grace and the Mackintosh sons and their wives were engulfed by sympathizers.

'Grace told me you'd resigned,' said Bonnie. 'When are you leaving?'

'Next week. This is goodbye, Bonnie. I'm sorry it has to be on such an occasion.'

Grief seemed to have flushed her of the uncertainty that had at times made her gauche and too young for her age: today she was a woman, dignified and in control of herself. 'How does Grace feel?'

He shrugged: he was not even sure how he felt himself, only knew that he was doing the right thing by leaving. He raised Bonnie's black-gloved hand and kissed it, no mockery at all this time in the gesture. 'Goodbye, Bonnie.'

'Thank you,' she said softly. 'For everything. And I think Grace is stupid. You're worth more than everything else she has opted for.'

'She's not entirely to blame. I opted for a few things myself. Keep her as a friend, Bonnie.'

Then he left her, moving away to rejoin his father and Lord Kenneway. They had delayed their departure to attend the Governor's funeral, but now the Jardine company plane was waiting at the airport to fly them to Seattle. Random paused on the edge of the crowd surrounding Grace, but she could not see him above the heads of the taller people around her, and he moved on.

He dropped his father and Kenneway at the airport. Kenneway, not entirely insensitive, left the father and son alone for a few minutes. 'I've talked to Ian,' said Nigel Random. 'The job in Scotland is waiting for you. Not as big as this, but it will keep you occupied until something bigger turns up. Will you come back to the Hall for a few days before you go up to Scotland?'

'We might do some shooting together. Birds instead of elk.'

'I'd like that. Take care of yourself.' Then, closer to his son now than he had ever been, he said, 'I'm sorry about you and Grace.'

Random nodded, but only said, 'Make sure the birds don't all head south before I get back to England.'

The following Tuesday Grace was elected to go to Washington. She won by 43,000 votes out of a total of 270,000; in Tozabe County her majority was 60 per cent of the vote. Cliff Pendrick phoned her to congratulate her.

'I'm calling from Miles City, Grace. You've come a long way from here.'

'That wasn't where I really started, Cliff.'

'No, I guess not. You're the most successful honyocker this state's ever seen.' She could not remember his calling her a honyocker before, not even back when they had first met. He was silent for a moment, then said, 'Well, I was wrong, wasn't I? I thought people cared enough about the issues I campaigned on. I said a few rough things about what you're planning to do. But there was nothing personal in it, believe me, Grace.'

'No hard feelings, Cliff. Maybe you can try against Mark Mountfield next time.'

'Maybe.'

'Well, if there is anything I can do for you in Washington or anywhere, let me know. After all I'm representing you as well as everyone else in the state.'

He chuckled, an echo from the young Cliff Pendrick she had been in love with ages go. 'Grace, you're already starting to sound like a real politician. Good luck.'

Grace hung up, staring at the phone for a while. As she had told Hugh Mackintosh in their last talk together, she was not dense. She was as aware of changes in herself as in other people; or so she told herself. Had she really changed so much in the past four months? Was she already a politician, already, as Ab Chartwell had counselled her to do, seeing people as voters first and only secondly as people? She couldn't believe it of herself, but maybe a woman should listen to the opinion of her first husband. After all, he had known her *when* . . . When what? she asked herself; and smiled. When she had been virgin territory? But there had been someone before Cliff, a honyocker boy who was lost in the mist of time and the dust clouds of the Great Plains.

On the Thursday morning, two days after the elections, Random parked his rented car in the driveway of the Jardine mansion, went up the steps and rang the bell. It was early, only eight-thirty, and he wondered if Grace was still asleep. But Lee, opening the door, told him Mrs Jardine was awake.

'I'll get her, Mr Random. She up in attic.'

He raised an eyebrow. 'No, I'll go up, Lee.'

He climbed the stairs, all at once conscious of the memory of the first time he had come to this house, made the same climb. The attic doors were open and he stood for a moment on the landing, wondering if he should turn back. But that would be cowardice and he did not want to be accused of that.

Grace, in a rich blue dressing-gown, her hair brushed but hanging loose, was standing in the middle of the ballroom. She turned as he stepped through the doorway, but if she felt any surprise she did not show it.

'Ma'am,' he said with a smile, 'may I have this dance?'

'You didn't touch your forelock.' But the banter was forced, a foreign language stiff on their tongues. She looked away from him, gestured at the room. 'I had planned a big celebration party, all dressed up. But it wouldn't be appropriate now. Not after what happend to Hugh. And to Jim,' she added.

'I talked to Wryman yesterday.'

'So did I. I called him to congratulate him and Sheriff Gauge.'

'He said they were closing the case on Harry. Coulson's name didn't have to appear in the records as Harry's murderer.'

'I asked him to do that. Pet Coulson has enough to bear now, without –'

He nodded. 'I suppose so. Nothing would be gained.' He

looked around the big empty room; he felt the ghosts watching them. 'Well, I have a long way to go –'

'I'm sorry you're going.' She knew how banal the words sounded, but she had none better at the moment.

'It wouldn't have worked, Grace.'

'We could have tried.'

'Being happy shouldn't be an effort.'

'At least we were faithful to each other while it lasted. That's something.' She reached for his hand, felt the pleasure of touching him again, almost wept. They still had so much to tell each other, but all the confidences, and the confidence, were gone. And she had Hugh Mackintosh's secret that she could never tell him or anyone else. 'I still love you, Jack.'

He raised her hand to his lips: he couldn't trust himself to hold her close. 'Goodbye, Grace. If you're still unmarried, perhaps I'll come back and vote for you at the next elections.'

'Words,' she said, leaned forward and kissed him on the mouth.

He stood for a moment, unable to move, tempted almost overwhelmingly to clutch her to him. But reason, the bane of lovers, held him. He turned quickly and went out of the huge room, leaving her to the ghosts.

He drove out of Helena, up past the ranch, up through Massacre Gap, down into Limbo Valley and on through Tozabe, looking neither to right or left as he went through the town. He had said his goodbyes yesterday to Chris Peeples and the others and he did not want to have to repeat them at some chance meeting. He drove out of the doomed town in the rented Gremlin, headed for Seattle and the Polar flight to London. Out along the highway he took the Juniper Creek road. At the second bend, as he began to climb, he stopped the car and got out. He took the binoculars, went to the edge of the road and looked back down the valley.

'Beautiful,' he said aloud. 'Christ, why do they have to do it?'

The snow suddenly blazed on the peaks as the sun came out from behind the gathering clouds. He felt something beneath his foot and he picked it up; it was a pine cone. He looked up at the tree beside which he stood, saw its heavy load of seed cones. That meant it was going to be a long, severe winter; and he felt a certain satisfaction. Anything that delayed the completion of the dam, the flooding of the valley, was all right with him. Nature was going to make its own protest at what was being done to it.

He looked out once again through the glasses, but he knew now it was time to go. He couldn't bear to look any more at the beauty of it; but he would always remember it. Just as he would always remember the other beauty who might have been his had he been a different man. He took the glasses from his eyes, looked at them, then set them down on a log in front of him. He set them down facing away from the valley, but it was unintentional and he didn't notice.